MW01483808

The Shattered Veil

ON
FATED
TIDES

The Shattered Veil

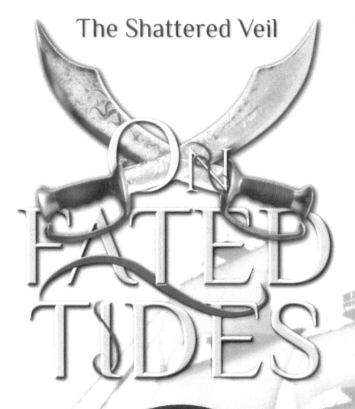

On
FATED
TIDES

Book One

M.R. POLISH

For Jym – My own heartmate, who taught me that even the fiercest storms can be weathered together.

Shadefall

Salty Sands

Arrowwood Forest

Ship Flats

Mistwood

Silverveil

Obsidian Ocean

Wraithmoor

Shadowed Reefs

The Nether Shores

King's Cove

So There I Was...

"I am Briar Firethorn, thief, guide, and a dman good swordswoman."

BRIAR

The darkness hunted me, creeping along the ground like a hungry shadow starved for mortal blood. The foul stench of death clung to the air. The roar of a Shadowborne echoed, sending goosebumps racing across my skin. Stopping now meant certain death—a gruesome fate of being torn apart by razor-sharp teeth and claws of the cursed fae lurking in the Waste.

They found me. They always found me. I could never mask myself from them, just as they couldn't hide from me. Their vile magic clawed at my senses long before their growls reached my ears, gripping my heart tighter as they closed in. A sixth sense I believed to be cursed with. I possessed a distinct and almost uncanny ability to discern whether someone harbored fae magic or was simply mortal. And every Shadowborne was once a fae, changed by a dark power, fated to stalk the earth forever stuck between human and beastly forms.

I was so close to the wall around Everfell that I could almost make out the scent of sandstone. Only a few more hours. Clutching my satchel, afraid of losing the precious contents, my lungs burned as I urged my legs to move faster. Running had become a hated but needed skill when using the Waste to travel. But it was the fastest way back to Everfell.

The roars turned into growls and snapping of teeth. I wasn't sure how many fae were out there, but I wasn't going to stop to find out. They were so close. Their scent permeated the air my lungs desperately craved.

The land shifted beneath me. I stumbled, barely avoiding a faceplant into the coarse, sandy dirt. A crack divided the earth with a deafening sound. The ground tilted, and I slid, clawing desperately at the edge as I dangled over the rift. My fingernails dug into the hard earth while I looked for any kind of purchase to climb out of the fissure.

Sweat stung my eyes as it trickled down my face and neck. "Blast! Gods, a little help?" I cursed under my breath, pleading with any deity that might listen as I struggled to regain solid ground.

My boots slipped, plunging me farther into the earth before I regained any footing. Resting my forehead on the crumbling wall, I focused on breathing. "It's okay, Briar. You've faced worse. I mean, you've never been swallowed by the ground before, but hey," I grunted, pulling myself up an inch. "It's gonna make for a *great* story."

I could hardly wait to see Asher's face when I told him of *this* adventure. He always missed the good stuff. As his friend, it was my duty to rub it in his face.

My arms shook, and I hated thinking I might not be strong enough to pull myself up.

"I am Briar Firethorn. Daughter of—" *Opph!* My foot slipped, and I bit off a curse. Kicking the earth to make a new hole for the tip of my boot to settle into. *Breathe in, breathe out.* "I am the daughter of Rowan and Selene Firethorn. Thief. Guide. And a damn good swordswoman." I could wield a blade better than most men—and they knew it.

At twenty-five years of age, I was past the childhood fantasies of settling down and being a docile lady. I scoffed at the thought. I'd rather chew off my arms than be a proper woman. Dresses were fine for some women, but trading my life for the prim existence held no allure.

Although, I was grateful I wasn't in a skirt now. My thick linen pants were saving my legs from becoming a scratching post to the rotten roots poking through the earth. The ground shuddered once more, and I slipped down the unstable wall. Rocks and dirt tumbled with me. I made the mistake of looking down. The hole was now too deep to see the bottom.

My heart raced. If the beasts didn't devour me, the ground would. I was half-surprised that the evil creatures hadn't tried jumping off the edge into the abyss, snapping their jaws in the hope of taking me down with them.

I swallowed the lump of fear forming in my throat. Blood dripped from my fingertips where my nails were split and lifted from clawing the ground. Thankfully, I hadn't registered the pain yet. One problem at a time.

Okay, so down wasn't an option. Up was becoming increasingly impossible. Carefully, I surveyed the wall behind and around me. If I could make my way to the right, I might be able to take a step back and work my way to the other side. There seemed to be larger clefts in the dirt where the crack narrowed, giving me hope that I might accomplish such a feat.

Wiping the sweat from my brow with my arm, I let loose a shaky breath. I pounded the dirt until I had a sufficient place to grab hold, then kicked in another foothold. Inch by inch, I made my way to the junction.

Stretching my leg back, I found some traction on the opposite wall. Pulling my body to stand—for the lack of a better word—upright in the massive hole, I steadied myself as I balanced between both sides, praying the ground would stay still.

A howl echoed around me. The beasts were closing in. "Blast!" I hissed through clenched teeth and pressed forward. Finding a place to grasp onto, I pulled myself to the other side and began climbing. I didn't trust the roots to hold me and avoided them. They were so dead I assumed they'd disintegrate beneath my touch.

Crawling onto solid ground, I nearly collapsed, my limbs trembling violently. But I couldn't stop. I didn't survive *that* to be slashed apart and drained of blood.

Pushing to my feet, I felt like I weighed more than the mountains protecting Everfell from the Crimson Coast. With each step, I found new strength.

Judging by the stars, an hour had passed, and the echoes of the Shadowborne faded into the distance, leaving nothing but another haunting memory behind. It was late, yet Everfell was wide awake. As a bustling port on the Ivory Gulf, tankards brimming with citrus rum were passed around until the early hours. Even then, a handful of coins could rouse a barkeep for another round.

Emerging from the Waste, I slowed my pace. This was my victory walk. Surviving another journey to Silvershade was no small feat. I held my head high as I entered town. Winding through the lively streets, I found myself drawn to Kracken's. An empty seat at the bar called to me, and I swiftly claimed it.

"Aye, girl. You look like you've tangled with a sea beast." Gephrey leaned on the bar, grinning wide.

I cocked my head, shooting him a sarcastic smile. "Worse. A Shadowborne."

The noise in the tavern dulled as a tense quiet settled over the room. Gephrey leaned forward, his grin fading. "You know better than to spin tales in here, Firethorn."

I tipped back on my stool, gesturing to my disheveled attire—dirt, sweat, and blood streaked every inch. "Does this look like a tall tale to you?" Nodding toward the barrel behind him, I settled back into my seat. "Don't be stingy. It's been a long night, and I'm parched."

His brow arched, skepticism etched into his face. Scoffing, I dug a piece of silver from my satchel and slammed it onto the bar.

He swiped the coin with a wide grin. "Ye've earned my gratitude, lass." With a wink, he shoved off the counter and filled a tankard, placing it before me.

The warm liquid slid down my throat, forcing the past few hours of dust to drown in my belly.

A tingle of magic pricked at my senses, teasing me from the back of the room. It wasn't unusual for fae to frequent Kraken's, but I had hoped they'd be elsewhere tonight. At least their magic wasn't tainted. No Shadowborne here.

I inspected my nails, relieved I hadn't lost any, but the splits would take a few days to heal. My fingertips stung and were definitely tender, but I supposed I should be grateful.

Whispers of earthshakes had circulated through parts of the Shadowmere Kingdom but not in the Evernight. And that was certainly too close to the city for my comfort. I nearly laughed. Being *in* the ground was too close.

I fished out another coin and tapped it on the bar. A hand clamped down on mine, snatching the precious silver from my fingers.

Spinning, I readied myself to throw hands and murder the poor fool who thought he could rob me.

Asher's hands shot up as he took a hefty step back, leaning away from me. "Hey, it's just me."

"Do you want to die?" I pried the coin from his hand, my glare lingering before I turned and settled back on my stool.

He leaned casually against the counter, flashing me a devilish grin. It probably worked on most girls, but it only made me laugh. Without breaking eye contact, I handed the coin over to Gephrey. "What are you doing here?"

"Looking for my second. You game?" Asher's brow furrowed as his gaze swept over my disheveled state. "You were supposed to be back hours ago. What happened?"

"One, you're *my* second. Never make that mistake again. Two, thanks for your observant skills." I tipped back my new drink, letting the warm burn settle in my throat. "Did you feel the ground shake?"

"Ha! First, the day you actually want a second, I volunteer. Hell, Briar, I'd go home with you if you asked. But you've never asked nor needed someone to help you sift through the roughage that litters these places."

Laughing with him came easily. "That's because I would never set my sights so low. Maybe you should consider finding a respectable lady?" I gestured to the room. "Though you won't find many in here."

As I swept my arm across the tavern, my attention snagged on the back corner. Three fae sat there, their eyes fixed on me. Covertly, I turned my back to them, pretending I saw nothing.

Asher shrugged and grabbed my tankard, finishing the last of my drink in one swig. He grimaced. "How do you drink that stuff?"

I stood, placing a hand on his shoulder. "It takes a strong woman to handle Kracken's brew. I'm not sure you're ready for it." The piercing gaze of the fae burned into my back, raising the hairs on my neck. "We should make this a more private conversation."

Asher straightened, his relaxed posture vanishing as he scanned the tavern. "After you."

One of the things I loved best about him was he never second-guessed me. If I told him there was a pit of venomous sea snakes under his feet and he needed to jump, he wouldn't hesitate. Our friendship was built on trust, and with that came intense loyalty.

Once outside, Asher kept my pace. "Want to explain why I've changed my nightly plans to accompany you out here with nothing as beautiful as M'lady Carmine?"

Carmine was probably the oldest barmaid and farthest thing from beautiful in any man's mind, but I digress—beauty was in the eye of the beholder. "I can't believe you can say that in my presence and still call yourself my friend."

"You are not in my league. I can't even pretend to reach high enough to be seen by someone like you."

I clutched my chest in mock indignation. "My honor is defended."

"Ah, my deary, you know I would fight a legion of pirates to defend your honor."

"A whole legion?" I feigned a gasp. "Including the pirate king himself?"

His brow cocked with his incredulous look. "Don't be ridiculous. No one fights him and lives to tell about it. Your honor would die with me."

Turning to walk backward, I playfully poked him in the chest. "Ah, but you would fight him."

He bumped into me, laughing softly. "I don't think you brought me out here to discuss my fighting skills."

Facing forward, I looped my arm through his. "There was a group of fae in the back corner of Kracken's. They had their eyes locked on me all night. I am not in the mood to deal with horny pirates tonight. I'm sure that's all they wanted."

Asher's face darkened, his good-natured grin vanishing as he stopped in his tracks. "So what you're saying is *I do* have to fight a legion of pirates tonight."

I tugged him forward to keep us moving. "No. I'm saying I want to get out of here. I need a bath, clean clothes, food, and a bed. It's been a long day and an even longer night."

He scrutinized me again. "You were saying something about an earthshake."

I nodded, steering us toward the Tower. It wasn't an actual tower, just something we called it. In all reality, it was nothing more than a den of thieves. We all shared the place like a dysfunctional family. "Did you feel it? Was there any damage here in Everfell?"

He shook his head. "No. But, Blackfoot said there was one not far from Stone Hollow."

"No one felt the one outside of Everfell?" My frown deepened as I recounted the ordeal with the ground opening and trying to swallow me whole.

As predicted, he grumbled about missing all the great adventures. When we neared the Tower's entrance, he tousled my hair before darting to open the door, making a grand gesture. "After you, my Shadowborne huntress, mistress of earthshakes, and the desire of all fae..."

I slugged his shoulder as I walked past. "You forgot greatest swordswoman in all of the Evernight Kingdom."

His laugh followed me down the hall and up the stairs, where he dropped me off near the washroom. Finally alone, I turned the rusted handles and waited as the tub filled with gloriously hot water. Setting my precious satchel to the side, I stripped and sighed as I sank into the metal basin. One of the few places with such luxury, the coveted hot springs that fed Everfell made us both hated and envied across the kingdoms. Running water was scarce, supplied through an ancient system of pipes and magic, but naturally heated water was truly precious.

I sank lower until only my face and knees were above the water. The past few days replayed in my head. Not only did I survive the Waste and outrun the Shadowborne, but also an earthshake. Yet, it was the candlestick that had my curiosity in full. It was probably the hardest heist I'd accomplished in all my years of thieving, but...

I sat up, water sloshing over the sides as I reached for the satchel. My fingers, wrinkled from the heat, fought with the leather flap. Leather and water didn't exactly mix well, but patience wasn't my strong suit.

Grabbing the candlestick, I dropped the bag and leaned back in the tub. The gold article didn't seem worth more than a few pieces of silver. Turning it over, I examined every inch. A subtle yet persistent hum of magic thrummed from within. It was that hum that had called to me, practically begging to be found. And once I took it, its magic had only grown stronger.

Okay, *took* is a light way of saying stole, but either way, that must be what made it so invaluable. My requester offered thirty pieces of gold. That was more than any thief has ever made. I wouldn't even tell Asher how much I was offered. Money like that can change people, and as much as I trusted him as my friend, I couldn't be sure he wouldn't resent me. It could also get me killed.

"A king cannot afford to falter, not when his people are drowning in shadows."

RHAYNE

The Tidecaller groaned and creaked, its timbers straining against the relentless fury of the storm. Each monstrous wave dragged the vessel into the depths of the sea before thrusting the bow violently back toward the sky. My men clung desperately to ropes and railings, their faces etched in determination. The Obsidian Ocean, a churning abyss of frothy whitecaps, seemed to seek out any weakness in our ship's defenses, eager to claim us as its prey.

Above, the sky was a rolling mass of impenetrable black clouds, their oppressive weight making the day indistinguishable from night. Lightning occasionally slashed through the murk, illuminating the ship in stark, fleeting flashes. The wind, an unending scream of anguish, lashed at the crew and ship alike, lamenting the lost and the warnings of those who had fallen before.

The Sliver had always been a treacherous expanse between the Nether Shores and the land kingdoms, but over the past year, it had been consumed by this ceaseless tempest. Originally, it had been created as a barrier between the mortal and fae realms, a safeguard after some fae sought to dominate the mortals. Our magic was never meant to enslave them; they had always been our equals in the eyes of those who valued harmony. The Sliver was more for their protection than ours, a testament to the balance we had once tried to preserve.

What had once been a navigable route from the veiled fae kingdom to the mortal shores was now a maelstrom of despair. Towering waves loomed like sentient beasts, eager to devour any who dared to cross. Its fury was relentless, and as I stared into the storm, I could feel the echoes of the ancient magic that had shaped it. Once a bridge between realms, the Sliver had become a ruthless guardian of the boundary, enforcing its separation with terrifying precision.

In the shadows of the storm, the true menace was not the tempest itself but the lurking horror of the Shadowborne sirens. Their haunting melodies whispered faintly amidst the storm's cacophony, promising not salvation but an eternal descent into the abyss where death was inevitable. Even now, the song tugged faintly at the edges of my mind, a sinister undercurrent beneath the thunder and wind.

Every roll of the ship was a reminder of our frailty. Immortal. King of the Pirates. Fae. Titles mattered not. Each passing moment tested the crew's resolve, their lives hanging by a thread as they battled both the storm and the ever-present threat of the Shadowborne's call. The Veil loomed ahead, unseen but felt, marking our passage back into the Nether Shores.

My hands tightened on the wheel, guiding us through the treacherous waters as the ship sailed toward the heart of the squall. Magic hung in the air, rolling over me like a welcome breath of life, urging me on.

The entrance to my kingdom was just ahead. The Veil, invisible to mortal eyes, could be felt by every fae. Few dared to cross between the realms, though it remained open to all. I didn't need to guard my kingdom—the storm did that for me.

Rain lashed at the ship, drenching every man aboard as if the towering waves hadn't already tried to swallow us whole. The wind threatened to shred the sails but they remained taut, pulling us relentlessly toward our destination.

"Ready the anchor!" My words were little more than a formality now, lost to the roar of the tempest.

The crew knew what needed to be done to pass through the Sliver. Our anchor wasn't ordinary iron—it was infused with magic, bound to my will alone. The sea seized us in its grip. Water and wind swirled violently around us, forming a barrier of magic and ocean that encircled us.

I braced myself as The Tidecaller shuddered under the storm's wrath. "Drop anchor!" My voice was sharp and commanding as I fought to keep the wheel steady. The maelstrom pulled us closer, dragging us toward the Veil with a force that would crush lesser ships.

The crew worked with practiced precision. Their movements were fluid despite the chaos. The Tidecaller roared in protest, but I held her steady, every fiber of my being focused on guiding us through.

We dove deeper into the vortex, the anchor plunging ahead, thrumming with power. I felt its magic ripple through the ship and up my arms, vibrating against my hands as I clung to the wheel. The iron sang as it dragged us down, deliberately guiding us to the seafloor. The moment the anchor struck the sandy depths, the spiraling walls of water collapsed around us, and the storm stilled.

The ship rocked as it rode a wave on top of the water. The deck glistened under the sun while the storm raged behind us. A cheer of good fortune erupted on deck.

"Alright, you heathens! Let's steer her home." I turned the wheel and guided us toward King's Cove.

It had been a year since I'd been home. Much too long for a king to be gone. I left a single ship in the mortal realm to search for the map—an elusive relic said to reveal the location of what its keeper desires. I had yet to lay eyes on this rare parchment, but I would not stop until I found a way to break the curse of the Shadowborne. No one knew how or why my people were changing, but I was determined to find a cure. I hoped the map would lead me to that very thing.

The Shadowborne curse was spreading faster, and every day without the map felt like another failure—as a King, as a leader, and as a man. Once strong and fierce, the fae were now becoming consumed by a darkness that twisted their minds and bodies. I'd seen it firsthand on a ship where an entire crew became too weak to stand, their bodies wracked with convulsions, drenched in sweat as they shifted into something unnatural. Half beast, half fae. Their humanity vanished, with not even a glimmer of their former selves left in their eyes.

But I could not afford to lose faith—not now, not ever.

The familiar sight of my kingdom emerged, bathed in the soft, silvery glow of twilight. The calm sea beckoned us to the island shores as the first twinkle of a star reflected on the water like a mirror to the sky above. My home was a place of magic and mystery, where wildflowers bloomed along the cliffs, and the wind carried the scent of salt and citrus. No matter how many times I returned, it was always a balm to my spirit—a reminder of everything I was fighting for. Here, the curse hadn't reached us, and for a moment, we were safe.

My crew was weary and ready to greet family and friends after such a long journey. Longer than I had anticipated. Leaving behind a ship with its crew on the other side of the Sliver to continue searching for the map was a hard decision. Yet not a single man balked at the prospect of enduring a few more weeks at sea.

As we docked, I felt the excitement ripple through the air. We were in dire need of a moral boost, and watching the crew race to the open arms of their loved ones reassured me this was the right thing to do. Though the curse loomed ever closer, I risked running my men into the ground if I maintained this relentless pace. A brief reprieve could strengthen us in this fight.

I stayed behind, ensuring the ship was secure, while my most trusted friend and second-in-command, Enric, remained at my side. Unlike many of the others, he hadn't found his heartmate or someone waiting for him to debark. Not that he nor anyone needed to find that connection to experience love. There were many fae who never found their heartmates and lived a life full of love. But it was a much deeper connection if a heartmate was found. One that transcended a mortal kind of love.

Or so I was told.

Enric leaned against the doorway to my cabin. He folded his arms, and a cocky grin lifted the corners of his mouth. "My King."

I nodded, gesturing for him to come in. I pointed to the map spread out on the table. "There are so many black markings on this you'd think we'd have found it by now."

"The men are off ship, and the kingdom is preparing for a night of feasting and dancing. It would not hurt you to join in and let this go for one night." He tapped the map. "Perhaps the others will find something more promising in the Evernight kingdom."

"The Waste has divided Evernight. It's doubtful they will find anything past Everfell." I had my own fears about any fae crossing the Waste. We'd already lost too many to the curse. I didn't want to foolishly sacrifice another.

His lopsided frown deepened the pull of his brows. "The map could be anywhere."

"But it is somewhere, and because of that, I will not stop searching."

"What if..." He shook his head.

"Oh, no, go ahead. You and I both know whatever you have to say will eat at you until it festers under your skin and you become an unbearable beast to have around." I chuckled. "Besides, you've never been one to control your tongue with me in private."

He cocked his head, and his smile returned. "I've never questioned your judgment as my king before."

"Is that what you're doing?" He had my attention now.

"I'm just curious. What if the map doesn't help us find a cure? What if it's not the answer to the curse? What if it isn't even real?"

"Ah, I see." I scratched over the days worth of stubble on my jaw. "The map is real. It will have answers. And I will find them." I said it with the conviction I wished I truly felt. In all honesty, I was worried about it being a dead end as much as he did, but as king, I couldn't afford to show uncertainty.

"Are you saying that as my king or my friend?"

"I say that because it's true."

Enric began searching the map once again. "I say if the others don't find it, we search here."

I followed his finger to Shadowmere, a place I had been hesitant to venture beyond Black Sands. Whispers of the curse echoed loudly, capturing the attention of all who dared to tread those lands. Many believed the Shadowborne origins lay deep within the kingdom's borders, and I couldn't bear the thought of exposing any more fae to the possibility of infection. Without a clear understanding of how the curse spread, it was wise to keep them as far from the threat as possible.

"The map could be hidden where we'd least expect it. Perhaps the rumors surrounding the curse are nothing more than a ruse to keep someone from finding it?" I straightened, stretching my neck muscles to release some tension.

"You have poured your life into these maps and across the sea as our king and protector. We have scoured the west and south with nothing to show but a fraction of the hope we set out with." Enric gave a knowing nod. "I will follow you through the cursed lands and beyond. Not just because you're my king, but you are my brother, even if not by blood. All I need is one reassurance, My King."

"You know as well as I that the map will lead you to what you desire most."

Enric hummed in agreement. A comfortable silence settled between us as we both regarded the map. I felt the weight of my role pressing down on me, the expectations of my people, and my own determination colliding in my chest.

With a deep breath, I turned to face him fully. "So, you say there is food and dancing?"

Enric's shoulders relaxed. A mischievous gleam lit up his eyes. "Aye. And women ready to make us very merry."

I laughed, shaking my head. "As tempting as that sounds, I'm afraid I'm not in a place to enjoy it."

My friend leaned over the table, peering at me as though he could unravel the reasons behind my restraint. "You're serious? Just think of the possibilities. The night could be one for the memories, especially when we're off to sea for months with nothing but salt air and the creak of the ship for company." He raised his brows, hinting at the indulgence he envisioned.

I clapped a hand on his shoulder, giving him a firm squeeze. "I hope you make plenty of memories tonight. But for me, temporary company doesn't have the same appeal it once did. Maybe when the time is right, I'll find someone I can truly connect with."

Enric scoffed. "A connection will have you beached! My King, men like us are meant for the sea, not to be kept ashore by the bonds of a woman." He gestured toward the cove. "What will you do if some fae temptress captures your heart and keeps you bound to land, eh?"

I laughed at the thought and shook my head. "Enric, my friend, I fear for the woman who'd even try. I'd sooner see her joining me at sea than anchoring herself ashore."

He gave me a knowing grin. "Aye, that's the spirit! But mark my words, My King, if ever there was a woman to tempt you from your ship, she'd have to have a spirit fiercer than the sea itself."

With a nod, I gestured to the door. "Come, let us not keep the feast waiting. The night is still young, and I'm sure you'll find someone with a spirit to match yours."

Enric laughed. His smirk deepened as he strode toward the door. "Aye. Feast, drink, and perhaps a little adventure. Who knows? Maybe the woman who could tame me is just beyond that door."

"Kidnapped by pirates. That wasn't how I planned my day, but then again, nothing ever went to plan."

BRIAR

The sun had not yet peaked over the sea as I hid behind crates and barrels, not yet ready to be seen. I was to meet the man who wanted the candlestick— the very object that had refused to let me sleep the night before. Its power had hummed and crackled under my skin until long past midnight. Now it rested, tucked safely in my pack, while I remained wide awake, grumpy from little sleep, and waiting for my buyer.

The docks stretched along the misty shoreline of the Ivory Gulf, weathered by salt and time, with rough-hewn planks that creaked underfoot, making it far from an ideal place to hide. Keeping still, I watched under the flickering lights of lanterns that hung from posts, lining the boardwalk. Runes were carved into the dock posts, supposedly remnants of old spells meant to ward off curses from the dark sea, yet only a smidgen of magic emanated from them.

The early morning fog rolled in from the water, swirling with tendrils reaching for the shore. Ships moored along the edges had patched and worn sails; their colors faded from years at sea. Each vessel bore scars from past skirmishes, while carved figureheads in the shapes of beautiful merfolk stood half-hidden in the shadows, watching the mortals who wandered too close.

Of course, it was all just a ruse.

The fae were nothing more than rowdy pirates looking for a good time. Why we had alliances with them, I would never understand. Our king—though I was sure my thoughts would get me killed—was a knuckle-brained cod. His stubbornness and lack of intelligence superseded that of even the most addle-headed deckhand. He'd march headlong into the Sliver, convinced it would bow to his authority. And woe to anyone with the sense to tell him otherwise. Wisdom had no place in that thick skull of his. The man would sooner have argued with a barnacle than admit he was wrong.

But now, with the Shadowborne curse spreading like a sickness, I feared he would run all of Evernight into the ground with his bullheaded pride and endless thirst for power. The tremors that shook our lands, once rare, were becoming unsettlingly common. Some whispered it was the curse digging its claws deeper into our souls.

Yet our king remained as blind as ever. His decisions grew more foolhardy with each passing day, dragging us deeper into the shadow of ruin. If he didn't change course, the entire kingdom would become nothing more than a broken memory, shattered by his arrogance and disregard for the curse creeping closer. For all his talk of alliances and loyalty, he refused to see the cost of his pride, and I feared Evernight would pay the price.

With my back pressed against the damp wood of a crate, I kept my eyes fixed on the shadows. The soft lapping of the water and the creak of the moored ships brought a fleeting sense of peace to my soul.

A slight movement caught my attention. I had expected my buyer to be stealthy—after all, what he came to purchase was no mere trinket. Still, his skill impressed me. He slipped through the shadows like a sly little mouse. For half a second, I wondered if he even knew I was there, but I doubted that, just as much as I doubted the candlestick's supposed value of only thirty pieces of gold. A deal was a deal, though. I might have been a thief, but I still had my integrity.

I turned, hoping to spot him again, but another shadow flickered as if there were two. I tensed, letting my fingers trail down to the hilt of the small dagger I wore at my waist. My gaze darted to the shadows, where now three of them skirted around me, creating the faintest rustle as they moved through the freight. Then... nothing. Silence.

I tried to steady my breath as I waited, straining to hear any movement. A faint clink, like a coin dropping onto the wooden planks, echoed somewhere behind me. My heart raced as I shifted to look, but a hand clamped over my mouth, silencing me. Another wrenched the dagger from my grasp as I was pulled back against a solid chest. I fought to break free, struggling against his grip, but he held me as if he were forged from stone.

"You are a clever little thief hiding in the shadows. Not easy to track down either." His voice, smooth as silk, was entirely too close to my ear.

My heart pounded as I was spun around to face the three fae pirates from last night at Kraken's. Maybe I should have let Asher fight up. Lifting my chin, I met their stares. With a mocking gleam in his eye, the taller one twirled my dagger between his fingers while the other kept a vise-like grip on my arms.

"Well, boys, it's been fun, but I'm not in the mood. You'll have to find another lady to fill your needs." My words were sharper than I felt, but I couldn't believe how relentless these three were. I had assumed they'd get their fill of trouble last night and by morning be satiated, already on their way to another port.

The fae holding me chuckled, his grip tightening slightly. "As tempting as that sounds, m'lady, I think you're the only one who can help us."

Keep it together, Briar. Think. There's always a way out.

I forced a playful expression and glanced between them. "Sorry, boys, but whatever twisted little fantasies you've got going, I'm not the willing participant you're hoping for."

The taller one laughed this time. "Ah, little thief, I would not need to abduct a woman to seduce her."

The one holding me glanced at the silent one beside him. "What do you think, Ciaus? Will the king approve of our little thief?"

Ciaus shrugged, his expression impassive. "If this goes wrong, he can kill you first. It was your idea. What about you, Nyx?"

The taller one, Nyx, grinned, the mocking gleam in his eye only sharpening. "I think I'm intrigued to see how this plays out."

Great. They have a plan, and I don't. I took a slow breath, steadying my nerves. Well, time to make one.

The man holding me wasn't just strong—he was smart. He angled himself in a way that blocked any real damage I might inflict with a kick. Not that I planned to let that stop me. Thrashing and struggling free might have worked, but I needed something more. Something bigger. He didn't seem like the kind of guy who would let go easily.

But...

My eyes darted around the dock, quickly assessing my surroundings. My mind raced with possibilities. I had seconds to decide. The crates I'd been hiding behind loomed above me, stacked precariously in a disorganized heap. If I could shift my weight just right against the base, I might topple them. It was a gamble—a risky one. There was a good chance I'd be injured in the process, but I was out of choices.

The thought of escaping through the confusion ignited a flicker of hope in my chest. I took a deep breath, shifting my weight subtly. The tension in his grip tightened as he registered my movements. Blast! I would have to be quicker. With a decisive push, I leaned my body against the crates, pouring every ounce of strength I had into the effort.

A loud crack thundered through the air as the top crate teetered, then crashed, sending its companions tumbling down like a rolling thunderstorm. The noise was deafening, and for a split second, my captor's grip faltered as he turned to assess the chaos.

Seizing the moment, I twisted free from his hold and darted into the shadows. My heart pounded as adrenaline surged through me as I ran.

Clutching my satchel with the candlestick pressed close, my chest heaved as I ducked through the docks, weaving between crates and barrels. The faint hum of its magic thrummed against my side, steady and insistent, like a heartbeat urging me forward.

The town loomed ahead, shrouded in early morning mist. A few people had begun to emerge from their homes as they prepared for the day before the sun fully rose.

Behind me, I could hear the fae. Their footsteps echoed on the planks, growing louder, their relentless magic prickling at the edges of my senses. It felt invasive, sharp, and unyielding, unlike the candlestick's steady pulse. My breath hitched as I pushed harder, every fiber of my being focused on staying ahead.

I needed a place to hide—or better yet, something I could use as a weapon. The small, cramped shop I'd stumbled into reeked of thick, sooty air. The tang of metal coated each breath, making my chest tighten. I squinted through the dim light and realized I'd stepped into a blacksmith's shop. I could kiss the gods for such luck!

Racks lined the walls, brimming with swords, daggers, and half-finished blades. Edging closer to a small pile of discarded scraps and tools, I crouched low, hoping the sharp tang of iron would mask my scent. Pressing myself against the wall, I held my breath and prayed I'd lost the fae.

The door creaked open, and a shadow filled the doorway. I bit back a curse as the three pirates slipped inside, their movements deliberate and predatory. Their eyes swept over the shop's dim interior, scanning every shadow. Caius's gaze locked onto me, his lips curling into a smug grin.

"There you are, little thief." His voice carried an edge of mockery, smooth and grating all at once. "You are clever, but fae are exceptional hunters."

The other two closed in, spreading out to block any chance of escape. My fingers itched for a weapon. Just inches away, lying on a cluttered workbench, was a dagger almost identical to the one I owned—the one Nyx now possessed.

I inched closer, my mind racing as I calculated the distance. With a sudden burst of energy, I pitched myself toward the blade and closed my fingers around the hilt. But before I could steady myself, one of the men lunged. Instinct took over. I brought the dagger up and twisted, slashing toward him. He stumbled back with a low growl, keeping his distance.

Ciaus sneered. "Feisty. This might be fun after all."

I backed up against the wall, my eyes darting over the cluttered workbench for anything to even the odds. The dagger in my hand felt small and inadequate against three opponents. My fingers brushed the handle of a sword, and I seized it, letting the dagger clatter to the ground. The sword's weight was unfamiliar, heavier than I preferred, but I welcomed it. Adjusting my grip, I squared my stance as they closed in, their smug, taunting expressions brimming with overconfidence. They didn't need to know how skilled I was with a blade.

The one who had seized me before held up his hands. "We just want you to help us."

"Help?" I scoffed, keeping the sword steady between us. "After you tried to kidnap me? Are you out of your minds?"

They exchanged glances as they circled, each poised to pounce. I held my ground, the weight of the blade a steady reminder of my resolve. Let the bite of steel speak for me.

Ciaus shook his head, his gaze shifting to the one I assumed was the mastermind behind their attempted kidnapping. "I hope this is worth it, Tavian."

Tavian rolled his shoulders, his grin widening with maddening confidence. "When the map is found, and the curse is gone, you can thank me. Until then, let's just get her to King's Cove."

King's Cove? Oh no. My chest tightened. I couldn't go there. I wasn't fae! There was no way I would survive going through the Sliver.

Nyx was the first to lunge. I parried, the strength of my desperation driving the blade against his. Metal clashed against metal, the sound ringing out in the cramped shop as I forced myself to hold steady. Every instinct screamed at me to run, but I knew my only chance of escape was to fight my way out. If I could make it to the streets, the morning crowd might offer enough cover to lose them, but that was only a hope.

My back pressed against the edge of the workbench as I blocked another strike. Gritting my teeth, I wrenched my dagger—the one he'd stolen—free from Nyx's grip and slashed out, the blade catching him across the arm. He hissed, retreating just enough for me to slip out of the circle they'd formed.

The blacksmith's shop was narrow, but that worked to my advantage. I only had to keep them in front of me. Raising both the sword and dagger, I let my gaze flick to the exit behind them. If I timed it right, I might still make it out before they blocked me again.

Tavian lunged, but I sidestepped and drove the dagger into his side, twisting sharply before spinning around Ciaus. My heart thundered in my chest as I bolted for the door. Casting one last defiant glare over my shoulder, I darted out of the blacksmith's shop and into the misty streets.

The first rays of dawn crept over the rooftops, casting the marketplace in a pink haze, but there was no time to appreciate the quiet beauty. Behind me, the shouts of the three faes surged closer. My pulse thundered as I veered around a corner, dodging past sleepy vendors setting up for the morning rush. I wove through carts and ducked between stalls and crates, desperate to shake them off my trail. But they were faster than I'd expected, and every time I glanced over my shoulder, one of them was there, closing in like a shadow that refused to let go.

"Enough games, little thief!" Nyx's voice sliced through the air, sharp and mocking. A faint shimmer of magic danced around him as he stalked closer.

Gritting my teeth, I pushed harder, darting down another alley, my heartbeat pounding in my ears.

Just ahead, I spotted a stack of barrels half-blocking a narrow passageway. A burst of adrenaline surged through me as I vaulted over them, hoping to put one last obstacle between us. But as I landed, Tavian stepped into view, his grin as dark as the early morning shadows. He spread his arms wide, blocking the alley's only exit. A small red stain bloomed on his shirt where I had stabbed him, but he didn't seem bothered.

"Going somewhere, little thief?" His voice was low and smooth, carrying a dangerous edge, and his eyes gleamed with malicious intent.

I spun around, only to find Ciaus and Nyx advancing from the other end, their expressions grim and unyielding. My chest tightened as they closed in, cutting off every possible escape. Backing up, I raised the sword and dagger defensively, but the odds were stacked against me.

"Stay back!" I warned, my voice steady despite the fear twisting in my gut. "I'm not about to make this easy for you."

Ciaus chuckled, crossing his arms. "Oh, I'd expect nothing less. But I think we've let you run long enough."

Nyx stepped closer, his magic sparking faintly in the air, wrapping around me like invisible binds. I felt my limbs grow heavy, like weights pulling me down, trapping me where I stood until I dropped both weapons. I tried to fight it, struggling against the invisible force, but it was useless. Their combined strength was too much, and every effort only seemed to drain me further.

"You're coming with us." Tavian looked almost amused as he watched me strain against the magic. "We did warn you."

My heartbeat drummed in my chest, defiant even as I felt myself weakening. They approached, their faces grim yet triumphant, fully aware I had nowhere to run.

Ciaus reached out, his grip firm as he seized my arm, and Tavian flanked me on the other side. I tried one last attempt to break free, twisting and kicking, but their hold was unbreakable.

"Don't take it personally, little thief." Nyx stepped closer, his voice carrying a hint of smug satisfaction as he grabbed my dagger. "We'd hate to harm you. After all, we're just here for your... cooperation."

With that, they led me forward, their grip inescapable, as the sun fully broke over the rooftops, bathing the narrow streets in a harsh, unforgiving light.

"She didn't know it yet, but she held the power to shatter me."

RHAYNE

estless energy prickled through me, keeping sleep at bay for the third night in a row. I stood at the edge of King's Cove, staring out over the dark expanse of the sea as dawn light began to creep across the horizon. The strange pull I'd felt for days was still there, like an itch just under my skin, refusing to be ignored. It was as if something—or someone—was calling me out to the waves.

The crew sensed it too. They'd been quick to ready The Tidecaller the moment I ordered it, moving with a quiet urgency that mirrored my own. We'd taken on a fresh set of hands for the journey, and though they were untested, they'd work hard to keep pace. I took my place at the helm, eager to be moving, the steady rumble of waves filling the silence as we left King's Cove and passed the island's cliffs, heading out toward the open sea.

On the other side of the Sliver, the pull grew stronger, a feeling that was both familiar and utterly foreign. The mist clinging to the waters was dense, thick with magic, its tendrils weaving around us like a spell. I caught sight of a ship in the distance, cutting through the haze, and a sense of recognition sparked within me. It was the one I'd ordered to remain on mortal shores for now. Yet here it was, headed toward the Sliver.

The sight sent a prickle of curiosity through me. Something was wrong, and I couldn't shake the feeling that whatever was drawing me here was connected to that ship. I signaled to my crew and adjusted our course to intercept it.

As we drew closer, I made out more details—the rigging, the darkened sails—everything in its place, yet a thick and strange tension hung in the air. My hands tightened on the wheel as I scanned the deck, searching for any hint of what had driven my men to act without orders.

"What in all the realms do they think they're doing?" My gaze narrowed as the distance between our ships closed. I saw my men now, their faces drawn and uneasy as they noticed us approaching. Whatever had pushed them this way had unsettled them deeply. I had every intention of finding out why.

We came alongside, the ships rocking together as my men secured ropes and boards to bridge the gap. As I stepped to the edge of the deck, Enric moved forward, his expression tense. "My King... with all due respect, maybe I should go instead. Let me find out what's going on over there before you put yourself in the middle of it."

The pull was unmistakable, like an invisible hand wrapping around my chest, tightening with each moment I lingered on my own deck. "Since when do you think I'd let you step into something I can handle myself?"

He crossed his arms, holding my gaze. "I'd just prefer not to bring you back with another scar—or worse. Let me get the answers, and I'll return to you the moment I have them."

I shook my head firmly. "I know you'd do it, Enric, but this is something I'll see with my own eyes. I won't leave it to chance or a secondhand report."

He huffed a breath, but I saw the loyalty behind his frustration. "Fine. Just... don't make me regret it. If anything seems off, you get back here. A king's too valuable to risk on a whim."

I gave him a faint smile, clapping his shoulder. "Aye, but this king is also capable of handling himself. You hold things steady here, Enric—I'll be back soon enough."

Enric watched me for a long moment, his jaw set, but finally gave a nod. "Aye, My King. Just don't make me come over there to haul you back myself."

Whatever strange magic stirred within me urged me toward the second ship. I boarded swiftly, the weight of something unknown yet distinctly powerful driving me forward.

Unease shadowed the crew's faces as they stepped aside, parting as I crossed the deck. They'd seen me in all manners of moods, but I knew they sensed something more dangerous simmering beneath the surface now. My eyes narrowed as I approached a cluster of them near the main mast. At the center, bound but very much alert, was a woman.

The moment I saw her, the pull turned electric, grounding itself in a single truth I hadn't known I'd been waiting for. She was mine.

The revelation hit me like a storm wave, both thrilling and infuriating. She'd been hidden here, under my nose, among my men, their eyes and hands far too close for comfort. And they were planning to take her across the Sliver—a reckless gamble that could very well cost her life.

One of the crew glanced my way, hesitant. "Captain... we found her on the docks. Thought she'd be worth bringing to your attention."

The rational part of me urged patience, but it was no match for the possessive fury seething beneath my skin. I forced myself to remain calm, though my voice lowered to a dangerous edge. "If any of you are close enough for your breath to touch her, it will be your last."

A shiver of silence fell over the men. I saw them step back instinctively, glancing at each other with wide eyes. I kept my gaze on the woman, feeling the war between anger and admiration as I took her in. She was bold, but that fire only fueled my need to keep her close and shield her from every eye that dared linger.

I stepped closer, my voice a command that brooked no argument. "You're coming aboard my ship." The words were firm and meant as much for her as my men, who remained frozen under my glare.

My fingers brushed against her skin as I unbound her. A jolt surged through me at the unexpected connection, and something deep within me shifted, anchoring itself to her. I swallowed hard, focusing on the ropes, forcing myself to stay composed as the truth settled in my mind. Whether she felt it too or had any inkling of what we were, she gave no indication. For now, I would keep that knowledge to myself.

Her long dark hair was messy after her journey this far. But it was her eyes that held me frozen to the deck. The icy blue stare that glared up at me was cold and spoke volumes, even though her voice did not. My tone softened, but only slightly. "This isn't a choice. You're coming with me."

I turned and led her across the board connecting the two ships, fully aware of my men's watchful gazes. The pull that had driven me here settled as soon as she was near, an inexplicable urge to protect her taking root. I couldn't explain it, but the thought of harm befalling her felt unbearable. Once aboard, I ordered my crew to prepare to set sail, unwilling to leave her on the mortal shores or anywhere beyond my reach.

I took her hand, guiding her toward the quarterdeck. With her beside me, I was acutely aware of every curve—the soft, tempting weight of her hips, thighs, and ample chest. She was enough to make a man question his own restraint. "Consider yourself under my protection now. And let's be clear—protection isn't something I offer lightly."

She looked up at me, defiant as ever, but I caught a flicker of something softer in her gaze. The pull finally settled in my chest as she stepped with me to the helm, where she belonged.

Without another word, I turned to the crew. "Prepare to set sail." There would be no leaving her behind, no chance of letting her slip from my sight. Whatever this pull was, it had brought her to me, and I'd be damned if I let her go.

"I assume you know who I am, but I would appreciate the same courtesy in return." My voice was calm, but my gaze never left her as I grabbed the wheel, watching every subtle shift of her stance. She glanced around, her eyes flicking toward the railings, the stretch of open water, and the distant horizon beyond. It was clear she was searching for an escape.

But there would be no escape. Not here. Out on the open sea, any attempt would be reckless. Her chances were as thin as the mist. And if she tried, it would lead to nothing but her death.

The thought clenched at me, a fierce tension coiling in my chest. No. That couldn't happen. I wouldn't let it. The idea of her risking her life, losing it before I even had a chance to understand the pull between us—it struck deeper than I cared to admit.

"Why does it matter if you know my name or not?" Her voice cut through the air, defiant, a challenge flashing in her eyes that was both maddening and... entertaining.

I allowed a faint smile to touch my lips. "Because you're on my ship, and I'm the one who decides who leaves it." I let the words linger, their weight clear. "So, humor me."

She held my gaze, and I saw the battle warring behind her eyes. But after a beat, her shoulders dropped, and a resigned sigh escaped her lips. "Briar," she muttered, almost too low to hear, as if giving up her name was the last thing she wanted to do. "Briar Firethorn."

"Briar," I repeated it, tasting the word, feeling the way it rolled over my tongue with a strange satisfaction. She'd given me her name, a small surrender, yet it felt like a victory—one I wasn't sure I could afford to let go of.

"Good." I eased my hand off the wheel. "Now that we're properly introduced, let's see if we can get along... for the rest of the journey."

"He stood there, like he owned the seas—and Gods help me, I hated how much he looked the part."

BRIAR

faint hum pulsed through the planks beneath my feet—The Tidecaller. A ship steeped in legend, rumored to have been forged in magic. Its timber was said to come from the Heartwood Tree, a mythical tree that grew only at the center of the Veil between realms. They claimed its wood carried the whispers of the ocean itself, alive and untamed.

The feeling underfoot grew into an unsettling weight. It was as if the ship itself were watching me, assessing. Blast! Gods, how had I ended up here? I bit back a curse, glancing around the polished wood and out to the endless sweep of the sea from the helm of the ship.

The Pirate King's ship.

A knot tightened in my throat, heavy and immovable. My skin prickled with unease, though I told myself it was nothing. Just a ship, just wood and sails and—I shook the thought off, focusing instead on how to keep myself alive aboard this cursed vessel.

The Pirate King stood just a few paces away, his back to me as he barked orders to his crew. Even without looking at me, he commanded the space, filling it with the kind of authority that made me feel both caged and... well, something I didn't dare put a name to. I clenched my fists, feeling the faint tremor in them and hating myself for it. There was no room for fear. Not here. Not with him.

But it was hard to ignore the reality of my situation. I was on Rhayne Whitehook's ship, halfway to gods-know-where, and the odds of escaping were looking slimmer by the second. I needed a plan, something to get myself out of this mess, but every angle I thought of dead-ended with the thought of that man standing just over there, as unyielding as the ocean itself.

I stiffened, crossing my arms in an attempt to steady myself as he turned to face me. Gods, he was a striking man... or fae, whatever he was. His long, white hair fell down his back, small braids woven throughout, and tattoos peeked out from beneath his shirt, hinting at a sculpted, well-muscled body.

I'd heard rumors about his magic, how anyone who struck a bargain with him carried his mark until their debt was paid. Though I'd never seen anyone with such a telltale sign, seeing him now, in the flesh, I had no doubt he'd revel in branding someone as his.

But then his gaze met mine, those intensely blue eyes locking onto me as if he already owned me. It stirred something deep inside me, something I had no business feeling. Something that should stay buried and forgotten. Now was definitely not the time to find my captor attractive.

"Enjoying the view?" His voice cut through my thoughts, low and almost amused. If I didn't know better, I'd think he knew exactly what was running through my head.

"Hardly. You know, most captors at least pretend they don't enjoy their work," I shot back, letting my words drip with as much venom as I could muster.

He cocked a brow, that infuriating smirk curling at the corner of his mouth. "Captor, am I? You wound me with such accusations."

I bit down on my response, refusing to give him the reaction he was clearly angling for. "If you wanted my cooperation, maybe a simple invitation would've sufficed."

He stepped closer, close enough that I could feel the weight of his gaze. "Invitations are for guests." His tone edged with curiosity. "So tell me, Briar, why would my men risk bringing you aboard a ship?"

I cursed under my breath. I didn't like the way he said my name, nor the pull in my chest every time he did. Anger flared hotly, chasing back the fear that simmered just beneath it.

"Whatever you think you're gaining by keeping me here, I promise it's not worth the trouble."

His gaze held mine, a mixture of amusement and something darker that sent a shiver down my spine. "That's for me to decide. For now, you'll stay on board."

I opened my mouth to argue, but nothing came. He wasn't exactly wrong. I'd seen the way his men watched me, eyes sharp with curiosity and something close to suspicion. If he hadn't stepped in, if he hadn't pulled me onto his ship himself... I shook the thought away, forcing myself to focus.

I turned toward the horizon, the vast stretch of ocean mocking me with its freedom. "If you think keeping me here will end well, you're as mad as they say."

He let out a low chuckle, the sound deep and rich. "I'd be disappointed if you didn't put up a fight, Briar. But be warned," his tone sharpened as he leaned in closer, "that fight ends with you staying here, on my ship, where you're under my watch."

I exhaled slowly, unable to look away, unwilling to give him the satisfaction of seeing how much this shook me. But as I gazed back at him, the weight of his presence, the sureness in his voice... I couldn't deny the flicker of fear and intrigue twisting in my chest.

Gods help me.

I watched as Rhayne moved to the helm, signaling his men to adjust our course. We were turning, the ship carving a smooth arc through the water. My stomach dropped as I realized where we were going. A dark, eerie light shimmered in the distance, like a whisper of doom at the edge of the horizon.

Panic rose, tightening in my chest. The Sliver. The temptress of the sea, with magic deep and deadly as the abyss. I'd heard the tales all my life—how only the fae could cross it and survive, how mortals who dared were pulled under by dark magic, never seen again. And now I was headed straight for it, on a fae king's ship.

41

Rhayne's gaze shifted back to me, and for a second, I could swear there was a flicker of something in his eyes—amusement, maybe, or some kind of twisted satisfaction.

"Frightened, are we?" His tone was too casual, the barest trace of a smirk on his lips.

I forced my voice to steady as I gripped the rail tighter than I'd like. "Only a fool wouldn't be. You're taking me straight into death's hands."

He turned, his azure eyes sharpening as they met mine, studying me as if trying to decide how much he'd tell me. "You think I'd risk that?" He let out a short breath, somewhere between a laugh and a scoff. "I don't know why you're on my ship, or what's led you here, but if you think I'm about to let the Sliver take you, you're sorely mistaken."

I tried to muster defiance, but the creeping mist of the Sliver was too close, its magic tugging at something deep inside me, and the fear took root before I could stop it. "You act like you can stop it."

"I can." He took a step closer, his gaze holding mine, a subtle intensity in his expression. "As long as you're on my ship, under my watch, nothing will harm you."

I wanted to challenge him, to fight against the strange pull he seemed to have over me, but something in his tone was almost... comforting. And terrifying.

"The sea obeys me." His voice was low and edged with something dark and powerful. "As long as you're with me, it won't touch you."

I stared at him, my mind at war with the flicker of hope his words ignited. He seemed so certain, so convinced he could hold back the magic that had swallowed sailors and ships whole. But still, doubt lingered.

"Just stay close and let me worry about the Sliver." His gaze softened, but there was no missing the possessive edge in his voice.

The Sliver teased us for a day, looming on the horizon until the first tendrils of mist slithered over the bow, curling around us like fingers reaching out from a grave. I clutched the railing, my knuckles white as my heart hammered wildly. The air grew colder, a chilling dampness sinking into my skin. My grip tightened until my nails bit into my palms.

A gentle but firm hand touched my shoulder, startling me. Rhayne's eyes met mine, steady and fierce, like the ocean itself. "Stay close," he murmured, his voice a low, calming rumble that cut through my panic. "I won't let the Sliver harm you."

He said it with such conviction as if he could simply command the storm into submission. But as I looked back at the towering clouds and the roiling, frothy waves, my fear only sharpened. Mortals didn't survive the Sliver—that much I knew. And yet here I was, inching closer to it with every roll of the ship.

"It's... alive," I whispered, shuddering as the mist thickened, wrapping itself around the ship like a shroud. The Obsidian Ocean stretched out before us, dark and wild, each wave a monstrous swell eager to claim us. Lightning cracked through the clouds, illuminating the endless expanse of black water, and I fought the urge to cry out as the ship swayed heavily.

Rhayne's hand moved from my shoulder to the small of my back, steadying me. "Briar, you're safe. Look at me."

I forced my eyes away from the storm and looked up at him. His gaze was unbreakable, calm as steel, and as he leaned closer, his hand slid up to rest just above my elbow in a gentle but firm hold. "Trust me. The sea obeys my will." The intensity in his voice settled deep inside of me, as if his very touch could anchor me.

I nodded, swallowing back the scream lodged in my throat as he turned back to the helm. His arm brushed mine, keeping me close, and I clung to that touch, focusing on the steady warmth of his presence instead of the terror unfurling around us.

"Drop anchor!" His command cut through the chaos, barely rising above the storm's deafening roar. I hadn't realized how loud the tempest had grown until that moment. The crew sprang into action, their movements swift and precise. Eyes forward, their faces were drawn but resolute. They knew what was coming.

Rhayne's hand tightened on my arm as the ship pitched forward, lurching into the mist. The anchor plunged into the depths, humming with an eerie, thrumming energy that seeped through the deck and into my bones. Suddenly, the ship tipped like some invisible hand dragged us downward. My heart leaped into my throat as we dropped, plunging straight toward the ocean floor.

A scream tore from my lips as the sea pulled us under, my voice echoing against the hull as the waters swallowed us whole. My knees buckled, and I clung to the rail, bracing myself as the ship tilted at an impossible angle. Rhayne's arm slid around my waist, steadying me, his grip firm and unyielding as he wrapped his body around mine.

"Hold tight." His voice was unwavering and calm, as if we weren't hurtling through a vortex. His touch was the only thing grounding me, the only solid thing in a world gone mad.

The ship groaned and shuddered, each timber straining against the weight of the sea pressing down on us. I could feel Rhayne's magic wrapping around the ship, holding it together, protecting us. The mist swirled, thick and dark, blocking out any trace of light, and I felt as though I were sinking into the abyss itself. My heart pounded wildly, fear clawing up my throat as I clung to him.

And then, as suddenly as it began, we stopped.

The ship steadied, floating gently on a calm sea. The mist lifted, revealing a surreal stillness, the water around us clear and almost tranquil. Blue skies starkly contrasted the distant storm raging behind us, as if some invisible barrier held it back. I caught my breath, my heart still racing as I realized we were... safe. Somehow.

Rhayne's arm stayed firmly around me, his warmth cutting through the cold, eerie quiet surrounding us. He glanced down, his gaze softening as it met my wide-eyed terror. "See?" His voice was low, steady, and reassuring. "You're safe with me."

I released a shaky breath, my fingers still gripping his sleeve as I nodded. Somehow, he'd guided us through the Sliver, defying every tale I'd ever heard. And despite my terror, I believed him.

Rhayne's hand slid to my arm, a steady warmth anchoring me in place as the world around us settled into an impossible calm. I felt his gaze on me, but I couldn't bring myself to look up—not yet. Not while my heart still raced with the memory of being dragged into the depths, and his hand was the only thing keeping me grounded.

"Welcome to my side of the sea." His voice was a low murmur, laced with a hint of pride and something deeper, something I couldn't quite name.

I looked up then, meeting his eyes, an unfamiliar steadiness in his gaze. The weight of what had just happened settled over me, sharp and undeniable: he had guided me through the Sliver, defied death itself, as if the storm had bowed to him and let us pass.

"Don't look so surprised," he added, a faint smile tugging at his lips. "I told you I wouldn't let anything happen to you."

I swallowed, forcing myself to release the lingering tension in my shoulders. "I didn't exactly have a choice in the matter, did I?"

He chuckled softly, the sound sending a prickle down my spine. His grip on my arm softened, though he didn't fully release me. "Not yet, Briar," he murmured, his tone carrying a subtle warning. "But if you cooperate, I won't have to make choices for you."

Before I could find a response, he turned back to the helm, calling orders to his men as they busied themselves, as if surviving a tempest was an ordinary feat.

I forced myself to breathe, to let go of the terror that had gripped me, though its shadow lingered. We crossed the Sliver. We survived. And now, as we drifted toward the fae kingdom, I couldn't shake the feeling that I'd crossed more than just an ocean. There was no going back—not from this, not from him.

And the worst part? I wasn't sure I wanted to.

6

"The sea demands loyalty, and so do I."

RHAYNE

The ship rocked gently in the quiet waters of the secluded cove. The setting sun bathed the deck in a golden glow, its light softening the sharp edges of the ship's timbers. I stood at the helm, watching as Briar was brought before me. Her gaze was fierce, her shoulders squared with a defiance that might have impressed me—if it hadn't been aimed at me. She met my eyes without a flicker of fear, her fiery stare brimming with unspoken questions.

"Care to explain why your men so rudely removed me from the bow? I was perfectly content far away from... you." She crossed her arms and tilted her chin up.

I held her gaze, resisting the urge to show even a flicker of the protectiveness that stirred within me. She didn't know the truth—that she was my heartmate. The realization hit me hard while we were crossing the Sliver. And, every pulse of her defiance only drew me closer, stirring something fierce and unyielding inside me. I kept my expression calm, my voice measured. "Patience, Briar. All things in due time."

Her eyes narrowed. "I don't think you understand. I don't intend to stay here, and I'm certainly not here to '*help*' you." Her voice was a low challenge, and I could tell she meant it. I respected her spirit, even admired it, but I couldn't let it dictate the terms.

Before I could respond, Ciaus, Nyx, and Tavian were brought in, each wearing slightly wary expressions. They were excellent pirates, skilled and trusted, yet I could see that they understood the fine line they had crossed by acting without orders. They each bowed slightly, waiting for me to speak.

"Explain yourselves." My tone was hard to keep calm—especially when it came to *her*. More precisely, to anyone who had touched her. "I didn't command you to bring a her here. We do not kidnap women."

Nyx stepped forward first, clearing his throat. "My King, we felt her magic the moment we saw her in a local tavern. We'd heard the rumors about a thief who could find *anything*, anywhere." He glanced briefly at Briar, then back at me, his voice carrying a note of admiration. "Word has it she's the best. That she's touched by magic."

Briar scoffed. "Magic? I don't have any magic. And even if I did, I wouldn't use it to help you find whatever it is you're looking for."

I watched her carefully, noting the fire in her eyes. She seemed genuinely baffled by the mention of magic, as if the idea was as foreign to her as the open sea might be to a mortal villager. She truly didn't know. Yet even I could feel the pulsing power radiating from within her.

The itch to move closer to her stirred within me, but I refrained, keeping my boots planted on the deck. "Regardless of what you believe, Briar, your presence here is no accident. And while their decision to bring you here was... unexpected, I have my reasons to believe they were right."

She shot me a glare, fists clenched at her sides. "I don't care who your men think I am. I'm not helping you. Not willingly."

Her defiance sparked something primal within me, but I held my composure. I wasn't about to let her out of my sight, not when she was so much more than she realized. I turned to the men. "Anything else?"

Ciaus shifted slightly under my gaze. "We overheard some talk. Other thieves say she's got a talent for finding what others can't. The kind of skill that's rare even among the fae."

Briar shot him a scathing look. "If you think rumors make me some kind of treasure-hunting fae, you're more deluded than I thought."

A small smile tugged at the corner of my mouth, but I quickly concealed it. "You may not see it, but something in you is beyond mere talent, but whether you choose to help or not... that's a different matter."

She let out a huff of frustration. "I'm not helping you, no matter what you think you know about me."

I met her glare, a flicker of admiration stirring in my chest despite the tension. "We'll see. You might find that certain... motivations change with time."

Her jaw tightened, but I could see a spark of uncertainty in her eyes. For now, I'd give her space to come to terms with her situation. Her defiance would prove entertaining, if nothing else, but I had other issues to deal with.

The Tidecaller rocked gently, but the tension on the quarterdeck was anything but calm. Ciaus, Tavian, and Nyx stood before me, their expressions ranging from sheepish to defiant. My crew gathered at a respectful distance, watching in tense silence. This wasn't just about disobedience—it was about ensuring that every man aboard knew who held the reins.

I stepped forward, letting the weight of my presence settle over them. "You acted without orders," I began, my voice low and steady, each word a sharp blade cutting through the stillness. "You kidnapped her. You brought her here, into my domain, without my command."

Ciaus cleared his throat, glancing at the others before speaking. "We thought it best, Captain. We believed bringing her here would help you... and the curse."

"You believed," I echoed, my tone biting. "And in your belief, you decided to take matters into your own hands. Did you think the chain of command didn't apply to you? Or did you think yourselves cleverer than your king?"

Tavian shifted uneasily, but Nyx, ever the bold one, met my gaze head on. "We acted for the good of the crew, Captain. For you."

"For me?" I stepped closer, the magic in my blood stirring like a restless tide. "You presume too much, Nyx. I decide what is for the good of my crew, not you. And you will not act in my name without my leave again."

They all stiffened as the air around us thickened. The sea's magic surged through me, answering my call. "You will make amends," I continued, my voice a low growl. "And you will do it under my terms."

I extended my hand, palm up, and the magic flared to life. Tendrils of water coiled around my fingers, glowing faintly with an otherworldly light. "A *bargain*," I said, the word laced with power. "You will bind yourselves to me until this curse is ended. You will obey my commands without question, and if you falter, the sea will claim you."

For a moment, silence hung in the air. Their hesitation rippled through me, sharp and unwelcome. Loyalty was not optional—hesitation was not acceptable.

Then, one by one, they nodded. "We accept," Nyx said, his voice steady despite the weight of the magic pressing down on them.

The delay lingered in my mind, a flicker of irritation rising before I buried it. They had crossed the line, but their acceptance was the bare minimum I demanded. Loyalty to me, to the ship, was not something they could choose when convenient—it was a duty, unyielding and absolute. They would learn that hesitation had no place here.

The magic surged, coiling like a living thing around their hands. As the glowing light seared into their skin, all three men grimaced. Tavian sucked in a sharp breath, Nyx clenched his jaw, and Ciaus hissed through his teeth, his hand trembling slightly. The marks—the same hook tattooed onto my arm—burned into their flesh, a permanent symbol of the bargain struck.

The pain wasn't just physical; I could feel the magic's weight settle over them, binding their very souls to mine. A hum echoed in my chest, faint but unmistakable, as if The Tidecaller herself had acknowledged the deal.

"This is no ordinary pact," I said, my voice low but firm. "The mark binds you to me. You are mine now, bound to The Tidecaller and to me. Betray me, and the magic will do worse than this brief sting."

They nodded, subdued but resolute. The crew murmured their approval, the lesson clear to all: disobedience had consequences, and loyalty was not optional under my rule.

I turned my attention back to Briar and gestured to Nyx. "Take her to my quarters." I clenched my jaw, burying the surge of emotions rising within me at the thought of her in my cabin.

Briar's eyes widened, her lips parting as she processed my words. "*Your* quarters?"

I held her gaze, allowing a faint smirk to play at the corners of my mouth. "Consider it part of your... *accommodations*, as a guest on my ship." I watched her bristle, the frustration flickering across her face. "As I said before, you are under *my* protection."

"Your idea of hospitality needs work." She crossed her arms tightly over her chest.

I took a step, closing the space between us. "You'll stay there, where I can ensure you won't find any mischief." It was hard to rein in the possessiveness simmering just beneath the surface.

Nyx moved to lead her toward the cabin, unable to deny my request, but the instant he stepped closer, I realized my mistake. Letting someone else be near her was out of the question. I held up a hand, stopping him in his tracks. "I'll handle it from here."

With that, I gestured for her to follow me. She hesitated, her eyes narrowing as if calculating an escape, but then, with a resigned sigh, she trailed after me down the narrow corridor.

I opened the door to my cabin and stepped inside, nodding for her to follow. She entered cautiously, her gaze sweeping over the room. The cabin was both practical and personal, with a single, well-worn bed tucked against the wall and a heavy desk cluttered with maps and navigation tools.

Her gaze fell to the bed, and she turned to me, raising a brow. "Where, exactly, am I supposed to sleep?"

I leaned against the doorframe, crossing my arms as I watched her. "The bed is yours. Unless you'd prefer the floor?"

She huffed, rolling her eyes. "Generous of you."

I kept my gaze steady on her, noting the tension in her posture and the faint flicker of nerves in her expression. "I'd suggest you rest. I'd like to avoid tying you to the mast if you get any ideas.

Her gaze narrowed. "I don't need to be babysat."

"Good." My voice dropped as I leaned slightly closer. "But you'll understand why I'll be close by. Just in case."

She met my gaze, the defiance in her eyes a flame I found myself eager to keep close. For now, I'd let her think she had some control, even if the bond between us told me otherwise.

As I left the cabin, a sense of satisfaction settled over me. But new questions raced through my mind. If she didn't know she had magic, she might not know what she was capable of. And if she was truly a thief that could find anything...

Perhaps the map was within reach after all.

Enric came to the bridge carrying a satchel. "She had this in her possession when they took her. Thought you'd like it."

"Anything interesting?" I took the offered bag and lifted the leather flap.

Enric raised a brow, barely containing his laugh as he looked between the bag and me. "Unless she's a trained candle warrior." His tone dripped with dry sarcasm, piquing my interest. "I'm still trying to figure out how it took three full-grown fae to bring her in."

Pulling out a large gold candlestick, I held it up and grunted a response. I'd wondered that as well. As I turned the heavy candlestick in my hands, its weight solid and cool against my palms, I couldn't help but frown. It was a fine object, but hardly a treasure worth fighting for—or so it seemed on the surface. Yet, according to Enric and my men, Briar had held onto it as if her life depended on it, refusing to let it go even after her capture.

"What's this about, then?" I murmured to myself, eyeing the intricate carvings along its stem. I could feel a faint pulse of something, almost a hum beneath the surface, but if there was magic woven into it, it was subtle, like a secret waiting to be uncovered.

Enric chuckled beside me, clearly amused. "Hardly looks like a weapon, does it?" He leaned against the railing, watching me with that familiar glint of skepticism. "But whatever it is, she thought it was worth fighting Ciaus, Tavian, *and* Nyx to keep it close."

I didn't respond, my focus entirely on the candlestick, its gold gleaming in the light. The more I studied it, the more questions arose. Briar had denied having magic, yet her actions contradicted that. I could feel her magic—or something like it—lingering on this object, though faint. And that made me wonder just what secrets she was hiding.

"I'll find out soon enough." Sliding the candlestick back into her satchel, I fastened the leather flap with a decisive pull.

Enric raised a brow. "You're planning to question her?"

I gave a curt nod, already turning toward my quarters. "She'll tell me why this was so important. Whether she wants to or not."

I walked through the corridor, the satchel heavy in my hand, its weight only added to my impatience. Reaching the door to my cabin, I hesitated, tempering the possessive edge I felt every time I thought of her. She was mine to protect, and that included understanding the secrets she carried.

Pushing the door open, I found her pacing, her defiance still simmering in her gaze as she looked up sharply. Her eyes fell to the satchel in my hand, widening slightly before narrowing, and a spark of resistance flared.

I held up the bag. "What's in this that's worth the trouble of three fae to keep you in line?"

She crossed her arms, tilting her chin up with that fiery spark I was quickly coming to expect. "That's none of your business."

"Considering you're on my ship, I'd say it's very much my business." I stepped closer, placing the satchel on the desk with deliberate care, then turned to face her. "You fought hard to keep it, Briar. There must be something about it I should know."

She shifted, casting a glance at the bag but keeping her lips pressed tight. "It's just a candlestick."

My gaze stayed steady on her. "Is it?"

"Yes." Her voice was firm, but her eyes betrayed her uncertainty. "I stole it fair and square."

"Interesting," I murmured, reaching into the satchel to pull out the object in question. I turned it slowly, holding it out for her to see. "So, you're telling me that this—just a gold candlestick—is worth throwing your life into chaos?"

She looked away, arms tightening around herself, her jaw clenched as if willing herself to keep silent. But I caught a flicker of something in her expression, a brief hesitation that only fueled my suspicion. She didn't know why it was important either.

"If it's just a candlestick, then you won't mind explaining why it feels... off," I pressed, watching her reaction closely. "I'm willing to bet there's more to this than you're letting on. When you're ready to stop pretending, you'll find I'm more than willing to listen."

She folded her arms, tilting her chin in defiance. "Or what? You'll brand me like you did those men?"

The idea of her wearing my mark stirred something I wasn't ready to confront—a pull, magnetic and undeniable. My lips pressed into a thin line as I shook my head. "A bargain with you would be dangerous."

Her brow arched, a spark of sarcasm in her gaze. "Something we both agree on."

I set the candlestick down firmly, the soft clink of metal on wood echoing in the silence. For now, I would keep it close, and if she had more secrets buried with it, I would find them. I didn't care if it took all night.

Pulling out a chair, I took a seat and watched as Bryer contemplated where she should sit. She yanked the second chair out from under the table. "Not touching the bed," she muttered, her tone edged with irritation.

She sat across from me, her shoulders squared and her gaze fiercely jumping from me to the candlestick. I could feel the faint hum of its magic, teasing me with its secret. Briar's defiance was matched only by her confusion.

"Tell me everything you know about this. Including how you came to have it. Leave nothing out." Though I kept my tone calm, my patience was wearing thin. If she truly was a thief who could find anything, we were going to have to find a way to work together. I needed to find the map, and if my men were right, then we might have found the one person to lead us to it.

Briar crossed her arms, leaning back in her chair. "I've already told you. I took it because someone asked me to. That's all there is to it."

"Aye, but this is the first time you've told me someone asked you to steal it. Who was it? Why did they want it?"

She shrugged. "I don't know. I don't ask names."

"Why did they ask you to steal it?" I wanted to hear the truth from her lips. I watched her carefully, noting the tension in her jaw and the slight flare of her nostrils. "You expect me to believe you went to such lengths for a mere trinket? Three of my best men dragged you onto this ship, and you fought them over a candlestick?"

Her eyes narrowed. "I was ambushed by your pirates. They didn't even know about the candlestick when they fought me, and then, because they are horrible swordsmen, they realized they were losing and had to resort to magic to force me onto their ship."

The corner of my mouth quirked up despite myself. "But that doesn't explain why I can feel magic in this... or why you were so determined to keep it."

Her gaze flicked to the candlestick, her expression unreadable. "Magic? If it's magic, that's news to me. I don't have any magic, so you'll forgive me if I don't see what all the fuss is about."

Interesting. Either she was an incredible liar, or she truly didn't know. I leaned forward, resting my elbows on the table, letting my eyes bore into hers. "You're telling me you're completely unaware that magic clings to this?"

She shrugged, though I didn't miss the flicker of doubt in her expression. "I'm not fae. I can't sense magic. To me, it's just a candlestick hardly worth the coins my buyer offered."

Silence hung between us, heavy and thick. I let her sit with her words, watching for any sign of faltering, any hint of recognition. But she held her ground, her eyes steady on mine, though I could see the faintest hint of something else—a wariness she tried to conceal.

"Then humor me." I lifted the candlestick and held it out to her. "Touch it. If it's just a piece of gold to you, then you won't mind."

Her jaw tightened, but she reached out, taking the candlestick from my hand. The moment her fingers wrapped around it, I felt a faint pulse, a surge of energy that resonated through the room. Her eyes widened, just a fraction, and her fingers tightened around the metal as if fighting the urge to let go.

"There." She kept her voice steady and her grip firm. "Satisfied?"

I studied her, noting the way her breath had quickened and her knuckles turned white as she held the candlestick. "If it's nothing to you, why do I feel the magic in you now?"

She flinched. A quick, involuntary reaction that told me I'd struck a nerve. She placed the candlestick back on the table, her gaze hardening. "You're imagining things."

"Am I?" Satisfaction curled within me. She was beginning to falter, and it was enough to confirm my suspicions. "If you have no magic, Briar, then why is it that the candlestick reacts to your touch?"

She scoffed, but there was an edge to her voice now, a hesitation that hadn't been there before. "It's just a piece of gold. Whatever you think you're feeling, it has nothing to do with me."

I leaned back, crossing my arms as I studied her. "You can keep telling yourself that if it makes you feel better. But I think we both know there's more to you than meets the eye."

Her eyes flashed with defiance, but there was something else beneath it, something closer to fear. She was beginning to realize that the story she'd told herself might not be the whole truth.

Gods, this woman was intriguing.

I let the silence stretch, watching her carefully. "This candlestick is no ordinary object. You may not know why, but I suggest you start trying to remember where you found it, or who might have wanted you to keep it."

She bit her lip, glancing at the candlestick, her expression conflicted. "It was… just an item among many. A piece I was offered a high price for."

"Then consider it fate. Whatever magic is bound to it—and perhaps to you—has brought you to this ship."

I stood, letting my words settle as I watched her. She might pretend it was just a piece of gold, but something about her reaction suggested otherwise. She held more power than she knew, more than she might even believe.

"A deal with the Pirate King was the only way."

BRIAR

eluctantly, I took the candlestick from the table, its weight familiar but somehow heavier now, as if it were holding onto secrets I'd yet to unearth. The dim light of the cabin cast soft shadows over its surface, and I frowned, touching the small, delicate engravings, like tiny stars clustered along the shaft, and strange symbols etched in a thin line around the base.

"These symbols…" I murmured, more to myself than to Rhayne, tracing my fingers over the intricate patterns.

As my fingers brushed one of the symbols, a faint shimmer glowed under my touch, like the soft spark of embers catching in the night. I jerked my hand back, staring at the candlestick in surprise, watching as the glow faded as quickly as it had come. My pulse quickened, but I kept my face neutral, unwilling to let him see my unease.

Rhayne leaned forward, his gaze intense, tracking every movement as if he could draw meaning from my reaction. "It's fae magic. Only someone with a connection to our realm could activate it."

I scoffed, rolling my eyes as I held the candlestick a little farther from myself. "Right. Well, I hate to disappoint you, but I don't have any mystical connection to the fae." I was mortal, plain and simple. This whole notion of *connection* was as foreign to me as the symbols themselves.

Rhayne watched me closely, his gaze unwavering, a hint of curiosity glinting in his eyes. "Then how do you explain that?" He gestured toward the candlestick, where a faint shimmer still pulsed softly, as if waiting for my touch to bring it to life again.

I swallowed, feeling the lingering tingle from where my fingers had brushed the markings. I didn't have an explanation, and a strange, unsettling warmth sank in my chest. "Maybe it's broken? Or maybe it's just reacting to the room? I'm sure fae magic has a way of misfiring every now and then."

But even I didn't believe my own words. The glow had been so clear, so certain, as if it recognized me in a way I couldn't understand. My gaze fell back to the symbols drawing me in.

Rhayne's voice was calm but laced with a knowing edge. "Magic doesn't *misfire*, Briar. It only responds to those it's bound to." He leaned back, crossing his arms as he studied me. "You may claim no connection, but that doesn't make it any less real."

I bristled, gripping the candlestick tighter as his words settled over me, stirring questions I'd never thought to ask. I was mortal; I'd always been mortal. But here, under his scrutinizing gaze and with the candlestick's faint shimmer betraying me, I felt the first crack of doubt.

I placed it on the table between us, trying to ignore the way it seemed to call to me, almost as if it knew me better than I knew myself. I had always felt magic, been drawn to it even. And it to me. But that didn't mean I possessed any magic.

I huffed as I ran my fingers along the candlestick. A flicker of light pulsed under my touch, only to disappear again, leaving me more exasperated than before.

I pressed on a small engraving, watching it glow faintly before fading. "It's just a glorified lamp if you ask me."

Across the table, Rhayne watched me with infuriating patience. His arms were crossed, and an almost amused expression sparked in his eyes. He didn't speak, didn't interfere, just watched. It was as if he were perfectly content to let me struggle while he studied the candlestick's reactions to my touch.

I tightened my fingers around the stem in frustration, feeling it twist slightly. I'd known when the buyer offered thirty pieces of gold this was too good to be true. I should have gone with my gut and declined the offer. But *noooo...* I loved a good challenge, and it had taken me almost two weeks to find this one! As soon as I felt its magic I should have tossed it in the sea and run the other way. But no, now I was on the other side of the Sliver, sitting with the freaking Pirate King, held as his hostage! Stupid candlestick.

I let out an audible groan and set the cursed gold down. "Are all fae objects this difficult?"

Rhayne's mouth twitched, a hint of a smile breaking his otherwise calm demeanor. "Perhaps the problem isn't with the object," he said, raising a brow, "but with technique?"

I scowled, thinking of all the things I wanted to say to him but didn't. The stories of Rhayne and his power weren't hushed tales. He was known for his strength and fighting skills, but also his magic. And it wasn't that long ago I'd watched him bind three souls to his. I for one, didn't want to be tied to this man in a magical bond. It didn't matter how extremely good-looking I thought he was, or how his muscles flexed while steering the ship. Or how his hand fit perfectly at the small of my back. Or even how his presence made me feel protected. Nope. None of that mattered. At least, I was going to tell myself that and make this entire thing as hard on him as I could.

I waved a gesture to the table. "By all means then, oh mighty Pirate King, what would you have me do?"

I couldn't tell if he was hiding behind a silent laugh or irritated by my words, but he ran his tongue over his teeth as he watched me. "Try turning the base counterclockwise. Fae items often conceal secrets within counterintuitive methods."

Of course they do. Everything with the fae felt backward.

Reluctantly, I did as he suggested, turning the base slowly to the left, expecting nothing more than a dead end. But to my surprise, there a subtle give beneath my fingers. My eyes widened as the base began to turn. The glowing intensified, sending a pulse of light up the length of the candlestick.

I glanced at Rhayne, and he nodded for me to continue. I twisted the base further, feeling the soft resistance give away until it became free, revealing a hidden compartment within. Inside was a slender, rolled-up piece of parchment with delicate worn edges.

Carefully, I tipped the stem to slide it out, unrolling it on the table as Rhayne leaned in closer to examine it. Symbols similar to the ones on the candlestick were scrawled across the top of the otherwise blank parchment. If I didn't know any better, I'd think this was a map. But it couldn't be. It felt like one, but I couldn't see one. Yet...

I touched the paper feeling the hum of its magic radiate through my fingertips like a welcome fire. Nothing lit up or began to glow, but it felt like it was just waking up. The more I looked at it, the more certain I became. I had no proof, but I knew what I knew. "It's a map."

Rhayne's gaze lingered on the parchment, but his attention shifted to me, a hint of something unreadable in his expression. "I have searched the seas and lands alike, and somehow the gods brought you to me."

"I don't know about the gods. They and I have a bit of a rough history, but I doubt they brought me here. In fact, I know exactly who brought me here, three obnoxiously strong fae that don't take no for an answer."

He shook his head. "This is the map we've been searching for."

I raised the parchment. "This? Good luck reading it. There's nothing on it. But I guess that means my job here is done, I found the map, and you can take me home."

Rhayne's gaze sharpened on me as he shook his head. "That is not an option."

The nerve of this man! I clenched my fist and glared back at him. "So that's it? I'm your captive until you find whatever it is this map will help you find?"

"This *map* has the potential to lead me to cure my people from the Shadowborne curse. And as much as you may or may not believe me right now, I think your connection to this magic is stronger than either of us realize."

Hearing his drive behind the need for the map buried some of my fury, but not enough. How dare he think he could just keep me a prisoner on his ship while he traipsed across the seas, looking for a cure that may or may not even be real! "I won't help you. Not willingly." I crossed my arms and stared at him, hoping my anger would sear his soul.

"If I helped you leave now, it would mean abandoning a chance to save my people. I won't let you go. Not until... No." He met my gaze steadily. "You may not want to stay right now, but I believe you will. This map brought you here, Briar, whether you accept that or not."

He glanced back at the delicate parchment. His fingers brushed gently over the faint symbols. "This was more than chance. Fate brought you to this ship for a reason."

I half-considered reminding him that it wasn't fate but those three brutes who had dragged me from Everfell. And as much as I hated having control over my decisions stripped away, the map—and the possibility that it could lead to a cure for the beastly Shadowborne—captured my intrigue. Not that I was about to let Rhayne know that.

I wondered if my buyer knew what was inside the candlestick. He must have; he offered thirty gold pieces. Knowing what I knew now, if this map truly could lead us to a cure, a hundred pieces wouldn't be enough. And now, I was stuck here, thirty pieces of gold poorer, and a captive of the infamous Pirate King.

At least my accommodations weren't as bad as they were on the other ship. There was at least a bed. One singular bed. A bed that there is no way I would share with the fae king. Posts enforced the corners of the grand bed, as if to hold the mattress even in rough seas. On top was a simple but thick quilt that looked like it would be perfect to wrap up in on a cold night.

The walls and floor were weathered wood that I was certain had seen their share of storms. Shelves lined the wall behind the table, filled with what I assumed were personal effects, as well as charts and bottles. A chest rested at the end of the bed with fae markings carved into it. I wondered what all he might have hidden inside.

Along the opposite wall there was a display of weapons I could use, but even I knew I was no match with a sword against Rhayne and his entire crew, so I buried the thought for later use. A single window with a view of the sea let in slivers of the last remaining rays of sunlight, casting a soft glow. A few trinkets and objects I wasn't familiar with filled the small space, giving me an insight into Rhayne. It was clear he was tidy, but also, he carried his responsibilities with him. It was obvious he loved his people and heritage.

I sighed, resigned to the idea that I might not be leaving tonight. "There's nothing more I can do. I know you think I have some sort of magical connection to this map, but I don't. I am not fae. I am nothing more than a mortal thief."

"Briar." The way he said my name had me wanting to lean in closer. "Who we are and what we are can be two very different things." He picked up the stem of the abandoned candlestick and held it out to me. "You stole this. It's not a secret. When you touch it, the fae magic embedded in it comes to life. I'm not sure why, and you may not understand, but some may say that makes you dangerous. Unknown magic isn't something fae take lightly. Leaving my protection isn't an option."

"Are you worried about me being dangerous? What if this mysterious magic harms your ship or crew?" I huffed. I was losing this argument, I could feel it. But it wouldn't stop me from pushing him a little more. "Maybe your men won't want me around?"

A spark of something dark flashed in his eyes. "It matters not what my men want. They know to trust me."

He wasn't budging. "But I don't."

"You will."

Blast. Gods, a little help? "Maybe there will be fae who think I'm dangerous enough to kidnap me? Or kill me? I am nothing to them... or to you. Get me past the Sliver and send me off in a jolly and I'll row to shore. You won't have to see me ever again."

A ping of sadness washed over me with that thought, and I hated it. He was my captor, not a friend.

The darkness deepened in his expression. "You are right. There may be someone who would want to harm you. I promised my protection." He stood up, his gaze softening, but it was the way he reached out for me, touching my cheek ever so gently, that had me nearly leaning into him. "And my protection you will have." The corners of his mouth lifted into a smile that I'm sure melted many women's hearts. "As my wife."

"Wait. What?" I quickly leaned away from him, clumsily shooting to my feet and taking a step away. "No."

I could not, would not, marry the Pirate King! He was out of his mind!

"Briar, my word is stronger than magic. I vowed to keep you safe. As my wife, no one would dare to touch you. My crew would trust you."

My heart raced. I couldn't be hearing what I was hearing. "I've heard better offers from street vendors."

"There will be no discussion on this." Rhayne turned his attention back to the map as if he genuinely thought I would stop my rejection.

"Excuse me, *Pirate King*, but I must refuse your proposal. As charming of an offer as it is, I can't. Besides, don't you think that would create a new problem? How well do you think your people would accept a thief as the wife of their king? You are not thinking this through."

Rhayne's slow, deliberate steps closed the distance between us, and I took a step back, only to feel the edge of the bed against my legs. I had nowhere left to go. He loomed over me, his presence overwhelming, filling every inch of space until all I could see was him.

"On the contrary, I think everything through. Thoroughly, I might add. My decisions may be swift, but trust me, Briar, thief of Evernight, soon-to-be wife of mine, I weigh every angle and consider everything. My choices are never without thought."

I swallowed hard, struggling to steady my breath as I looked up at him. His words burned right through me, striking places I hadn't known were vulnerable, sparking a fire I had no intention of letting him feed.

"You like deals, don't you?" My voice trembled slightly, despite my desperate need to remain calm. Desperate times called for desperate measures.

He cocked his head, watching me curiously. "You'd like to bargain with me? I thought we agreed that could be dangerous."

I nodded, heart thudding in my chest. "We did. But that's what you do, isn't it?"

His lips curved in that infuriatingly confident way. "A deal could be... effective." He stepped closer, his torso almost brushing mine, the warmth of him making it hard to focus. "Tell me, Briar," he murmured, his voice low, "what kind of bargain did you have in mind?"

I held his gaze, steadying my breath as I squared my shoulders. "If I'm going to go along with this, I want the choice to walk away when it's over. Once that map shows us what you need to see, our deal ends. I'll be free to go."

Rhayne's expression flickered, a glint of something unreadable in his eyes. His silence unsettled me, but I pushed forward. "And one more thing." I straightened, refusing to let him see any hesitation. "No mark. I won't be branded for everyone to see. I don't need a reminder that my life isn't mine."

The edge of amusement in his gaze faded, replaced by something far more intense. "If anyone so much as doubted the permanence of our union, they would be begging me for a deal to save their lives. But," he added, his tone softening just a fraction, "if my mark would make you feel bound... I'll forgo it. As long as you understand that this binding is no simple charade."

I swallowed, his words carrying a weight that almost made me falter. "Then we're agreed?"

He tilted his head, studying me with a small, knowing smile. "Until the map reveals what we need to see." He took a step back, his voice darkening with a subtle challenge. "But I'd think carefully, Briar, about what it is you're hoping to walk away from."

"I've faced storms fiercer than most men can survive, yet nothing prepared me for her fire."

RHAYNE

Gods, the woman was exhilarating. Briar wanted to strike a deal with me—not a forced bargain, but a choice made entirely of her own free will. I'd spent years mastering the art of crafting every deal to my advantage. And this one—this would be almost too easy.

She folded her arms but kept her head held high. "As long as I get to walk away, the deal will be worth it."

Her words were like a punch to my gut. I had to find a way to keep her with me. "I've never had such a beauty bound to me before. Perhaps this will be a deal well made after all."

She rolled her eyes. "Your flattery does nothing to sway my decision, Pirate King."

I stepped closer, drawn by the heat of her body and the rapid beat of her heart. My fingers brushed her cheek, the back of my hand lingering near her lips, where her warmth tempted me to stay. "My beautiful Pirate Queen, my flattery was not meant to deter you."

She gulped, her breath faltering as I let my hand fall. "I am not your queen."

Cocking my head, I studied her. The gods had crafted a perfect temptation, setting her in my path to test the limits of my restraint—and my sanity. A soft chuckle rumbled in my chest. "Oh, I assure you, you are."

A clatter on the deck broke the moment, snapping us both back to the present. She sidestepped, ducking to get around me. "You are just as delusional as your men."

The soft light of the sunset crept through the window, streaking a red and purple shadow across the table and over Briar. The cabin seemed to shrink around us as the distance between us widened. The air hummed with unspoken tension.

Briar's defiant gaze locked on mine. "So, do we have a deal? How does this work?"

I stepped closer. "Yes, Briar, we have a deal. But deals with me are not just words. They are binding. A promise sealed with intention, magic, and trust." I watched her for any sign of hesitancy. "How it works is simple: you agree and so do I. The magic does the rest. But once it's made, there's no undoing it. So, I'd think carefully before you agree."

I'd never tried to talk anyone *out* of a deal before. But I didn't want her to think she was forced into it. She had options. None of which included me letting her go, but if this gave her the illusion of control, I'd allow it.

Her brow arched. "Trust?" She scoffed. "You've got an interesting definition of it, considering I'm being held here against my will."

"Correction, you're being held here for your protection."

"And marrying you is an act of my free will?"

"It is if you don't want to die."

Her gaze narrowed on me as if searching for a loophole. But there wouldn't be one. Only I would know the bargain's true ties. She huffed. "Fine. Let's get this over with. Just don't expect me to be impressed by your magic tricks, and remember, it's on my terms."

"Your terms." I let the words roll over my tongue as I closed the distance between us, crowding her space. "Until the map reveals its secrets."

As appealing as the thought was to be bound to her through magic, I had no intention of keeping it that way. She was mine, yes, but I wouldn't force her. No, I smiled deeply inside. She would stay because she wanted to.

She nodded sharply, though her breathing quickened. "And no marks."

Holding her gaze, I reached out. "A deal without a mark. But it still needs to be sealed. That's how magic works. It demands recognition. An exchange."

Her eyes narrowed. "What kind of exchange?"

"A touch, a promise, a tie of intention. Simple, yes, but very binding." I took her hand in mine, feeling her pulse flutter beneath my touch. I had no intention of letting this hurt her and silently vowed to take that part of the bargain for her.

Her eyes darted to our joined hands before flickering back to mine. "Just get it over with."

I couldn't stop the faint smile tugging at the corner of my mouth. Her defiance was exhilarating. I let my magic unfurl. A ripple of power danced between us as a stream of water slid over the floor until it reached up to curl around my fingers. She gasped softly as the energy moved through her, tethering itself to her will and mine.

The magic pulsed brighter for an instant, as though it were alive. I tightened my grip on her hand, locking the promise into place. Pain shot up my arm as though I had reached inside a fire, but I kept my face free from any expression. I didn't want her to know I'd taken that for her. "It is done."

She pulled her hand back quickly, rubbing it as if to dispel the lingering sensation. "That's it?"

"That's it." Though the magic still thrummed between us, invisible to her but unmistakable to me. "For now."

Her gaze narrowed, but she didn't press further. I turned away to give her a moment, though my mind was already racing. The binding was complete, but the threads of magic now tied her to me in a way she couldn't yet understand.

And gods help anyone who tried to pull her away.

Briar held her hands up, inspecting them. "No mark."

If anyone else had said that, I would have taken it as a sign of disrespect. But with her, I laughed. "I am a man of my word."

"I am beginning to see that." She held up a finger, nearly pushing it to my chest. "But that doesn't mean I am happy about this."

I mocked a half frown on her behalf. "Of course not. How could the woman about to be the fae queen be happy?"

She swallowed and dropped her finger, looking away. "I didn't ask for that. I didn't ask for any of this. I still don't fully understand what's going on, or why."

76

It was the first time I saw a flicker of insecurity in her, and I hated it. The doubt twisting inside her mind infuriated me. Gently, I tipped her chin up, forcing her to meet my eyes. "You didn't ask for life. Did you? And yet you've lived. You've succeeded because you used what you were given and took charge of it. You embraced life and thrived."

"As a thief." She folded her arms, looking at me with a fierce yet determined glare. The woman I was just beginning to know resurfaced.

"As a thief, yes. But also, as a woman. As a fighter." I chuckled, unable to resist the thought. "Do you know what I would have given to see you fight off Nyx, Ciaus, and Tavian?"

A smile tugged at her lips. "I can give you a repeat if you let me borrow a sword."

I let my fingers trail lightly over her chin before dropping my hand. Watching the spark return to her eyes and the faint curve of her lips as she finally smiled filled the knot of unease in my chest with a quiet satisfaction. "Once you are my queen, you can have any sword, any time. What is mine will be yours."

Her gaze flicked briefly to the wall of weapons before returning to me, her weight shifting. "I won't be held as a hostage?"

I stepped closer, forcing her to move back, her legs hitting the table, blocking her in. "You will be my equal." I leaned down, brushing her hair back, savoring the way her heart raced under my touch. "Do I look like a hostage to you?"

She shook her head, but no words escaped her mouth.

Standing upright, I towered over her. She was so dainty compared to me, and it made me feel even more protective of this spirited creature before me. "Good. Now, we have a bargain to fulfill."

Leaning back, she braced herself on the table's surface, her face flushed. "If you gave me an inch of space to breathe, maybe we could focus on something else. Like, the map."

"Aye." With her this close, I doubted I'd find anything else that could hold my attention. Reluctantly, I stepped back, grabbed her chair, and yanked it out, gesturing for her to sit before pulling one for myself.

Her hesitation was almost amusing, but she took the seat.

"I'm not sure how I even know this is a map. It doesn't make sense." She shook her head and dropped her hands to her lap.

"Briar, are you certain your parents never kept anything from you? Is there a history I should know about?"

Her glare, sharp enough to cut steel, hit me. "My parents were good people."

"I didn't ask if they were good."

"It was implied. You can't just go around asking people if their parents lied to them." She rolled her shoulders back. "I didn't know my mother. She died when I was just a baby. And my father was... well, let's just say he taught me how to be what I am. Last I heard, he was headed to the Silverveil kingdom. He may be a thief, but I can't see him lying to me."

Interesting. "Your father just left you to your own accord?"

"It's not like I am a child."

"No. You are very much a grown woman. I just wonder how a father would leave his daughter alone without knowing she was safe and taken care of."

"You mean married off to some man? I am quite capable of taking care of myself."

"Clearly." Amusement flickered inside me. Pushing her to the edge was quickly becoming my favorite pastime. "What about grandparents? You're certain your parents were not of fae decent?"

Her expression faltered, and I could almost see her mind rolling with new questions. A lifetime of memories and thoughts trying to back up her claims of not understanding magic—or having any herself.

"No." She shook her head. "This is ridiculous. I am not fae. I don't have magic. It's the blasted candlestick that's causing all this, not me."

"Briar, the magic it contains comes to life under your touch. That is not something to overlook. Magic doesn't lie, even if we wish it did. Whether you admit it or not, it's responding to you—not the other way around. And denying it won't make it any less true."

She let out a scoffing laugh. "Gods, you are insufferable."

"I think you mean irresistible."

"Hardly."

"And yet, here you are."

"Against my will. At least until this thing shows us whatever you need." She picked up the map and glared at it. "Asher will never believe me when I tell him a map forced me into a bargain with the Pirate King."

The way another man's name left her lips stirred something primal inside me, deep and dark.

Her eyes snapped to mine. "Did you just growl?"

"Did you just mention another man on my ship? In my cabin?"

She leaned closer, her smile almost sweet. "It's not like this whole marriage proposal is real. Why does it matter?"

I closed in, stealing the air between us. "It matters because you're mine, Briar. Deal or not, real or not—you're mine. And I won't hear another man's name cross your lips like that again."

Her chest rose with a shaky breath. Slowly, she crossed her arms, leaning back as if to put distance between us. "Yours? Last I checked, I'm no one's property, least of all yours, Pirate King." She tilted her head. "You really think a deal gives you that kind of claim on me? That's bold, even for you."

A smirk tugged at the corner of my mouth. "Bold? Little thief, you have yet to see bold. But I assure you, you'll know it when you do." Taking a breath, I leaned back in my chair. "Now, let's focus on the map. Worry about our wedding tomorrow."

Her mouth opened, ready with a retort, but she quickly shut it. Instead, she tugged the parchment closer, scooting in with a huff.

The light dimmed as night descended upon us, but the ancient fae symbols along the top of the map glimmered faintly. I focused on those, hoping for a clue. The faded markings were a beacon of hope, a sign that this map could lead me to find a way to save my people. After a year of searching, it was fate that brought the map to me.

As I looked at Briar, the woman who held the key to it all, I couldn't help but think it was more than fate that brought her to me.

"The magic hummed beneath my skin,
like it was waiting for me to remember
who I was."

BRIAR

The gods should have just let the ground swallow me in the earthshake. But no, they allowed me to be kidnapped and bound in a soul-binding deal with the Pirate King. And worse? I was beginning to think he was serious about forcing me to marry him.

I thought striking a bargain with him would make him back off, but he was still adamant.

I'd never met another man so infuriating.

High and mighty.

Unrelenting.

Unbearably annoying.

And yet, somehow, here I was, stuck with him.

The idea that I had some magical ties to the fae was absurd. Sure, I'd always been able to sense magic, but that didn't mean *I had* magic.

I huffed, slumping into the chair. The map lay across the table between us, its faint markings catching what little light remained from the setting sun. I glared at it as if sheer willpower might force it to give up its secrets.

Rhayne leaned over the table, his broad shoulders casting long shadows across the parchment. "The magic will reveal itself when it chooses."

"Or not at all," I muttered under my breath, running a finger over the faded lines. "What kind of map hides its secrets from the people trying to use it? Shouldn't it want to be helpful?"

"Magic doesn't work that way," he said, clearly amused at my frustration.

"Of course it doesn't." I threw up my hands, letting out a frustrated groan. "Because everything about this—" I gestured wildly to the map, the cabin, and him—"is designed to make my life miserable."

"Not everything." His voice was low, and when I glanced up, I caught the hint of a teasing smile tugging at his lips. The way he looked at me made my stomach tighten, and I quickly turned my attention back to the map.

I traced a symbol with my finger, careful not to tear the fragile parchment. "These markings—do they mean anything to you?"

"They're fae symbols." He leaned closer, his presence looming, making the air feel heavier... *warmer*. "Ancient ones. They might be directions, a riddle, or something entirely different. It's hard to say without context."

"Great." I rubbed my temples. "So, we have a map that's practically unreadable, with markings that don't make sense, and no clue where to start."

"Welcome to my world," he replied dryly, his voice tinged with a hint of amusement.

I shot him a glare. "How have you been looking for this thing for years and still not figured out how to use it?"

"I didn't have the map, until now."

I let out another huff of frustration. "Well, now that you do, it's not exactly being cooperative."

As if to mock me, the light in the cabin continued to dim, the shadows lengthening across the table. The details of the map became even harder to make out. Rhayne stood, moving to light the lantern.

But something flickered across the map's surface—a faint shimmer, like starlight, just for an instant.

"Wait." I shot to my feet, grabbing his wrist before he could strike the flint. "Don't."

His brows furrowed, but he stopped. "Don't what?"

"The light." I nodded, pointing toward the map. "Something... happened. Look."

We both stared down at the parchment. A sliver of moonlight streamed through the window, pale and silver against the darkening room. And where it touched the map, the symbols began to glow, faint at first but growing brighter.

"What in the..." My voice trailed off as I leaned in closer, mesmerized by the shifting light. "Did you see that? The markings—they're changing."

Rhayne's expression darkened with intrigue. "It's reacting to the moonlight."

A spark of excitement surged through me, cutting through the frustration that had been building all evening. I reached for the map, carefully lifting it. "We need more light. Real moonlight."

"Briar—" His tone carried a warning, but I was already moving toward the door.

"I'm not waiting around in here!" I called over my shoulder. "If the map wants the moonlight, it's going to get it."

He muttered something under his breath, likely a curse, as I shot toward the door. His broad frame blocked my path, but I wasn't about to let him slow me down. Without thinking, I leapt forward, aiming to push him out of the way and clear him entirely.

It didn't go as planned.

In my mad rush to move the mountain of a man, I rammed my elbow into his side and tripped over his boots. With a startled grunt, he staggered back, one hand shooting out to steady himself against the wall. "What in the gods' name—"

I landed less gracefully than I'd hoped, stumbling into the door before yanking it open. "Move faster, Pirate King!" I called over my shoulder, not bothering to check if he was okay. "The map's doing something!"

Behind me, I heard him mutter another sharp curse, followed by the heavy thud of his boots as he stormed after me. "Briar, if you try that again, you'll find yourself tied to the mast!"

I couldn't help the grin spreading across my face as I bolted out onto the deck, the cool night air rushing over my face. The moon slowly rose to hang above us, its silver light spilling over the ship like a blanket. I tightened my grip on the map and took a few steps away from the cabin, holding it up toward the sky.

The parchment came to life in my hands, faint symbols glimmering along its edges. My breath caught as a soft, golden glow began to spread across the surface. The markings became clearer, sharper, and undeniably alive. Arrows and symbols emerged as if they'd been etched there all along, waiting for this very moment.

I stared in disbelief, the frustration and irritation that had been clawing at me moments ago vanishing like smoke. "It's working." My voice trembled with excitement. "It's actually working!"

The faint sound of Rhayne's boots approaching didn't distract me. I spun to face him, holding the map out triumphantly, practically shoving it into his face. "Look! I figured it out! The map—your stupid map—it needs moonlight! That's it, right? It's showing us what you need."

He slowed as he stepped into the moonlight, his sharp blue eyes narrowing as he took in the glowing symbols. But his expression didn't change—no awe, no surprise, just that frustrating calm he always wore like armor.

I frowned, pulling the map closer to me. "What? What's wrong? Why do you look like that?"

"Briar," he said, his tone measured, "what exactly do you see?"

I blinked, confused. "What do I see? The symbols, the arrows—it's glowing, clear as day. Don't you—" My words faltered as I glanced at him, then back to the map. The excitement that had been bubbling inside me began to dim.

"You don't see it, do you?" My voice was quieter now, the realization settled like a stone in my chest.

"No." His gaze deepened as he studied me. "To me, it's still a blank parchment. But I can feel the magic reacting to you." His voice dropped. "Only to you."

My grip tightened on the map, a swirl of confusion and unease rising in me. "That's... impossible. You're fae. If this thing is magic, shouldn't you—"

"It's not about me, Briar. It's about you."

The certainty in his tone hit me harder than the glow of the map. I shook my head, trying to shove away the thought forming at the edges of my mind. "No. That doesn't make sense. I don't have magic. I'm not—"

The words choked in my throat, refusing to come out as my chest tightened. I turned back to the map, desperate to find an answer in its glow. If this was what Rhayne needed, then surely it meant I could be done with this madness, with him.

"This proves it, doesn't it?" I asked, trying to sound more confident than I felt. "You've got what you need. So you can let me go now."

He stepped closer, his presence impossible to ignore, but I kept my eyes on the map. "Briar," he began, his voice low and careful, but I cut him off.

"No. Don't start. Don't try to tell me this means something else. The map works, so the deal is over. You got what you wanted."

The silence that followed was heavy, broken only by the faint creak of the ship and the soft lapping of water against the hull. I could feel his gaze on me, the weight of it pressing against my skin, but I refused to meet it.

"Briar," he said finally, his tone soft but unyielding, "this map hasn't revealed everything yet. It's only just begun."

The map flickered faintly in my hands, the glow shifting as though responding to his words. My excitement drained, replaced by a hollow dread as I realized this was far from over.

"Did I just hear right? You've found the map?" Enric jogged up the steps to the deck outside Rhayne's cabin. He saw the map, and his hand brushed mine as he grabbed the parchment. I swore there was a low rumble coming from Rhayne. I turned to face him, but his glower fell on Enric, not me.

"There's nothing here." Enric's entire countenance shifted as if all hope had vanished.

"There is." I took the map and pointed. "There are gold markings and arrows. I'm not sure where or what it is showing us, but it's there. I don't know how you two don't see it."

Rhayne and Enric seemed to have a silent conversation before the king nodded and then gestured to me. "It appears our little thief can see what others cannot. She's just full of surprises." Rhayne smirked, crossing his arms. "Some more useful than others."

Enric's brow furrowed, his gaze flicking between me and the map. "If she's the only one who can see it, then what good is it to the rest of us?"

I tightened my grip on the map, glaring at him. "Well, lucky for you, I'm here to explain it. Not that I'm thrilled about being the only one with this particular *talent*." I used the word like it tasted sour in my mouth.

Rhayne stepped closer. The weight of his presence was impossible to ignore. He plucked the map from my hands with a gentleness that belied his strength, his eyes locked on mine. "And you're certain of what you see?"

"Yes," I snapped, frustration bubbling to the surface. "I wouldn't waste my time if I weren't."

He nodded once, his expression unreadable, and held the map out toward Enric. "Prepare the crew. We follow wherever this leads."

Enric hesitated, clearly unsure. "And what happens if her *sight* isn't reliable?"

Rhayne's jaw tightened, and for a moment, the air between them grew heavy. "It is."

Enric nodded reluctantly and turned, leaving me alone with Rhayne.

Rhayne's piercing gaze locked on me. "And you, little thief, had better be right."

"Right about what? The glowing map that you can't see?" I shot back, folding my arms. "That's not exactly something I'm making up for fun."

His lips quirked into something that wasn't quite a smile, more like a challenge. "If this map leads us where I hope it does, you'll prove to be more valuable than even I anticipated."

"Wow, thanks for the compliment." I rolled my eyes. "You've really mastered the art of flattery."

Before I could say more, he stepped closer, the intensity in his eyes making my breath hitch. "Careful, Briar. Flattery isn't something I waste on people I don't intend to keep."

His words hit me like a wave, and for a moment, I couldn't tell if it was anger or something else curling in my chest. "You're impossible," I muttered, snatching the map back from him and holding it to my chest. "Let me make one thing clear—I'm not doing this for you. I just want to get this over with and go home."

"You've made that very clear," he said, his voice low and calm. "But you might find that getting what you want isn't as simple as you think."

I glared at him, but the glow of the map caught my eye again, pulling my attention back to its markings. I had no idea where it was leading us, but one thing was certain—it wasn't going to be anywhere easy.

"No one touches her. No one.
She's mine to protect, even if she doesn't
know it yet."

10

RHAYNE

I couldn't believe it. My little thief was part fae. She had to be. And the map was connected to her. Fate truly was surprising, but nonetheless, it was fate that brought her to me—that bound her to me.

I barely had time to process the magic I sensed—feeling the map come alive under her touch in a way that defied her belief—when she bolted. Her movement was a blur of panic and defiance. The door to my cabin slammed shut behind her with a force that rattled the frame.

Taking a slow, measured breath, I reigned in the instinct to follow her immediately. She needed space, or at least, she thought she did. I would give her a moment, just long enough to let the tension simmer.

The gentle waves lapped at the side of the ship, and the slight sway helped me temper the urgency surging through me to rush in after her.

When I reached the cabin, I found it locked—or rather, barricaded. The faint scrape marks on the floor and the slight give in the door told me everything I needed to know. She'd wedged something under the handle. My jaw tightened as I ran my fingers over the edge of the doorframe, debating my next move.

I wasn't sure if I wanted to laugh or curse. She was stubborn, that much was clear. But even as frustration simmered beneath my skin, I couldn't help the flicker of admiration. Few would dare defy me, let alone a woman barely half my size.

"Briar," I said, my voice calm and measured. The last thing she needed was to feel cornered. But she would know I wouldn't walk away.

A muffled reply came through the door. "Go away."

A chuckle rumbled low in my chest, more instinct than intention. I leaned closer, resting one hand against the solid wood. "Open the door, little thief."

"No," she snapped back, her tone like a blade—quick and sharp. But there it was, hidden beneath the edge of her defiance: uncertainty.

I let the silence stretch, long enough for her to wonder what I might do next. The tension in the air thickened, each passing second pressing against the fragile barrier she'd tried to put between us.

Leaning forward, I let my voice drop, soft and deliberate, though the steel in my tone was unmistakable. "Briar, I'll give you one chance to open this door. After that, you lose the choice."

I heard her scoff on the other side. "I'm not opening it. You don't get to decide when I need space, Pirate King."

"Space?" I let the word roll off my tongue, tilting my head slightly. "You think space will change anything? It won't. Open the door, or I will."

Her silence was telling. I could almost see her pacing, weighing her options, her mind working furiously to find a way to outmaneuver me.

Still, I waited, my palm flat against the door, feeling the faint vibrations as she shifted on the other side. I could sense her resolve cracking, no matter how tightly she held onto it.

Finally, her voice came again, quieter this time but no less stubborn. "I'm not afraid of you."

The corner of my mouth lifted in a faint smile. "Good. Because you have no reason to be. But don't mistake my patience for weakness, Briar. If you think a chair and a bit of wood will keep me out, you don't know me as well as you think you do."

The scrape of the chair against the floor was soft, almost reluctant, and then the door opened just enough for her face to appear. She glared at me, her eyes blazing, though her uneven breathing betrayed the storm within her.

I stepped inside, closing the door gently behind me. For all her strength, all her fire, I couldn't ignore the faint tremble in her hands as she crossed her arms over her chest.

"What do you want?" she asked, her voice steady despite the vulnerability she tried so hard to hide.

I met her gaze. "To make sure you understand something, Briar. You're not alone in this. No matter how much you fight it, you're mine now. And I protect what's mine."

Her lips pressed into a thin line as she stopped in front of the desk, her back to me. The faint glow of the map reflected against her skin, but her shoulders were taut. She reached out, tracing the edge of the parchment with her fingertips, hesitant and unsure.

"I'm not yours," she said finally, her voice quiet but laced with steel. "I agreed to a bargain. That's all this is."

My gaze locked on her as I took a deliberate step forward, the space between us shrinking again. "Is that what you think?"

She spun around to face me, her hand still braced on the desk as though it might anchor her. "It's what I know."

Her words were sharp, but her trembling hand betrayed her. I leaned closer, careful not to touch her but ensuring she felt the weight of my presence. "You can tell yourself that, Briar. But the truth? It's written all over you. The map responds to you, the magic hums for you. Even you can't deny it."

Her chest rose and fell with shallow breaths, her glare fixed on me with a desperation I couldn't quite place. "I don't care what the map says. I don't care what you say. I know who I am, and it's not… this."

I raised a brow, watching the way her defiance flickered, teetering on the edge of something deeper. "Not what, Briar? Not fae? Not magic? Or not mine?"

Her jaw clenched, and she looked away again, her voice dropping to a murmur. "Not anyone's."

I let her words hang in the air before speaking softly. "You're stronger than you think. But you can't run from who you are, no matter how hard you try."

She let out a bitter laugh, crossing her arms again. "You think you know me, don't you? Just because of some glowing map and a deal I didn't have much choice in making?"

I stepped closer, and this time, I didn't stop. My hand brushed against her arm, a gentle, grounding touch. Her breath hitched, but she didn't pull away. "No," I said, my voice low. "I don't think I know you. I do know you. And not just because of the map. I see you, Briar. I see your fire, your fear, your fight."

Her gaze snapped to mine, the vulnerability in her eyes stark against her anger. "You don't know me."

"I know enough," I countered, my thumb brushing the soft fabric of her sleeve. "Enough to know that whatever you're running from isn't bigger than what you could be if you stopped fighting it."

She stared at me for a fraction of a second before she pulled back, retreating to the desk as if it might shield her. "Why do you care?"

"Because you're mine," I said simply, the truth undeniable.

Her laugh was harsh, her lips curling into a smirk that didn't quite reach her eyes. "Right. Yours. Because a deal makes it so?"

"Because I make it so."

Her glare burned brighter, her hands curling into fists at her sides. "You're insufferable."

I chuckled, letting her anger roll over me like waves breaking against the shore. "So you've said."

"And I'll keep saying it," she snapped, her voice rising.

"Good." My voice dropped. "Keep fighting me, little thief. It only makes this more fun."

Her lips parted, a retort poised on the edge of her tongue, but she caught herself, turning away again. This time, she leaned on the desk, her head bowed as she stared at the map.

Silence settled over the cabin, heavy but not uncomfortable. I let it linger, watching the rise and fall of her shoulders as she wrestled with herself.

Finally, I stepped back, giving her the space she seemed to crave. "I'll leave you to think," I said, my tone softening. "But don't take too long. We've waited long enough to find that map and where it will take us. I cannot postpone a day to find the cure. Not even for you."

She didn't reply, her focus fixed on the parchment, but I didn't need her words to know she'd felt the weight of mine.

As I turned to leave, my gaze lingered on her, a pull I couldn't resist. The storm within her wasn't one I could calm—not yet. But I would stand beside her through it, just as I was always meant to.

For now, I'd give her this moment. But someday, she'd see the truth that burned as brightly in me as it did in the stars—that she wasn't just bound to me by chance or bargain. She was mine, as I was hers.

And while giving her the time to realize it would test every ounce of my patience, letting her think she could outmatch me might just be the most fun I've had in years.

The inky black sky twinkled with more stars than the gods could count. The moon was now high overhead, teasing me with its light. Briar had been given enough time to pout, sulk, or throw whatever tantrum suited her mood. It was time to go. If the map only revealed its path under the moonlight, then we needed to put as much distance behind us as possible before dawn stole the sky.

Marching to my cabin, I half expected to find the door barricaded again, but when I turned the handle, it opened smoothly.

Briar sat on the edge of the bed, her gaze distant and unfocused as though lost in some thought she couldn't—or wouldn't—share. A small shiver coursed through her, making her body tremble.

Crossing the room, I opened my sea chest, revealing clothes and a few personal effects. I grabbed a jacket and stood, carefully placed it over her shoulders. My hand lingered on her shoulder. For a moment, I worried she would shrug me off, but instead, her hand came to mine, covering it in a fleeting gesture.

"Thank you." Her voice was softer than I'd heard before.

I paused, letting the silence stretch between us for just a moment longer. "We need to leave, Briar. The moon is already being chased out of the sky."

Her fingers tightened briefly on mine before she let go, pulling the jacket closer around her as though it offered more than warmth. I stepped back, giving her space to rise, but I couldn't ignore the way her movements seemed slower.

"Are you ready?" I asked, though the question felt heavier than it should have, carrying more than its intended weight.

She nodded, but confidence flickered faintly in her expression. "I'm always ready. Let's get this over with."

A faint smirk tugged at my lips as I gestured for her to follow me. The storm in her eyes hadn't dimmed, and I found myself grateful for it. Let her fight me, challenge me. Her defiance was tempered but far from extinguished. If anything, it burned hotter, waiting for the right moment to strike.

Enric approached us on the quarterdeck, his stride steady as always, though the tension in his face gave him away. "The crew's ready, My King. Supplies are loaded, and the tide is on our side."

My little thief used the distraction to keep walking. She grasped the railing and stared out over the water. I loved how the moonlight gave her an ethereal glow.

I nodded, but my attention stayed on Briar. "Good."

Enric followed my gaze, his brow arching with skepticism. "Are we certain she knows how to lead us? It's not exactly easy to follow a map we can't see."

"She'll figure it out," I said, my tone steady. "She's more capable than you realize."

Enric crossed his arms, but his expression was full of concern. "Let's hope so. This isn't a journey we can afford to lose to chance."

I turned to face him fully, my voice calm but carrying the weight of conviction. "She'll guide us, Enric. I trust her."

His brow lifted further, and he gave a dry laugh. "You trust her? A thief? That's a bold sentiment, even for you."

The heat of my gaze locked onto his, leaving no room for doubt. "She's more than a thief, and you know it. The same fire that drives me burns in her. She'll rise to meet this, just as I would."

Enric's brows drew together, his confidence flickering for the first time. "The same fire... What are you saying, My King? That she's like you? That she's—"

"I'm saying she belongs here," I cut in, my tone sharper than intended. "She has the strength to see this through. That's all you need to know."

Enric let out a slow breath, raking a hand through his hair. "Gods... you're putting a lot of faith in her. I hope it doesn't come back to bite us."

"You've stood by my side long enough to know I don't take chances I'm not prepared to win." I stepped closer, holding his gaze until he looked away.

His jaw tightened, and he shook his head as if trying to dispel his unease. "She'd better be worth it."

"She is," I murmured, my eyes lingering on Briar. "More than you know."

I settled in at the wheel, silently enjoying the closeness of Briar as she stepped up beside me, holding the map out as if she were memorizing every detail. Magic emanated off it as if it were alive.

The crew's shouts echoed across the cove as they hoisted the final sails and secured the cargo. The Tidecaller swayed gently against the dock, its dark wood glistening under the moonlight.

The ropes were pulled, the sails unfurled, and the ship began to drift away from the cove. I watched as King's Cove faded into the distance, the island's silhouette swallowed by the horizon.

The Sliver awaited, its storms brewing just beyond the calm waters. The crew moved with practiced precision, but the tension was palpable. Everyone knew the risks of crossing the Sliver—but this time, there was more at stake.

I turned back to Briar, who stood silently at the railing, her gaze fixed on the darkening sky. For all her fire, there was a quiet strength in her, one that I was beginning to understand—and one I would protect at all costs.

The air thickened as we passed into the Sliver, the world shrouded in an unnatural mist. The moon above was barely a faint glow, the stars swallowed by the haze. Even the sea seemed quieter, as though it, too, held its breath.

I tightened my grip on the wheel, every muscle in my body braced. The Sliver had always been treacherous, but this...this was worse than I'd ever seen it.

From the corner of my eye, I saw Briar standing near the railing, her arms crossed, her expression defiant despite the unease rolling off her in waves.

The first note of the siren song was soft, almost gentle, like a whisper against the back of my neck. The crew stiffened as one, their eyes darting toward the mist.

"Focus!" My voice barely cut through the growing melody. "The song is nothing but a trick. Keep your wits, or you'll lose them."

Briar glanced at me, her brows knitting together. "It sounds like a wail or cry."

Of course she could hear it. The magic in her would make her more susceptible. "Stay close to the mast," I ordered, sharper than intended.

A few of the men wandered closer to the edge of the ship. "Eyes forward! Ignore the song. It's not real."

"Not real?" Briar shot me a sharp look from where she braced herself near the mast. "You mean the cursed fae singing it aren't real?" Her voice dripped with sarcasm.

I gritted my teeth, summoning a swell of magic to counteract the pull of the melody. "The sirens are as real as the sea itself, but their song is a trick. Don't let it in."

Another wave slammed into the hull, this one harder than the last. A clawed hand emerged from the mist, gripping the railing with inhuman strength. A Shadowborne siren hauled itself up, its glowing eyes fixed on the deck.

"They're here!" Enric shouted, drawing his blade as another Shadowborne appeared on the opposite side of the ship.

Briar's knuckles whitened as she gripped the mast, her eyes narrowing on the creatures. "You didn't mention they'd crawl aboard."

"They don't usually get this bold," I muttered, summoning a surge of water to crash into the nearest Shadowborne, dragging it back overboard. "Stay close."

Her lips parted as though to argue, but another wave struck, and the ship pitched violently. A crack split the air as a section of the railing gave way. Briar stumbled, her hand slipping from the mast as the deck tilted beneath her feet.

Before I could move, a Shadowborne lunged toward her, its claws outstretched.

"No!" The word ripped from my throat as I unleashed a torrent of magic. Water rose like a living shield, slamming into the creature and hurling it into the sea. I reached her just as she lost her footing, pulling her against me before she could fall. "Stay close to me. I can't protect you if you keep running toward danger."

Her glare flared. "I wasn't running toward danger."

"Then you have a remarkable talent for finding it." My grip tightened for a fraction of a second before I let her go.

The ship groaned beneath us, a siren clung to the main mast as another clawed its way toward the bow. My magic surged again, the sea responding with waves that crashed over the deck, sweeping the creatures away.

The Tidecaller's hum intensified, its magic weaving through mine. The damaged railing began to mend itself, the planks creaking as they knitted back together. The ship was alive, its power a mirror to my own.

Briar stumbled back a step but caught herself. Her gaze darted between me and the ship, suspicion flickering in her eyes. "Your ship just...healed itself."

"It's magic," I said simply, not taking my eyes off her. "And as long as I'm here, it won't fail."

Her lips parted as if to argue, but then she looked down at her hands, her fingers trembling slightly. "And what happens if you're not here?"

"That's not something you'll need to worry about," I replied, my tone softer. "I don't plan on leaving."

The final wave of Shadowborne surged toward us, their clawed hands reaching for the deck. With a roar, I unleashed everything I had, the water rising like a living wall. The wave crashed down, dragging the creatures into the depths.

The mist began to lift, the oppressive weight easing as the Shadowborne retreated. Silence fell over the deck, broken only by the creaking of the masts and the ragged breaths of the crew.

Briar stepped out of my hold, her chin lifting despite the slight tremble in her hands. "I hope this isn't a regular occurrence."

"It's the Sliver," I said simply. "Nothing about it is regular."

Her gaze lingered on the sea, her defiance softening into something closer to resignation. "Then let's get through it before they change their minds."

The Sliver loomed ahead, a dark wound between realms that churned with restless magic. The sea mirrored the chaos above, its waters black and heaving, dotted with frothy whitecaps that threatened to swallow the ship whole. The crew's movements were sharp and efficient, but the tension in the air was palpable. Even the Tidecaller seemed uneasy, her timbers groaning as if warning us of the danger ahead.

"Brace yourselves," I called out, gripping the wheel as The Tidecaller's timbers groaned in response to the approaching chaos. "Prepare the anchor."

The crew sprang into action, their movements fluid and efficient, though tension crackled in the air. This passage was not one any of them took lightly.

Beside me, Briar stood near the helm, her gaze fixed on the storm ahead. She wasn't trembling or clinging to anything for support. Instead, there was an intensity in her eyes, a curiosity that even the Sliver's terrifying beauty couldn't quell.

"How does it work?" She spared a glance at me. "Getting through, I mean."

"Watch closely, little thief."

Her eyes narrowed, but she said nothing, shifting her focus back to the storm.

The Tidecaller lurched as the first wave slammed against the hull, the water roaring like a beast hungry for its prey. I planted my feet firmly, drawing on the connection between the ship and my magic. The ship responded immediately, its power humming beneath my hands as I steered toward the heart of the vortex.

"Drop anchor!" I commanded, my voice cutting through the cacophony.

The iron anchor, inscribed with ancient runes, was released, plunging into the depths of the churning sea. Its descent wasn't just physical—it was magical, a tether that connected us to the ocean floor and steadied our passage. The Tidecaller's magic surged, weaving through the ship and into the waters around us, creating a protective barrier against the storm's fury.

The whirlpool ahead widened, its swirling walls rising impossibly high. Briar's grip tightened on the railing, but her expression remained composed. If she was afraid, she wasn't showing it.

She turned to me. "It's not like the last time."

"No, the curse has grown stronger."

The ship began to descend, the anchor pulling us downward with deliberate precision. The waters closed over us, and the world turned dark, illuminated only by the faint glow of the runes etched into The Tidecaller's hull. The crew worked in tense silence, their trust in me and the ship unwavering.

Then, a ripple of movement caught my attention. It was subtle, almost imperceptible, but I felt it—a shift in the magic, a disturbance in the balance.

"Something's here," I said, my tone sharp. "Stay alert."

Briar's gaze snapped to mine, and she stepped closer, her hand instinctively moving to her satchel. "What do you mean, *something?*"

As if in answer, a Shadowborne siren emerged from the shadows, its form twisted and grotesque. It clung to the railing, its glowing eyes locked on Briar. The air around it crackled with dark energy, the remnants of the fae it had once been.

"Get back," I ordered, stepping in front of her. My magic surged, coiling around me like a living thing as I faced the creature.

The Shadowborne lunged, its claws raking through the air. I struck back with a wave of water, slamming it against the deck. It snarled, its movements jerky and unnatural, but it wasn't giving up.

Briar darted to the side, grabbing the dagger from my side, flashing it as she moved with precision and purpose. She struck the creature's side, driving it back, but its focus remained on her.

I let out a growl, my magic surging to its peak. With a sharp gesture, I unleashed a torrent of water that engulfed the siren, dragging it off the ship and into the abyss below. The creature's snarls faded into silence, and the tension on the deck eased.

Briar straightened, her chest heaving as she wiped her blade clean. "That was... new," she said, her voice steadier than I expected.

"Aye." I glanced around at the mist swirling around us. "They seem to be coming for you." I wondered if it was Briar they were after or the map. Either way, they had to get through me first, and there was no way I'd let them.

The ship continued its descent, the waters around us glowing faintly as The Tidecaller's magic held steady. Briar's eyes followed the patterns etched into the ship's hull, her curiosity evident despite the danger.

"This ship," she said softly, almost to herself. "It's alive, isn't it?"

"In a way," I replied, my voice quieter now. "Its magic is tied to mine, as much a part of me as my blood."

Briar didn't respond, her gaze lingering on the runes. She didn't need to say anything—her silence spoke volumes. The storm outside the barrier raged on, but the ship held firm, carrying us toward the other side of the Veil.

As we emerged into calmer waters, the crew let out a collective sigh of relief. The Tidecaller hummed softly, her magic already beginning to repair the damage. I turned to Briar, finding her watching me with a look I couldn't quite place.

"That's the second time you've saved me through the Sliver."

"We had a bargain, did we not? I promised you my protection." She did not need to know that our deal had ended nearly as quickly as it began. As soon as the map revealed itself to her the binding broke. It was how I knew she could see it and wasn't tricking us.

For the first time since we'd entered the Sliver, I allowed myself a small smile. Briar Firethorn, thief of Evernight, mate of the Pirate King, had one more deal to fulfill...

"We've survived the Sliver. Now, let's see if you can survive being my wife."

11

"He said I was his queen, but I wasn't
sure if he meant to protect me
or to keep me."

BRIAR

e've survived the Sliver. Now, let's see if you can survive being my wife.

His words burned through me, sparking a defiance I clung to like a lifeline. My fists clenched at my sides, and I spun to face him, my lips already parted to lash out, but the sight of his self-assured smirk stopped me cold.

"Your wife?" I bit the words out. "I'm here because of a bargain, not by choice. Don't mistake this for anything else, Pirate King."

He remained infuriatingly calm as he leaned closer. "Bargain or not, Briar, you'll wear the title."

The heat of his proximity made my thoughts falter. I hated how effortlessly he seemed to dismantle my resolve with a single glance. And I hated myself more for letting him.

The crew's distant murmur broke through my spiraling thoughts. Torches along the deck cast flickering shadows over the planks. The moon hung high above us, its silver light glinting off the railings and reflecting in the calm sea below.

My heart raced as I contemplated the absurdity of throwing myself overboard. Would Rhayne's magic haul me back onto the ship like an unruly catch? Would the binding we'd made stop me from ever truly leaving him? The memory of the Shadowborne siren in the waters sent a chill through me, and I stepped back from the railing.

"I don't understand why you're so adamant about marrying me," I said, crossing my arms. "Surely there must be a hundred women vying for the honor of becoming your wife. I'd hate to deprive them." My tone dripped with sarcasm, a skill I was beginning to think should count as one of my talents.

He closed the distance between us in a single, deliberate step. "You're the only woman I've ever offered protection."

The words hit me harder than I wanted to admit, but I wasn't about to let him see that. Hardly believable. He had to be a thousand years old. Okay, maybe not that old, but there was no way he'd gone hundreds of years and not once found a woman he was willing to—

Wait.

"Are you seriously telling me that in all your years—centuries, probably—you've never offered your so-called protection to anyone else?"

He didn't flinch, didn't so much as blink. His gaze was steady. "Not once."

I huffed, crossing my arms tighter. "I don't believe you."

His lips curved into a smug grin, the kind that made me want to smack it off his face—or maybe kiss it, which only made me angrier. "Believe what you like, Briar. But it doesn't make it any less true."

"Maybe it's because no one else was foolish enough to get tangled up with you."

"Perhaps." He tilted his head slightly, the moonlight catching the silver in his hair. "Or maybe it's because I've been waiting."

The weight of his words settled between us, heavier than I was prepared for. I swallowed hard, refusing to let the warmth rising in my chest show.

"Waiting for what?" My voice wavered.

"For you."

Rhayne's gaze lingered on me for a moment longer before he turned sharply, his voice cutting across the deck as he walked away. "Enric!"

The crew froze mid-motion, their murmurs falling silent as Enric stepped forward. His expression was neutral, but his eyes betrayed a flicker of confusion.

"My King," Enric said, bowing his head slightly.

"Prepare the deck," Rhayne commanded.

"For what purpose?" Enric's gaze briefly shifted to me before returning to his king.

"A ceremony." Rhayne's words were calm yet carried a weight that silenced any immediate objection.

"A ceremony," Enric repeated slowly, his brow furrowing. "On The Tidecaller?"

"Aye." Rhayne stepped closer to me, wrapping an arm around my waist and pulling me in. "The Nether Shores will have a queen."

It was almost worth marrying the king just to see Enric's face. He quickly sobered, but his expression turned hard. "My King, it is not for me to question your... love life? But, I have to ask—"

"You are correct. It is not for you to question. There will be a wedding. Tonight."

Enric bowed slightly. "A wedding on The Tidecaller. It shall be done."

It didn't take Enric long to gather the men and soon the ship was alive with excitement. The deck buzzed with activity. Men shouted to one another, their voices rising over the rhythmic thud of boots on wood, the clinking of metal, and the scrape of barrels being rolled aside. The cacophony made my head pound.

I stepped away from Rhayne, gripping the railing tighter than I cared to admit as I watched the chaos unfold. The crew's faces were lit with anticipation, their eyes gleaming as though they were about to witness something legendary.

But me? I felt like I was about to throw up.

A group of pirates passed by, laughing and gesturing animatedly toward the deck being cleared. I only caught snippets of their conversation.

"A wedding! On The Tidecaller! Imagine that."

"First in its history, no less. The king doesn't do anything halfway."

"Lucky woman, isn't she?"

Lucky? I wanted to laugh. If only they knew.

The weight of it all pressed down on me like a lead anchor. My chest tightened as I watched their preparations. A wedding. A marriage. To him.

"Do they think this is some sort of fairytale?" I whispered bitterly to myself. My stomach churned as I glanced at the deck, which had been transformed into something almost... romantic. Torches lined the edges, casting a golden glow, while the sea beyond shimmered under the moonlight. It was beautiful, I couldn't deny that. But it felt like a noose tightening around my neck.

Turning away from the bustling crew, I wrapped my arms around myself as if the gesture could shield me from what was coming.

"Feeling shy, Pirate Queen?"

His voice sent a shiver down my spine—low and teasing, yet with an edge of steel beneath it. I didn't have to turn to know Rhayne was behind me.

I bristled at the title. "I'm not your queen," I snapped, my voice sharper than I intended.

"Not yet," he replied smoothly, stepping closer. His presence was impossible to ignore, his confidence radiating like the heat of the torches. "But you will be."

I spun to face him, my fists clenched at my sides. "Why? Why are you doing this? You barely know me. You don't even like me."

His smirk deepened, maddeningly calm. "You think I'd marry someone I didn't like? How little you understand me, Briar."

"Oh, I understand plenty," I shot back, my voice rising. "This is about control. About your ridiculous obsession with binding me to your side, all for some stupid map."

His gaze darkened, the teasing glint in his eyes replaced by something harder, more intense. "This is about protection. You've seen the dangers of the Sliver and the Shadowborne. My kingdom has enemies, Briar, and you're a part of this now—whether you want to be or not."

"That's not protection," I hissed. "That's possession."

His jaw tightened, but his voice remained steady. "Call it what you will. But you'll see soon enough that it's the only way to keep you safe."

The hum of the crew's excitement grew louder as their preparations neared completion. My head spun as I glanced back at the deck. The realization hit me like a wave. This wasn't a ceremony for them. It was for me.

I took a shaky breath, my voice softening as panic crept into my words. "You can't force me to say yes."

Rhayne stepped closer, his presence consuming the space around us. "I don't need to," he said, his voice low and resolute. "Because you already agreed. A bargain, remember? This is just the next step."

My chest heaved as I glared at him, hating the way his calm certainty contrasted with my spiraling thoughts.

"And what if I refuse?"

He leaned in. "You won't. Because whether you admit it or not, you know this is the right choice."

The sounds of the crew preparing for the ceremony swirled around us, but I barely heard them. All I could focus on was him—his unwavering gaze, his maddening confidence, and the way his words wrapped around me like a net I couldn't escape.

"Rhayne—"

He reached out, his hand brushing against my arm in a way that sent an unwanted shiver through me. "Briar," he said softly, his voice almost gentle now. "Trust me, just this once."

And damn him, I hated how tempting that sounded.

The crew had gathered along the edges of the deck, their faces a mix of solemn respect and barely restrained curiosity. Enric stood closest, his arms crossed, his sharp eyes tracking every movement. I tried to ignore them all, focusing instead on the man beside me.

Rhayne.

The Tidecaller hummed beneath my feet, as if the ship itself were watching. There was no escape now, not with the ocean stretching endlessly around us and Rhayne's magic binding me in ways I didn't fully understand. It had to be why I didn't feel like running too far from him. Blasted bargain.

I glanced at him, standing tall and confident, his silver-white hair catching the moonlight like some cursed halo. His expression was unreadable, but there was a glint in his eyes that unnerved me.

"You could at least pretend to be nervous," I muttered.

His lips curved slightly. "Why would I be nervous? I'm about to wed the most formidable thief in all the realms."

I shot him a glare, but the heat rising to my cheeks betrayed me.

The ceremony began with a low chant, one of the crew stepping forward to trace a circle of water around us. The seawater shimmered faintly, glowing with an ethereal light that pulsed in time with my racing heartbeat.

"What is this?" I whispered, my voice tight.

"Tradition," Rhayne replied, his tone maddeningly calm. "The sea bears witness, just as the gods do."

As the water completed its circle, I felt the magic settle over me, heavy and undeniable. My pulse quickened, my breath coming shallow as the weight of the moment pressed down on me.

Rhayne took my hand, his grip firm but not unkind. He looked into my eyes, and for a moment, the world around us faded.

"I, Rhayne Whitehook, of sea and storm, bind my name, my power, and my soul to yours. By the will of the tides and the stars above, I vow to shield you from all who dare harm, to honor your strength, and protect what is ours. You are mine, Briar Firethorn, until the sun sets on my final day, and the sea calls me home. By magic and blood, by oath and intent, I claim you."

His words sent a shiver down my spine, the magic thrumming between us intensifying with every syllable.

"Your turn," he prompted gently, his thumb brushing over my knuckles.

I swallowed hard, every nerve in my body screaming at me to run. But I didn't. Instead, I lifted my chin, meeting his gaze with as much defiance as I could muster. In that moment, everything disappeared. It was just Rhayne and me on the deck. I wasn't sure what to say. A faint ripple of magic danced across my skin, subtle but undeniable. Whatever words I spoke next would be more than a promise—they would seal me tighter than any bargain I'd struck with the Pirate King. There would be no loopholes, no escape, no undoing the vow. The weight of it pressed against me, and for a moment, I wasn't sure if I could force the words past my lips.

"I, Briar Firethorn, of land and shadow, bind my word and my will to this vow. Though I step into this union uncertain, I will walk beside you through storms and seas, unyielding in my strength and purpose. While my heart is my own, I will share it beyond the shadow of fear, and I will stand with you, not because I am claimed, but because I choose to be here. Let this be the beginning of what neither of us can yet see."

The moment the words left my lips, the air between us seemed to change, charged with something I couldn't quite explain. The magic of the vow flared, and a spark of energy felt as though it had sunk into my very bones. Rhayne's gaze fixed on mine, as if he could see straight into the depths of my soul.

"Spoken like a queen," he murmured, his voice low and reverent, the sound brushing over me like a caress.

I stiffened, unsure whether to take his words as sincere or another of his ploys. His expression was unreadable, a mix of pride and something darker, deeper. It wasn't anger, though—it was something far more unnerving. Something possessive. My pulse quickened, and I hated that he could probably hear it.

Before I could step back, he reached for my hand. His touch was warm, steady—confident. The magic between us pulsed again, faint but undeniable, like a silent reminder of the bond we'd just forged. He didn't speak for a moment, and when he finally did, his words made my stomach twist.

"You have my vow, Briar. And may the gods help anyone who dares to come between us."

The weight of his voice settled over me like a cloak I hadn't asked for but couldn't take off. He meant every word—I could feel it in the way his grip on my hand tightened ever so slightly, as though he thought I might vanish if he let go. His conviction was both unsettling and, in some twisted way, reassuring.

I forced myself to meet his gaze, hoping to find some flicker of doubt or hesitation. But there was none. His expression was as unyielding as the sea, and I realized with a sinking feeling that I'd just tied myself to a man who didn't lose.

The crew erupted into cheers, stepping back as the glowing circle faded.

Rhayne turned to me, his hand still holding mine. "You're trembling."

"I'm not trembling," I snapped, even though I very much was.

His gaze softened, and he reached up to brush a strand of hair from my face. "There's no need to fear me, Briar."

"I don't fear you," I lied, yanking my hand free. It wasn't just him I feared, it was what I felt. There was something more than just a vow between us, something strange and foreign, something that tethered me to him in ways I didn't understand.

He chuckled, the sound rich and maddeningly confident. His lips curved into a faint, knowing smile, one that sent a ripple of unease and curiosity through me. "Fear has never been nor ever will be what I want from you." His voice was a low rumble that carried both challenge and promise.

I opened my mouth to retort, but he stepped closer, leaning down so that his voice was a whisper against my ear.

"And, Briar, do try to remember—you're not just my wife. You're my queen."

His words sent a wave of heat and fury through me, but before I could respond, he turned and strode away, leaving me standing there with the weight of the vows heavy on my soul.

I glanced down at my hands, half expecting to see some mark, some physical proof of what had just happened. But there was nothing. Nothing except the knowledge that I had just sealed my future with a man who was as dangerous as he was compelling.

And gods help me, I wasn't sure if I hated him for it— or if some part of me was beginning to understand why I couldn't escape him.

12

"Every look, every touch, every word she threw my way only tightened the bond between us."

RHAYNE

The Tidecaller cut through the waves with the elegance of a predator, her magic humming faintly beneath my feet. Beyond the Sliver, the seas should have been calmer, but the air held a tautness, like a bowstring stretched to its breaking point.

The Shadowed Reefs loomed ahead, hidden beneath the dark waters like the bones of ancient mariners. It wasn't a place anyone ventured willingly, and yet, here we were, chasing the whims of a map only Briar could read.

Briar.

My gaze shifted to her, a figure outlined in moonlight as she leaned against the railing. Even from here, I could feel her defiance—radiating off her like a flame stubbornly refusing to be extinguished. Her silence since the wedding unsettled me, louder than her sharpest words. Was she resigned or scheming? Likely both.

Enric approached, his boots quiet on the deck. "The crew's restless, My King. The Shadowed Reefs aren't exactly a sailor's paradise."

"They'll follow orders," I said, my tone leaving no room for debate.

"They will," he agreed, though his brow furrowed. "But what about her? If she's the only one who can see the map, what happens if she decides she's done with this?"

That was an impossibility as far as I was concerned. "She won't."

"And if she does?" His voice softened, though there was no mistaking the worry beneath the surface. "You're placing a lot of faith in someone who was running from you not long ago."

I turned to him, meeting his gaze evenly. "The same faith you've placed in me for years. She's not just anyone, Enric."

He studied me for a moment, his lips thinning. "I've never heard you speak of anyone like this before."

"She's my queen." The weight of those words settled between us. "And she's more than that."

His eyes widened slightly before he nodded, stepping back without another word. He didn't need to question further—not yet.

I approached Briar, the soft creak of the deck accompanying my steps. She didn't turn as I neared, but I knew she felt me. She always did.

"Enjoying the view?" I asked, leaning against the railing beside her.

Her head turned, and she fixed me with a sharp glare. "If you're here to gloat, don't waste your breath."

"Not gloating," I said casually. "Merely reminding you that we're nearing the Shadowed Reefs. I'll need you to guide us."

"Guide you?" She laughed bitterly, holding up the shimmering map. "You mean with this?"

Even from where I stood, I could feel the pulse of magic in the air, responding to her touch. She had no idea how much power she carried—or how much it tethered her to me.

"Yes," I said, my voice calm. "That."

Her eyes narrowed, flicking between the map and the horizon. "Northwest. Toward the reefs. The symbols—they're shifting."

"Shifting?" I stepped closer, intrigued. "Explain."

She turned the map toward me, though all I saw was a blank glowing parchment. "They move, like they're alive. It's… hard to describe, but it's taking us somewhere."

Her focus was unwavering, her brow furrowed in concentration. She wasn't lying. Whatever the map revealed, it was drawing us forward with purpose.

"We'll follow it," I said firmly. "And you'll lead us."

Her lips tightened, and she shot me a pointed look. "Not like I have a choice."

"You always have a choice, Briar." My words softened, meant for her ears alone as I left her once again to ensure we maintained the proper heading.

As the crew adjusted our course, the waters grew darker, the waves rolling with an unnatural rhythm. The air was heavy, charged with an energy that sent a prickle along my skin. Even The Tidecaller's usual hum felt subdued, as if she, too, sensed the danger ahead.

Briar stood at the bow, her hair whipping in the wind. I joined her, my presence looming at her side.

"What are you thinking?" I asked, my voice low.

Her gaze didn't waver from the horizon. "That this map better be worth it. And that you better know what you're doing."

I chuckled, the sound low and deliberate. "I always know what I'm doing."

Her eyes darted to mine, sharp and challenging. "Confident, aren't you?"

"It's not confidence. It's certainty," I replied. "And you'll see it too, in time."

Her lips parted, likely to deliver some sharp retort, but a sudden shift in the wind stilled her. The air grew heavier, thick with an almost tangible tension that set the crew on edge. Even The Tidecaller seemed to sense it, her magic pulsing faintly.

Briar's gaze flicked to the horizon, her posture stiffening. "What is that?"

I followed her line of sight, catching the faint silhouette of sails cutting through the moonlit water. My chest tightened as the distant shapes resolved into a ship moving swiftly, their intentions unmistakable.

The call came from the crow's nest, cutting through the quiet, "Ship ahead!"

My eyes narrowed, and my magic coiled, ready for whatever lay ahead. "Stay here," I said, already turning toward the helm.

Briar, of course, ignored the command. She followed me, her steps quick and determined. "Who are they?"

"Not friends," I said, glancing back at her. "And definitely not here by accident. Fate brought you to me, Briar, just as it gave you the ability to read that map. I'm not so naïve as to think no one else is searching for it." I gestured to the map in her hands. "Or for you. But they'll have neither. You are mine." I offered her a quick smile. "Wife."

Enric appeared beside me, his expression grim. "They're moving fast, My King. Too coordinated for scavengers."

"Prepare the crew," I ordered. "We'll meet them head-on."

Briar stepped closer, her unease hidden behind a defiant stare. "What's the plan?"

"The plan," I said, turning to face her fully, "is for you to stay out of harm's way."

Her eyes narrowed. "And if I don't?"

I leaned closer, my voice low but edged with steel. "Then you'll see exactly what I meant by certainty."

She held my gaze, her defiance flickering like a flame, but I didn't wait for her reply. The crew was already moving into position, The Tidecaller rocked with anticipation. The night air was charged with the promise of a fight—and whatever awaited us beyond those sails, I would face it head-on. But if it came to a fight, defiance alone wouldn't keep Briar safe.

I stepped toward her, the creak of the deck under my boots drawing her attention. She turned, her expression guarded.

"What?" she asked, her tone sharp, though I saw the flicker of unease in her eyes.

I held out the hilt of my dagger, the steel catching the light. "Take it."

Her gaze flicked from the weapon to my face, suspicion clear in her features. "Why?"

"Just in case." My voice was even, but the weight behind the words was unmistakable.

"I can handle myself," she said, crossing her arms. But she didn't move away.

"I know," I said, stepping closer and pressing the dagger into her hand. Her fingers curled around it, the defiance in her eyes softening for just a moment. "But I'd rather not test your skills tonight."

She snorted, tucking the weapon into her belt. "How considerate of you."

The corner of my mouth tugged into a faint smirk. "I have my moments."

Her retort was cut short by a shout from the crow's nest. "They're closing in!"

The crew sprang into action, the hum of preparation buzzing through the air. Briar stepped back, her hand instinctively brushing the hilt of the dagger at her side.

"You're staying here," I said, my tone leaving no room for argument.

She raised an eyebrow. "Like hell I am."

I took a step closer, lowering my voice so only she could hear. "This isn't a negotiation, Briar. You're not a part of this fight unless you absolutely have to be."

Her jaw tightened, but she didn't argue further. She was smart enough to know when to pick her battles.

I turned back to the crew, my magic surging as I prepared for the coming fight. Briar might have the fire of a warrior, but hoped she wouldn't have to use it.

Magic surged through me, a steady force I let flow into the ship itself. The Tidecaller responded, her magic amplifying mine, the hum beneath my feet growing into a roar. The crew snapped to their stations, and the air crackled with tension.

Briar stood beside me, gripping the hilt of a sword one of the crew had tossed her way. Her knuckles were white, but her jaw was set in that determined way I'd come to admire.

"I can fight, you know," she said, her voice steady despite the chaos building around us.

I spared her a glance, my magic keeping the waves at bay. Gods, this was a bad idea. "Stay where I can see you."

Her eyes flashed with defiance, but she nodded, her grip tightening on the blade.

The enemy ship loomed closer, its cannons roaring as they unleashed a barrage of iron and fire. The Tidecaller moved like a predator, weaving through the assault with a grace that belied her size. I focused, pulling the storm tighter around us, the lightning casting everything in eerie flashes of white and blue.

"Get the girl!" a voice bellowed from the enemy ship. The words sliced through the cacophony like a blade.

Briar froze for a heartbeat before turning to me, her eyes wide. "Did you hear that?"

I didn't answer, my magic surging as I lashed out with a wave, slamming it against their hull to rock the ship.

Another shout followed, "She has the map! Don't let her escape!"

I cursed under my breath. So they knew. Whoever had sent them had made sure they understood exactly what they were after.

"They're after me," Briar said, her voice quieter now but no less fierce. "And the map."

I gritted my teeth, unleashing another burst of power that sent a wall of water crashing over their deck. "They won't have either."

The enemy ship closed the distance, grappling hooks biting into The Tidecaller's sides. The clash began in earnest as their crew poured onto our deck. Steel met steel, the sharp clang of blades ringing out over the storm.

"Behind you!" I shouted, sending a surge of water that swept an attacker off his feet, flinging him into the sea.

Briar whirled, her blade catching another enemy across the arm. Her movements were raw but effective, her determination carving through the chaos. She fought like someone who had been cornered too many times to let it happen again.

More shouts from the enemy reached my ears.

"Don't kill her! The girl is no use to us dead!"

The confirmation sent a chill down my spine. They wouldn't retreat. Even if they had to burn their own ship, they would take Briar or sink us in the process.

Lightning split the sky, illuminating the deck as I surged forward, cutting down an enemy who had his sights on Briar. She glanced at me, her breath coming fast.

"I told you I could fight," she said, her voice tinged with a mix of pride and challenge.

"I never doubted it," I said, deflecting another attack with a twist of my blade. "But they won't stop until they have you."

"Then we make sure they can't follow us." Her gaze flicked to their ship, and I understood her meaning.

A grim smile tugged at the corner of my mouth. "We sink them."

With a nod, she moved closer to my side as I unleashed the full force of The Tidecaller's magic. The ship thrummed beneath us, the planks glowing faintly as the storm obeyed my command.

The tide surged, the waves towering and crashing against the enemy ship, battering it from all sides. The crew fought valiantly, cutting down the invaders one by one, but the sheer numbers threatened to overwhelm us.

"Enric!" I barked, catching my second-in-command's attention. "Signal the cannons. Focus on their hull."

"Aye, My King!"

As Enric relayed the order, the cannons roared, sending deadly iron tearing into the enemy's ship. The grappling hooks loosened as their crew began to falter, their confidence shaken by The Tidecaller's fury.

I turned my attention to the enemy captain, a burly man shouting orders from the other deck. He met my gaze across the chaos, his expression twisted with rage.

"This isn't over, Pirate King!" he bellowed. "We'll find her! The map belongs to us!"

"Not today," I muttered, my magic surging one final time.

With a deafening crack, the enemy ship's mast splintered and fell, taking much of their rigging with it. The ship began to list, water pouring into the breaches we'd created.

The remaining invaders scrambled back to their ship, some shouting for retreat while others clung to the wreckage. I didn't relent, ensuring they wouldn't have the strength to regroup.

The Tidecaller pulled away, her magic repairing the damage to our hull as the storm began to subside. I glanced at Briar, her chest heaving as she leaned against the railing, her blade still in hand.

"You're reckless," I said, my voice sharp.

"And you're overbearing," she shot back, though there was a faint smile on her lips.

I stepped closer, letting the storm quiet within me as I met her gaze. "You were brilliant."

Her breath hitched, but she didn't look away. For a moment, the chaos faded, leaving only the two of us standing amidst the aftermath of battle.

The tide had shifted—and I wasn't sure who was pulling whom anymore.

The Shadowed Reefs loomed ahead, unseen but undeniably felt. With each passing mile, the air grew heavier, pressing against my chest like an unseen weight. The sea itself darkened to an inky black, its surface swallowing the faint light of the moon. Even the stars faltered here, their distant glow dimmed as if reluctant to illuminate what lay ahead.

The Tidecaller thrummed, her magic humming with a strange resonance. It wasn't her usual song of command and certainty; this was something else—an undercurrent of anticipation, perhaps even warning.

Around me, the crew moved with quiet efficiency, their usual banter replaced by tense glances and muttered prayers. Every man aboard knew the legends of the Shadowed Reefs—ships lost to unseen barriers, entire crews dragged beneath the waves by forces no one could name. The stories had teeth here, sharp enough to cut through even the bravest hearts.

I stood at the helm, my gaze fixed on the horizon, though there was nothing to see. Just the infinite stretch of water and the foreboding sense that we were heading into something far greater than ourselves. The battle behind us had rattled the men, but the fear of what lay ahead had sunk its claws deeper.

Briar leaned against the railing near the bow, her figure outlined in the faint glow of the moonlight. She hadn't spoken much since the fight, but I could feel the tension radiating from her. The map would guide us through, but only she could see its shifting path—and only she could lead us forward.

Enric approached, his steps deliberate and heavy with meaning. He stopped just short of me, his voice low to avoid carrying to the others. "The men are holding steady, My King, but the reefs... You can feel it, can't you?"

I nodded, my gaze fixed ahead. "The Tidecaller will see us through."

"And her?" He tilted his head toward Briar, who remained near the bow, her hands gripping the railing as she studied the map. "You trust her?"

"With my life," I said without hesitation. "She's not just a guide, Enric."

Enric didn't press further, but his silence spoke volumes. He understood the stakes, even if he didn't fully grasp the bond that tied me to Briar.

I left the helm in his hands and made my way to her. She didn't turn as I approached, but I could see the tension in her shoulders, the way her fingers tightened around the parchment as if it might slip from her grasp.

"The reefs are close," I said, my voice low. "What do you see?"

She held up the map without looking at me. "The symbols are moving faster, like they're pulling us toward something. But I can't tell what."

Her honesty was disarming. There was no bravado, no attempt to mask her uncertainty. It only made me trust her more.

"Then we follow," I said, placing a hand lightly on her shoulder. She tensed but didn't pull away. "But know this: I'll get us through. The Tidecaller answers to me, and I won't let anything happen to you."

Her laugh was dry, almost bitter. "I'm not worried about myself. It's your crew I'm thinking about. They didn't ask to follow your map or your madness."

"They follow because they believe in me." I stepped closer, lowering my voice. "And so will you."

Her eyes snapped to mine, a spark of defiance flickering in their depths. "We'll see."

Before I could respond, a voice rang out from the crow's nest. "Reefs ahead! Jagged rocks to starboard!"

I spun, barking orders. "Helm, steer us starboard! Watch the wind!"

The Tidecaller groaned as she shifted, her sails straining against the sudden gusts. The air crackled with energy that sent shivers up my spine and raised the hairs on my arms. The crew sprang into action, their movements fluid and efficient despite the tension.

Briar gripped the railing beside me, her knuckles white. "This feels wrong," she muttered, her voice barely audible over the wind. "The map is leading us straight into it."

"It always feels wrong before it's right," I said, though even I couldn't shake the unease creeping over me.

The ship tilted sharply as a rogue wave slammed into us, spraying the deck with warm seawater. Briar stumbled, and I caught her arm, pulling her close to steady her. "Stay near me," I said, my voice firm.

She nodded, her usual defiance replaced by something more fragile. Fear, perhaps, though she'd never admit it.

As the ship steadied, I felt The Tidecaller's magic surge, a deep pulse resonating through the wood and into my bones. She was responding to me, to the command of my magic, as we navigated the treacherous waters.

"Drop anchor!" My voice rang out, commanding and sharp. The crew obeyed without hesitation, the heavy iron anchor plunging into the swirling depths with a splash. The Tidecaller groaned as the anchor caught, steadying her against the currents threatening to push us off course.

Briar's knuckles were white as she gripped the railing, the map clutched tightly in her other hand. Her wide eyes flickered toward me. "What are you doing?"

I moved to the center of the deck, my magic coiling within me like a restless tide. "Pushing us through. The waters here aren't natural—they resist passage. This isn't just sailing; it's a battle with the sea itself." I gave her a pointed look. "Trust me."

"Trust you?" she snapped. "We're about to get swallowed whole!"

"No," I said calmly, raising my arms and focusing on the waters around us. "We're about to break through."

The ocean surged beneath us, an invisible force straining against the Tidecaller. My magic flowed outward, weaving into the currents, bending them to my will. It was like threading a needle with a tempest, the resistance strong and unrelenting. The ship trembled, her timbers groaning under the pressure.

The crew exchanged wary glances but stayed at their posts, trusting the bond between my magic and The Tidecaller to carry us through. The ship's magic thrummed in response, amplifying mine as I forced the water to part around us.

Briar's voice cut through the tension. "What's happening? Why does the sea feel... alive?"

"It is alive," I said through gritted teeth. "The magic here is ancient and stubborn. It pushes back, testing us. Testing me." I pressed my hands forward, the water bending and reshaping, creating a path ahead that shimmered faintly under the moonlight.

The Tidecaller glided forward, its movement unnaturally smooth as the waters rolled away like curtains. The air was heavy with the scent of salt and magic, vibrating with power.

Briar leaned closer to the railing, her curiosity overcoming her fear. "You're... controlling the sea?"

"I'm guiding it," I corrected, sweat beading on my brow as I fought to maintain the flow. "The waters here obey no man. But they listen to me."

Her lips parted slightly, but she said nothing, her gaze darting to the shimmering waves surrounding us. The crew worked in tense silence, their movements precise and deliberate as we pressed onward.

The map in Briar's hand shimmered faintly, catching her attention. "The symbols... they're brighter," she murmured, more to herself than anyone else.

"Good," I said, my voice strained. "That means we're heading the right way."

A sudden, sharp wave crashed against the side of the ship, breaking through the protective current I'd created. The Tidecaller jolted, throwing several crew members off balance. Briar stumbled, clutching the railing for support.

"Hold steady!" I called out, summoning another surge of magic. The waters hissed and churned as I pushed them back, regaining control. "We're almost through."

The ship rocked violently again, and I felt the resistance intensify as though the sea itself sought to swallow us whole. My magic flared, pulling harder, The Tidecaller responding with a low hum that vibrated through her hull.

Finally, with a final push, the waters calmed. The oppressive force that had surrounded us dissipated, leaving a stillness that was almost unnerving. The crew released a collective breath, some exchanging nervous glances.

Briar's gaze snapped to me. "What just happened?"

I turned to her, my chest rising and falling with exertion. "The sea tried to stop us. But it failed."

Her eyes narrowed. "Why does it feel like it's going to try again?"

The tension in my shoulders eased and I took a steadying breath. "Because the sea will always test us here. But next time, I'll make sure it doesn't get that close."

Briar turned to look out over the endless sea. "What now?"

"Now," I said, stepping closer, "we find out what your map wants to show us."

13

"The map didn't lead to gold or jewels. It led to something far more dangerous."

BRIAR

The horizon began to shift, the faintest sliver of light breaking through the night sky, softening the deep blue into streaks of gray and pale gold. The stars, bold and bright only moments ago, began their slow retreat, leaving the sea and sky to prepare for a new day.

I glanced down at the map in my hands, its once-glowing symbols fading as if the encroaching daylight was a balm for its magic. The parchment grew still, its secrets slipping back into whatever shadows had birthed them.

"It's going to sleep," I muttered, running my thumb over its surface, half expecting it to spark back to life. But it didn't. The map was as blank as it had been when we first looked at it.

Rhayne, standing just behind me, leaned in closer, his voice low and steady. "The magic of the map rests when the sun rises. It'll show you more when the time is right."

I turned to look at him, his calm confidence aggravating and oddly reassuring all at once. "Convenient."

"It's the way of fae magic. And a reminder that even we need rest." He tilted his head toward the fading night. "The Tidecaller will anchor here for now. The crew needs sleep—and so do you."

I bristled at his tone, the way he said it like an order masked in concern. But as much as I hated to admit it, my body ached from the tension and chaos of the past few days. My legs wobbled slightly beneath me, and I cursed myself for showing even a hint of weakness.

"Fine," I said, turning on my heel. "Lead the way, oh mighty Pirate King."

His chuckle followed me as he gestured toward the cabin. "My Queen, your quarters await."

I rolled my eyes but stepped past him, the faint hum of The Tidecaller beneath my feet an ever-present reminder of the ship's magic. The crew moved about in quiet efficiency, their fatigue evident but their respect for Rhayne unwavering. They didn't so much as glance at me as I entered the cabin.

The door shut behind us with a soft click, and the air inside felt heavier, more intimate. I stopped short, my gaze locking on the single bed dominating the small space.

My stomach twisted, a mix of annoyance and something I couldn't quite name. Of course there was only one bed. Why would the Pirate King need more than one?

"Where am I supposed to sleep?" The words came out sharper than I intended, but the question felt necessary to mask the sudden, unwelcome rush of heat in my cheeks.

Rhayne crossed the room in two strides, shrugging off his jacket and tossing it onto a nearby chair. "There," he said simply, gesturing to the bed.

I folded my arms, narrowing my eyes. "And where will you be?"

He paused, his movements deliberate as he turned to meet my gaze. "There."

My mouth dropped open slightly before I snapped it shut. "You're joking."

"I'm not." His voice was calm, almost amused, but his expression was unreadable. "It's a bed, Briar. I'm not asking for anything else."

The implication in his words sent a shiver down my spine, and I hated how easily his presence could unsettle me. He was too close, too steady, his confidence a stark contrast to the chaos of my thoughts.

"I'm not sharing a bed with you," I said, my tone defiant, though even I could hear the crack in my voice. "We may be married, but this is ridiculous."

He took a step closer, the space between us shrinking. "Ridiculous or not, it's what we have. And if you're worried, don't be. You have my word, Briar. I won't touch you... unless you ask."

My breath hitched, and I hated the way his words hung in the air, heavy and charged. The way his eyes darkened, watching me, as if he knew exactly what effect he had on me.

I turned away abruptly, focusing on the small desk cluttered with maps and navigation tools. "I'll sleep on the floor."

"You won't." His voice was firm, leaving no room for argument. "You'll take the bed, and I'll take the chair."

I risked a glance at him, surprised by the offer. His expression was unreadable, but there was no mockery, no trace of the teasing smirk he so often wore.

"Fine," I said, moving toward the bed with slow, deliberate steps. "But if you so much as—"

"I know," he interrupted. "You'll stab me in my sleep."

I huffed, climbing onto the mattress and pulling the blanket over me. The bed was softer than I expected, the gentle sway of the ship lulling me despite my resolve to stay guarded.

Rhayne settled into the chair, his long frame looking far too large for the small space. He leaned back, his arms crossing over his chest as he watched me with an intensity that made my skin prickle.

"Goodnight, wife," he said, the faintest hint of amusement returning to his tone.

"Don't call me that," I muttered, turning my back to him.

The room fell quiet, but the tension lingered, wrapping around us like the magic of the ship itself. And as I closed my eyes, I couldn't shake the feeling that sleep wouldn't come easily—not with Rhayne so close, and not with the weight of everything unspoken between us.

When I awoke, the first thing I noticed was warmth. A solid, infuriating warmth pressed against my side. My eyes snapped open, and there he was. Rhayne. In the bed. His silver-white hair spilled across the pillow, his arm draped loosely over the blanket as if he hadn't a care in the world.

"Are you kidding me?" I hissed, shoving at his shoulder with all the force I could muster.

His eyes cracked open, lazily meeting mine as if I hadn't just jarred him awake. "Evening, wife."

"Don't," I growled, shoving him harder. He rolled onto his back, his eyes holding a mischievous grin.

"I couldn't sleep in the chair," he said, stretching like a damned cat. "So, I improvised."

"You improvised," I repeated, my voice rising. "By invading my space?"

"It's *our* space," he corrected, propping himself up on one elbow. "You're my queen, remember?"

My hands clenched into fists as I resisted the urge to throw the nearest object at him. "Get out."

He raised an eyebrow, his smirk widening. "You were perfectly fine with me here until you woke up. Seems like a *you* problem."

"It's a me problem because you're in my bed!" I practically shouted, throwing the blanket off and leaping to my feet.

"Our bed," he said, his tone maddeningly calm.

I pointed a finger at him, my chest heaving. "If you don't get out of this bed right now, I swear I will—"

"You'll what?" he interrupted, his voice dropping to a low, dangerous murmur. "Push me again? Throw me overboard? Face it, Briar, you're stuck with me. And you might as well get used to it."

My mouth opened and closed, words failing me as his gaze held mine. There was something infuriatingly smug in his expression, but beneath it, I caught a flicker of something else. Something softer.

"I hate you," I muttered, though my voice lacked conviction.

"Good," he said, settling back into the bed with a satisfied sigh. "Hate me all you want, as long as you stay close."

I grabbed a pillow and threw it at him, relishing the soft *thwack* as it hit his face. "You're impossible."

"And yet, here we are," he replied, his chuckle chasing me as I stormed out of the cabin, slamming the door behind me.

The cool morning air hit my skin like a balm, though it did little to temper the storm raging inside me. Being married to Rhayne was going to drive me mad.

I took my time on deck. The Tidecaller's anchor held firm as we drifted just at the edge of the Shadowed Reefs. I stood at the railing, staring out at the jagged maze of black stone rising from the water like the broken teeth of some ancient beast. The air here felt different—thick and heavy, as though the sea itself held its breath.

The reefs shimmered faintly, streaked with an unnatural, faintly glowing seaweed that swayed with the water's slow pulse. It should've been mesmerizing, but it only set my nerves on edge.

Many of the faces were now becoming familiar, but no one spoke to me. I wasn't sure if I was grateful or irritated.

In a way, I felt entirely alone, but on the other hand, I was now married to Rhayne Whitehook, the freaking Pirate King. I definitely wasn't alone. The fact that I woke to him sleeping in my bed was proof.

Ugh.

The nerve of that man!

After pacing the deck once more, it became painfully clear—I needed to relieve myself and find a change of clothes. Just because I was being held prisoner on this ship didn't mean I had to smell like I belonged in the brig. Gods, what I wouldn't give to be back home at the Tower, with fresh linens, steaming hot water, and a proper bath.

As I returned to the cabin, the bright afternoon sunlight filtered through the windows, painting everything in gold. My stomach growled, a sharp reminder that I hadn't eaten since before the wedding—which, somehow, already felt like an eternity ago.

I glanced at Rhayne, who stood near the door, his gaze fixed on the horizon as though the answers to the universe might appear there.

"I don't suppose your magical ship serves breakfast," I said, breaking the silence.

He turned to me, his gaze sweeping over me as if he were memorizing every inch. "I was just about to suggest we eat."

"Together?" My voice pitched higher than I'd intended.

"We are married, Briar," he said smoothly, his tone dripping with amusement. "Sharing a meal won't kill you."

I huffed and crossed my arms. "I guess I don't have a choice."

Rhayne opened the cabin door, gesturing for me to follow. "You always have a choice, little thief. But skipping meals isn't a wise one."

I bit back a retort and followed him to the galley, the scent of bread and something savory wafting through the air. The crew bustled about, their movements accompanied by a hum of activity and laughter. It felt at odds with the chaos of the night before.

In the corner, a modest spread was laid out on a small table: warm bread, cured meats, and fruit that looked surprisingly fresh for a ship. Rhayne pulled out a chair for me, and I hesitated before sitting, eyeing him warily.

"You're playing at being a gentleman now?" I asked, arching a brow.

"I'm always a gentleman," he replied, his voice a perfect blend of charm and mock offense. "You just don't appreciate it."

"I don't trust it," I muttered, grabbing a piece of bread and tearing into it. The bread was soft, the perfect balance of chewy and crisp. Damn it.

Rhayne sat across from me, his movements deliberate as he poured a steaming cup of tea. "You'll find that trust is something we'll need to work on, wife."

"Stop calling me that," I said, my words muffled around a bite of bread.

"But it's what you are," he countered, leaning back in his chair, his blue eyes glinting with mischief. "Unless you've forgotten our vows already."

"I haven't forgotten anything," I snapped, reaching for the fruit. "I just think this whole situation is absurd."

"Absurd or not, it's real." He took a sip of his tea, watching me over the rim of his cup. "And if you're going to continue being this feisty, I'll need to make sure you're well-fed."

"Feisty?" I repeated, glaring at him. "You're lucky I'm even speaking to you."

"Ah, but you *are* speaking to me." He set his cup down and leaned forward, his gaze locking with mine. "And every word you speak only confirms what I already know."

"Which is?" I challenged, refusing to look away.

"That you and I are more alike than you'd care to admit," he said, his voice low and sure. "Stubborn, defiant, and entirely too captivated by the challenge of the other."

I scoffed and stood abruptly, grabbing my plate. "The only thing captivating me right now is this bread."

Rhayne chuckled softly, watching me as I moved to sit at another table. "Wherever you go, Briar, I'll follow."

I shot him a look over my shoulder. "Then you'd better stay seated, because I'm not moving far."

As I sat down with my back to him, I could feel his gaze lingering. Damn him. Even when he wasn't saying anything, he was impossible to ignore. And yet somehow, the bread tasted even better knowing he was annoyed.

The galley door swung open, and a large man with arms as thick as oak branches and an apron dusted with flour stepped inside. His dark hair was tied back in a leather strap, and his sharp green eyes swept over us with a look that suggested he was no stranger to tense dining situations. It was also impossible to ignore the hook tattoo on his hand, and I wondered what kind of bargain he was bound to.

"You two are either plotting something or about to kill each other," he said, his voice warm and rich with humor. "Either way, I'd rather not clean up the mess."

Rhayne leaned back in his chair. "Briar, meet Corwin, The Tidecaller's cook. He's been with me since the beginning."

Corwin rolled his eyes. "Not by choice, mind you. I've just yet to find a better kitchen that floats."

I couldn't stop the smile tugging at my lips. Corwin's presence was like a balm, smoothing out the ever-present tension that seemed to follow Rhayne. "Nice to meet you, Corwin. It seems your bread is the only reason I haven't lost my mind yet."

His grin widened. "That's what they all say. But don't get too attached—I've a reputation to maintain as the surliest cook on the seas."

"I think I can handle a little surliness," I said, taking another bite of bread. "Especially if it comes with food like this."

Corwin barked out a laugh, moving to the table and grabbing a piece of fruit. "Careful, lass. Flattery like that might get you an extra slice of pie."

Rhayne's gaze flicked to Corwin, his grin fading slightly. "She's not here to win you over, Corwin."

Corwin waved him off with a flour-dusted hand. "Relax, My King. If she's putting up with you, she deserves a bit of kindness."

I couldn't help the chuckle that escaped me. "Finally, someone with sense."

Corwin winked at me, then leaned closer, mock whispering, "Don't let him fool you. Beneath all that brooding, he's just a softie. Thinks he's mysterious, but he's an open book."

Rhayne's eyes narrowed, though there was no real heat behind it. "Corwin, I'd tread carefully."

"Or what? You'll find another cook who makes that ridiculous stew you like so much?" Corwin shot back, grinning as though he lived for moments like this.

I liked him immediately. Where Rhayne was all tension and control, Corwin brought a levity that was sorely needed. He didn't seem the least bit intimidated by the Pirate King—or me, for that matter—and that alone made him invaluable.

"Briar," Corwin said, straightening up, "if you ever need a break from His Majesty's brooding, you'll find me here. I make a mean tea to go with that bread."

"Noted," I said, already feeling a little lighter. "Thanks, Corwin."

"Anytime, lass." He turned to Rhayne, his grin softening into something more genuine. "But seriously, My King, if you're headed to the reefs, keep her close. The crew talks, and you know how rumors spread."

Rhayne's expression hardened, but he gave a curt nod. "I know."

With that, Corwin left, leaving the faint scent of spices and the lingering echo of his laughter. For the first time since the wedding, I felt a sliver of normalcy—however fleeting—settle over me.

After I'd eaten my fill of bread and fruit, I washed it down with a mug of warm citrus rum that, annoyingly, was better than the Kracken's. Rhayne sat across from me, his silence louder than any words. His steady, unreadable gaze followed my every movement, and it was starting to grate on my nerves.

Setting the mug down harder than necessary, I stood abruptly, determined to put some distance between us. "If you're going to sit there like a shadow and stare, maybe find someone else to haunt."

He leaned back in his seat and crossed his arms, watching me intently. "I was merely ensuring my wife is well-fed. Corwin could prepare something else if bread doesn't suit you."

I huffed, crossing my arms. "I'm perfectly satisfied with the bread, thank you very much."

"Good. It would be a shame if my queen went hungry."

I shot him a glare, heat rising to my cheeks. "I'm going to the deck." Without waiting for a response, I turned sharply and headed for the stairs, my steps clipped and deliberate.

"Do try not to fall overboard," he called after me, his tone laced with amusement.

I bit back the urge to throw something at him and instead kept walking, muttering curses under my breath. As I climbed the stairs to the deck, my hands clenched into fists at my sides. How did he manage to get under my skin so effortlessly? One smirk, one infuriatingly calm word from him, and I was ready to throw myself overboard just to get away from it.

The nerve of him, sitting there like he owned the world—and me along with it. I inhaled deeply, the salt-tinged air stinging my lungs, but it did little to cool the heat crawling up my neck. The man was impossible, and worse, he knew it.

I reached the quarterdeck and paused, letting the open air wash over me. The ocean stretched endlessly in every direction, aside from the dark, jagged steeples of the reef, an unrelenting reminder of how far I was from everything familiar. I leaned against the railing, the breeze tugging at my hair, and let my thoughts drift to Asher. Was he looking for me? Or had he given up, assuming I'd disappeared for good?

A pang of homesickness tightened my chest. As much as I wanted to believe I could hold my own here, the truth was harder to face. I missed the Tower, the warmth of Asher's laughter, and the quiet certainty that came with having someone at my side who didn't infuriate me at every turn.

And yet, as my gaze wandered to the endless horizon, I couldn't deny the pull of this place—the magic of the sea, the unspoken promises of The Tidecaller, and the maddening man who'd somehow become the axis of my world.

Blast it all, I was trapped in more ways than one.

Rhayne's voice pulled me from my thoughts. "We'll need to search the reefs while we wait for night to come so you can read the map."

I turned to him, frowning. "You're seriously suggesting we need to go in there?" I gestured toward the ominous spires.

He gave me one of those infuriatingly calm smiles, the kind that made me want to punch him and kiss him at the same time. "The map led us here for a reason. It's our duty to uncover what it wants us to find."

The Tidecaller swayed gently beneath my feet, her magic humming faintly as if it, too, questioned the wisdom of leaving her safety. I stared after Rhayne, who was already descending the rope ladder toward the longboat waiting below, its narrow frame bobbing on the waves.

"You can't be serious," I muttered under my breath, glancing at the dark, jagged reefs.

"Move along, little thief." His voice carried up to me, calm and unbothered, as if we were heading off for a casual stroll rather than into certain danger. "Unless you plan to stay behind and miss all the fun."

The crew was already preparing the longboat, their murmured words blending with the creak of oars and the slap of water against the hull.

I grabbed the railing, my fingers tightening. "You honestly want me to get off this magical ship that repairs itself to go traipsing around the Shadowed Reefs in that?" I gestured to the longboat, which looked pitifully small compared to the towering waves and the treacherous waters around us.

Rhayne paused halfway down the ladder, turning to glance up at me, his silver-white hair catching the faint sunlight. "I could always carry you if you prefer." His challenge sparked my irritation—and my curiosity. He wouldn't. Would he?

My stomach twisted, but I forced myself to step forward. "If I die out there, I'm coming back to haunt you," I muttered, gripping the ladder with both hands.

"You'd make a charming ghost," Rhayne replied, his smug grin audible even without seeing his face. "Now hurry up before I change my mind and leave you behind."

I descended the ladder carefully, the rough rope scratching against my palms. The salty spray of the sea stung my face, and the longboat rocked violently as I climbed aboard, my boots skidding on its slick surface. Rhayne was already there, steady and assured, his hand outstretched to help me. I hesitated, glaring at him.

"Don't make me say *please*," he drawled.

I reluctantly took his hand, his grip strong and warm as he pulled me into the boat. "There. Happy?" I muttered, brushing past him to sit as far from him as the small space allowed.

Rhayne took his place at the helm, nodding to the crew who'd climbed aboard with us. The oars dipped into the water, their rhythmic strokes propelling us toward the reefs. The further we went, the darker the water seemed to grow.

I glanced back at The Tidecaller, its imposing silhouette fading into the mist. It was strange to leave her behind, like stepping away from a lifeline. The longboat felt exposed and vulnerable against the reef.

"Do you even know what we're looking for?" I asked, breaking the heavy silence.

"No. But the map does."

I snorted. "The map. Right. The magical piece of parchment that only I can read. Comforting."

Rhayne's gaze flicked to me, steady and unyielding. "Trust yourself, little thief."

I opened my mouth to retort but stopped short as the reefs loomed closer. My pulse quickened, and I tightened my grip on the edge of the boat. Whatever we were about to find, I wasn't sure I wanted to be part of it.

The longboat glided closer to the reefs, the sound of the oars cutting through the water the only thing breaking the tense silence. I kept my eyes on the towering rocks, their surfaces slick with seaweed that shimmered faintly in the dim light. They rose high above us, their jagged edges sharp enough to gut a ship or a careless intruder. This place felt wrong. The kind of wrong that made my skin crawl and every instinct screamed to turn back.

Rhayne sat relaxed as if the ominous surroundings didn't faze him in the slightest. Typical. I, on the other hand, was gripping the edge of the boat so tightly my knuckles ached.

The crew exchanged uneasy glances, their usual banter replaced by wary silence. I caught snippets of muttered prayers to gods I didn't recognize. Even the air felt different here, heavy and charged, like a storm waiting to strike.

Rhayne's voice cut through the tension, low and calm. "Bring us alongside that opening." He pointed toward a narrow gap between the rocks, where the water churned unnaturally, as if something below the surface was stirring.

"You can't be serious," I muttered, glaring at him. "That doesn't look like an opening. It looks like a trap."

His gaze went straight to me. "Afraid, little thief?"

"Smart," I shot back. "There's a difference."

The crew maneuvered the longboat through the narrow gap, their movements precise but edged with tension.

I leaned forward, straining to see into the shadows ahead, but the darkness was impenetrable, swallowing the light entirely.

The boat slowed as we entered a small cove, the water eerily still. The cliffs loomed around us, enclosing the space like the walls of a prison. In the center of the cove stood a cluster of rocks, rising like a natural pedestal. Atop it lay something small and gleaming, faintly reflecting the dim light that filtered through the overcast sky.

"What is that?" I asked, my voice barely above a whisper.

"Let's find out," Rhayne said, standing with an easy grace that made me want to throw him overboard. He reached for an oar to steady the boat as we drew closer to the rocks.

As the longboat scraped gently against the pedestal, Rhayne turned to the crew. "Stay here. Keep watch."

"And me?" I asked, crossing my arms.

"You're coming with me." He didn't wait for a response, stepping onto the slick rocks with the kind of confidence that suggested he'd already accounted for every possible mishap. He turned, holding out a hand to me. "Unless, of course, you'd rather wait here and trust the tides to keep you safe."

I scowled but took his hand, my boots slipping slightly as I climbed onto the rocks. His grip tightened, steadying me, and for a brief moment, I hated how solid and unshakable he felt.

The object on the pedestal came into sharper focus as we approached—a small, ornate box, its surface etched with glowing symbols. I hesitated, the hairs on the back of my neck standing on end.

"This feels like a trap," I said, my voice low.

Rhayne crouched beside the box, his expression thoughtful. "If it is, it's a well-crafted one." He glanced up at me, his blue eyes sharp. "Do you feel anything?"

"Feel anything?" I echoed, frowning. "What is that supposed to mean?"

"You're the one who can read the map. If this is part of its magic, it might respond to you."

I stared at him. "And what if it explodes when I touch it? Or summons some cursed sea creature to drag us all under?"

He smiled faintly, that infuriatingly calm expression never faltering. "Then I'll save you. Again."

I rolled my eyes but stepped closer, my pulse hammering in my chest. The box seemed to hum faintly, its glow intensifying as I reached out. My fingers brushed the surface, and a sudden jolt of energy shot up my arm, making me gasp.

"What is it?" Rhayne asked, his voice sharp.

"I don't know," I said, shaking my hand as the sensation faded. "It... it feels like...home." It was hard to explain. Whatever it was, it was full of magic. But the familiar burst of energy left me homesick for something I couldn't remember.

The box clicked softly, the lid shifting as if it had been waiting for my touch. I hesitated, glancing at Rhayne. He nodded once, his gaze steady.

I opened the lid.

Inside lay a small crystalline shard, its surface swirling with dark, shadowy tendrils. It was both beautiful and ominous, like a piece of the night sky trapped in solid form.

Rhayne's expression darkened as he studied it. "A fragment of something greater," he murmured, almost to himself.

"What is it?" I asked, my voice edged with unease. But even as I said the words, I knew. Just like the map, I knew without a doubt this was something bigger than anything we could have prepared ourselves for. "It's a heart."

Rhayne's brow rose. "A heart?"

"Obviously not human." The thrumming pulse of magic collided with my soul, wrapping around it like an embrace—familiar, comforting, and terrifying all at once.

"I've seen a few of those, and I concur, not human."

I rolled my eyes. "I'm sure you were the reason someone was missing their heart."

His soft chuckle echoed in the cove. "You'd be right. Sometimes a bargain doesn't end well."

"So, if I broke our deal, you'd rip out my heart?" I was skeptical. I was beginning to think I may be the only one safe with the Pirate King, but it wasn't going to stop me from barbing him.

"Little thief, are you offering me your heart?" His grin vanished, replaced by sharp focus. "We aren't alone."

I turned sharply, following his line of sight. In the shadows of the cliffs, movement rippled through the darkness. Figures emerged, their forms cloaked and indistinct, their eyes glinting like shards of broken glass.

"Shadowborne," Rhayne said, his voice a low growl. He stepped in front of me, his hand resting on the hilt of his sword. "Get back to the boat. Now."

I didn't argue. Gripping the box tightly, I scrambled back toward the longboat as the figures closed in. The crew shouted, readying their weapons as the Shadowborne siren emerged from the water and fully into the light.

The battle that followed was brutal and swift, the air filled with the clash of steel and the crackle of magic as Rhayne unleashed his power. I clutched the box to my chest, my heart pounding as I watched him fight, his movements precise and lethal.

When the last of the Shadowborne fell, dissolving into shadowy mist, Rhayne turned to me, his expression grim.

"Let's go," he said, his voice tight. "We have what we came for."

As we pushed off from the rocks, I couldn't shake the feeling that the crystal in my hands was more than just a piece of the puzzle. It was a warning of what was to come.

The longboat bumped against the hull of The Tidecaller, its rocking motion a stark contrast to the steady thrum of magic emanating from the heart tucked inside a cloth sack in Rhayne's grip.

I climbed the rope ladder, the strain on my arms and legs barely registering past the hum of the stone's presence. Rhayne followed close behind.

The crew gathered silently on deck as we stepped aboard. Their gazes shifted to the sack in Rhayne's hand, curiosity flickering like the first spark of a fire. The faint glow from the heart seemed to press against the fabric, teasing its presence without fully revealing itself.

Enric stepped forward, his expression unreadable save for a slight crease in his brow. "What did you find?"

Rhayne held the sack up, just enough for a subtle glimmer to escape. The faint light was enough to draw murmurs from the crew, their eyes widening in awe—or apprehension.

"Something worth the trouble," Rhayne said, his voice low and steady. "Though what it is, we'll have to figure out."

I crossed my arms, keeping my distance from the sack. The magic pulsing from it felt alive, unnatural, like it could slip past the edges of reality if given the chance. "Whatever it is, it feels like it's old and extremely powerful. Don't think for a second it's just a shiny rock."

Rhayne shot me a glance, a faint smile tugging at his lips. "Noted."

The sun was sinking fast now, painting the sky in streaks of deep orange and violet. The weight of dusk pressed on us, the kind of heaviness that came not just with the loss of light, but with the knowledge that the map would soon come alive again, urging us onward.

The crew returned to their duties, their movements tense but efficient. The heart's faint glow seemed to pulse in rhythm with the hum of The Tidecaller, as though the ship recognized something about it. The thought sent a shiver down my spine.

Rhayne's eyes were fixed on the horizon, his expression sharp but contemplative. "We're getting closer to something," he murmured, more to himself than anyone else.

I frowned, resisting the urge to demand answers he didn't have. "Closer to what? Something useful, I hope."

He didn't answer right away, his focus still on the horizon as the sun's last rays vanished beneath the waves. The first stars began to dot the sky, their faint light barely illuminating the sea. Finally, he turned to me, his gaze softening, though his words carried weight.

"Whatever it is, it brought us here for a reason. That's enough to keep going."

I glanced at the sack, unease stirring in my chest. "You sound awfully sure about that."

"Because I am." His tone left no room for argument, but the look in his eyes was less certain than his words.

The ship's bell rang out, signaling the shift change as night fully enveloped us. Rhayne adjusted his grip on the sack, his other hand resting on the hilt of his sword as though preparing for anything.

"Stay close," he said, his voice lower now. "Whatever this map leads to, it's only going to get harder from here."

I nodded, though my mind churned with questions. The shard's faint glow seemed to echo the unspoken tension between us, a reminder that we were chasing something neither of us could yet name.

As the night deepened, I looked back toward the reefs, their jagged shadows now hidden beneath the dark waves. Whatever the heart was, or whatever it belonged to, it had brought us one step closer to answers—or destruction. Maybe both.

"I didn't betray her because I wanted to, I betrayed her because I had no other choice. Or so I keep telling myself."

ASHER

The seat beneath me was hard and cold, but it was nothing compared to the icy weight pressing down on my chest. My palms were clammy despite the chill in the dimly lit chamber deep within the mountains off the Crimson Coast. The flickering lantern light cast twisted shadows on the rough walls. Across from me, he loomed—an entity cloaked in darkness, his very presence steeped in something unnatural. The air around him rippled, faint traces of magic leaking into the room. It felt wrong, as though it had seeped through a crack in the fabric of the world itself.

"You lost her?" The accusation hit like a hammer, solid and unyielding.

I swallowed hard, my usual charm nowhere to be found. "She slipped through faster than I expected. The crew she's with… they're not ordinary."

A low growl rumbled from the shadows, resonating with a depth that made my teeth ache. The figure shifted, and for the briefest moment, I thought I saw something—a jagged outline, dark tendrils curling against the faintest light. "Not ordinary? She's not ordinary, you fool. She is the key. And now you've let her fall into their hands."

"She doesn't know," I said quickly, leaning forward as if proximity could soften the weight of my failure. "She has no idea what she is. No idea what she can do."

"And yet, she's with them." The disdain in his tone was enough to strip me bare, every word a lash. "Do you think they'll hesitate to use her? To wield her against the very balance we shattered?"

I clenched my fists, nails biting into my palms to keep them from trembling. "I'll fix it," I said, my voice steadier than I felt. My mind raced, desperate for a solution. "I'll bring her back."

The shadow shifted again, leaning closer, and this time the chill was palpable, like frost creeping into my lungs. His eyes glinted faintly, an unnatural shimmer that didn't belong in this world—proof of his origin. "If you don't, Asher, there will be nothing left of you to fix."

The words echoed in the still air, sinking deep into my bones. I stood, my knees threatening to give way, but I forced myself upright. The weight of his gaze followed me as I backed toward the door.

The room felt smaller. The air heavier. My chest tightened with the promise of failure, but I pushed it down. I had to find her.

Because if I didn't... I wouldn't live long enough to regret it.

"When my lips found hers, it wasn't about want anymore ~ it was about need, raw and undeniable."

RHAYNE

The waning light settled over the sea, creating shadows that stretched like a dark mirror beneath The Tidecaller. Briar stood at the railing, her figure rigid, as though sheer will alone could ward off the weight of the day.

I approached, the hum of the ship beneath my feet a steady reminder of our bond. She didn't turn, but I knew she felt me.

"You should be resting," I said, my voice low enough not to carry to the crew.

She huffed, gripping the rail tighter. "Resting? On this floating prison of yours? Hardly."

I leaned against the rail, my gaze flicking to the horizon. "You've seen more today than most would in a lifetime. A little gratitude wouldn't kill you."

Her head snapped toward me, those fierce blue eyes locking on mine. "Gratitude?" She laughed. "You want me to thank you for dragging me into this mess? For turning my life upside down?"

I turned to face her fully, the moonlight catching the defiance etched into her expression. "You're alive because of me. The mess, as you call it, would've found you with or without my help. At least now you have a fighting chance."

Her chest rose sharply, her lips parting as if to unleash another barb. But she hesitated, her gaze dipping for a fraction of a second before snapping back to mine. "You think you're my savior? You're nothing but a self-righteous, arrogant—"

The words cut off as I stepped closer, the space between us vanishing in a heartbeat. "Careful, Briar," I murmured, my voice rougher than I intended. "You're treading dangerous waters."

She didn't back away. Of course, she didn't. "Maybe I like dangerous waters."

Gods, the woman was maddening. A storm in human form, all fire and fury. My hand rose before I could stop myself, my fingers brushing a stray lock of hair from her face. Her breath hitched, her pulse fluttering at her throat.

"Do you?" I asked, the words a challenge and a question.

She didn't answer—not with words. Her gaze dropped to my lips, a fleeting, involuntary glance that sent heat surging through me. And then, like the sea itself, she shifted. Her defiance wavered, replaced by something raw and unguarded.

It was all the invitation I needed.

I closed the distance, capturing her lips in a kiss that was as much a clash as it was a connection. She froze for a moment, her body stiff against mine, but then she responded, her hands gripping the front of my shirt as if to push me away—or pull me closer.

The world narrowed to her—her warmth, her fire, the taste of defiance mixed with something sweeter beneath it. It was intoxicating. Infuriating.

And over too soon.

She broke away, her breaths ragged as she stared at me, eyes wide with a mixture of shock and anger. "What the hell was that?" she demanded, her voice unsteady.

"Something we both wanted," I said, my voice even despite the tightness in my chest. "Even if you won't admit it."

Her hand flew to my chest, shoving me back a step. "Don't you dare do that again."

A slow smirk curved my lips, the lingering taste of her still on my tongue. "If you don't want it to happen again, little thief, don't look at me like that."

Her glare burned hot and her cheeks flushed as she stormed past me toward the cabin. I let her go, the moment replaying in my mind.

Whatever storm we were heading into, it was nothing compared to the one brewing between us.

The moon hung heavy in the sky, its silvery glow casting long, uneven shadows across the deck of The Tidecaller. The crystal pulsed faintly with an ethereal light where it rested on the table in my cabin, its presence as unsettling as it was fascinating. It was unlike anything I had encountered before—a relic of immense power, but its purpose and origin remained shrouded. Briar called it a heart, and I agreed. The way it ebbed with magic was like a pulse. But it was more than that, it felt alive.

The crew was quiet, their earlier excitement dimmed by the weight of what we had found. Even the hum of The Tidecaller seemed subdued, its magic thrumming softly as if whispering secrets I couldn't yet decipher.

I stood at the helm, my gaze fixed on the horizon, though my thoughts were filled with Briar. I could still taste her. The kiss was something I hadn't planned on, but now it consumed me. *She* consumed me. And I wanted more.

She was below deck, likely pacing, her mind working through every possible way to defy me without breaking her vow. The thought stirred an unbidden smile, but it faded quickly. The weight of what lay ahead pressed heavily on my shoulders.

The heart had revealed itself to her. Not to me. Not to my crew. Her.

There was no denying it now—Briar was tied to something far greater than either of us understood. And yet, she was oblivious to her significance, still clinging to her defiance, still fighting to maintain her independence.

A rustle of movement pulled me from my thoughts. Enric approached, his footsteps deliberate but soft, his expression unreadable.

"My King," he said, his voice low, careful not to disturb the quiet of the night. "The crew is uneasy. The crystal... they feel it."

I nodded, my jaw tightening. "As they should. It's not our magic that it holds."

Enric hesitated, his gaze flicking briefly toward the cabin door where Briar was. "Do you trust her?"

I turned my head sharply, pinning him with a look. "She's my queen."

"That's not an answer," he said quietly, his tone more that of a friend than as my second.

I exhaled, the tension in my chest loosening slightly. "She doesn't know what she is. But I trust her spirit. Her fire." I thought about Briar for a moment and her fiery demeanor, almost chuckling. "And, of course, I trust my ability to handle her."

Enric huffed a laugh, though it lacked humor. "She's not like anyone we've dealt with before."

"No, she's not," I agreed, my voice softening as my gaze drifted back to the horizon. "And that's why she's here."

Enric didn't press further, retreating silently as I turned my focus back to the cabin door. The soft glow of the heart spilled through the cracks, beckoning me like a siren's call. I moved toward it, the sound of my boots against the wood echoing in the stillness.

The door creaked as I pushed it open, revealing Briar seated cross-legged on the floor, the map spread out before her. The crystal sat beside it, faintly glowing, its light pulsing in a slow rhythm like a heartbeat. She didn't look up when I entered, her attention locked on the interaction between the two artifacts.

"What's it doing?" I asked, my voice low.

Her head jerked up, her wide blue eyes shimmering with an unfamiliar hint of apprehension. "It reacts when I get close to it. See?" She extended a tentative hand toward the gem, and its glow intensified, as if drawn to her.

I crossed the room. Magic thrummed in the air, faint but unmistakable. The shard wasn't just powerful—it was alive in its own way, responding to her as the map did.

"It's like it knows me," she said softly, her fingers hovering near the crystal. "But that doesn't make any sense. I don't understand how or why."

"Magic rarely offers clarity," I replied, crouching beside her. "But it doesn't lie either. Whatever this is, it's tied to you."

Her jaw tightened, but she didn't pull away. Instead, she gestured to the map, its markings faintly shimmering under the moonlight streaming through the window. "The map's been shifting again. The arrows are changing direction."

"To where?" I asked, leaning closer.

"Northeast." Her voice was steady, but there was a flicker of hesitation in her tone. "I think it's pointing to Silverveil."

The name struck me like a wave crashing against the hull. Silverveil. A kingdom of light and unspoiled magic. It was said to be the last remnant of the Veil's original power, untouched by the curse.

"Silverveil," I repeated, my gaze locking on hers.

She nodded, biting her lip. "I'm not certain, but... the markings on the map—they're faint, but they're starting to resemble the old paths described in stories about the kingdom. The ones my father used to tell me."

Her father. Of course, she would make the connection. "You believe that's where he was heading?" I asked, keeping my tone neutral.

"I don't know," she admitted, her voice tight. "It's been years. If he was there, why wouldn't he have come back? Why wouldn't he have sent word?"

"Maybe he couldn't," I said simply. "If Silverveil is what they say it is, it's not a place you leave easily."

Her gaze flickered back to the heart, and I could see the war raging within her. She was a woman who lived by her wits, her ability to outmaneuver and outthink anyone in her path. But this—magic, fate, and a kingdom of myth—was beyond anything she could rationalize or manipulate.

I placed a hand on the map, drawing her attention back to me. "Whether it's Silverveil or something else, the map has chosen a direction. We follow it."

Her lips pressed into a thin line, but she nodded. "It's three days, maybe less if the wind favors us."

"Then we won't stop," I said firmly. "Not during the day. Not for anything."

She glanced at the crystal again, the faint glow reflected in her eyes. "Do you think this has something to do with the map?"

"Without a doubt," I said. "And likely everything else to come."

Her hand trembled slightly as she reached for it, stopping just short of touching it. "It feels... familiar. Like I should know what it is."

"Do you?" I pressed, watching her closely.

She shook her head, frustration flashing across her face. "No. But I wish I did."

I leaned back, letting the silence settle between us for a moment before standing. "Get some rest," I said, my tone softer now. "We'll need you sharp when we reach Silverveil."

She snorted lightly, the tension breaking just enough to let her usual defiance surface. "You mean you'll need me to read the map."

"That too," I teased.

Her gaze lingered on the crystal as I moved toward the door, her expression a mix of curiosity and unease. I paused, glancing back at her.

"Briar," I said, my voice steady. "Whatever this is— whatever it means—we'll figure it out."

She looked up at me, her blue eyes searching mine. For a brief moment, there was something unspoken between us, a connection I couldn't ignore. Then she nodded, her attention returning to the map.

I stepped out into the cool night air, the weight of Silverveil's name settling heavy in my mind. Whatever waited for us there, it wasn't just about a map or a heart. It was about Briar—and the truth she carried, whether she was ready to face it or not.

The curse, Briar, the map, the crystal... they were all bound together.

The Tidecaller's deck buzzed with muted energy as I stepped into the night. The crew moved like shadows, their murmured conversations carried away by the sea breeze. The stars above glinted like shards of the Veil itself, casting an eerie glow over the water.

"Rough night, My King?" Enric's voice carried a note of dry amusement as he approached, his boots clicking softly against the wood.

I glanced at him, catching the faint smirk tugging at the corner of his mouth. "The night's young, Enric."

His brow arched, but he didn't press further. Enric had always known when to pry and when to hold his tongue. A skill I valued more than I often acknowledged.

"What's the state of the crew?" I asked, my tone brisk.

"Restless." He gestured toward the shadows of men working at the rigging and keeping watch.

I nodded, my eyes narrowing as I scanned the horizon. "The map points us northeast, toward Silverveil. The crew needs to be ready for anything."

Enric crossed his arms, his expression turning thoughtful. "Do you think *the thief* knows more than she lets on? About the crystal, the map, her connection to all of this?"

I met his gaze, my voice low and firm. "Briar's secrets are her own—for now. But she's not the enemy, Enric. She's the key. And she is also your queen."

He tilted his head slightly, his skepticism plain, though he held back whatever doubt lingered. "As you say."

The Tidecaller hummed faintly beneath our feet as the wind shifted suddenly, carrying with it the unmistakable taste of storm-churned seas.

I looked back at Enric. "The weather?"

He stepped to the railing, holding out a hand. A faint glow pulsed at his fingertips, a ripple of silvery light that spread into the air like frost over glass. The magic hung there for a moment before dissipating, leaving only the cold bite of the wind in its wake.

"Shifting winds. A storm's brewing to the south, but it won't reach us if we stay the course," he said, his tone matter-of-fact. "The seas ahead, though... they're temperamental. More than usual."

"Magic?" I asked, though I already knew the answer.

Enric nodded. "The same kind that thrums through that gem. Whatever it is, it's stirring things up."

"Good." My lips curled into a faint smile. "A restless sea keeps our enemies cautious."

"And our crew on edge."

"They'll hold." I glanced toward the helm, catching the faint flicker of lantern light as it illuminated the ship's wheel. "The Tidecaller won't let us down."

"And if it's not the ship that needs watching?" Enric asked, his gaze lingering toward the cabin where I'd left Briar.

My jaw tightened. "She's my queen, Enric. She doesn't need watching."

"She doesn't strike me as the type to follow orders blindly," he said, though his tone lacked judgment.

"She doesn't," I agreed, my tone softer but no less firm. "And that's why I trust her. Briar isn't a liability—she's the reason we'll find what we're looking for. Don't mistake her defiance for weakness."

Enric let out a quiet chuckle, shaking his head. "Fair enough, My King. Just try not to let her burn the ship down before we reach Silverveil."

As he turned to oversee the crew, I allowed myself a moment of quiet. The distant stars blurred into the sea, the horizon stretching endlessly ahead. Silverveil awaited, its mysteries tied to the map, the heart, and Briar herself.

Whatever lay ahead, it would test us all. But I'd be damned if I let anything take her—or the answers we sought—from me.

"No one had ever looked at me like that, as if I was worth an entire kindgom and more."

BRIAR

The salty tang of the sea breeze hit me as I stepped out of the cabin and onto the deck. The chill of the early morning air crept beneath my clothes. My fingers grazed the edge of the railing as I leaned into the view. The horizon blazed with golds and oranges, the sun rising to chase away the lingering shadows of the night. It was breathtaking.

I hated that it was breathtaking.

The crew stirred around me, their movements purposeful but not hurried. End of the night routines unfolded like clockwork—ropes tightened, sails adjusted, laughter spilling out in bursts. For all their gruff exteriors, they worked like a family. A loud, boisterous, occasionally smelly family.

My stomach grumbled, reminding me I hadn't eaten since... I frowned. When was the last time I'd eaten? The thought drew me toward the galley where Corwin's voice carried over the sound of clanging pots.

"There she is!" Corwin greeted me with a grin that could've powered a lighthouse. "Morning, lass. You're just in time for breakfast."

I approached cautiously, eyeing the assortment of bread, dried meats, and fruits laid out. "What's the catch?"

"No catch." He winked, sliding a plate toward me. "Though I wouldn't rule out the odd fish bone in the stew."

I smiled despite myself, picking up a hunk of bread. "You're too kind."

He leaned on the counter, watching me. "I like to think so. But you, lass, you've got that look about you this morning."

"What look?"

"The one that says you're either going to cause trouble or walk straight into it." Corwin chuckled, turning back to his work. "Just don't forget—trouble's more fun with company."

His words stayed with me as I carried my plate back toward the railing. The bread was stale, the fruit slightly overripe, but it was food, and it gave me an excuse to linger. The sunrise painted everything in soft hues, a rare moment of peace that I wasn't sure I trusted.

The sun climbed higher, chasing away the last traces of dawn. The crew moved with renewed energy, their banter and shouts blending with the steady rhythm of the ship. I lingered by the railing, watching the endless stretch of water ahead, the weight of the map and its secrets gnawing at the edges of my thoughts.

Corwin's words from earlier echoed faintly in my mind: *Trouble's more fun with company.*

Trouble seemed to be all I'd found since stepping foot on The Tidecaller. And Rhayne—*my husband*—was the embodiment of it. My stomach churned at the memory of the kiss, unbidden but burning just beneath my skin.

With a sigh, I turned toward the cabin, needing space from the open air and the curious stares of the crew. The sound of the door closing behind me was almost comforting— until I saw Rhayne, still at the desk, his broad shoulders hunched over the map. Though why I didn't know, unless he could suddenly read it. In that case, I would no longer be needed. That thought was a lot sadder than I wanted to admit.

"You missed breakfast," I said, setting my empty plate on the small table near the door.

"Did I?" He didn't look up from the map, his tone light but distracted. "I'll mourn the loss."

I crossed my arms, leaning against the doorframe. "Don't worry. Corwin promised to save you something special. Pretty sure it involved hardtack and a questionable piece of salted fish."

That earned me a dry glance, his lips twitching faintly. "How thoughtful of him."

"Very," I replied with mock sincerity. "He said it was fit for a king."

"And you let him get away with such disrespect?"

I shrugged, enjoying the momentary break in his usual guarded demeanor. "Figured you'd handle it. You're the king, after all."

His smirk deepened, a slow, calculated expression that always put me on edge. "Careful, Briar. You're starting to sound concerned for my well-being."

"Hardly," I shot back, straightening. "I just prefer my captor to be well-fed. Makes the escape plans easier if you're too full to chase me."

He chuckled, the sound low and infuriatingly confident. "Don't mistake my restraint for leniency, little thief. You'd find escaping me far more challenging than you imagine."

I rolled my eyes and moved further into the cabin, determined not to let him see the heat creeping up my neck. "Relax, Pirate King. I'm not going anywhere. Not until that map tells us where we're supposed to go next."

I stepped further into the room, the tension in the air shifting with every step. "So, what's the plan, oh fearless Pirate King? Or are you still staring at the map, hoping it will read itself?"

He turned fully now, leaning against the desk with his arms crossed. "The plan is to keep moving until it shows us what we need. And to make sure you don't cause trouble in the meantime."

"Me? Trouble?" I placed a hand on my chest, feigning innocence. "I'm a model prisoner."

"My wife is not a prisoner. She has more freedom than anyone on this ship." The way he looked at me sent a warm chill through me.

I scoffed. "But not *off* the ship?"

His smug grin lifted the corners of his eyes as he raked over me. "Little thief, there are two things you need to remember. One, you are mine. And two..." He crossed the space between us and touched my chin, forcing me to look up at him. "I will churn the seas and drown the kingdoms for

173

you. On or off the ship, you are not, nor ever will be, my prisoner."

"Stop looking at me like that," I said, turning my head to break the connection.

"Like what?" he asked, his voice low and rough, tinged with something that made my pulse stutter.

"Like you... like you..." My words faltered, and I hated the way he made me feel off-balance, vulnerable. I pushed past him, heading for the bed. "Forget it. Just go sleep in your damn chair."

"I'm not sleeping in the chair," he said, the firmness in his voice stopping me in my tracks.

"Yes, you are," I said, turning to face him, my hands on my hips. "That's how this works. You're the one who dragged me into this mess. The least you can do is give me the bed."

"I'm not sleeping in the chair, Briar," he repeated, stepping closer, his tone unyielding. "And neither are you."

My heart thundered as he came closer, his presence overwhelming in the confined space. "So what, you expect me to just... what? Share the bed with you like we're—"

"Like we're married?" he cut in, his voice softer now, though no less intense. "We are."

"That doesn't mean—"

"It means you'll take the bed," he said, his voice brooking no argument. "I won't have you curled up in that chair, waking up sore and miserable."

I bristled, the weight of his words and the heat of his gaze making it impossible to think straight. "And you think I'll be comfortable sleeping next to you?"

His lips curved into a faint smile, though his eyes remained serious. "You'll survive."

I opened my mouth to argue further, but the exhaustion of the night finally caught up with me. The idea of fighting with him all morning over who slept where seemed as tiring as the thought of sharing the bed itself.

"Fine," I muttered, kicking off my boots and tossing them near the door. "But stay on your side."

"As you wish," he said, his voice laced with something that made me doubt his sincerity.

I climbed onto the bed, keeping as much distance as possible between us. The mattress dipped slightly under his weight as he settled on the opposite side, his movements slow and deliberate.

I turned my back to him, pretending to focus on the faint glow of the morning sun against the wall. But no matter how hard I tried, I couldn't ignore his presence. The steady rhythm of his breathing, the heat radiating from his side of the bed—it was all too much.

"You're tense," he said, his voice soft and close enough to make my pulse jump.

"Because you're in my bed," I snapped, though my voice lacked conviction.

"Our bed," he corrected. "And you don't need to be afraid of me."

"I'm not afraid of you," I said quickly, the words more defensive than I intended.

Silence stretched between us, heavy and charged. My mind raced, thoughts colliding as I tried to make sense of the pull I felt toward him. It was more than the forced marriage, more than the kiss we'd shared. It was something deeper, something that both terrified and intrigued me.

The memory of his lips on mine crept into my thoughts. The way he'd kissed me, like I was the only thing keeping him tethered to the world. It had been overwhelming, consuming—and I hated that I couldn't stop thinking about it.

I squeezed my eyes shut, willing sleep to come, but it eluded me. The warmth of his presence, the steady hum of his breathing, the weight of the bond I didn't fully understand—it was all too much.

And yet, despite everything, I couldn't bring myself to move away.

When I opened my eyes, it took a moment for them to adjust to the dim light. Had I slept all day? I stretched and rolled over. Rhayne's side of the bed was empty, but a trace of his warmth still lingered under the quilt. Sliding over, I curled up in the blanket and settled onto his pillow. His warmth wasn't the only thing clinging to the bed. His scent was everywhere. I swore I smelled it in my dreams.

I pulled the covers over my head and groaned. My dreams were even filled with him. I couldn't escape. He was everywhere. And that kiss... I relived it at least a dozen times in my sleep.

The door to the cabin creaked opened. Heavy steps filled the space, a rhythm I recognized without looking. Even in the short time I'd known him, I could tell the sound of Rhayne's footsteps from anyone else's.

"I brought you some dinner." His voice still had the sleepy timbre that warmed every inch of me. Despite hating the man, he was easily the most enjoyable man to look at. And listen to. And I hated to admit it... but sleep next to.

Poking my head out from under the quilt, I spied the food. "Did you poison it?"

"Aye. It was the first thing I did after I asked Corwin for a meal fit for a queen." He placed the plate of something that looked like fish stew and a slab of bread on the table.

The smell wasn't as unpleasant as it looked. I sat up and crinkled my nose. The food might not stink, but I did. "Do you have a way to bathe on the ship?"

"Are you asking for me, or for yourself?"

I sniffed the air. "Possibly for both." Gods. The man didn't need a bath. He still smelled incredible. It wasn't fair. But there was no way I would tell him that.

He laughed. "I had cleaned up for my queen this morning before bed, but I suppose I could do for another bath. Perhaps you would like to join me?"

"I think you have mistaken me for one of your swooning admirers."

"I mistake you for nothing, Briar Firethorn. Queen of the Nether Shores, wife of the Pirate King—*my* wife."

"You forgot best thief of Evernight and most talented swordswoman this side of the Veil."

"My apologies." He came closer to the bed. "Speaking of. I believe this is yours. I think Nyx was rather fond of it." He held out my dagger.

I didn't think I'd ever see it again. It wasn't much. Nothing fancy. But it was mine. I took it, placing it in my lap. "Thank you." I eyed him curiously. "You aren't afraid I'll cut out your heart while you sleep *in my bed?*"

"*Our* bed. And my heart is yours to do as you wish." He leaned down, kissing the top of my head before turning to leave.

I sat there stunned. I should have said something. Anything. But no words came.

He stopped at the door. "I will have a private bath prepared for you. Eat first."

The evening sun flooded the room as he opened the door and left, leaving me speechless.

My heart is yours to do as you wish.

It was absurd. Ludicrous, even. The Pirate King couldn't possibly mean it—not the man who kissed me like he wanted to devour me, who stole my freedom with a binding vow, who made my pulse race with a mere glance. He was just playing his game, toying with me like a cat with a cornered mouse.

And yet...

I touched my fingers to my lips, the memory of his kiss burning against my skin. It hadn't been just a kiss; it was a declaration, unspoken and raw. And now this—offering me his heart, as though I could trust that mine wouldn't shatter the moment I reached for it.

The map lay on the desk, quiet in the daylight, its mysteries temporarily hidden. My gaze flicked to it before wandering to the faint glow of the crystal heart on the shelf. Both reminders of the dangerous waters I was navigating. Rhayne was no different. A man bound by tides and shadows, powerful and unpredictable, yet somehow tethered to me.

A soft knock at the door startled me. I turned as it opened, and Corwin peeked inside, his grin as wide as ever.

"I have a bath to prepare for the queen," he said, waggling his eyebrows. "Captain's orders." Corwin chuckled as he entered, balancing a tray in his hands. "And he thought you might want something sweet while you wait."

Another man followed him in carrying a large half-barrel looking tub. It had ropes for handles and was bound with metal bands around the middle. So much for soaking in a spacious bath. At least I would be clean.

Corwin set the tray on the desk—a small array of fruit and what looked like delicate pastries dusted with sugar. I eyed them suspiciously.

"Don't worry," Corwin said, his eyes lighting up with a playful smile. "I didn't poison them. Captain wouldn't be too pleased if his queen started foaming at the mouth."

I grabbed a slice of fruit, mostly to avoid responding to the word queen. Corwin lingered, his grin fading as he tilted his head. "I was hoping you'd like them."

I nodded shoving another bite in my mouth. It was much better than the fish stew.

The other man left, returning moments later with another crewmate. Together, the two of them began making trips from the galley with heated water, filling the tub.

Corwin ensured they were precise in their duties before leaving. I was about to slip off my shirt when the door opened again, this time revealing Rhayne. He stepped inside, his presence filling the room with an intensity that made my breath hitch.

"Really?" I said, straightening with an exaggerated huff. "You couldn't knock first?"

His eyes flicked over me, his expression unreadable. "I did knock. You didn't answer."

"Because I'm about to get into a bath." I waved at the tub for emphasis.

He ignored my indignation and glanced at the tub. "Water's still warm. Good."

I folded my arms, glaring at him. "And you're still here. Not good."

Rhayne met my glare with a calm intensity, stepping further into the room. "I wanted to make sure everything was ready."

"It's a tub of water. What more do you need to check?"

"Your safety," he said simply, his tone leaving no room for argument. "This ship may be mine, but that doesn't mean it's without risks."

The words disarmed me more than I cared to admit, and I hated the way they lingered in the space between us. I quickly deflected with sarcasm. "Ah, yes. I'd nearly forgotten about the hordes of pirates and rogue barrels waiting to ambush me mid-bath."

His gaze stayed steady. "You might joke, but I've seen enough to know it's better to be thorough."

I rolled my eyes, the tension in my shoulders refusing to ease under his scrutiny. "Well, congratulations, Your Majesty. The bath is up to standard. Now if you'd kindly leave."

He stepped closer, his movements slow and deliberate, until the space between us was nearly nonexistent. The warmth of his presence brushed against my skin, and I suddenly felt far more exposed than I was.

"Call if you need anything," he said, his voice low. "I won't be far."

I opened my mouth to reply, but no witty retort came. Instead, I watched as he turned and left the cabin, the door clicking shut behind him.

The room felt too quiet, the stillness pressing in on me. I exhaled sharply, running a hand through my hair. Damn him. Damn his insistence, his protectiveness, and the way he seemed to see right through me.

With a muttered curse, I pulled off my boots and turned toward the tub. If I had to endure this madness, I might as well enjoy a moment of warmth and solitude. The tub wasn't spacious, but I managed to fit. With my knees pulled up to my chest, I leaned back as much as the space allowed and tried to relax.

The hot water lapped gently at my skin, as steam rose faintly kissing my skin. Warmth sank into muscles I hadn't realized were sore. I trailed my fingers along the water's surface, watching the ripples spread, my mind as restless as the waves beneath The Tidecaller.

I should have been relaxing, but my thoughts kept circling back to him—Rhayne, with his maddening smirks and the way he said things that made my chest tighten. Like when he told me his heart was mine. What did that even mean? And why had it left me so... unbalanced?

The door creaked open, and I instinctively sank deeper into the water. "I thought I said I wanted privacy," I snapped, expecting to see Rhayne.

Instead of his deep, steady voice, I heard Nyx's startled exclamation. "Oh, hells—!"

My eyes snapped to the doorway where Nyx stood frozen, his usual cocky demeanor replaced by wide-eyed panic. "What are you—?"

"Briar," he stammered, backing up with his hands raised, "I didn't—"

The door slammed open, and there he was. Rhayne. His presence filled the room like a thundercloud, crackling with barely-contained fury.

"Nyx," Rhayne said, his voice low and dangerous, "you've just made the worst mistake of your life."

"Captain, I didn't know—" Nyx didn't have time to finish.

"Out," Rhayne snapped, his magic stirring the air, the faint hum of it like the charge before a storm.

Nyx didn't argue. He practically tripped over himself in his rush to leave, muttering apologies as he disappeared. The door slammed shut behind him, and then it was just the two of us.

I sat frozen in the tub, my heart pounding as Rhayne turned to me. His blue eyes burned with something primal, something that made my breath hitch.

"Are you alright?" he asked, his voice softer now but no less intense.

"I'm fine," I said quickly, though my cheeks burned. "It's not like he saw anything."

His jaw clenched, and he crossed the room in three long strides, his presence towering over me. "No one should have even had the chance," he said, his voice low and rough. "You deserve more respect than that."

I blinked up at him, unsure whether to feel indignant or... something else entirely. "I can take care of myself, you know. You don't have to play the overprotective husband." He crouched down beside the tub, his gaze steady but softer now, his intensity tempered by something almost tender. "I'm not playing anything, Briar. You're not just my wife—you're my queen. And no one disrespects you on my ship."

His words sent a shiver down my spine. "A little dramatic, don't you think?"

His gaze didn't waver. "Not when it comes to you."

The air between us seemed to thicken, charged with unspoken things that neither of us dared put into words. I was suddenly very aware of the water lapping at my skin, of the way his eyes flickered, not with desire alone, but with something deeper—something that scared me.

"You should leave," I said, my voice faltering despite myself.

He stood slowly, his gaze never leaving mine. "If I leave, you'll just convince yourself this didn't happen. That you don't feel what I feel."

I opened my mouth to retort, but the words caught in my throat as he turned his back to me. He didn't go far, though. Instead, he picked up a towel from the chair and held it out without turning around.

"Get out, Briar. We need to talk."

I hesitated for a long moment, the tension between us crackling like static. There was no denying the pull, the way my heart raced and my magic hummed faintly at the edges of my senses. Finally, I reached for the towel, the cool air brushing my skin as I stood.

Once I was wrapped securely, he turned back, his expression unreadable. And then he stepped closer. Too close.

"Rhayne—"

Whatever I was about to say vanished as his lips crashed against mine. The world tilted, the heat of him overwhelming as his hands came to rest on my waist. He didn't pull me closer, didn't force anything. But gods, the way he kissed me...

I didn't want to think about what it meant. I didn't want to think at all.

When he finally pulled back, his breathing was ragged, his forehead resting against mine. "This isn't over," he said, his voice hoarse.

And then he stepped away, leaving me standing there, breathless and confused, as the door clicked shut behind him.

*"No one gets to see her like that. No one.
Not while I still draw breath."*

RHAYNE

The moment I stepped onto the deck, the crew's voices fell to a tense murmur. Word had already spread— Nyx had walked in on Briar during her bath. The air was heavy with unspoken tension, the kind that ripples through even the saltiest pirates when they sense a storm brewing.

I planted my boots firmly at the center of the deck, letting the silence stretch, drawing their attention like a rip current. My gaze swept across the men who served me faithfully—loyal, skilled, and yet so deeply flawed in their carelessness.

"Nyx," I called, my voice a low rumble. The man stepped forward reluctantly, his usual swagger muted. His gaze flicked to the floor, avoiding mine.

"My King," he said, his tone subdued.

I crossed my arms, my presence towering even without raising my voice. "Tell me, Nyx, what exactly compelled you to enter my cabin without knocking?"

He shifted uneasily, his shoulders hunching. "I didn't think... I mean, I wasn't trying to—"

"You didn't think," I cut in, my voice sharp as a blade. "A habit I find increasingly dangerous aboard my ship."

A ripple of unease passed through the crew. I let the silence settle before speaking again, my tone softer but no less commanding. "You've all served me long enough to know the rules. Privacy aboard The Tidecaller is scarce, but it is sacred. My cabin is not yours to enter at will, and my *queen*," I emphasized the title, "is not to be disrespected."

Nyx's head dipped lower, his shame palpable. "It won't happen again, My King."

"No, it won't," I said, the weight of my magic briefly brushing the air, a subtle reminder of the power I wielded. "Because if it does, the consequences will be swift and final."

I turned my gaze to the rest of the crew, letting my words sink in. "This is not just a ship; it is our home, our sanctuary. If anyone forgets that again, they'll find themselves tossed to the mercy of the sea. Is that understood?"

A resounding "Aye, My King!" echoed across the deck.

"Good." My tone softened, but my expression remained stern. "Now, get back to your duties."

The crew dispersed quickly, their movements brisk and purposeful. Only Enric lingered, his gaze steady as he approached.

"You handled that well," he said, his voice low enough for only me to hear.

I nodded, my jaw tight. "I won't tolerate her feeling unsafe here. Not for a moment."

Enric's brow arched slightly. "She really is more than just your queen, isn't she."

I met his gaze but said nothing. He didn't press further, giving me a small nod before retreating to oversee the crew.

When I returned to the cabin, the tension from the deck still coiled tight in my chest. Briar sat on the edge of the bed, her wet hair clinging to her shoulders. The lantern's light flickered softly, casting golden shadows across her face.

She had found a change of clothes in my chest. They were entirely too large for her, but I couldn't shake the pride I felt seeing her in my clothing.

She didn't look up as I closed the door behind me. "You didn't have to make such a fuss," she said, her voice calm but edged with something I couldn't quite place.

I stepped closer, stopping just a few feet from her. "You think I should've ignored it? Let them believe there are no consequences for disrespecting you?"

Her eyes met mine then, sharp and challenging. "I don't need you to fight my battles."

"I know you don't," I said, my voice low. "But that doesn't mean I won't."

She stood, closing the distance between us. Her defiance burned as brightly as ever, but there was something else there too—something softer, more uncertain. "Why?" she asked, her voice quieter now. "Why does it matter so much to you?"

I hesitated, the weight of my answer pressing heavily against my chest. Because you're my heartmate. Because the thought of anyone causing you harm makes me want to raze the seas. But I couldn't tell her that—not yet.

"Because you're my wife. And whether you want to believe it or not, you're part of this crew now. You're part of this ship. And I protect what's mine."

Her lips parted, a retort ready, but she didn't speak. Instead, she stepped back, her gaze dropping to the floor. For a moment, we were both silent, the tension between us crackling like a storm waiting to break.

"You said we needed to talk," she said finally, her voice barely above a whisper.

I nodded, stepping closer until I was just within arm's reach. "I needed you to know that no one will touch you—not without answering to me. You're safe here, Briar."

Her eyes flicked back up to mine, searching, questioning. "And if I don't want to be here?"

My jaw tightened, the answer coming unbidden. "Then I'll find a way to change your mind."

Her breath hitched, and for a fleeting moment, I thought she might step closer. But instead, she turned away, her hand brushing against the edge of the bed.

I watched her, my chest tightening with an ache I didn't fully understand. She didn't trust me yet—not fully. But I could be patient. For her, I could weather any storm.

For now, I left her to her thoughts, stepping back toward the door. But as I turned the handle, I glanced over my shoulder. "The moon is rising. We'll need you up top soon."

At the helm, Enric stood with his usual steadiness, his gaze fixed on the horizon. He'd been uncharacteristically silent since we left the reefs, though the occasional glance my way told me his mind was far from idle. The man was loyal to a fault, but even loyalty had its limits when uncertainty clouded the path ahead.

I descended from the bridge and crossed the deck toward the bow, where Briar stood with the map spread out before her on a makeshift table. The moonlight caught the golden symbols etched into the parchment, their faint glow pulsing in rhythm with the waves. She traced a finger over the markings, her brow furrowed in concentration.

"Anything new?" I asked, stepping beside her.

She didn't flinch—she never did—but her shoulders stiffened slightly, a sure sign she'd been deep in thought. "It's shifting again. The markings keep changing, like they're trying to tell me something. But it doesn't make sense."

"It will," I said, my voice steady. "The map hasn't led us astray yet."

Her head tilted toward me, a skeptical arch to her brow. "That's easy for you to say. You're not the one trying to decipher cryptic glowing symbols in the middle of the sea."

"True." I dipped closer to whisper, loving how goosebumps raced along her skin. "I'm just the one ensuring we don't sink before we get there."

She shivered but quickly recovered. "Well, congratulations. The ship hasn't sunk *yet*."

"High praise," I drawled, folding my arms as I leaned closer to the map. "What's the latest revelation?"

Her fingers hovered over the map that shimmered faintly. "It's still pointing northeast. It feels... insistent."

"So it is taking us to Silverveil."

Briar twitched her mouth to the side as she contemplated the map. "I think its more than just Silverveil. I'm not sure what it is, but we are definitely headed for land."

"Another two days and we shall see, maybe less if the winds favor us."

Her gaze shifted back to the map, her fingers tracing the edge of the parchment as if it could answer the questions swirling in her mind. "And what exactly do you think we'll find there?"

"I don't know," I admitted. "But whatever it is, the map believes you're the one who needs to find it."

Her laugh was soft, almost bitter. "The map believes in me. That's comforting."

I straightened, studying her profile in the moonlight. "You don't have to believe in it, Briar. Just follow it. Trust it."

Her head snapped toward me, her eyes flashing with something fierce. "Trust it? Like I'm supposed to trust you?"

"You don't trust me?" I asked, feigning offense.

Her glare could have turned the sea to stone. "Trust is earned, Pirate King."

"Then consider this my ongoing effort," I replied, gesturing toward the map. "Lead the way, little thief. Silverveil awaits."

Her eyes narrowed, but she didn't argue. Instead, she folded the map carefully, tucking it under her arm as she turned toward the helm.

"Enric," I called as we approached. "Continue the heading. Northeast, straight for Silverveil."

He nodded sharply, his hands steady on the wheel as he made the necessary adjustments. "Two more days, if the winds hold."

"They will," I said, more to myself than anyone else. The Tidecaller had a way of answering my needs, and this was no exception.

Briar lingered near the railing, her gaze distant as the ship surged forward. The pull of the map was undeniable, but so was the storm brewing within her. Whatever awaited us in Silverveil, it wasn't just answers she was seeking. And whatever those answers were, I knew they would change everything—for both of us.

The moonlight painted The Tidecaller in silvery hues as I stepped out onto the deck. The familiar hum of its magic pulsed beneath my boots, but tonight, there was something lighter in the air—laughter.

My gaze traveled toward the center of the deck, where a cluster of my crew had gathered around an overturned barrel. Nyx, Ciaus, Tavian, and a few others were deep into a game, their raucous voices carrying above the gentle lapping of the waves. And there, sitting among them, was my wife.

Briar was perched on the edge of a crate, her arms crossed, a smug grin on her face as she traded barbs with Nyx. The moonlight caught her hair, turning it into a cascade of midnight shadows against her silhouette. She looked... comfortable. At ease in a way I hadn't seen since she'd set foot on this ship. It was a strange contrast to the sharp edges of defiance she usually wore.

As I approached, the group fell silent for a moment, their gazes flicking toward me as if bracing for rebuke. I waved a hand, stepping closer. "Carry on."

Nyx grinned, gesturing toward the empty spot beside Briar. "Care to join us, Captain? Even the odds a bit?"

Briar rolled her eyes, the smirk never leaving her lips. "You think he can help you? I've already figured out your tells, Nyx."

Her confidence sparked something in me—an urge to test her. I stepped closer, letting the anticipation linger before lowering myself onto a crate opposite her. "If Briar's playing, I'll have to. Wouldn't want her walking away with all your coin, would we?"

Her eyes met mine, amusement flickering in their depths. "Bold assumption, Pirate King. Let's see if you're as good with cards as you are with commands."

Tavian shuffled the cards, the rhythmic snap breaking the air. He dealt the hands with practiced precision, and the game began. It was a straightforward game—easy to learn, hard to master. It demanded quick thinking and a keen eye for deception. Perfect for someone like Briar. And, if I were honest, for me.

The crew's banter flowed freely, weaving through the rhythmic creak of The Tidecaller and the slap of cards on the makeshift table. Tavian leaned back, grinning as he teased Nyx for his terrible bluff. Nyx retorted with a dramatic flair that had the others roaring with laughter.

I barely glanced at my own hand, my attention fixed on Briar. She was sharper than I'd anticipated, her bluffs subtle, her strategy nimble and unpredictable. She played to win, but there was something more—a fire in her eyes that burned brighter with each hand. She was enjoying herself, even if she'd never admit it outright.

"Nyx, you're worse at cards than you are at sneaking through a port," Briar quipped, throwing down her hand with a flourish. Her grin widened as she swept the pile of coins toward her.

Nyx groaned, throwing his cards onto the barrel. "She's a menace, Captain. Call her off before we're all ruined."

I leaned forward, resting my elbows on my knees, my gaze steady on her. "You're quick, I'll give you that. But how long do you think you can keep it up?"

She tilted her head, meeting my stare without hesitation. "Long enough to take everything you've got, if you're not careful."

The crew roared with laughter, Nyx clapping Tavian on the back as they commiserated over their losses. Briar's grin softened slightly, but the glint in her eyes remained. She was loosening up, her sharp edges relaxing just enough to let me catch a glimpse of the woman behind the walls.

The cards shuffled again, but my mind was already elsewhere. She was a puzzle, one I hadn't yet solved.

Tavian dealt another round, the cards slapping against the barrel. The crew leaned in, watching with barely concealed amusement as the game unfolded. Nyx, his usual lopsided grin firmly in place, tapped his fingers on the edge. "Careful, Captain. She's got the devil's luck, this one."

"Luck?" Briar arched a brow, her confidence lighting up the space around her. "I've won three hands in a row because you can't keep your tells to yourself, Nyx. You practically screamed when you drew that king."

The crew burst into laughter, Nyx groaning as he threw his hands up. "It's a strategy! Keeps you guessing."

"More like keeps you losing," Tavian muttered, earning another round of chuckles.

I smirked, laying down a pair of aces. "Guess I'll just have to see if her so-called luck holds up."

Briar's eyes met mine, amusement flickering in their depths. "Luck's got nothing to do with it, Pirate King. I'm just better at this than you are."

"Is that so?" I leaned back in my seat, studying her. "We'll see."

Nyx leaned toward Tavian, loud enough for all to hear. "You think he'll let her win? You know, for morale?"

Tavian snorted, shaking his head. "Not a chance. He's got that look—the one that says he's already plotting her downfall."

I let a slow grin spread across my face. "You're not wrong, Tavian. Shame you don't use that keen observation to fix your own game."

Tavian glanced at his cards, quickly flipping them over as if I might have seen them. "It's called the element of surprise, Captain."

The laughter rippled across the deck, easing the tension of the day. Briar didn't hold back, calling out Tavian's nervous shuffle, Nyx's fidgeting with his rings, and even Ciaus—silent and brooding—for the way his jaw clenched whenever he bluffed.

"Ciaus," she said, her voice dripping with mock concern, "you might want to work on that jaw thing. It's giving away all your secrets."

The crew roared, and even Ciaus shook his head, a rare grin tugging at his lips. "I don't know what you're talking about," he said flatly.

"Sure you don't," Briar quipped, tossing her cards onto the barrel. "Four of a kind. Thank you very much."

Nyx groaned, dropping his head into his hands. "She's cleaning us out."

Tavian threw his cards down with a laugh. "I think she's stealing our dignity, too."

When the game came to its final hand, I laid my cards down with deliberate precision, revealing the winning set. The crew erupted into cheers, pounding the railing in approval.

Briar narrowed her eyes at me, her smile changing into something sharper. "I see. So the Pirate King cheats."

I chuckled, leaning forward just enough to make her hold my gaze. "Only when necessary."

The crew's laughter echoed around us, filling the deck as they exchanged jabs and jests. Briar leaned back, arms crossed but a faint smile tugging at her lips.

As the night wore on, the game shifted to stories, each member of the crew taking their turn. Nyx's tales were absurd as ever, Tavian's were full of exaggerated heroics, and Ciaus's were laced with dry wit. The men hung on every word, their camaraderie thick in the air.

When it came to Briar's turn, she hesitated, her confidence faltering for the first time that night. But then, with a glint of determination in her eyes, she launched into a story from her thieving days—a daring escape involving a merchant, a rooftop chase, and a cartload of stolen goods.

"And what was so valuable it was worth all that trouble?" Ciaus asked, leaning forward.

She deadpanned. "Lemons."

The crew burst into laughter, and even I felt a chuckle escape me. It was a rare sound, one that felt foreign in my throat, but it lingered as I watched her. She'd held her own tonight, not just in the game but with the crew. It wasn't just her sharp wit or quick thinking. It was the way she carried herself, as if she belonged here—even if she didn't think so herself.

When the game wound down and the men began to disperse, I stood and made my way to her side. She glanced up at me, her expression unreadable.

"Not bad," I said, tilting my head toward the dwindling group.

She shrugged, her smirk returning. "They're tolerable. When they're not pointing swords at me."

A smile tugged at my lips. "That's progress."

Her gaze lingered on me for a moment, something unspoken passing between us. The ship swayed gently beneath my feet as I stood there, watching her walk away. In that moment, nothing else had ever mattered—nor ever would—but her.

The sky began to lighten, ever so slightly. Dawn was awakening the day, and the sun would soon be pushing the moon from its place overhead. The majority of the crew were waking and starting their day, and those of us on the night shift with Briar and the map would be heading to bed.

I glanced at my cabin door. For two days it had been almost impossible to sleep with Briar that close. I didn't see today being any different. Pushing the door open, I was hit by the fresh scent of citrus soap from her bath earlier. She was already curled up under the blanket on her side of the bed, against the wall. Even if she hadn't taken that side, I would have insisted on it. There was no way I would let her sleep between the door and myself. If someone should come in, they would have to get through me to get to her.

The soft glow of the lantern cast shadows across her figure, and for a fleeting moment, I let myself look at her without pretense. She'd shed the tension she carried during the games with the crew, her posture now softer, more relaxed.

"You missed the part where Tavian almost fell overboard during his dance," I said, my tone light as I crossed the room.

She turned her head slightly, her voice muffled by the pillow. "I didn't miss it. I just decided sleep was more important than watching your crew act like fools."

"And yet, you seemed to enjoy yourself."

She rolled over fully, resting her head on her hand as she leveled me with a pointed stare. "It's called distraction. I'm not about to let myself enjoy being on this ship."

I raised a brow, leaning casually against the wall near the bed. "Is that so? From where I stood, it looked like you were having fun."

Her glare deepened, but there was no real bite to it. "Don't flatter yourself, Pirate King. If anything, I was letting them distract me from you."

"From me?" I echoed, stepping closer, unable to resist the way her gaze flicked toward me before darting away.

She huffed, shifting under the blanket. "Don't look so smug. If you're expecting me to invite you to bed, you'll be waiting a long time."

I stopped at the edge of the bed, the smirk I couldn't suppress curving my lips. "Is that an invitation?"

Her eyes narrowed, glinting in the low light. "You're insufferable."

"So you keep saying." I sat on the edge of the bed and tugged my boots off.

She groaned, rolling back onto her side to face away from me. "I hate you."

I chuckled softly, sinking into the bed beside her, rolling to watch her. "Sleep well, wife."

She didn't respond, but as her breathing evened out, I stayed where I was, watching the faint rise and fall of her shoulders, unable to deny the pull she had on me—even now.

"He offered his hand, not as a captor, but as something far more dangerous — an equal."

BRIAR

e had left King's Cove four nights ago, and I could honestly say I had never been away from land for so long before, and I wasn't sure I ever wanted to return. The vastness of the sea stretched endlessly around us, calling to me in a way I couldn't have anticipated. It was like a soothing song for my soul, a balm I didn't know I needed until now.

The gentle sway of the ship had become a comfort, almost like an embrace. Even when the waters turned rough and waves crashed into the hull with unrelenting force, I found myself in awe of their power rather than fear. There was a wild beauty in their strength, something untamed and freeing. And as much as I despised Rhayne, it was impossible not to be drawn to his presence—the man who could command both the ship and the sea with equal ease.

He was the Pirate King, after all, and it wasn't just his magic that made him such. His confidence was magnetic, his every movement a deliberate assertion of his authority. It didn't help that he was ridiculously pleasing to look at. Gods help me, but his powerful stance was enough to stir something I didn't want to name. The way he looked at me, though—that was another battle entirely.

His gaze had a weight to it, as if he could see straight through me, peeling back my defenses and leaving me bare. And when his eyes lingered, my body betrayed me in ways I couldn't control.

I leaned on the railing, letting the wind cool my cheeks as I watched him out of the corner of my eye. The early morning sun spilled golden hues across the deck, setting the polished wood aglow. Rhayne stood at the helm, his focus fixed on the horizon. The light painted him in warm tones, softening the hard edges of his features, though nothing could dim the sheer presence he carried.

His arms flexed as he gripped the wheel, his movements as assured as the sea itself. He adjusted our course with practiced ease, and for a moment, I hated how effortless he made it look. Hated how the confidence that rolled off him in waves made it even harder to look away.

"Land ahead!"

The cry rang out from the top of the mast, breaking through my thoughts. My head snapped up, heart thudding as I spun toward the bow. Squinting against the morning light, I searched the horizon but saw nothing. "I can't see it."

Rhayne gestured past the hull. "Silverveil awaits. It looks like a shadow from here, but by nightfall we should be there."

Nightfall. So soon. And yet… so far. I wasn't sure what we would find in Silverveil. Or what the map wanted. But, I would be lying if I said I wasn't a little bit curious.

If only Asher could see me now. He'd be so sad he missed another adventure. I could already hear him teasing me about being married… to a freaking pirate. The Pirate *King,* to be precise.

But then, a darker thought crept in. Was Asher even looking for me? Did he know I was missing? Did he care? The questions swirled like the waves below, and I forced myself to focus on the horizon, squinting for any sign of land.

The crew bustled around the deck, the morning's golden light softening their hardened edges. There was a strange camaraderie among them, a rhythm to their movements that spoke of years spent navigating the seas together. It was as if they were all threads woven into the same tapestry—rough, frayed, and yet unbreakable.

I turned my attention back to Rhayne. He stood steady at the helm, his presence commanding without effort. His gaze flicked to me, catching me watching him. Heat bloomed in my cheeks, and I quickly looked away, pretending to be fascinated by the distant horizon.

"Briar," his voice called out, steady and deep.

I glanced up, meeting his eyes.

"Come here," he said, his tone leaving no room for argument.

I hesitated for a moment before pushing off the railing and walking toward him. The sway of the ship made my steps uneven, but I held my head high, refusing to let him see any hesitation.

As I reached the helm, he gestured to the wheel. "Take it."

I blinked, startled. "What?"

"The wheel." His lips lifted into a faint smirk. "Go on."

"You want me to steer The Tidecaller?" I asked, my voice tinged with disbelief.

"You're my queen, aren't you?" he said, the title rolling off his tongue with infuriating ease. "It's only fitting you learn to command her."

I narrowed my eyes at him, searching for any hint of mockery, but his expression was unreadable. Reluctantly, I stepped closer, placing my hands on the wheel. The wood was smooth and warm beneath my palms, humming faintly with the ship's magic.

"Steady hands," he instructed, moving behind me. His arms brushed against mine as he adjusted my grip. His presence was overwhelming, the heat of his body a constant reminder of how close he was.

"Like this?" I asked, my voice quieter than I intended.

"Good," he murmured, his breath grazing my ear. "Now feel the rhythm of the ship. She'll guide you if you let her."

The wheel felt alive beneath my hands. It wasn't just the smooth warmth of the wood or the faint hum I'd noticed before—it was something deeper, something that seemed to pulse in time with the beating of my heart. The Tidecaller's magic wasn't just humming anymore; it was reacting, responding to my touch like a living thing.

I stiffened, gripping the wheel tighter. The sensation wasn't unpleasant, but it was unsettling. The ship seemed to lean into my hands, the gentle sway of the waves beneath her shifting in harmony with the pressure of my fingers.

"Briar," Rhayne's voice broke through the haze, low and careful.

I turned my head slightly, catching the sharp focus in his gaze. He was watching me—no, not just me. He was watching the ship, his attention flicking between my hands on the wheel and the faint shimmer of energy that now danced along the edges of the wood.

When Rhayne stepped closer, the air seemed to change. His magic stirred the faint hum of The Tidecaller into a resonant thrum, the vibration coursing through the wheel and into my hands. It wasn't just the ship reacting—it was responding. To me.

My breath caught as I tightened my grip on the wood, unsure if I wanted to let go or hold on tighter. It was unnerving, but beneath that unease was a strange sense of belonging, as though the ship and I shared some unspoken understanding.

"You feel that, don't you?" Rhayne's voice was quieter now, carrying a weight that matched the thrum beneath my fingers.

I nodded, unable to trust my voice. "It's... alive," I finally managed.

His lips curved faintly, his gaze fixed on the wheel as he placed his hand just above mine. A pulse of energy surged between us, sharp and undeniable. The ship hummed louder, and for a fleeting moment, I swore the ocean itself whispered my name.

"She's more than wood and sails," Rhayne murmured. "The Tidecaller is part of the sea, and the sea knows magic when it feels it. She knows you."

The intensity in his tone made me look up, meeting his gaze. His eyes held something deeper than curiosity—something reverent, almost like he was seeing a piece of a puzzle fall into place. "And you," I asked softly, "do you trust me?"

He didn't answer immediately. Instead, he released my wrist with a deliberate slowness, his fingers brushing against my skin as if reluctant to let go. "I trust the sea," he said, his words carefully chosen, before stepping back.

The loss of his touch left a strange emptiness, colder than the ocean breeze. And yet, the faint hum beneath my feet was a reminder that I wasn't entirely alone.

"Wind's shifting! Adjust the sails!" Enric's sharp voice broke the moment like a stone thrown into still water.

Rhayne moved seamlessly to the wheel. I stepped aside, my heart still racing as I watched him command the crew.

Silverveil was ahead, but for now, the sea was ours.

I woke to the sunset and the cheering of the crew. Apparently, we were docking. I ran a hand over the cold side of the bed. Rhayne didn't come in today. I hated that I was disappointed.

The chill of the sheets under my fingers should have been a comfort, a reminder that I had the space to myself. Instead, it gnawed at me—a stupid, unnecessary disappointment that I refused to acknowledge. I should be happy Rhayne had stayed away, that I didn't have to deal with his smug grins or maddening confidence.

The cheering outside grew louder, a muffled roar that rumbled through the cabin walls. I swung my legs over the edge of the bed, stretching briefly before pulling on my boots. The crew's excitement was palpable even through the floorboards, and it tugged at something in me. Curiosity, perhaps. Or nerves.

I splashed water on my face from the small basin near the corner, the coolness jolting me fully awake. The map and the crystal still lay where I'd left them, their presence a constant weight in the back of my mind. Whatever awaited us in Silverveil wasn't going to be simple. It couldn't be.

Pushing the thought aside, I headed for the door. The ship swayed gently underfoot. The scent of salt and wood filled the air as I climbed the steps to the deck.

The scene that greeted me stole my breath.

The Silverveil Kingdom rose before us like a dream. The docks stretched out toward The Tidecaller, their dark wood kissed by the soft glow of lanterns that hung from intricate iron posts. Beyond the harbor, the land opened up to a lush forest, its trees draped in pale, silvery leaves that shimmered faintly even in the fading light. Mist curled along the ground, weaving between the trunks like a living thing.

The sky above was painted in hues of deep orange and gold, the last remnants of the sun's descent giving way to twilight. The sight was otherworldly, ethereal in a way that made my chest tighten.

"You're awake."

Rhayne's voice pulled me from my reverie. I turned to find him standing at the helm, his hands resting casually on the wheel. The fading sunlight caught in his white hair, making it glow like starlight. His gaze was fixed on the docks, but the slight curve of his lips told me he'd been watching me.

"Of course I'm awake," I said, brushing past him toward the railing. "Kind of hard to sleep through all the noise."

He chuckled. "The crew is eager. Mistwood is a rare sight for most, even those who've sailed these waters for years."

I leaned against the railing, my fingers gripping the worn wood as I took in the scene again. "It's beautiful," I admitted softly.

Rhayne joined me, his presence a steady weight at my side. "Beautiful," he echoed, though when I glanced at him, his eyes weren't on the forest or the shimmering trees. They were on me.

I looked away quickly, clearing my throat. "So, what's the plan? Dock the ship, explore the woods, and hope the map tells us something?"

"That's the gist of it," he said, his tone laced with amusement. "Though I imagine Mistwood will provide more answers than you think."

"What makes you so sure?" I asked, my brows lifting.

He tapped the wheel lightly, his expression unreadable. "Because Mistwood rarely welcomes anyone who doesn't belong."

The words settled uncomfortably in my chest. Before I could press him for more, the crew's shouts intensified as The Tidecaller neared the dock. Lines were thrown, ropes secured, and the ship stilled as it came to rest against the mooring.

"Come," Rhayne said, his voice quiet but commanding. "It's time to see what Silverveil has in store for us."

I hesitated, my feet rooted to the deck. Something about the place—its beauty, its stillness—felt too perfect, like a veneer hiding something much darker.

But when Rhayne extended his hand toward me, his blue eyes steady and unyielding, I pushed the unease aside and took it.

Rhayne's hand was warm and steady around mine. It was maddening how much comfort I found in it, though I would never admit that to him—or to myself, if I could help it.

The gangplank creaked as we stepped onto it, the wood worn smooth from countless feet before ours. The crew's excited murmurs filled the air as they disembarked, their gazes darting to the trees and the mist. Even Nyx and the other fae looked uneasy, their usual confidence subdued in the face of Mistwood's eerie beauty.

"Keep sharp," Rhayne said, his voice carrying over the crew. "Mistwood isn't a place to let your guard down. Stay near the ship unless instructed otherwise."

The crew nodded, their chatter quieting as his words settled over them. Rhayne's authority was absolute, his presence commanding in a way that left no room for argument. Even I felt it, though I tried to pretend otherwise.

The moment my boots touched the dock, a strange sensation rippled through me. It was subtle, like the hum of The Tidecaller, but different—lighter, more inviting. I glanced down at the boards beneath my feet, half-expecting them to glow. They didn't, but the feeling lingered, a quiet pulse that made my heart beat faster.

Rhayne's hand slipped from mine as we stepped onto solid ground. I tried not to notice the absence of his touch, focusing instead on the forest ahead. The silvery leaves whispered in the faint breeze, their soft rustling the only sound in the stillness.

"What's the map saying?" Rhayne asked, his voice low as he came to stand beside me.

I pulled the parchment from my satchel, unfolding it carefully. The symbols shimmered faintly in the dim light, shifting and twisting. I traced them with my eyes, their movements almost hypnotic.

"It's pointing further into the forest," I said, my voice quieter than I intended. The weight of the place pressed down on me, as if Mistwood itself was listening.

Rhayne glanced at the map over my shoulder, his breath warm against my cheek. "Then that's where we'll go."

"Just like that?" I asked, turning to face him. "You're willing to wander into an enchanted forest because of a map that no one else can read?"

His lips curved into a faint smirk. "I trust the map."

"Do you trust me?" It was the second time I'd asked that.

Rhayne's gaze locked onto mine, the smile fading. For a moment, the weight of his answer hung between us, heavier than the air in the forest.

"Yes," he said simply. "I trust you."

The words knocked the breath out of me, leaving me scrambling for something to say. Before I could find it, Rhayne turned to the crew, his voice cutting through the stillness.

"Nyx, Tavian, Ciaus, prepare to go with us. Enric, stay with the ship and ensure the crew keeps watch. Briar and I will lead."

I blinked, his words sinking in. "Lead?"

"You're the only one who can see where we're going," he said, his tone leaving no room for argument. "Unless you'd prefer to stay behind and let me blindly walk in there?"

I glared at him, stuffing the map back into my satchel. "Fine. Let's get this over with."

The path into Mistwood loomed ahead, its shadows deep and inviting all at once. My heart thudded in my chest as we stepped forward, the weight of the forest closing in around us.

The outskirts of Mistwood were alive with muted activity as we passed through the edge of the village. People lingered in doorways or bustled around dimly lit stalls, their faces half-hidden in the hazy glow of lanterns. Their eyes followed us, curiosity mingling with wariness. Every glance sent a ripple of unease down my spine, though I forced my head high and my steps steady. I wouldn't let them see my discomfort.

The satchel on my hip felt heavier with every step, as if the heart inside carried a weight of its own, its magic thrumming faintly against my side. Rhayne led the way, his posture rigid, his hand never straying far from the hilt of his sword. The rest of the crew followed in a loose formation, their usual banter replaced by an oppressive silence. Even Nyx, who always seemed to have a smug remark ready, kept his mouth shut.

The town itself wasn't what I'd expected. For a place called Mistwood, I thought it would be more grandeur? Instead, the buildings were simple, made of pale stone and dark wood. The mist clung to every surface, making the town seem ethereal, almost dreamlike. Or nightmarish, depending on how you looked at it.

A child darted across our path, his laughter echoing through the quiet street. I flinched, my hand instinctively brushing the edge of the satchel. Rhayne glanced over his shoulder, his eyes catching mine.

"You alright?" he asked, his voice low enough that only I could hear.

I forced a nod. "Fine. Just... odd."

He frowned, his gaze lingering on me for a moment longer before he turned his attention back to the road ahead. "We'll find out what it's leading us to soon enough."

I wasn't sure if that was meant to be reassuring, but it didn't stop my heart from hammering in my chest.

A woman selling flowers on the corner called out to us, hoping to make a last minute sale, her voice sweet and melodic. "Travelers! Would you like a blessing for your journey?"

"No," Rhayne said firmly, not even glancing her way.

I hesitated, looking at the bundle of pale blooms in her hand. They weren't like any flowers I'd seen before—delicate, almost translucent, as though they'd been spun from mist itself. There was something hauntingly beautiful about them.

"Briar." Rhayne's voice broke through my thoughts, sharp but not unkind. "Stay close and keep moving."

I clenched my jaw and fell into step behind him, ignoring the woman's disappointed murmur.

The road narrowed as we left the last of the houses behind, the mist growing thicker and heavier with each step. The towering trees loomed ahead, their silvered bark gleaming faintly in the dim light. The air was colder here, carrying with it the faint scent of pine and something else—something metallic and sharp that twisted my stomach.

Each step into Mistwood felt like crossing an invisible threshold. The crunch of leaves underfoot was muffled by the mist, and the faint rustle of the trees seemed to carry whispers just out of reach. The shard pulsed faintly against my hip, its magic a quiet rhythm that matched my racing heartbeat. I brushed my hand against the satchel, feeling its warmth bloom beneath my fingers.

"This place feels... wrong," I muttered, my voice low enough that only Rhayne could hear.

He slowed, falling into step beside me. "Mistwood has its secrets," he said, his tone even, though his silver eyes flicked warily toward the trees. "Keep your wits about you."

"Don't worry," I said, tightening my grip on the satchel's strap. "I have no intention of letting my guard down."

His lips curved into a faint smile, but it didn't reach his eyes. "Good."

Ahead, the forest opened into a faint path shrouded in mist. The hum of magic I'd felt since arriving in Mistwood grew stronger, wrapping around me like an invisible thread, tugging me toward something unseen. Whatever lay ahead, I couldn't shake the feeling that it was watching us as much as we were heading toward it.

19

"The forest whispered secrets I couldn't hear, but I didn't have to. My only focus was keeping her safe."

RHAYNE

he Arrowwood Forest was quieter than I liked. The silvery leaves overhead hissed faintly with the breeze, their blade-shaped edges glinting like drawn steel. I'd been through these woods before, and though the treaty between my kingdom and Silverveil was supposed to keep us safe, I knew better than to rely on politics out here. There were always those eager to test a king's defenses.

My magic hummed in my veins, coiled and ready. Being this far from the ocean put me on edge—summoning water inland took more out of me than I cared to admit. But if anything threatened Briar, I'd drown this place, sea or no sea.

She walked slightly behind me, the map clutched in her hand. A breeze ruffled her dark hair, and I caught a glimpse of the tension lining her jaw. The map's magic pulled at her, impossible to ignore, and she was too stubborn to show fear, even if a forest full of hidden dangers should have put anyone on guard.

Glancing over my shoulder, I made sure she stayed close. "Watch your step," I said, eyeing the ground where fallen leaves were sharp enough to slice through boots.

Her lips pressed into a tight line. "I'm not a child," she muttered, shifted a little nearer. "I've managed worse than a few leaves. Remind me to tell you about the time I was nearly swallowed by the ground." She snickered a tiny laugh.

I raised a brow, letting my gaze sweep the treen line. "I would have loved to see that. But, Arrowwood isn't just *a few leaves*, little thief. It's bandits, beasts, and gods know what else. The treaty doesn't stop rogue mercenaries from testing their luck."

She started to retort but paused, a flicker of uncertainty crossing her features as she looked down at the map again. I couldn't see what was on the parchment, but I felt the buzz of magic every time her fingers grazed over it.

"You see anything?" I asked, keeping my voice low.

She shook her head. "Not precisely. It's more like... a pull. We're headed in the right direction, but I can't tell if it's a good thing or a trap."

A trap. Always a possibility. A quick glance over my shoulder confirmed that Nyx, Tavian, Ciaus, and a few others were trailing a short distance behind us, each on high alert. Even they'd gone uncharacteristically silent in these woods.

Steeling myself, I pushed a low-hanging branch aside and offered Briar my hand to step through. She hesitated, then batted it away on her own—stubborn as ever. I bit back a grin. She might resist every protective gesture I made, but that wouldn't stop me from doing it. If something did come for us, I'd stand in front of her without a second thought, vows or not.

A twig snapped, echoing too loudly in the hush. My fingers twitched toward my sword hilt. She froze. For one tense moment, my magic leapt, ready to pull any water from the soil. But it was only a small animal darting behind the brush.

Briar's eyes shone with mischief as she surveyed the looming forest. "You're looking a little tense, Pirate King. I've fought krakens more intimidating than that innocent creature. Maybe you should stay behind me this time."

I let out a low chuckle, curling my fingers around the hilt of my sword. "You'd like that, wouldn't you?" A smirk tugged at my lips. "The day I hide behind you, wife, is the day the ocean runs dry."

She lifted her chin, feigning a casual shrug. "Suit yourself. Just don't blame me if you end up with a leaf blade in your backside."

My grin widened, and I moved closer, lowering my voice so only she could hear. "If I do, you'll be the first to patch me up, right?"

"Keep dreaming," she tossed back, stepping ahead on the trail. But her brief, sidelong smile told me more than words ever could.

She shrugged, feigning confidence, but I knew her better than that by now. She was as uneasy as I was. She was just better at hiding it.

We pressed on, the thick trunks narrowing our path. The Arrowwood canopy filtered the light into a silver haze that set everything on edge. If the map wanted us here, it had better give us whatever it was leading us to quickly, before the forest decided we weren't welcome after all.

A breeze rustled the leaves, creating a harsh, metallic whisper. Briar clutched the parchment tighter. For a heartbeat, neither of us moved. But the moment passed, and I set my jaw, determination rising. I might not have the sea's full strength beneath my feet, but I had enough power—and more than enough will—to protect what was mine.

"Lead the way," I said, softer this time.

She inhaled deeply, her eyes meeting mine. There was something there—an unspoken trust, despite her constant defiance. Without a word, she walked on, and I kept stride at her side, ready for whatever the forest dared throw at us.

The leaves overhead shimmered under the moonlight, all but hissing whenever the wind trickled through them. Our footsteps were muted on the soft, silver-strewn ground, yet each creak of a branch or distant rustle had Tavian gripping his sword hilt a little tighter. Even Nyx stayed mostly silent, his eyes combing the shadows.

Briar walked ahead of us, clutching the map. Its magic stirred something in the air—a slow pulse that made the hairs on my arms rise. I didn't like letting her lead, but I liked being blind even less.

"You sure it says to keep going straight?" Tavian asked in a hushed tone, breaking the silence.

Briar sighed, not slowing her pace. "It doesn't exactly say anything. I can just... see the lines, the symbols." She glanced back at me. "If you have a better idea, Pirate King, I'm all ears."

I met her gaze, catching the way the moonlight turned her eyes icy blue. "Not unless you'd like me to wrestle the ocean inland to carry us. But I don't imagine you want to be waist-deep in saltwater right now."

She let out a faint scoff. "Well, I've been craving a swim—"

"Keep walking, little thief," I cut in, though my tone held a trace of amusement.

The hours dragged as we pressed deeper into the forest. Shadows stretched long and deep, turning every distant rustle into a potential threat. No one spoke. Even Nyx, whose tongue could cut through silence like a blade, kept his sharp comments to himself.

The path narrowed, the dense Arrowwood canopy pressing in on all sides. My magic thrummed beneath my skin, restless without the pull of the sea. The further we went, the more the forest seemed to push back, its presence both ominous and watchful.

Briar slowed ahead of me, clutching the map with one hand while the other brushed aside a low-hanging branch. I didn't have to see the map to feel its magic shifting like a faint pulse in the air.

"The lines are fading," she murmured, her voice tight with frustration. She held the parchment closer to a sliver of moonlight breaking through the trees. "I can barely make out the path."

"Then we stop," I said, scanning the area for any sign of a clearing. "We're blind without the map's guidance."

Tavian groaned, rolling his shoulders. "Finally. I thought we were going to walk until dawn."

Nyx snorted. "Don't get too comfortable. We're not out of this yet."

The crew exchanged uneasy glances, their tension palpable. No one wanted to linger in the forest longer than necessary, but pushing forward without direction was a greater risk. My gaze swept the tree line, searching for anything resembling a safe haven. The Arrowwood Forest wasn't known for its generosity.

"There." I pointed to a break in the dense foliage ahead, where the silvered leaves gave way to a small patch of open ground. The faint glow of moonlight illuminated the space, making it feel less oppressive than the surrounding woods. "We'll set up there."

The clearing was less than ideal. Sharp, blade-like leaves littered the ground, and the towering trees on either side made it feel more like a cage than a sanctuary. Still, it was the best we'd find in these cursed woods. I gestured for the crew to move forward, my hand resting instinctively on the hilt of my sword.

"Keep your guard up," I warned, my voice low but firm.

Nyx muttered something under his breath but didn't argue. Tavian and Ciaus moved ahead, clearing the worst of the debris while the rest of the crew formed a loose perimeter around the clearing. Even in their exhaustion, they worked with practiced efficiency, their movements quick and deliberate.

Briar stood in the center of the clearing, her eyes scanning the map one last time before folding it carefully into her satchel. The tension in her shoulders betrayed her frustration, but she said nothing as she knelt to clear a patch of ground for herself.

I approached her, my boots crunching softly against the leaves. "We'll wait here until the sun sets," I said, keeping my voice steady. "The map will show us the way again when it's ready."

She looked up at me, her blue eyes glinting in the moonlight. "And if it doesn't?" Her tone was sharp, but there was an edge of uncertainty beneath it.

"It will," I said, more certain than I felt. "It hasn't led us astray yet."

She blew out a breath, her expression unreadable as she turned away to finish her task.

As the clearing settled into an uneasy quiet, I leaned against a tree at the edge of the camp, my gaze flicking between Briar and the surrounding woods. The forest whispered around us, its presence a constant reminder that we were intruding on something ancient and unwelcoming. My magic stirred, ready to lash out at the first sign of danger.

Briar finally sank onto her makeshift bed. She fought her exhaustion with a stubbornness I couldn't help but admire, her eyes darting to the edges of the clearing as if daring the forest to challenge her.

My grip tightened on the hilt of my sword as I leaned against the trunk of a twisted Arrowwood, keeping watch. But as the minutes stretched, her figure pulled my attention again and again. The vulnerability of her sleeping form tugged at something deep in my chest. She was usually all sharp words and stubborn pride, but now, she looked almost fragile.

The crew's whispers faded into the background as I let myself watch her. And for the first time in days, I allowed my guard to slip—just a little.

A soft rustle. My eyelids flicked open instantly. Briar stirred, though she didn't fully wake, and shifted closer, reaching out as though searching for warmth.

To my surprise, she rolled toward me, her arm draping across my leg. Then her head settled gently onto my lap. Her breathing hitched before smoothing out again, and she curled in like she'd done it a hundred times before.

Everything in me stilled. The edges of my mouth tugged upward despite my best attempts to maintain my composure. Carefully, I lifted one arm to rest across my bent knee, the other hovering near her, close enough to brush her hair aside if I dared.

My magic, ever coiled, hummed in my veins, but it felt... quieter, somehow. Like it had found a new current, something less frantic than the surging tide. Without the ocean, I'd been on edge since sunset, yet with Briar's head on my thigh, all the tension in my muscles eased.

A soft chuckle drew my attention. "Still watching her." Nyx leaned against a nearby tree, his arms crossed and his sharp gaze flicking between me and Briar.

"Careful, Nyx," I said, my tone carrying an edge. "You're treading on thin ice."

Nyx smirked, though there was no challenge in it, just the kind of knowing look that had grated on my nerves since the day I brought him aboard. "No offense, My King. Just making an observation. She's holding her own, your queen. The crew's noticed."

"She's my wife," I said evenly, meeting his gaze. "Her place is beside me. And if anyone questions that, they'll answer to me."

Nyx's smile faded into something more serious. "No one's questioning it. But they've noticed how you are with her. How she's different."

"And?" I said, arching a brow.

"And they're watching," he replied. "That's all I'm saying. She's earned some of their respect, even if they don't fully understand why yet."

Nyx stepped closer, his voice dropping even lower. "They know she's your queen, Captain. Your wife. That's why they'll follow her lead if it comes to it. But they're still looking to you to make sure she belongs here."

"She does," I said firmly. "And they'll see it soon enough."

Nyx inclined his head, the respect clear in the gesture. "Of course, My King. Just thought you should know where things stand."

With that, he turned and made his way back toward the fire, his sharp eyes scanning the edges of the clearing as he passed Tavian and Ciaus. They didn't speak, but I caught the subtle exchange of glances between them—acknowledgment, maybe, or silent agreement.

I leaned my head back again, letting Briar's steady breathing soften the edges of my wariness. Nothing could make me move from this spot. Not until she stirred on her own and decided we had to face the path ahead again. Until then, the forest could howl. I was content right here, steady as the roots beneath us, with my thief-wife curled against me like I was the safest harbor she could find.

The sun rose higher, staining the Arrowwood's silvery foliage with streaks of pale gold and Briar's head remained on my lap, her cheek pressed against my thigh as she slept. Her warmth seeped through me, chasing away the chill of the forest's lingering menace. I kept one hand resting lightly on her shoulder, the other hanging at my side. I told myself it was just to maintain vigilance. But I knew better.

She shifted in her sleep, her arm sliding closer across my legs. A jolt of awareness shot through me, an ache that had nothing to do with fatigue. Everything about her—her scent, her nearness, the gentle weight of her against me— invaded my senses. I swallowed, desperately willing the rush of desire back under control. There was no place for such distraction out here, not with the forest still brimming with unknown threats.

But the flicker of that feeling refused to be contained. It pulsed beneath my ribcage, reminding me of vows made, of lines crossed. She was my wife now—my heartmate in truth as well as law—and though we carried plenty of sharp words for one another by day, this quiet moment revealed the tenderness we never spoke aloud.

I shifted slightly to keep from waking her. My body hummed with a renewed awareness, magic mixing with something purely human. Even the hush of the forest seemed to magnify the sound of her breathing. Every brush of her hair against my hand, every twitch of her fingers in sleep, amplified the tension coiling low in my spine.

Pressing my head back against the smooth trunk, I kept my eyes open, half-listening to the rustle of leaves overhead. But soon, the steady cadence of her breathing lulled me, and the weariness of the past few days tugged heavily at my eyelids.

I tried to resist. One of us needed to stay vigilant. Yet her warmth, the reassuring weight of her head on my lap, and the relative quiet of the forest worked against me. My arms felt leaden. My pulse slowed, and the flicker of longing that had been burning in my chest softened into an almost comforting ache.

Finally, I let my eyes slip shut with my hand still resting on her shoulder. In sleep, my thoughts dissolved into fleeting images: a glimpse of Briar's dark hair fanned across a ship's railing, the echo of her laughter over crashing waves. Images that made my lips tilt in a faint, unguarded smile.

I'd meant only to drift lightly, half-aware of my surroundings. But sleep beckoned deeper, drawing me down. My grip on her tightened slightly, possessive even in slumber, as if I feared she'd disappear the moment I was truly gone to dreams. The forest might be full of dangers, but with her in my arms—and my magic ever-coiled beneath my skin—I allowed myself a moment's peace.

The last thing I felt was her breathing, gentle and warm against me, and a quiet surge of pure, unfiltered want. Then darkness claimed my senses.

I jerked awake at the sound of Nyx's low voice. My hand instinctively dropped to the hilt of my sword, but I forced myself to stillness, mindful of Briar's head resting on my lap.

"Captain," Nyx repeated, his tone careful to avoid waking her. "I believe we're being watched."

My gaze snapped to his, heart still pounding from the remnants of sleep. He didn't look alarmed, but his usual confidence was edged with unease. His sharp eyes darted between the spindly trunks and silver leaves of the Arrowwood, scanning for movement. Gently, I slid my hand from Briar's shoulder and motioned for him to continue.

"I've sent Tavian and Ciaus to scout ahead," he said, nodding toward the shadowy outline of the trees where the two had disappeared moments before. "It's a group—five, maybe six. They've made camp nearby."

"Armed?" I asked, my voice low.

Nyx nodded once. "Swords, bows. Nothing marked or official. They don't look like soldiers, but..." He hesitated, glancing at Briar. "There's something about them. Something off."

Before I could press him, Tavian and Ciaus reappeared, picking their way silently over the forest floor. Tavian rubbed the back of his neck—a nervous habit that always betrayed his unease. "Small group," Ciaus reported, his voice low. "They're not heavily armed, but there's a feel to them. Like they're waiting."

"For us?" I asked sharply, my eyes narrowing.

He shifted his weight, avoiding my gaze. "It's not just that, Captain." His voice dropped further. "One of them... I've seen him before. Back in Everfell."

A prickle of unease crawled up my spine. "You're certain?"

Ciaus hesitated, his gaze flicking to Briar, who continued to sleep peacefully on my lap. "In the tavern, the night we found her. He was in the back corner, watching her. I thought he might have been her buyer, but he never approached. Just sat there, watching." He paused, his jaw tightening. "I don't think they're here by accident."

The weight of his words settled heavily. Whoever they were, their presence wasn't a coincidence. My chest tightened with an unfamiliar tension. Someone was after Briar.

Carefully, I shifted her off my lap, setting her head on the folded cloak beside me. She muttered a soft protest but didn't wake. Rising, I rolled out the stiffness in my neck, then knelt beside her to rouse her gently.

"It's time to wake, little thief," I murmured. The urgency in my voice must have bled through, because her eyes fluttered open immediately.

She blinked up at me, her voice groggy. "The map— did it do something?"

"Not yet," I said, offering my hand to help her up. "But it's time we kept moving. The forest doesn't feel so hospitable."

She frowned but accepted my hand, standing with a stretch. Her eyes scanned the clearing, taking in the dismantled camp and the tension etched into the crew's faces.

"What aren't you telling me?" she asked, too perceptive for her own good.

"Nothing you need to worry about yet," I said smoothly, brushing past her question.

Her eyes narrowed slightly, but she didn't press further. She glanced down at the map, its surface still blank in the daylight. Frustration flickered across her features before she tucked it away, nodding reluctantly. "Fine. Let's go."

The crew moved quickly, their movements efficient as they packed the last of our gear. Nyx lingered near the edge of the clearing, his sharp gaze cutting into the shadows. Tavian and Ciaus fell in behind us, their unease palpable in the heavy silence.

The Arrowwoods closed in around us as we moved deeper into its depths, the silvered canopy filtering the light into an eerie, shifting haze. Each step felt heavier, the forest's magic pressing against my senses. I stayed close to Briar, my hand never straying far from the hilt of my sword.

"What's the plan?" she asked quietly, her voice low enough not to carry.

"To keep moving," I said, my tone deliberately neutral. "We follow the map as soon as it gives us direction again."

Her brow arched, skepticism flickering across her face. "And until then?"

"Stay alert," I replied, keeping my gaze ahead.

I didn't elaborate. The last thing I needed was for her to start imagining worst-case scenarios. She was already tense enough, her magic a faint hum in the air between us.

Her fingers brushed the edge of her satchel, her expression unreadable. For a moment, I thought she might push further, but then she nodded, her pace quickening to match mine.

20

"I wasn't sure what unnerved me more, the forest's magic or the way Rhayne made me feel safe when I didn't want to need him."

BRIAR

I trudged behind Rhayne, trying to ignore the dull ache in my legs—and the sharper jab of irritation burning in my chest. We'd agreed to wait until the map lit up again, yet here we were, marching deeper into this cursed forest like we had all the answers. The magic from the place we'd camped tugged at me, an invisible thread pulling at my ribcage, urging me to turn back.

But the oh-so-imperious Pirate King had declared a sudden change of plans, and I, apparently, had no say in the matter.

I wanted to call him out, to demand answers, but the glint in his eyes when I tried told me this wasn't a whim. Something had spooked him—though he'd never admit it. Fine. If he wanted to drag us all into this unsettling maze of silver-leafed shadows without explanation, I'd make damn sure he knew exactly how displeased I was.

My irritation wasn't helped by the fact that I was starving, my bladder uncomfortably full, and my body aching from days of trekking over roots and razor-edged leaves. Couldn't I get two seconds of privacy or comfort? And speaking of comfort…

My thoughts wandered longingly to a real bath. Not a splash from a tiny barrel, but a proper hot bath—soap, steam, and maybe a lock on the door. Surely I'd earned at least that before we set sail again.

The toe of my boot caught on an exposed root, and I stumbled, catching myself just in time to avoid landing face-first in the dirt. I hissed under my breath, glaring at Rhayne's broad back. "Can you at least tell me why we're moving?" I demanded, my voice sharper than I intended. "You said we'd stay put until the map gave us a direction."

He glanced back at me briefly, his jaw tight. "Change of plans."

"That's not an explanation," I muttered, loud enough for him to hear.

If he noticed my tone, he didn't react. His expression was carved from stone, offering nothing but a flicker in his eyes that told me he was hiding something. That only fueled my frustration.

My stomach growled loudly, and I threw up my hands. "We better stop soon, or I'm going to start gnawing on Arrowwood leaves."

Rhayne slowed just enough to cast a glance at me, his gaze flicking over me. "We will. Just a little farther."

I rolled my eyes, falling back into step as the forest's eerie silence pressed in around us. Every sharp leaf and twisting root felt like a personal insult, as if the woods themselves were mocking my exhaustion.

A bath. That was what I needed—a steaming, blissfully private bath in some cozy inn, far from the endless tangle of trees and shadowy dangers. Maybe they'd even have fresh bread and something warm to drink. I snorted at my own fantasy. If the Pirate King wanted to keep his secrets, then fine—I'd cling to the dream of hot water and peace to keep myself moving.

For now, I had no choice but to endure, ignoring the insistent tug that urged me to turn back and the gnawing unease of not knowing where we were headed. One way or another, I'd get answers out of Rhayne. And if he was half as considerate as he pretended to be, maybe—just maybe—he'd find me that bath I so desperately craved.

Moonlight fell in silvery shafts through the canopy, casting a ghostly glow over the forest. The silvery leaves overhead hissed faintly in the breeze, their edges catching the light like shards of glass. My heart thudded against my ribs as I pulled the map from my satchel, my fingers trembling slightly. It had been stubbornly blank for hours, but the moment the sun dipped below the horizon, faint lines and runes began to shimmer across its surface.

"We're here?" I breathed, confusion knotting in my chest. All I saw was more forest—razor-edged leaves, gnarled roots, and endless shadows. But the map's meaning was unmistakable: this was the spot.

Nyx let out a low whistle behind me, his tone tinged with disbelief. "You sure about that?"

I half-turned, holding up the glowing parchment. "See for yourself. It says we're right on top of it."

Rhayne's brow furrowed as he stepped closer, his gaze scanning the trees. "Stay alert. We're not alone out here."

I rolled my eyes, though unease prickled at the base of my spine. He was always suspicious, always bracing for danger. To be fair, though, everything about these woods screamed ambush. The oppressive quiet, the faint metallic rustle of the leaves, the way the shadows seemed to shift when you weren't looking.

A sudden rustle broke the stillness, followed by the sharp snap of a twig. My hand instinctively drifted to the hilt of my dagger as I scanned the trees, my pulse quickening.

Leaves rustled above, something moving just beyond the edge of my vision. I took a cautious step forward—but before I could blink, a figure stepped out of the shadows. His features came into view, and my breath hitched.

"Asher?" The name escaped my lips before I could think.

My feet moved on their own, closing the distance between us. I barely registered Rhayne's sharp shout behind me, his voice heavy with warning. All I could see was Asher, his familiar face etched with disbelief and relief.

He caught me in his arms, lifting me off the ground as though I weighed nothing. "I can't believe I finally found you," he said, his voice rough with emotion.

A laugh bubbled out of me, half a sob. "How—? Why—?"

But as he sat me down, I felt his posture shift. His grip on my wrist tightened, his gaze sliding past me. I turned, following his line of sight, and my stomach dropped. Rhayne was stalking toward us, his expression carved from stone, his crew bristling at his back. The air thickened with unspoken tension, and Asher's hand on me felt suddenly suffocating.

"Briar," Rhayne's voice was sharp, cutting through the clearing like a blade. "Get back."

I opened my mouth to argue, to demand an explanation, but before I could speak, a shrill cry pierced the air.

An arrow hissed past my ear, close enough that the wind of it stirred my hair. I spun in time to see Ciaus stagger, his hand clutching at an arrow embedded in his side. Blood bloomed across his tunic, stark and crimson against the forest's silver haze.

"Ciaus!" I shouted, adrenaline surging through me. The clearing erupted into chaos.

Figures emerged from the shadows, their movements quick and precise. Bandits or mercenaries, it didn't matter. They came at us with blades and arrows, ruthless in their attack.

"Form up!" Rhayne's command rang out as he drew his sword, a flash of steel catching the moonlight.

Asher let go of me and launched himself at the nearest attacker, moving with brutal efficiency. His blade flashed, cutting down one opponent before turning to face another. A blade slashed across his forearm, but he barely flinched, driving his elbow into the attacker's throat.

I darted toward Ciaus, who had collapsed to one knee. His face was pale, his breaths shallow. A bandit loomed over him, sword raised. Without thinking, I hurled my dagger, the blade burying itself in the man's shoulder. He fell with a howl, and I reached Ciaus, gripping his arm to keep him upright.

"Stay with me," I said, my voice steady despite the chaos around us.

Nyx and Tavian fought nearby, their blades clashing against the enemy's. Nyx dispatched one attacker with a swift, vicious strike, while Tavian drove another back with a well-timed blow. For a moment, it felt like we might gain the upper hand.

But more figures pressed in from all sides. My heart thundered as I fought to keep Ciaus from collapsing completely. "Just a scratch," he muttered, his attempt at a grin failing miserably.

"Liar," I shot back, ducking as another blade arced overhead.

Asher moved to cover us, cutting down an assailant with a ferocity I'd forgotten he possessed.

Rhayne was a force of nature. He moved through the fray with lethal precision, his blade slicing through attackers like a storm cutting through the sea. Even without the ocean to bolster his power, I could feel the raw magic coiled within him, thrumming beneath his skin. He was unstoppable. His eyes met mine briefly, a silent promise to keep me safe, before he turned to face the next threat.

The fight ended as abruptly as it had begun. The remaining bandits fled into the shadows, leaving their wounded and dead behind. The clearing fell into an uneasy silence, broken only by the heavy breathing of the crew and the groans of the injured.

Asher wiped blood from his blade, his eyes scanning the clearing. "They won't be back," he said grimly, his voice rough.

Rhayne sheathed his sword and strode toward me, his gaze flicking over Ciaus. "Is he going to make it?"

Ciaus gave a weak nod, though his teeth were clenched. "I've had worse," he rasped, the strain in his voice betraying the lie.

Rhayne's jaw tightened, his gaze sweeping over the clearing. "We need to get him back to the ship," he said firmly. "Tavian—escort him and one other."

Relief flickered through me as Tavian moved with precision, gathering supplies and rigging a makeshift stretcher. Their efficiency was a small comfort in the chaos. Meanwhile, Asher hung back, his attention flicking between Rhayne and me, his expression tight as if he were trying to piece together a puzzle.

Rhayne turned to him, his gaze cool and unreadable. "Thanks for the help. You're...?"

"Asher," he said brusquely, brushing dirt off his sleeve before offering me a broad grin that didn't quite reach his eyes. "So, care to explain how you ended up in a forest ambush?"

I let out a shaky laugh, the adrenaline still buzzing in my veins. "How did you even know I'd be here?"

Asher shrugged, his gaze flicking to the shadows before settling back on me. "I was already here, trying to find your father. I thought he could help me find you. Then I heard about a large ship arriving in Mistwood and I thought... what if? Turns out, I was right."

He said it so casually, but something in his tone grated against my nerves. The words felt rehearsed, too easy. And there was no way he could have known I'd be here, only just arriving. I pushed the thought aside—he had, after all, just fought by my side.

He reached for my arm, his grip too firm to be reassuring. "I'm just glad you're safe," he murmured, his voice soft but his eyes sharp.

Before I could respond, Rhayne's voice interrupted, steady and edged with quiet authority. "She's safe now. That's all that matters."

I stiffened as Asher's gaze darted past me to Rhayne, his expression flickering with recognition—or maybe challenge. His grip on my arm tightened, and I felt the rising tension ripple through the clearing like a storm building on the horizon.

"Who are these people, Briar?" Asher demanded, his tone hardening. "How did you end up here?"

I forced a shaky exhale, trying to calm my frayed nerves. "It's... complicated. Let's just say I crossed paths with them when they, uh, borrowed me."

"Borrowed?" Rhayne echoed dryly, his lips curving into a smirk that didn't reach his eyes.

Asher's brows shot up. "They kidnapped you?" His fury flared, and he stepped closer, his hand tightening on my wrist. "Briar—"

"It's not what you think," I interrupted, glancing toward Rhayne for a moment, seeking his steady presence without entirely meaning to. "I'm fine, Asher. I'm here now, aren't I? And, well... things didn't exactly go as planned, but they've worked out. Mostly."

"Mostly? What does that even mean?" Asher pressed, his voice dropping as he leaned closer.

Rhayne stepped in, closing the distance with calm authority. He rested a hand on my shoulder, his presence a wall between Asher and me. "For one, she's married."

Asher froze, his jaw slackening in disbelief. "Married. To who?"

"To me," Rhayne said smoothly, his tone laced with finality.

Heat surged to my cheeks as Asher's grip fell away, his expression twisting into something between shock and betrayal. The silence that followed was heavy, broken only by the faint groans of the injured and the rustle of leaves overhead.

In the corner of my eye, I saw the map lying where I'd dropped it during the fight, its glow faint but insistent. It was clear we were exactly where it wanted us to be, but the purpose remained out of reach.

I tugged my arm free, taking a shaky step back. "Can we do this later? Ciaus needs help, and we still need to figure out what the map wants."

Rhayne's hand lingered on my shoulder, steady and protective. Asher, meanwhile, stared at me as though I'd just handed him a dagger and dared him to use it.

Rhayne broke the tension first, turning to Asher. "You're welcome to come with us. But understand this: you'll follow my command."

Asher crossed his arms, his gaze hardening. "And if I don't?"

"Then you'll leave," Rhayne said flatly, his tone brooking no argument.

A beat passed, the air crackling with unspoken tension. Finally, Asher dipped his head in reluctant agreement. "I'll follow your lead. For now."

The qualifier didn't escape me, but I chose to stay silent. The last thing we needed was another fight, especially with the map's guidance still shrouded in mystery.

Rhayne motioned for the crew to move. "Let's go. We'll regroup further out."

I slipped the map back into my satchel, casting a wary glance at Asher. "So... you just happened to find us at exactly the right time?"

A faint smile tugged at his lips, though it didn't reach his eyes. "Just good luck, I guess."

I wanted to press him further, to dig into the gaps in his story, but Rhayne's warning glance held me back. For now, we had bigger problems to face.

The forest pressed in around us as we moved, the metallic hiss of the leaves overhead a constant reminder of the danger lurking in every shadow. My nerves hummed with leftover adrenaline, my senses hyperaware of every movement around me. Nyx kept a wary eye on Asher, while Rhayne's steady presence at my side felt like a lifeline I hadn't realized I needed.

Whatever lay ahead, I knew one thing for certain: the tension in our group had just reached a breaking point. And with Asher's arrival, the path forward had become even murkier.

21

"She didn't ask for my protection, but I'd give it anyway. The forest wouldn't take her from me."

RHAYNE

I kept my hand near the hilt of my sword, every muscle coiled as we ventured deeper into the forest. The leaves above whispered like drawn blades, their silvery edges glinting in the moonlight. The air was thick with a tension that mirrored a storm brewing at sea. I could almost taste the tang of lightning on my tongue, though I knew it was my own magic stirring beneath the surface, coiled and ready to lash out at the first sign of danger.

The bond between Briar and I made it harder to keep a clear head. Even now, with Asher trailing too close to her, my pulse quickened in a way I didn't entirely trust. I told myself it was simple suspicion—he was a stranger who had appeared out of nowhere at precisely the wrong time. But deep down, I knew the truth was more tangled. Briar's presence pulled at me in ways I couldn't always control. Her heartbeat, her every step, resonated with something within me. It wasn't just duty that made me protect her. It was something far more dangerous.

I'd felt it the first time I saw her, on that ship. A spark, faint but insistent, had lodged itself in my chest, refusing to fade. The longer we were together, the stronger it grew—a second pulse beating in rhythm with my own. Her magic called to mine, even though our powers were worlds apart. She was tied to secrets that pulled her toward this cursed forest, while I was bound to the ocean, its tides answering only to me. Yet something about her spirit felt as wild and unrelenting as the waves I commanded. A heartmate bond, the old stories would call it—a tether forged in fate and magic.

No matter the distance between us, I could sense her mood like the shifting winds before a storm. Her unease prickled along my skin, urging me to shield her from whatever loomed ahead. Her amusement, rare as it was, coaxed a smile to my lips before I even realized it. The bond was an enchantment I hadn't sought—one I didn't fully understand. Yet I knew, without question, I'd never willingly let it go. It was my strength, even as it exposed my greatest vulnerability.

Tonight, it felt more like a tempest—chaotic and relentless. Briar's relief at seeing Asher battled with my instinctive distrust of him. Her happiness stirred something possessive in me, but her wariness of my reaction added weight to the storm brewing in my chest. The bond magnified it all, every emotion twisting together until I could barely tell where hers ended and mine began.

I glanced back at Asher, my gaze sharp and assessing. How simple it would be to lay the blame for the ambush at his feet. My instincts screamed caution, my magic simmering beneath the surface as if readying for a fight. But as I studied him, the worry etched into his face gave me pause. He hadn't hesitated during the fight, matching the ferocity of my crew to defend Briar. He'd been as focused on her safety as I was. Loyalty? Or a calculated ploy?

For Briar's sake, I couldn't afford to dismiss either possibility.

Letting Asher remain with us was the wisest course—for now. But it wasn't just about strategy. He was walking a thin line, and the moment I sensed any threat, I would not hesitate. I might be far from the tides, but I'd tear open the sky itself to keep Briar safe. No forest, no curse, and no fate would stop me. Because when her heart called, mine answered.

Briar shot me a sidelong glance, and that quiet, unspoken thread between us thrummed to life. Her concern pulsed as clearly as my own heartbeat, tugging at the bond we shared. My mouth curved into a faint grin, meant to reassure her, and I let my hand brush against her back—a brief, grounding touch. The warmth of her nearness coursed through me like the pull of the tide, potent and undeniable, a reminder that I wasn't the only one who felt this pull.

I forced my focus onto practicalities: counting our remaining supplies, gauging how far Ciaus and the others would need to travel to reach the ship, estimating how long we had until the sun rose and the map fell dormant again. Even as I calculated, my gaze flicked between Briar and Asher, unable to fully suppress the protective edge simmering in my chest.

Nyx moved past me like a shadow, silent as the breeze stirring the trees, scanning the undergrowth for signs of pursuit. He caught my eye more than once, cutting me sidelong glances that carried unspoken questions. *You sure about letting that man stay?* his expression seemed to say.

I wasn't sure. Not entirely. But for Briar's sake—for the quest's sake—I couldn't afford to act rashly. My doubts lingered, sharper than the bladed leaves overhead. One glance at Briar, though, tempered my instincts. She was scowling at Asher over some offhand remark, irritation flashing across her face. Yet beneath the exasperation, there was something softer—relief. The way her posture eased when he was near spoke volumes. It gnawed at me, more than I wanted to admit.

I clenched my jaw, my grip tightening instinctively on the hilt of my sword. Keep him close. The mantra echoed in my mind. It was better to have Asher here, under watchful eyes, than to let him disappear into the shadows unchecked. The forest, the map, the ambush—it all felt too well-timed, as if we were playing into a design not our own. If Asher was part of that, he'd slip eventually, and when he did, I'd be ready.

I slid a glance at Briar. Her knuckles were white against the satchel strap, her shoulders tight with tension. She carried the map and crystal like a weight pulling her down, yet she bore it with a determination that sent an odd mix of pride and concern through me. When her gaze flicked to mine, the heartbond flared to life, a tangible connection crackling in the air between us. No matter what storm lay ahead, I could feel the threads of her magic wrapping tighter around us both.

When Briar finally broke eye contact, I dragged in a steadying breath and forced my attention back to the silver-black path stretching ahead. The forest loomed, its dense shadows pressing in as if it could sense our unease. Each step felt like a test, like we were being measured for how far we'd go and how long we'd last.

The map didn't make it easy. Its glowing runes shifted like quicksilver, pointing one way and then another. Briar was frustrated. Every time she found a heading, the lines flickered, faded, and re-formed, sometimes leading us back the way we'd come. We pressed on, even as irritation simmered among us, every reversal sapping what little patience we had left.

Briar came to an abrupt halt, her voice sharp with annoyance. "We're running in circles."

She wasn't wrong. I stopped beside her, looking at the map I couldn't see. Behind us, Asher watched silently. His presence prickled at the edge of my awareness, his gaze on Briar a constant annoyance. Yet he said little, his questions about the map carefully measured, his curiosity veiled. Was he trying to figure out its secrets—or gauge how much we already knew?

I turned slightly, catching Asher's steady gaze. The mistrust between us hung in the air like a blade waiting to fall. He didn't flinch, didn't offer a single tell, and that made him all the more frustrating to read.

Nyx prowled at the edges of the group, a silent sentry keeping watch for threats. Every so often, he melted into the shadows, reappearing a few paces ahead or behind us, his sharp eyes sweeping the dense undergrowth. Though he said nothing, I could feel his unease, the subtle tension in his movements. He didn't trust this place, and neither did I.

Briar groaned and ran a hand through her hair, her frustration crackling through the heartbond. "This map is useless. What's the point of magic that leads us in circles?"

Her voice trembled slightly, a rare crack in her usual resolve, and it hit me harder than I cared to admit. "It's not useless," I said, keeping my tone steady, even as my own patience wore thin. "It's a guide, not a guarantee. We'll figure it out."

She shot me a skeptical look but said nothing. I could see the strain in her expression, the exhaustion of carrying the map's burden along with everything else. A piece of me ached to take some of it from her, to shield her from the weight of whatever the forest demanded.

"We might be following something," Asher offered, his voice cutting into the silence. "If the map keeps shifting, maybe it's reacting to a moving target."

His suggestion wasn't far from my own suspicions, though I hated the idea of chasing something—or someone—that stayed just out of reach. The thought of being led deeper into the forest, farther from the sea, set my teeth on edge.

Nyx reappeared at my side, his voice low. "The forest is too quiet. If they're trying to lead us somewhere, they're doing a damn good job of keeping us on edge."

I nodded, my grip tightening on my sword hilt. "Then we'll follow for now. But the moment this map stops making sense, we hold our ground."

Briar shot me a look that was equal parts frustration and determination. "And if it doesn't lead us to anything?"

"Then we find it on our own," I said, my voice firm. "Whatever we're chasing, it won't stay hidden forever."

The metallic rustle of leaves echoed around us, a sound like knives scraping together. The forest seemed to lean closer, its shadows stretching toward us as if to swallow us whole. I kept my gaze forward, my senses sharp, and the mantra repeated in my head like a vow: Keep him close. Keep her safe. No matter what the forest had planned, I wouldn't let it win.

"So which is it, map?" Briar muttered, exasperation roughening her tone. She dragged a hand through her hair, leaving it more disheveled than before, her gaze darting across the parchment's shifting lines. "East? West? Do you want us to lie down right here and wait for whatever is messing with us to find us?"

I resisted the urge to snatch the map from her hands, though my own patience was running thin. The magic tied to it wasn't mine to command, and no amount of effort on my part would make it obey. I remembered how it had practically sung in her hands back on the ship, reacting to her presence in ways that were impossible to ignore. Something about her connection to it felt personal, though she couldn't fully explain it.

Stepping closer, I placed a hand on her shoulder, the bond between us sparking faintly at the touch. "We'll figure it out," I said, keeping my voice low and even. "The map isn't infallible. It's trying to guide us, even if it feels like it's working against us."

Briar glanced up, her agitation clear, but her lips pressed into a thin line as she gave a reluctant nod. "I just don't understand what it wants." Her voice was softer now, tinged with something close to defeat.

Nyx emerged from the shadows, his movements as silent as ever. He sheathed his dagger, his sharp gaze scanning the perimeter as he spoke. "The map's going to get us killed at this rate," he said darkly, though his tone lacked accusation. He'd follow my orders without hesitation, no matter his doubts. But his unease was clear.

I turned to Briar, then to the map. The faint glow of its runes reflected in her eyes, and I could see the exhaustion weighing on her. A sense of futility tugged at me, but I shoved it aside. Giving in to frustration wouldn't get us out of this forest. "One more sweep," I said finally, my voice firm enough to cut through the tension. "If the markings vanish again, we find solid ground and wait for dawn. Wandering blind isn't going to help anyone."

No one argued. Weariness hung heavy in the air, and the memory of Ciaus's injury lingered like a warning. Even Asher, who I half-expected to push back, merely gave a curt nod. The unspoken understanding was clear: the forest wasn't on our side, and every step deeper felt like stepping into a trap.

We started forward again, the faint shimmer of new lines weaving across the map guiding our path. Briar walked ahead, her brow furrowed in concentration as she tried to make sense of the shifting symbols. I kept close to her side, my hand hovering near the hilt of my sword, every muscle coiled.

This place won't claim her, I vowed silently. Whatever game the map is playing, it won't win.

Briar's steps faltered, and she let out a soft groan. "We're running in circles," she muttered, frustration thick in her voice. She held the map up again, the runes only she could see almost mocking in their refusal to settle on a clear direction.

"Not circles," I said, my voice calmer than I felt. "Patterns. It's trying to guide us somewhere, even if it's making us work for it."

She shot me a skeptical look, her lips twitching as if she wanted to argue. But she didn't. Instead, she adjusted her grip on the satchel and pressed on, her resolve steady despite the map's maddening behavior.

I touched Briar's back gently. "We can rest here. We can regroup and come up with a new plan to find whatever we are chasing."

Briar nodded, muttering under her breath as she cleared a patch of ground, kicking aside the leaves. Asher moved to assist her, but one sharp glance from me stopped him in his tracks. He hesitated, then turned to help Nyx secure the perimeter instead.

The clearing we'd found wasn't ideal—too exposed for my liking, with the silvery branches overhead casting shifting shadows that made it impossible to fully relax. But it was the best we could manage without venturing even deeper into this cursed forest.

Briar sat down heavily, her back against a tree with the map clutched tightly in her lap. I could see the tension in her shoulders, the way her fingers traced the edge of the parchment as if willing it to offer answers.

"Try to rest," I said, kneeling beside her. The bond between us thrummed faintly, a steady current that tethered my focus to her. "We'll make better progress once the sun's up."

She looked up at me, her expression caught somewhere between defiance and exhaustion. "And if the map decides to change its mind while we're sitting here?"

"We'll deal with it," I replied, my voice firm but not unkind. "For now, it's not doing us any good to keep chasing shadows."

Her lips pressed into a thin line, but she didn't argue. Instead, she exhaled sharply and leaned her head back against the tree, closing her eyes for a moment. I stayed close, not trusting the forest—or anyone in it—to give us even a moment's peace.

Nyx returned from his sweep, his movements nearly silent as he approached. He crouched a few feet away, his sharp gaze scanning the clearing. "Nothing nearby," he reported. "But it feels too quiet."

I nodded. "Stay sharp. If whoever we're following knows we're here, they might try to turn the game against us."

Nyx's jaw tightened, but he gave a curt nod before slipping into the shadows again, his presence blending seamlessly with the forest's eerie gloom.

Asher chose that moment to settle on the opposite side of the clearing, his back to a tree and his blade resting casually across his lap. He caught my gaze briefly, his expression unreadable. For all his careful movements and measured words, I couldn't shake the sense that he was waiting for something—an opportunity, perhaps, or a sign that Briar might trust him enough to let her guard down.

"Get some rest," I said to Briar again, softer this time. "I'll keep watch."

She opened one eye to study me. "You're not going to sleep either, are you?"

"I don't need to," I replied, leaning back against the nearest trunk but keeping my hand near my sword. "Not when you're here."

Her expression softened for the briefest moment before she nodded, pulling her cloak tighter around her shoulders. Within minutes, her breathing steadied, though I doubted she was fully asleep. Briar was too wary for that—too aware of the dangers lurking just beyond the edge of the firelight.

The hours stretched on, the forest alive with faint sounds that kept my senses on edge. A rustle here, a distant creak there. Every noise felt like a prelude to something darker, and my magic churned beneath my skin, ready to rise at a moment's notice.

22

"The worst part wasn't being tied up or dragged away – it was the realization that I might never see Rhayne again."

BRIAR

I woke slowly, cocooned in warmth—a stark contrast to the biting chill of Arrowwood's perpetual night. My thoughts felt sluggish, like they were slogging through fog, but I became sharply aware of the steady rise and fall of a chest beneath me. My head rested against a broad shoulder, an arm draped protectively around me. My heart jumped when I realized who that arm belonged to.

Rhayne.

For a moment, I considered pulling away, pretending I hadn't just spent the night curled into his side like I belonged there. But I didn't move. I couldn't. The comfort of his warmth, the safety of his hold, was too much to give up. It was a feeling I'd never admit aloud but couldn't deny.

The forest's dangers felt distant in this moment, his steady breathing soothing the tension coiled in my chest. A week ago, I would've laughed at the idea of finding peace in the Pirate King's arms. Now, I found myself lingering, listening to his heartbeat like it was a melody meant for me.

But reality intruded. My cheeks burned at the thought of anyone seeing us like this, and I shifted, lifting my head to glance at him. Dawn filtered through the treetops, casting shadows over his face. Even in sleep, his brow was furrowed slightly, as if his mind refused to fully let go of the weight he carried.

An irrational urge rose within me—to smooth that line away, to see if his features could soften further. I shook the thought from my head. *Don't be ridiculous, Briar.* There's no room for foolish daydreams when danger could be lurking a heartbeat away.

I eased myself free of his arm, careful not to disturb him, but the moment I pressed a hand to his chest to steady myself, his eyes flickered open. That sharp, intense gaze pinned me in place, his voice a low rumble.

"Running off so soon, little thief?" he drawled, amusement threading through his words despite the roughness of sleep.

I snorted, fighting a grin. "Don't flatter yourself, Pirate King. I just need a moment alone."

He arched a brow, his lips curving into that infuriating smirk. "Alone? Should I be worried? Or are you planning to rob the forest blind while I'm not looking?"

I rolled my eyes. "I'll restrain my thieving impulses. You, on the other hand, behave yourself. I don't need you charming the trees into doing your bidding."

He chuckled, letting his arm fall away. "Charming? No need. They'd follow me willingly."

"Exactly what I'm worried about," I muttered, brushing stray leaves from my clothes as I stood. "One wrong move, and these trees will slice you to ribbons."

His grin widened. "But you'd save me, wouldn't you?"

I tossed a mock glare over my shoulder. "Don't push your luck."

His soft laughter followed me as I slipped into the shadows beyond the camp. Despite the tension that clung to us like mist, I found myself smiling faintly as I picked my way through the underbrush.

The forest was unnervingly quiet. I wrapped Rhayne's jacket around me tighter to ward off the slight chill. A faint glow on the horizon hinted at dawn, but the darkness still clung to every surface. My skin prickled with unease as I moved further away, searching for a moment of solitude.

I sighed, leaning against the rough bark of a towering tree. My hand drifted reassuringly to the map tucked in my satchel. It had been leading us in circles, and frustration coiled in my chest at the thought. Maybe I was losing my touch—or maybe the map was just as confused as I was.

A flicker of light caught my attention, faint and ethereal, just at the edge of my vision. My breath hitched as I turned, my heart thudding heavily in my chest. The glow pulsed, a ghostly shimmer weaving through the trees like a living thing. It wasn't firelight, nor the glow of the moon breaking through the canopy. No, this was something else. Something... wrong.

I stepped closer, my boots silent against the mossy ground. The shimmer grew brighter, revealing a jagged line stretching across the air itself. It looked like the world had been torn open, the edges of the rift fraying like threads pulled too tight. The Veil. Or what was left of it.

I stood frozen, watching as the rip widened, the edges unraveling with an almost hypnotic rhythm. Tendrils of shadow seeped through the tear, writhing like smoke before dissipating into the night. The ground beneath me felt unsteady, the pulse of magic intensifying with each passing second. I clenched my fists, my nails biting into my palms.

So this was why the map kept leading us in circles. It wasn't broken. It was following this. Chasing the seam as it unraveled. The realization sent a shiver down my spine.

"What are you?" I whispered, my voice barely audible. But I knew. Deep down, I knew. This was the heart of the curse. The source of everything that had gone wrong. And it was spreading.

I swallowed hard, stepping back as the shadows seemed to reach for me, drawn to the magic they could sense thrumming under my skin. My connection to the Veil—it terrified me. I didn't want to understand it, but the truth pressed down on me with the weight of inevitability. If this rip wasn't stopped, there wouldn't be a map, a kingdom, or even a world left to save.

The sound of a distant branch snapping jolted me from my thoughts. My instincts screamed danger, but I didn't dare tear my eyes away from the rift. Not yet. It was mesmerizing in the worst way, beautiful and terrible all at once.

Another crack of wood. Closer this time.

I turned sharply, the eerie glow of the Veil still seared into my vision. My hand flew to the dagger at my belt, heart pounding as I turned toward the noise.

"Asher?" I blurted, startled as his familiar form stepped out from the gloom. He raised his hands, a sheepish smile playing on his lips.

"Sorry," he said softly. "Didn't mean to scare you. Just wanted to check on you."

I frowned, my grip tightening on the hilt of my dagger. "You're not on watch. Rhayne—"

"I know what the Pirate King said." His tone sharpened, and he took a step closer. "But you shouldn't be out here alone."

Instinct prickled at the back of my neck as he closed the distance. I straightened, my unease growing. "I'm fine, Asher. We've known each other a long time, but you're freaking me out—"

Before I could finish, he moved. His hand clamped around my wrist, twisting it until my dagger fell to the ground. Pain shot up my arm, and I bit back a cry.

"Asher, what the hell are you doing?" I hissed, struggling against his grip.

"I'm sorry," he said, his voice low and urgent. "But this was the only way. I needed to get you away from them."

His other arm wrapped around my waist, hauling me back against him. Panic surged in my chest as I kicked and twisted, trying to break free. "Let me go!" I snarled, managing to jab my elbow into his ribs.

He hissed in pain but held firm. "Stop fighting. I'm trying to keep you safe."

"Safe?" I spat. "You're insane! Let go of me!"

Before I could land another blow, a second figure stepped out of the shadows—a tall, man who moved with chilling precision, grabbing my arms and pinning them behind me. A rough hand clamped over my mouth, muffling my screams.

Panic clawed at my throat as I thrashed, but their grips were unyielding. Asher's face swam into focus, his expression filled with regret. "This is bigger than you, Briar. Bigger than any of us. You'll see."

I fought harder, but the taller man struck the side of my head. Pain flared, and the world spun. As my vision darkened, the last thought that raced through my mind was of Rhayne. Would he find me in time? Would he even know where to look?

Darkness swallowed me whole.

I surfaced groggily from the haze of unconsciousness, a dull ache throbbing in my skull. My body swayed in a steady rhythm, far too smooth to be the uneven jolt of forest ground. A sick twist gripped my stomach as I blinked, struggling to make sense of the strange sensation.

Dim light filtered through a small, barred window, confirming the suffocating truth—I wasn't in the forest anymore. The air was different, thick with salt and the metallic tang of rust. My heart pounded as realization sank in. The creak of wood, the rush of waves against a hull.

I was on a ship.

I jerked upright—or tried to. The ropes binding my wrists to the cot stopped me with biting force, sending a sharp jolt of pain shooting up my arms. Panic surged, hot and immediate, but I shoved it down, forcing my sluggish mind to focus. The last thing I remembered was the forest—Asher and his accomplices, the man pinning my arms, the suffocating press of silence as everything went black.

And now, I was far from Silverveil.

The realization hit me like a blow to the chest, knocking the breath from my lungs. My vision swam as I fought to piece together the situation. The rhythmic sway beneath me wasn't just a trick of my pounding head—this ship was moving, fast, cutting through the waves. I was being taken, hauled away from everything familiar and safe, dragged toward an unknown fate.

How long had I been unconscious? Hours? Days? My throat went dry as the questions churned in my mind. My stomach twisted with dread as the possibilities unfolded. If the ship was already this far out, how could anyone find me now? Rhayne... Nyx... even Tavian—they wouldn't know where to start looking. I could be halfway to the end of the world before they even realized where I'd gone.

The ropes dug into my wrists as I twisted against them, desperate for some slack, some way to get free. The rough fibers bit into raw skin, sending flares of pain with every movement, but I didn't care. Helplessness burned in my chest, stoking a spark of anger to life. This wasn't how it was supposed to go. I was smarter than this. I should've seen Asher's betrayal coming.

And Rhayne... A bitter laugh bubbled in my throat, too choked to escape. What would he think when he realized I was gone? Would he think I planned this? That I escaped? Would he even care? The memory of his warmth, his steady presence in the forest, flickered at the edges of my mind, but I shoved it away. He had a kingdom to save, a mission to complete. I was just a piece of that puzzle—a means to an end. He wouldn't risk his people, his crew, just to save me.

Would he?

A splinter of longing pierced through the chaos in my mind, sharp and unbidden. I clenched my jaw, swallowing the thought. It didn't matter. It couldn't. Whether Rhayne cared or not, I couldn't count on him—or anyone else—to come for me. I'd learned long ago that relying on others only led to disappointment.

Footsteps echoed down a narrow corridor, dragging my attention to the door. The muted creak of boots on wood grew louder, closer, until the latch clicked and the door swung open.

Two figures entered. One was Asher, his familiar frame lit by the faint lantern glow spilling into the room. His expression was tight, his eyes unreadable as they flicked to me. Behind him loomed another man, taller, sanding with his hands clenched into fists. The menacing man glared at me. The set of his shoulders and the deliberate way he moved made my skin crawl.

Asher stopped a few paces away, his gaze trailing over me, assessing. "You're awake," he said, his voice quiet but lacking its usual warmth.

I glared at him, refusing to show the knot of fear twisting in my chest. "What in the gods' names are you doing, Asher?"

He didn't flinch, but I saw the faint tightening of his jaw. "I didn't have a choice, Briar. You wouldn't have come willingly."

"Willingly to what?" I spat, straining against the ropes. "Being dragged onto a ship like cargo? Betraying me?"

The stranger chuckled—a low, grating sound that made the hairs on the back of my neck rise. "She's got spirit," he said, his voice like gravel. "That'll make this easier. Or harder, depending on her cooperation."

My stomach churned. "Cooperation for what?"

Asher hesitated, his gaze flickering to the stranger. "Careful, Helix." His attention turned to me. "We need you, Briar. Your magic. The map. You're the only one who can destroy the Veil."

I froze, the weight of his words sinking like a stone in my chest. The Veil? They wanted me to destroy it? "Do you even realize what that will do?"

I wasn't even sure I could do what he thought I could, but that moment in the forest right before he kidnapped me, I saw something... Was it the Veil? If it was, it was ripping. Tearing open like a fissure. But what was seeping from it was worse.

Asher's expression hardened, his voice dropping. "The Veil shouldn't be there, Briar. Destroying it will change everything."

"Change what?" I snapped. "And at what cost? You have no idea what you're dealing with."

"He doesn't need to know," Helix cut in, his tone dripping with arrogance. "That's why we have you."

A chill ran through me as his words settled over the room. My mind raced, searching for some way out, some plan to stall them long enough to figure out my next move. But the ropes held firm, and the ship's walls felt like a cage closing in.

Asher stepped closer, his voice softening. "I didn't want it to happen like this, Briar. But it's done. Just... don't make it harder than it has to be."

Rage flared, white-hot and unrelenting. I leaned forward as much as the bindings allowed, my voice sharp as steel. "You have no idea what you've unleashed, Asher. What you *will* unleash. And when this all goes to hell, don't expect me to save you."

His face flickered with something—guilt, regret—but he turned away, leaving me to the stranger's unsettling gaze. I swallowed hard, steeling myself. They might think they had the upper hand, but I wasn't about to make this easy for them.

Because if there was one thing I knew for certain, it was that I wasn't done fighting. Not yet.

The door to the cell creaked open, and I flinched instinctively, pulling back from the sudden flood of light. Asher stepped inside, his face shadowed, the grim lines of his mouth betraying no warmth. Behind him, muffled voices buzzed faintly, their tones tense and hurried, blending with the creak of the ship's timbers. My pulse quickened, but I kept my gaze fixed on the damp wood planks beneath me, refusing to meet his eyes. Refusing to give him the satisfaction.

The ache in my wrists flared as I shifted against the ropes that bound me, the raw skin stinging with every small movement. The stench of the hold was suffocating—a pungent mix of saltwater, rotting wood, and the bitter tang of despair. I clenched my jaw, trying to focus on anything other than the sinking realization that I was far from help.

Asher's boots thudded across the cell's floor, stopping just in front of me. I tensed, every muscle coiled, expecting another blow. Instead, he knelt, shoving a stale piece of bread and a tin cup of warm rum onto the floor near my feet. I glared at the offering, my stomach churning at the sight. The bread was hard, the rum sour-smelling. I didn't trust it—didn't trust him. Asher might have once been my friend, but that person was long gone, replaced by a man willing to sell me out for whatever power he thought the Veil held.

My stomach growled, but I shoved the hunger aside. If they thought they could break me with scraps of comfort, they didn't know me.

The voices outside faded, leaving me in silence, save for the creaking of the ship and the distant crash of waves. The dim light from the barred window did little to push back the shadows, and the weight of the betrayal settled heavily on my shoulders. Asher had crossed a line, and I couldn't fathom how long he'd been planning this. Weeks? Months? Had every moment of our friendship been a lie?

My jaw tightened, and I forced my mind away from the questions that would only drive me deeper into despair. I had to think—had to find a way out. Because no one was coming for me. Rhayne wouldn't risk his kingdom, his people, for someone like me. Why would he?

And yet, a small, treacherous part of me whispered otherwise. That part reminded me of the way his gaze lingered on me, the protective edge in his voice when he spoke my name. But hope was a dangerous thing, and I'd learned the hard way not to rely on anyone but myself.

I clenched my fists, ignoring the sting of the rope. I'd get out of this. I had to. Because one thing was certain—if they thought I was just a pawn in their game, they were about to find out how wrong they were.

I wasn't going to sit here and wait for rescue. I wasn't going to let Asher or anyone else decide my fate. And if I had to destroy the crystal to keep it from falling into the wrong hands, I would. Whatever power it held, they wouldn't get it from me. Not without a fight.

23

"The sea churned with my rage as I vowed to bring her back. Whoever dared to take her would learn the price of crossing the Pirate King."

RHAYNE

I felt it deep in my bones, like the first rumble of a storm on the horizon. Briar. She was gone.

Moments earlier, the tether between us had burned with her despair and anger, sharp and urgent. Then, suddenly, there was nothing. A hollow void where she should have been. My chest tightened, and I raced through the forest, Nyx hot on my heels.

We burst into the clearing where she had been. The ground was a mess—leaves scattered, branches broken, and soil churned as if there had been a struggle. My heart dropped as I scanned the scene, my instincts roaring louder than any reason.

"She was here," I growled, my voice low and dangerous. I crouched, brushing my fingers over the disturbed earth. "There was a fight."

Nyx's expression was uncharacteristically grim as he crouched beside me, his sharp eyes scanning the faint trail leading into the trees. "They didn't cover their tracks," he said, his voice tight. "Either they're careless, or they don't think we'll follow."

"Then they're fools," I said, rising to my feet. My magic thrummed faintly, tugging at the tether that linked me to Briar. It wasn't strong, but it was enough—a faint pulse, like a whisper in the back of my mind, guiding me.

We reached the ship faster than I thought possible, and Enric was waiting at the gangplank, his sharp eyes narrowing as he caught sight of us. He didn't need to ask; the tension radiating off me was answer enough.

"She's gone," I said, my voice clipped as I strode past him onto the deck. "They've taken her."

Enric fell into step beside me, his tone steady despite the storm brewing in my chest. "Do we have a direction?"

"West."

Enric nodded, already barking orders to the crew. Men scrambled to gather supplies and weapons, their usual banter replaced by a tense efficiency. The air on the deck was charged, the weight of my fury pressing down on everyone around me.

"They don't know what they've done," I muttered, my voice low but laced with menace.

Enric's gaze flicked to me, his expression unreadable. "What about you, My King? Are you ready for what comes next?"

My jaw tightened, and I turned my eyes to the horizon, where the faint glow of dawn began to touch the sky. "They've taken what's mine, Enric. I won't stop until I get her back. If it means tearing apart the sea, I'll do it."

Enric's nod was sharp, his faith in me unwavering. "Then we'll make them regret it."

I stared out over the darkening coast, my hands curling into fists. They didn't know one thing. I was tethered to Briar. And no matter where they took her, I would find her.

The charts and maps scattered across my cabin table blurred as my vision tunneled. My pulse thundered, a visceral drumbeat that echoed through the bond. My chest constricted, the pressure sharp and unforgiving. She wasn't in the forest anymore—that much was clear. She was farther away now, out of reach. My magic surged in response, a maelstrom building beneath my skin, dragging the sea into its thrall.

The Tidecaller responded instantly. Her timbers groaned as if she shared my rage, the ropes straining as if eager to snap free. The water beneath the hull churned violently, matching the rhythm of my fury. The sea rose to meet my anger, waves cresting higher, the salt spray lashing against the wood like a feral beast unleashed.

I gripped the edge of the table, the wood creaking under my fingers. The bond between Briar and me pulsed with an unrelenting force, filling me with the echoes of her fear and frustration. But what cut the deepest was the unmistakable sting of betrayal. The pieces fell into place with brutal clarity, and my teeth clenched as Asher's face burned in my mind—his calculated charm, his lies, and now, his unforgivable theft.

"Cast off!" I barked, my voice raw with rage. My crew moved in hurried efficiency, their sharp movements reflecting the crackling tension that gripped the ship. The Tidecaller swayed as the ropes snapped free, and I seized the wheel, every nerve in my body taut with purpose. The ocean itself seemed to bend to my will, the waves roaring their agreement.

"Captain," Nyx said, stepping closer, his voice calm but his eyes sharp as flint. "We're heading toward the Crimson Coast. The wind's with us—we'll make it in less than a day."

"Good," I growled. The word was rough, guttural, barely scratching the surface of the storm brewing inside me. I didn't need his reassurance. I could feel the pull, guiding me to her like a thread of magic stitched through the very waters. The Tidecaller knew where to go, and so did I.

Nyx hesitated for a beat, then said, "You think she's still...?"

I turned on him, my glare sharp enough to cut. "She's alive." My voice was a growl, low and lethal. "I'll feel it until she's not."

Nyx gave a curt nod and stepped back, his expression unreadable but his movements efficient. He knew better than to press further. The rest of the crew moved in synchronized chaos around us, readying the ship for whatever storm we were heading into, whether it was born of my fury or something far worse.

Images of Briar flashed in my mind—her defiant grin, the steel in her gaze when she stood against me, the softer moments when the bond between us hummed like a quiet tide. I clenched my jaw, pushing down the fear that threatened to surface. She was strong. She was fighting. I could feel it through the bond, her resistance a flicker of light in the darkness. But she wasn't invincible. And Asher knew how to twist the knife.

The wheel groaned under my grip as the ship surged forward, cutting through the water like a blade. The storm inside me seeped into the world around us, thickening the air with static and promise. The waves were with me, each one carrying me closer to her.

"Ready the crew," I ordered, my voice like the crack of thunder. I glanced at Nyx, whose steady presence grounded the chaos spiraling inside me. "We're not stopping until she's back. I don't care how many ships we have to sink or how many men we have to kill. If they've hurt her—" My words faltered, the rage coiling tighter in my chest. "They'll wish the sea had swallowed them whole before I get my hands on them."

Enric nodded sharply, already turning to relay the orders. The crew moved with precision, their trust in me unwavering. They knew the stakes—they'd seen me wield the fury of the tides before. But this wasn't just about vengeance. This was about her. My wife. My heartmate.

The Tidecaller groaned beneath my feet, as if sensing my thoughts, eager to answer my call. The waves rose higher, and the wind tore at the sails with relentless force. I gritted my teeth, every muscle straining as the ship lunged forward.

No one takes what's mine. No one.

With every passing wave, the bond between us thrummed stronger. I could still feel her, faint but unyielding. She was out there, and she was waiting. I would find her. I would burn the Crimson Coast to the ground if that's what it took. And when I held her again, I'd make damn sure no one ever dared to take her from me.

Because Briar was mine. And the sea always brings back what belongs to her king.

24

"It wasn't fear that gripped me – it was rage. Pure, burning rage at the man I once called a friend."

BRIAR

Gods, it felt like days since we left Silverveil. I didn't know where we were headed, but the relentless pitch and roll of the ship told me we weren't near calm waters. The storm raged outside, its fury battering the hull as rain pelted down in heavy torrents. The sea seemed alive with anger, as though reflecting my own tumultuous thoughts. I might've laughed at the irony if the crazed state of my mind wasn't already teetering on the edge of hysteria.

My head throbbed from whoever had whacked me in the forest. Each movement sent sharp, stabbing pain radiating from the lump on the side of my skull. I bit back a groan, unwilling to show weakness even though no one could hear me in the dark, damp cell. The ropes binding my wrists chafed with every twist and pull, and my raw skin stung worse than the salt air biting my lips.

The smell of the hold was unbearable. Wet wood, decay, and the metallic tang of rust filled my nostrils. I'd tried to adjust to the rank atmosphere, but every breath felt like I was swallowing seawater and rot. It was the kind of place that made the soul shrink. And yet... something else lingered, hidden beneath the oppressive stench—a scent faintly familiar but buried under layers of damp and despair.

A jolt of the ship threw me sideways, my shoulder colliding painfully with the rough boards of the wall. My breath hissed out between clenched teeth, but the impact did more than jar me; it dislodged the broken cot I was tied to, loosening the leg just enough to make the ropes slacken. My pulse jumped. An opening.

I shifted carefully, ignoring the splinters biting into my palms as I worked the weakened ropes against the jagged edge of the cot's wood. Minutes—or maybe hours—passed as I wiggled and twisted until, finally, the bindings gave way. I yanked my hands free, hissing as the blood rushed back into my numb fingers.

The faint sound of voices above told me I didn't have long. Gathering my courage, I pressed my hands to the floor to steady myself before creeping toward the door. It was locked, as I'd feared. My lip curled in frustration, but as I leaned my weight against the frame, the wood creaked—not in protest, but weakly, as if the hinges were straining against rot. This ship was old. Maybe too old to hold anyone captive effectively.

I shoved harder, bracing myself against the wall, until the door gave way with a sharp snap. The sound echoed through the narrow corridor beyond, and my heart leapt into my throat. I paused, listening, but the voices above didn't falter.

Moving quickly, I slipped out, my boots quiet against the damp wood. The corridor smelled worse than the cell, the air thicker here, tinged with sweat and something metallic. My gut twisted as I followed the scent, an inexplicable dread curling in my chest.

The ship groaned and tilted sharply, nearly throwing me into the wall. I caught myself and pushed onward, following the dim light of a lantern swinging at the far end of the passage. The metallic scent grew stronger, undercut by something acrid and sour that churned my stomach.

I hesitated at the edge of the light, squinting into the shadowy room beyond. Chains clinked softly, a faint noise that sent a chill skittering down my spine. The lantern's glow illuminated a figure slumped in the far corner, bound and unmoving.

My breath caught. No. It couldn't be.

I stepped into the room, the floor beneath me slick with seawater that seeped through the hull. My heart pounded painfully as I approached the figure, each step heavier than the last.

"Gods," I whispered, dropping to my knees beside him. His face was gaunt, pale, with deep hollows beneath his cheekbones. His once-strong frame was now frail, the muscles of a man who had once carried me on his shoulders wasted away. Blood crusted the edges of his wrists where chains bit into his skin, and his breathing was shallow, ragged.

"Father?" My voice cracked, barely audible above the sound of the storm. I reached out, my trembling hand brushing against his shoulder. He flinched at the contact, his

269

eyes snapping open—dull, glazed, but still holding a flicker of recognition.

"Briar..." His voice was hoarse, barely more than a whisper, but it was enough to undo me.

Tears blurred my vision as I gripped his arm. "What did they do to you? How—how are you here?"

He tried to speak, but the effort seemed to sap what little strength he had left. His head lolled forward, and I scrambled to support him, my heart pounding with desperation. "Father, stay with me," I pleaded. "I'm going to get you out of here, I promise."

His lips moved, forming words I couldn't hear over the roar of the storm and the creaking of the ship. I leaned closer, pressing my ear near his mouth.

"The... Veil..." he rasped, his breath ghosting over my skin. "They... can't destroy it... stop them, Briar. Stop..."

Tears spilled down my cheeks as his head drooped against my shoulder. I clutched him tightly, panic clawing at my chest. "No, don't you dare give up on me," I whispered fiercely. "I'm going to save you. You hear me? You're not leaving me again."

The sound of heavy footsteps in the corridor made my blood run cold. I shifted, placing my body between the door and my father as the realization hit me: I wasn't just a prisoner on this ship. Neither was he. We were pawns in whatever twisted game Asher was playing.

The door swung open, and the lantern light caught the glint of a blade. I swallowed hard, squaring my shoulders. My pulse hammered as I moved instinctively, crouching over my father like a shield. My fingers tightened around the only weapon I had—a splintered piece of wood I'd grabbed from the broken doorframe. Hardly ideal, but it would have to do.

"You really think you can fight your way out of this, Briar?" A low chuckle came from the doorway.

Asher.

The sight of him twisted my stomach. He stepped further into the room, his face shadowed but his voice dripping with that maddening mix of regret and condescension. Behind him, another figure loomed—the same hulking man from earlier, his expression void of sympathy.

"Asher," I snarled, straightening slightly but keeping myself between them and my father. "What is this? Why is he here? What did you do to him?"

"I told you I went to Silverveil for your father." Asher's gaze flicked to my father, and for a moment, something like guilt crossed his features. But it was gone as quickly as it came, replaced by cold resolve. "But, this isn't about him. It's about you. And the Veil."

"I'm not doing anything for you," I snapped. My voice wavered, but the anger burning in my chest kept me steady. "You want to destroy it? Do it yourself. I'm not helping you."

Asher sighed, shaking his head. "I was hoping you'd cooperate, Briar. Really, I was. But you've left me no choice."

He stepped closer, and I tightened my grip on the splintered wood. My father groaned softly behind me, his shallow breathing a painful reminder of how weak he was. I couldn't let them hurt him again.

"Stay back," I warned, raising the makeshift weapon. My hands trembled, but I held my ground.

Helix came in behind him, smirking. "She's got spirit. Shame it won't last."

I clenched my teeth, my mind racing. The odds were against me—two armed men, no real weapon, and my father barely clinging to consciousness. But I couldn't just give in. Not now. Not ever.

"You don't have to do this," I said, trying to keep my voice steady. My gaze locked on Asher, the betrayal still fresh and raw. "Whatever you think you'll gain from this, it's not worth it."

Asher's jaw tightened. "It's not about what I gain, Briar. It's about what's necessary. The Veil is bigger than you or me. And if you'd just listen—"

"Listen?" I snapped, my voice rising despite myself. "You want me to listen after you betrayed me? After you dragged me onto this gods-forsaken ship and hurt my father? You think I'd believe a word you say now?"

His eyes darkened, and for a moment, I thought I saw a flicker of regret. But then Helix moved, and the moment was gone. He lunged forward, and instinct took over.

I swung the splintered wood, catching him across the forearm. He hissed in pain, but the blow wasn't enough to stop him. He grabbed my wrist, twisting it painfully until I dropped the makeshift weapon.

"Briar!" Asher barked, but I didn't hear what else he said. I was too busy thrashing, kicking, clawing—anything to break free. My foot connected with Helix's shin, and he stumbled, giving me just enough room to twist away.

Asher cursed, stepping closer. "Enough!"

I ignored him, lunging for the lantern hanging on the wall. If I could just—

But Asher was faster. He caught my arm, spinning me around and pinning me against the wall. His grip was firm but not cruel, and his expression was twisted with something I couldn't name.

"Stop fighting me, Briar," he said, his voice low and urgent. "I don't want to hurt you. Just—stop."

The storm outside seemed to echo the turmoil inside me, the ship rocking violently as the waves crashed against the hull. My heart pounded, and for a moment, I thought about giving in—about what it might mean to stop fighting, to save my father without risking more pain.

But then I looked past Asher, to the frail figure of my father slumped on the floor. To the blood crusted around his wrists. To the betrayal that burned like fire in my chest.

I met Asher's gaze, my voice shaking but defiant. "You already hurt me."

The words hung between us, heavy and final. Asher flinched, his grip faltering just enough for me to shove him back. I didn't waste the opening. I darted past him, grabbing the lantern and hurling it toward Helix. It shattered against the wall, flames licking at the wood and casting jagged shadows across the room.

"Briar!" Asher shouted, but I was already at my father's side, tugging at the chains that bound him. My fingers were slick with sweat and blood, the metal biting into my skin, but I didn't stop. I couldn't.

"Come on," I whispered, my voice breaking. "We're getting out of here."

The fire spread quickly, smoke curling into the air. The chaos in the room was palpable—Asher shouting orders, Helix cursing as he tried to douse the flames. But all I could focus on was my father, on the shallow rise and fall of his chest, on the faint flicker of life that told me it wasn't too late.

"Briar, wait—" Asher's voice cut through the haze, but I didn't look back.

I wouldn't stop. Not until we were free.

The flames flickered against the walls, their dance casting chaotic shadows across the room. Smoke curled through the air, acrid and biting, and for a moment, I thought the chaos might provide a chance. But then Helix snarled, yanking a cloak from a nearby hook to smother the fire, and Asher was suddenly there, pulling me back from my father with rough but controlled strength.

"Enough!" he barked, his voice tight with both anger and frustration. "You'll kill him faster if you keep this up."

I froze at the words, my chest heaving. My father lay slumped against the wall, his skin pale, his breathing shallow. The firelight illuminated the deep lines on his face, the bruises around his wrists, the sheen of sweat on his forehead.

"Father," I whispered, my voice cracking. I tried to move toward him, but Asher's grip tightened on my arm, keeping me in place. "Let me go! He's dying!"

Asher hesitated, his jaw clenched, before nodding to Helix. "Undo the chains. Let her have this."

Helix growled something under his breath but obeyed, kneeling to unlock the manacles binding my father's wrists. The sound of metal hitting the floor was deafening, and the moment he was free, I wrenched out of Asher's grasp and dropped to my knees beside him.

The sway of the ship rocked beneath me, but it did little to calm the storm raging in my chest. The air in the hold was still thick with smoke, almost suffocating, as I knelt beside my father. He was pale, far too pale, his chest rising and falling in uneven, shallow breaths. Blood stained his tunic, his hands, the floor—and I couldn't stop it. I couldn't do anything but press my hands against his wounds, willing him to stay with me.

"Father, stay with me," I begged, my voice cracking under the weight of my desperation. "I-I can get us out of here. Just hold on."

His lips quirked in a faint smile that hurt more than any blade could. "Still... so stubborn," he rasped, his voice a fragile thread. "You've got your mother's fire."

"Then don't leave me!" The words tore out of me before I could stop them. "You didn't come this far just to give up now."

He coughed, his body shuddering with the effort. "I didn't leave you... to give up. I left to protect you."

"From what?" My voice shook as I clutched his hand, the warmth already fading from his skin. "You should have stayed. We could've fought together."

"You don't understand." His eyes, dim but determined, locked on mine. "Your mother... was a Veil Guardian... from the other realm."

The words slammed into me like a wave. "What are you talking about?" I whispered, shaking my head.

275

He nodded weakly, his breaths coming in shorter, sharper bursts. "Your mother's magic... it passed to you. Makes you... a beacon. They can find you... through the rifts."

The weight of his words settled over me, suffocating. A beacon. My magic, my connection to the heart and map—it was all because of her. "So you left," I murmured, my throat tightening. "To protect me."

"I thought... if I found the fractured pieces first... if I could find a way to fix the Veil before they could..." His voice faltered, his hand trembling in mine. "But they were faster. I failed."

"No." I shook my head vehemently, tears blurring my vision. "You didn't fail. I'll fix it. I'll finish what you started."

His weak laugh cut me to the bone. "You're brave... just like her. But you won't do it alone. You can't."

I leaned closer, gripping his hand as if it could anchor him here. "I'm not alone. I'll find a way."

His hand tightened around mine, a last surge of strength. His gaze sharpened, more focused than it had been since I found him. "Rhayne."

The name struck me like a bolt of lightning. "What?" I asked, my breath hitching. "What about him?"

His lips parted, the word barely a whisper. "Heartmate."

My stomach plummeted, my thoughts reeling. Heartmate? What the gods' names did that mean? I stared at him, but his eyes were already dulling, his grip loosening in mine.

"Father?" Panic surged, and I shook his hand. "No, no, no! Father, stay with me! Please!"

But he didn't. His head lolled back, his chest falling still, and the silence that followed was deafening. I clung to his hand, tears streaming down my face as the weight of his loss crushed me.

Heartmate.

The word clawed at my mind, refusing to let go. I whispered it under my breath, tasting the unfamiliarity of it. I had no idea what it meant, but I knew who did. Rhayne. My pulse thundered as the pieces started to click into place—the pull I felt toward him, the way his presence seemed to anchor me, the unspoken tension that thrummed between us.

Had he known?

I stared at my father's lifeless body, anger and confusion warring with grief. He'd left to protect me, sacrificed everything to try to keep me safe. And with his dying breath, he'd given me this—Rhayne, heartmate. It didn't make sense. But I couldn't let it rest.

If I made it out of this alive, Rhayne was going to give me answers. And I wasn't going to stop until I understood exactly what my father's last words meant.

Asher's voice broke through the haze, sharp and impatient. "We don't have time for this—."

"Shut up," I snapped, the venom in my voice startling even me. I rose slowly, turning to face him with tears still streaming down my face but fury burning in my chest. "You're not getting anything from me. Not now. Not ever."

His jaw tightened, but he didn't argue, his gaze flicking to Helix as if debating his next move.

Good. Let him hesitate. Let him doubt. Because I would fight, and I would win. For my father. For my mother. For the Veil—and for myself.

And gods help anyone who stood in my way.

"Every roar of the sea, every pulse of magic, screamed her name. She was my queen, my heartmate, and, I'd lay waste to kingdoms for her return."

RHAYNE

The Tidecaller cut through the violent waters, closing in on the rocky shore of the Crimson Coast. No dock, no welcoming party—just jagged cliffs and the enemy ship anchored in the bay, its silhouette black against the stormy sky. The sight sent fury burning through my veins. She was here. I could feel it.

"Lower the boats!" I barked, stepping away from the wheel. Enric was already by my side, his sword ready.

"The ship's crew won't go down without a fight," he said, his tone calm but edged with steel.

"Let them try." My magic surged, a storm brewing inside me that echoed the churning sea.

The boats hit the water, and I jumped down into the lead one, taking the oars with Enric and Nyx at my side. The waves battered us as we rowed toward the enemy ship, rain pelting down in heavy sheets, but nothing could dull the pulse of the bond pulling me forward. Briar had been here. She was close.

When we reached the side of the ship, I didn't wait for anyone to lead the charge. My hands gripped the rope ladder, hauling myself up with a single-minded focus. The moment my boots hit the deck, my sword was in my hand.

A shout went up as the first man charged me, but he barely got within striking distance before my blade sliced through him. Blood sprayed across the planks as chaos erupted.

"Find her!" I roared over the clash of steel and the roar of the storm. "Take down anyone in your way!"

Enric was already at my back, his blade cutting through another attacker. "We'll clear the deck first," he said, his voice steady despite the madness around us.

The enemy was disorganized, fighting more out of desperation than strategy. They didn't stand a chance against us. My men moved like shadows, their blades flashing in the dim light, cutting down resistance as we swept across the deck.

I grabbed one of the enemy crew by the collar, slamming him against the mast. "Where is she?" I snarled, my blade pressed to his throat.

His eyes were wide with terror, his voice a shaky rasp. "I don't—don't know! Below deck! They—she was there!"

I didn't wait for more. Shoving him aside, I charged toward the hatch, Enric at my heels. "Nyx, Tavian—clear the rest of the ship. Don't leave anyone standing!"

The hold was dark and cramped, the air thick with the stench of damp wood and unwashed bodies. My magic coiled tighter the farther I went, the bond pulling me forward like a lifeline.

"Here!" Enric called, his voice echoing down the narrow corridor.

I reached him just as he kicked open the door to a small cell. The ropes on the floor were frayed, lying discarded where they'd held her. The air inside was suffocating, but I could feel it—her presence, faint but unmistakable.

She had been here.

My jaw clenched, my grip tightening on the hilt of my sword as I stepped inside. The remnants of her presence clung to the air like a whisper, the bond vibrating with a faint echo of her emotions. Fear. Anger. Pain.

"She's gone," Enric said grimly, scanning the empty cell. "Whoever took her didn't leave her behind." His gaze flicked to the ropes on the floor. "They can't have gotten far. The storm would've slowed them down."

"Then we keep moving." I turned on my heel, stepping back into the corridor. The rage inside me was a living thing, fueling the storm that raged beyond the ship's walls. "Search every inch of this vessel. Someone here knows where she is, and they're going to tell me."

Nyx appeared from the shadows, blood streaking his face. "Deck's clear. No sign of her topside."

"She was here," I said, my voice low and dangerous. "They moved her before we got here. We'll follow the trail."

Enric nodded. "If they've anchored this far from shore, there's a reason. They didn't take her far."

I stepped back out into the storm, the wind howling around me as the sea churned beneath the ship. The

Tidecaller rocked in the distance, waiting for my command. I gripped the railing, letting the fury inside me fuel my magic.

"We'll find her," I said, more to myself than to anyone else. The bond pulsed faintly, a beacon in the storm. "And when we do, I'll make them regret ever laying a hand on her."

The ship creaked under the weight of the storm, the sea roaring in the distance. But no sound could drown out the promise thrumming in my chest. Briar was mine. And I was coming for her.

The longboats scraped against the red sand, their hulls grinding to a halt as the first pale streaks of dawn painted the sky. The Crimson Coast. It was as ruthless as its name. Under the dim light, the beach shimmered like blood, each grain of crimson sand glinting with an ominous sheen. Now, with daylight creeping in, it was easy to see why this stretch of land had earned its grim reputation.

I leapt from the boat before it fully grounded, boots sinking into the strange, gleaming sand. The bond thrummed in my chest, more distinct now, stronger than it had been on the ship. Briar had been taken here. I knew it with every fiber of my being. My magic coiled like a serpent beneath my skin, restless and ready to strike.

"Spread out!" I barked, my voice carrying over the roar of the waves. The crew moved quickly, scattering in pairs across the shore, their weapons drawn. Enric was at my side, his blade glinting in the faint light. Nyx followed close behind, his steps silent as ever.

The sea behind us churned, the swells rising and falling with an unnatural rhythm. My anger fueled the ocean, pulling it toward me with each step I took. The waves slammed against the shore, sending spray into the air, and the Tidecaller groaned in the distance.

"She's close," I muttered, more to myself than to anyone else. The bond pulsed in my chest, guiding me like a compass. But anger clouded my focus, and the sea responded to my lack of control. The water surged higher, curling in on itself like a beast ready to pounce.

"My King." Enric's voice was steady, but there was a note of caution in it. "The swells—if they rise any higher..."

I stopped abruptly, planting my feet in the sand. The ocean hissed and crashed behind me, its fury mirroring my own. Enric was right. If I let the sea run unchecked, it would tear apart the very ground we stood on—and everything in its path. Including Briar.

I clenched my fists, forcing myself to breathe. My magic writhed inside me, resisting the restraint I tried to impose. The bond between Briar and me pulsed harder, louder, feeding my need to act. To find her. To bring her back. But if I wasn't careful, I'd destroy everything in the process.

"She's not in the ocean," Enric said carefully, his tone the same he used to soothe an unpredictable storm. "We'll find her on land. Keep the sea with us, but don't let it lead."

I exhaled sharply, forcing the waves to settle with an effort that left my muscles trembling. The sea grumbled in protest, the swells receding reluctantly, but it obeyed. For now.

The red sand sparkled mockingly under the growing light, but the pull in my chest was undeniable. "I can feel her. She's not far."

Nyx knelt in the sand, running his fingers through the grains as if searching for clues. He held up a strand of dark hair caught in a clump of seaweed, his sharp eyes meeting mine. "She was dragged this way. Tracks head inland."

I was already moving before he finished speaking, my boots pounding against the strange sand. The crew followed without question, their weapons drawn and ready. Every instinct screamed at me to run faster, to tear apart anything in my path until I found her. The bond guided me, the faint echo of her presence keeping me steady.

"She's alive," I growled, my voice low and resolute. "I'll feel it until she's not."

Enric jogged beside me, his sword at the ready. "Then let's make sure she stays that way."

The crimson sand beneath our boots glittered ominously as we moved inland, every step dragging us closer to the dense, jagged cliffs that loomed over the coast. The sun had crept higher, igniting the blood-red grains like embers in a fire, and a faint mist curled up from the shoreline, thickening with each step we took.

Nyx was ahead of me, his hands subtly moving through the air. Though invisible to most, I could feel the pull of his magic like a net spreading out before us. His tethers brushed against the edges of unseen things, warning him before we stumbled into danger. Behind me, Enric muttered incantations under his breath, his magic weaving into the air to steady the winds, keeping them from scattering the mist completely and revealing us too soon.

"Hold," Nyx said, stopping abruptly. His fingers twitched, his focus narrowing to the space directly in front of him. "Something's here. Feels... taut, like a snare."

I stepped forward, squinting against the rising mist. My magic thrummed uneasily in my veins, the sea at my back whispering warnings I couldn't yet see. "What kind of snare?"

"Magic," he replied tersely. "Old. Strong. It's wound around this whole place like a fishing net."

Enric strode up beside us, his brow furrowing as he waved a hand in the air, summoning a faint breeze to part the mist. For a moment, the landscape beyond us came into focus—a narrow pathway winding up the cliffs, flanked by jagged rocks and thorny vines that seemed to writhe on their own. And there, barely visible in the sunlight, glimmered threads of silvery light stretched across the path, humming faintly with power.

"It's a ward," Enric said grimly. "A nasty one."

Nyx nodded, his hands lowering slightly as he traced the invisible lines. "Step through it, and you'll be torn apart."

I gritted my teeth, the image of Briar—trapped or worse—spurring my pulse into a dangerous rhythm. "Can you disarm it?"

Nyx hesitated, glancing at Enric. "Not easily. It's keyed to something... alive. Probably whoever set it. If they're still near, tampering with it will alert them immediately."

The ocean inside me surged with impatience, the waves battering against my control. Every second wasted felt like another second Briar was slipping further from my grasp. "Then we don't tamper," I growled. "We go through."

Enric raised a brow. "Through? Rhayne, this isn't a simple trap—this is magic older than you or me. You can't just brute force your way—"

"I'm not leaving her behind!" My voice lashed out like a whip, the force of it making Enric take a half-step back. I steadied myself, gripping the rising tide of my anger before it could consume me.

Nyx exhaled slowly. "If you're serious about going through, I'll guide us. I can hold the tethers just long enough for us to slip past—but it'll take everything I've got. One wrong move, and we'll be shredded and then no one can help her."

"Do it," I said, my voice cold with determination. I stared at Nyx, tugging on the bond of our bargain to force him to do my will. "Enric, keep the mist thick but controlled. If anyone's watching, I don't want them seeing us until it's too late."

Enric sighed, but his hands lifted, the air around us twisting with his power. The mist swirled denser, cloaking us in an ethereal shroud that felt both protective and foreboding. Nyx's magic sparked, faint and shimmering like threads of spider silk, as he moved forward.

"Step exactly where I step," Nyx murmured, his voice taut with focus. "And don't touch the lines."

We followed, each step feeling like a gamble with death. The ward hummed louder the closer we got, the silvery threads vibrating like plucked harp strings. I could feel their power brushing against my skin, a cold, biting sensation that made my magic stir in defense.

A sudden crackle split the air, and I froze. Nyx hissed, his hands twitching as he struggled to stabilize the tethers.

"They're shifting," he said through gritted teeth. "The ward's reacting to our presence."

"Keep moving," I ordered, my voice low but firm. "We're not stopping now."

Enric muttered another incantation, and the mist thickened, muffling the ward's growing hum. But as we pressed on, I felt it—a pulse, faint but distinct, coming from the cliffs above. Someone was watching us.

"Nyx," I said quietly, my gaze scanning the ridges. "Can you feel it?"

He nodded stiffly, sweat beading on his brow. "Whoever set this trap, they're close. They're waiting for it to spring."

The pulse grew stronger, and I knew we had to act fast. "Enric," I said, my tone sharp. "When we clear this ward, I want a storm ready. I don't care how small—just enough to scatter them."

"And what about you?" he asked, his voice edged with concern.

"I'll deal with whoever's waiting for us," I said, my grip tightening on my sword. The sea raged within me, ready to crash down on anyone who stood in our way.

As we neared the final stretch, the ward's hum reached a fever pitch. Nyx's hands moved like a conductor's, guiding the invisible threads just enough to let us slip past without triggering the trap. My magic coiled tightly, ready to strike at the first sign of danger.

And then, with a final step, we were through. The air beyond the ward felt heavier, charged with the remnants of its power. But there was no time to celebrate.

A shadow moved above us, and a voice rang out—sharp and mocking. "You should've stayed at sea, Pirate King."

The trap wasn't just the ward. It was an ambush.

The voice sliced through the mist like a blade, sharp and taunting. I didn't need to see the speaker to feel the danger coiling around us. The ambush was perfectly laid—high ground, hidden vantage points, and the ward behind us ensuring no easy retreat.

I drew my sword, its steel catching the faint glow of the mist. My magic surged, an instinctive response to the threat, and The Tidecaller's power pulsed through me. The waves beyond the cliffs whispered their readiness, eager to rise at my command.

"Show yourselves!" I barked, my voice carrying like thunder through the stillness.

Laughter echoed, a cold and hollow sound. Figures emerged from the shadows above, their silhouettes sharp against the crimson glow of the sand. Archers, perched like vultures, their arrows nocked and aimed. Below them, more figures stepped out from the jagged rocks, blades glinting in the faint light. They outnumbered us easily, but numbers had never intimidated me before.

Nyx cursed under his breath, his fingers twitching as his tethers flicked out like searching tendrils. "They're spread wide. Too wide."

"Enric," I said, my voice low and steady. "Cover us. Now."

Enric nodded, lifting his hands. The mist thickened instantly, rolling in heavy waves around us, blurring the enemy's sightlines. The archers hesitated, their forms shifting uneasily as the haze swallowed the cliffs.

"Hold steady," the voice called from above, sharp and commanding. "The mist is a trick. Hold your positions."

I didn't wait for them to adjust. "Nyx, take the left. I'll cover the center. Enric, keep the mist thick and prepare to pull the wind. We scatter them, and we find who's in charge."

Nyx vanished into the fog, his tethers pulling him toward the enemy like a shadow slipping through cracks. I surged forward, my magic thrumming in tandem with the sea. The ground beneath me vibrated with the tide's call, a low hum that promised devastation if unleashed.

The first man I encountered didn't even see me coming. He swung wildly at the sound of my approach, but my blade was faster, slicing through his defenses with ease. The spray of red on the rocky ground barely registered as I moved past him, my focus honed on the higher ridge.

A faint hiss warned me of an arrow flying toward my chest. I twisted, the projectile skimming past my shoulder and embedding itself in the rock behind me. My magic responded instinctively, the ocean's pull tightening in my veins.

Another figure lunged at me, his sword raised high. I sidestepped, catching his blade with mine and shoving him backward into the jagged rocks. He crumpled, winded but alive. I had no time to finish him. My focus was already shifting higher, to the archer who had loosed that arrow.

Enric's winds howled through the pass, catching the archers off guard. Several stumbled, their shots going wide as they fought to keep their footing. The mist churned with the wind, blinding them further.

A familiar shape darted through the haze—Nyx. His magic hummed faintly, invisible threads wrapping around an archer's legs and yanking him off balance. The man toppled, his bow clattering to the ground. Nyx didn't stop, moving fluidly from one target to the next, a ghost among the chaos.

"My King!" Enric's voice cut through the din, strained but steady. "The mist can't hold much longer—they're regrouping!"

I growled under my breath, my grip tightening on my blade. The trap had been well-laid, but they hadn't accounted for my crew—or the force of the ocean's fury. "Then we don't give them the chance."

Reaching the base of the cliff, I summoned the sea with a sharp flick of my wrist. A surge of water roared up the narrow pass, smashing into the rocks and scattering our attackers like leaves in a gale. Shouts and curses rang out as they scrambled for cover, their formation breaking apart under the onslaught.

The leader's voice rose above the chaos, angry and commanding. "Hold the line! He can't keep this up forever!"

They were wrong. I could.

"I didn't want to believe there was a bond between us, but in the darkest moments, it was the only hope I had left."

BRIAR

he bindings bit into my wrists, raw and unforgiving as I stumbled along the uneven path. Every step was a fight to keep my footing, the sharp rocks and twisting roots seeming to conspire against me. Asher's hand gripped my arm tightly, his hold unrelenting as he pulled me forward, and I bit down on the inside of my cheek to keep from crying out.

He had my satchel slung across his shoulder, the map and crystal inside. The loss of it felt like a piece of me had been ripped away. It wasn't just the physical absence; it was the way the magic inside it pulsed, calling to me faintly like a song I couldn't quite hear. The pull was maddening, a persistent tug at the edges of my mind, and I couldn't tell if it was the shard, the map, or something far more dangerous.

"Move faster," Asher barked, his voice harsh above the roaring wind.

I glared at him, planting my feet in defiance. "You'll have to drag me."

He sighed, his patience clearly fraying. "Don't make this harder than it needs to be, Briar."

"Harder for you, you mean." My voice dripped with venom. I twisted against his grip, trying to wrench free, but his fingers only tightened. "Why don't you drop dead and save us both the trouble?"

His jaw clenched, and for a moment, I thought he might hit me. Instead, he jerked me forward, nearly sending me sprawling. "Keep fighting, and you'll regret it."

"I already do," I shot back, my pulse pounding with adrenaline. I didn't care how dangerous he looked, or how hopeless this seemed. I wasn't going to stop fighting. Not for him. Not for anyone.

The wind howled through the trees, and the storm raged overhead, a chaotic symphony of thunder and rain. Each crack of lightning illuminated the crimson-tinted world around us, the red sand shimmered like blood under the violent light. The path was slick with rain, turning the ground into a treacherous mess, but I refused to let it slow me down.

A particularly loud crack of thunder made me flinch, my heart leaping into my throat. The storm was relentless, almost alive in its fury, and a part of me wondered if it was natural. It felt... wrong, somehow. Too focused, too angry. Like it was looking for something—or someone.

Another pulse of magic thrummed through me, sharper this time, and I stumbled again, gasping. It wasn't just the heart or the map. It was something else. Something powerful, dark, angry... and it was getting closer.

Asher noticed, his eyes narrowing. "What was that?"

I shook my head, not trusting myself to speak. My legs felt heavy, my breath coming in short bursts as the magic pulsed again, closer and more insistent. It wasn't just calling to me—it was demanding something. My skin prickled, and I bit back a curse, refusing to let Asher see how much it rattled me.

"Don't play dumb, Briar." His grip tightened, and he leaned in close, his breath hot against my ear. "I know you feel it."

I whipped my head around, glaring at him. "I feel your lies choking the air. Does that count?"

He scowled, dragging me forward with renewed force. "You'll wish you hadn't said that."

The storm roared louder, drowning out his threats. My heart raced, every nerve in my body on edge. The rain lashed against my skin, cold and biting, but it was nothing compared to the fire burning in my chest. I didn't know what was coming—only that it was close, and it was dangerous.

The magic pulsed again, and this time, it felt like it was tearing through me. I cried out, my knees buckling as the power surged. Asher cursed, hauling me upright before I could collapse completely.

"What's happening?" he demanded, shaking me.

"I don't know!" I shouted back, the truth slipping out before I could stop it. The magic was too strong, too overwhelming. It wasn't mine, and it wasn't the crystal's. It was something else entirely.

And it terrified me.

Lightning struck a tree just ahead of us, splintering it in a deafening explosion of wood and fire. The path was blocked, and Asher let out a string of curses, his frustration spilling over.

"We keep moving!" he barked at the others, his men scrambling to find a way around the fallen tree.

I seized the moment, twisting against his grip with all the strength I had left. My nails raked against his arm, and he hissed, loosening his hold just enough for me to stumble back a step.

"Briar!" he roared, lunging for me.

But I was already moving, my legs carrying me blindly through the chaos. The storm raged around me, the magic pulsing in time with the thunder, and I didn't know where I was going. All I knew was that I couldn't stop.

Another flash of lightning illuminated the path ahead, and I skidded to a halt, my breath catching in my throat. The ground dropped away into a sheer cliff, the churning sea raging far below. My stomach twisted as I teetered on the edge, the wind threatening to push me over.

Asher's hand closed around my arm, yanking me back from the brink. "Enough!" he snarled, his voice barely audible over the storm. "You can't escape, Briar. Stop trying."

I struggled against him, my chest heaving with effort.

Asher yanked me back from the cliff's edge with a force that nearly knocked the air from my lungs. His grip was iron, his fingers digging into my arm like talons. I twisted against him, but it was no use. My legs wobbled, the proximity to the sheer drop making my head spin. The churning sea below seemed to echo the storm in the sky, a relentless fury that felt too close, too alive.

"Stubborn to the last," Asher muttered through clenched teeth, his eyes cold as he looked me over. "Fine. Let's see how far that gets you."

Before I could spit out a retort, he pulled a length of rope from his belt and tied it around my wrists, looping it tighter than before. The rough fibers bit into my skin, and I winced, biting back a cry as he secured the knot with brutal efficiency.

"I don't have time for your games," he growled, tugging the rope to ensure it held. "You try running again, and I won't be so forgiving."

Forgiving? I glared at him, my chest heaving. The bindings burned against my already raw wrists, but I refused to give him the satisfaction of seeing me break. "You call this forgiving?" I spat. "You're nothing but a coward hiding behind stolen power."

His jaw tightened, and for a moment, I thought he might lash out. But instead, he straightened, his expression hardening into something even colder. "Keep moving," he barked to the others, shoving me forward.

The ground beneath us shuddered violently, cutting him off. A sharp crack split the air as the earth groaned and shifted. I stumbled, my heart leaping into my throat as the rock beneath my feet gave way, crumbling into a narrow ravine that hadn't been there a moment ago.

"Asher!" I scrambled back, my hands scraping against the sharp stone as I struggled to find solid footing.

"I've got you," he said, grabbing my arm and pulling me to safety just as another tremor shook the mountain.

We both froze, staring at the gaping rift that had torn through the earth. A dark, pulsing light shimmered faintly in the depths, its edges frayed and writhing like smoke. My stomach twisted as the familiar hum of magic reached me, sharper and more malevolent than before.

The Veil.

This tear was different from the one I'd seen in the forest. It was deeper, darker, the shadows within it almost alive. Tendrils of black mist coiled outward, brushing against the edges of the ravine like they were searching for something—or someone.

My skin prickled as the magic tugged at me, a cold, relentless pull that made my breath catch. "It's here too," I whispered, the words trembling on my lips. "It's spreading."

Asher's gaze darted to me, his jaw tightening. "You can feel it?"

"Of course I can feel it!" I snapped, taking a shaky step back. The Veil's magic crawled under my skin, familiar and horrifying all at once. "It's unraveling, Asher. This isn't just some curse—it's tearing the world apart."

He didn't answer, his eyes fixed on the rip as if it might reach out and pull us in.

A low rumble echoed through the mountain, and I felt the ground shift again, this time beneath my soul. This wasn't just an earthshake. This was a warning.

"Come on, we need to get to Kael." Asher yanked on my ropes, practically dragging me with him.

The rain lashed at us with unrelenting force as we trudged along the muddy path. My boots slipped against the wet ground, but Asher's grip on the rope kept me from falling completely. The storm raged on, a cacophony of thunder and wind that seemed to grow louder with every step. It wasn't just the weather—it was the magic. The pulse I'd felt earlier was stronger now, vibrating through my very bones.

Whatever was coming, it was close.

I stumbled again, and Asher yanked the rope impatiently. "Stay on your feet," he snapped.

I shot him a glare over my shoulder. "Maybe if you didn't tie me like a hog, I'd have an easier time."

He didn't respond, his attention fixed ahead. His men flanked us, their faces grim as they navigated the treacherous path. The red sand clung to our boots, glittering like blood in the faint light of the approaching dawn. The storm's wrath seemed to paint the landscape in shades of chaos, and I couldn't shake the feeling that it wasn't entirely natural.

The pull of the shard—or whatever magic was tangled with it—was growing unbearable. It wasn't just calling to me anymore; it was screaming. Each pulse sent a wave of heat through my chest, like a heartbeat that wasn't mine. I staggered under its weight, my breath coming in shallow gasps.

"What's wrong with her?" one of Asher's men muttered, his voice barely audible over the storm.

"She's feeling it," Asher replied, his tone clipped. "Kael's magic."

His eyes flicked toward the horizon, where the storm clouds churned in restless fury. He didn't look confident. He looked worried.

Good. He should be.

I stumbled again, this time falling to my knees. The rope burned as Asher yanked me upright, and I gasped, the magic's pull nearly overwhelming me. "Who is Kael?" I demanded, my voice cracking. "Why does his magic feel like this?"

"Shut up and keep moving," Asher snapped, dragging me forward.

But I couldn't shut it out. The storm, the magic, the pulsing energy that vibrated through the air—it was all too much. My head throbbed, my vision swam, and for a moment, I thought I might collapse entirely. Yet even through the haze of pain and exhaustion, I felt something else.

Hope.

Because the storm wasn't random. The magic wasn't random. It was him.

Rhayne.

I didn't know how, but I knew. The storm's fury, the way the waves churned with violent purpose—it was him. It had to be. And if he was close, if he was coming for me, then I just had to hold on a little longer.

Asher's grip tightened as he pulled me forward, his pace quickening. He didn't realize it yet, but his time was running out. And when Rhayne found us—and I knew he would—there would be hell to pay.

The rain lashed against my skin, sharp as needles, as we trudged higher up the jagged cliffs. My legs burned with every step, exhaustion weighing down on me like lead. I had no idea how long we'd been climbing but the storm only seemed to grow fiercer. Thunder cracked overhead, a deafening roar that made me flinch every time, and the wind whipped so fiercely it felt like it might tear me off the narrow path.

The heart called to me.

I didn't understand how I knew, but the sensation was undeniable—a rhythmic pulse thrumming in my chest, in time with the storm's furious beat. It was faint at first, like the whisper of a heartbeat beneath layers of noise, but the further we climbed, the stronger it grew. As if it were countering Kael's magic.

Each pulse was like a thread pulling me forward. Or backward. I couldn't tell. My thoughts flickered back to my father's dying words—*Rhayne... heartmate*—and the truth he'd revealed about the Veil. He had been trying to protect me, to stop this exact situation from unfolding. But now, here I was, climbing a gods-forsaken mountain in the Crimson Coast toward an evil I couldn't see, only feel. I was certain whoever Kael was, he was what the Veil was supposed to protect us from... his magic felt wrong, dark, and unlike anything I'd ever felt before.

"Keep moving!" Asher barked, shoving me forward when I faltered on a loose rock. My wrists strained against the coarse rope that bound them. I bit back a curse, stumbling but refusing to let him see me falter more than necessary.

The storm's howls drowned out my thoughts. I swallowed hard, pressing forward despite the growing ache in my ribs and the sharp sting of rain cutting into my cheeks.

The storm shifted suddenly, the wind howling in a different pitch, and I stopped dead in my tracks. The heart's pulse surged, almost like it was in sync with the storm itself. My chest tightened, and my breath hitched.

"What was that?" Asher's voice snapped through the gale, sharp and suspicious.

I shook my head, keeping my expression blank. "Nothing. Just… trying not to fall off this gods-forsaken cliff."

But Asher wasn't convinced. His dark eyes narrowed, tracking my gaze to the satchel slung across his chest. He stepped closer, his boots crunching against the wet rock. "You're not a very good liar. I know you, Briar. Years of being your friend, I know when you're lying."

My stomach flipped. I glared at him. "You don't know me."

"We'll see," he hissed, his voice barely audible over the storm.

I rolled my eyes, feigning exhaustion. "Whatever you think I can do, you're wrong."

He wasn't buying it. He grabbed my arm, spinning me around to face him. "Don't lie to me. You're the key to all of this, and we both know it."

"And who told you that? Kael?" I tried to yank my arm back, but his grip tightened, making me wince.

"Enough," he growled. "You think I haven't noticed? You think I don't see how this pulls at you?" He lifted my satchel, flaunting the brown leather. "How you look at it like it's speaking to you? You know more than you're letting on."

I leaned in slightly, a bitter smile tugging at my lips. "You think you're so clever, don't you? You think you can force the answers out of me like some cheap trick?" My voice dropped, cold and biting. "Here's the truth: I don't know anything about the Veil or the crystal in that bag. I don't know what that stupid map wants. And I don't know why you think I would help you. But I promise you, Asher, if there is magic out there—it doesn't like you."

His jaw clenched, and for a moment, I thought he might strike me. Instead, he shoved me back, hard enough that I nearly lost my footing. "Careful," he said, his tone low and dangerous. "Keep pushing me, and you'll find out just how far I'm willing to go."

The storm continued its wrathful symphony as Asher barked orders to his men, securing my bindings tighter and forcing me to move again.

The relentless climb was killing me. My legs trembled with every step, and the bindings around my wrists burned like fire. My breath came in shallow gasps, and the world tilted and blurred at the edges. The storm wasn't helping, its fury battering against me with the force of a hundred angry gods.

Each step felt like dragging a boulder uphill, and yet I forced myself to keep going, if only to deny Asher the satisfaction of seeing me collapse. He was always just a step behind me, his eyes sharp and calculating, watching me like a hawk.

The heart's pulse had dimmed, and I wasn't sure if it was because we were moving further away from whatever it was calling to or if I was just too exhausted to feel it anymore.

"Keep moving," Asher snapped, shoving me forward when I stumbled over a loose rock.

I bit back a retort, too drained to even glare at him. His men trudged ahead, forming a loose line that looked more disorganized than intimidating. They weren't used to the terrain any more than I was. If I weren't bound, if my legs didn't feel like lead, I might've taken advantage of that.

But what would be the point? Even if I escaped, I had no idea where we were or how far I'd get before the storm swallowed me whole.

"Pick up the pace," Asher barked again, and his tone made my teeth grind.

"Why don't you carry me, then?" I snapped back, my voice rasping from disuse.

His jaw tightened, but he didn't respond, which I counted as a small victory. The group pressed forward, and I focused on putting one foot in front of the other, the world blurring into rain and rock and misery.

I didn't notice we'd stopped until I nearly walked straight into one of the men in front of me. He turned, glaring, but Asher silenced him with a sharp gesture. The group had gathered near the edge of a rocky outcropping, overlooking a stretch of forest that seemed to drop into nothingness below. A small cave hid behind the trees.

Asher stepped forward, the wind tearing at his coat, and turned to face his men. "We camp here," he announced, his voice cutting through the storm. "We're close. One more day, and we'll be there."

My heart stuttered. One more day?

I sagged against the nearest boulder, too tired to care if anyone saw. Asher's men began setting up a crude shelter, their movements sluggish and clumsy in the storm. The wind howled louder, and I closed my eyes, trying to block out everything but the pounding in my head.

Close. That's what Asher said. Close to what? Where will we be? I didn't know of anything that was in these mountains.

"Don't get comfortable," Asher muttered, crouching beside me. His face was shadowed, rain streaking down his cheekbones like tears. "You'll be in there tonight." He gestured to the cave.

I forced my eyes open, fixing him with a glare. "Why are you doing this?"

His lips curled into a humorless smile. "If you think really hard, you already know the answer."

"Enlighten me," I said dryly, even though my pulse raced. He leaned in, and for the first time, I saw something raw and desperate in his expression.

"The Veil," he said quietly. "Power is worth the sacrifice, and there is no greater power than the barrier between the realms."

I froze, my mind spinning. "And you want me to destroy it? Asher, that doesn't make sense."

His hand shot out, gripping my chin and forcing me to meet his gaze. "If it's destroyed then everything it is hiding can become mine."

"And you truly think that whatever is in the other realm will just hand over its power to you?" My voice wavered despite my effort to sound defiant.

His smile turned sharp and cold. "I know that there will be nothing stopping me from taking what should be mine."

My blood turned to ice. The Veil wasn't just some relic—it was a barrier, something that kept... things in their place. If Asher wanted to destroy it, to rip open the realms, there was no telling what kind of chaos he'd unleash.

"You're insane," I whispered.

He stood, towering over me like a storm cloud. "Maybe. But I'm also right. And you're going to help me prove it."

The crystal's pulse throbbed faintly against my skin, and for the first time, I felt the weight of what was at stake. My father's warnings hadn't been just about protecting me—they'd been about protecting the world.

"If Asher thought the mountain could keep her from me, he underestimated the fury of the tide and the man bound to it."

RHAYNE

he enemy was unrelenting, their attacks a tide that refused to ebb. My blade sang through the air, striking down another man foolish enough to step into my path. The crimson sand beneath us was slick with blood, but the battle was far from over. Every swing of my sword, every surge of water I summoned, was a push against the growing weight of exhaustion. And still, they kept coming.

The storm churned above, its winds howling in my ears. Enric and Nyx fought fiercely beside me, their magic weaving through the chaos. Nyx's tethers snapped around an attacker, wrenching him off his feet and slamming him into the jagged rocks. Enric's winds roared, scattering arrows before they could find their mark.

The ground shook with a deafening crack as the mountain threatened to split apart. I felt Briar's panic through the bond and my heart raced. She told me she was almost swallowed by the ground once, and I imagined her falling into a fissure to her death. But she was still alive. I felt her heartbeat next to mine like an echo. Her panic changed to anger... anger I could handle. Hold on, little thief. Be angry. I'm coming.

But then, the shadows shifted, unnaturally thick and cold. A low growl echoed from somewhere deeper within the mist. My stomach twisted as a foul scent, like rot and iron, seeped into the air. I didn't need to see them to know what was coming.

Shadowborne.

The first one emerged like a nightmare given form— its figure gaunt, almost skeletal, but unnervingly fast. Its claws scraped against the rocks, teeth snapping as it lunged for one of the attackers. The man's scream cut through the night as the creature tore into him, dark ichor spilling from its maw.

"Fall back!" I roared to my crew, my voice carrying above the chaos. "Don't let them get too close!"

The Shadowborne weren't just beasts—they were a plague. The curse that twisted them spread like wildfire though we knew not how. It was said claw marks, bites, or even the faintest touch could infect fae. Fever would follow, then madness, and finally... transformation. I wasn't taking any chances with my crew.

Another creature lunged from the darkness, its glowing, inhuman eyes locking onto me. I raised my blade, slicing through its gnarled arm as it swiped at my chest. The limb fell to the ground, writhing like a severed snake. The creature howled, an ear-piercing wail that sent shivers down my spine, but I didn't falter. One clean strike through its neck silenced it for good.

"Enric!" I barked. "Push them back! Use the wind to keep them away!"

Enric's magic surged, a powerful gust tearing through the mist and shoving the creatures toward the cliff's edge. Several of them stumbled, their clawed feet scrabbling for purchase on the slick rocks. One slipped, its twisted body plummeting into the crashing waves below.

Nyx appeared beside me, his usually calm demeanor strained. "They're too fast. If we don't end this quickly, someone's going to get—"

A sickening snarl cut him off, and we turned just in time to see one of the Shadowborne leap for one of our crew. The young man, Orrin, dodged, but wasn't quick enough. The creature's claws raked across his chest. My heart stopped for a beat.

"Nyx, pull him back!" I commanded.

Nyx's tethers whipped out, wrapping around Orrin's waist and yanking him away from the fray.

Another wave of fury surged through me, and I let it loose. The ground trembled as water exploded from the rocky shoreline, a wall of liquid fury that swept through the remaining Shadowborne. Their wails echoed into the night as the wave carried them away, leaving only silence in its wake.

I stood there, chest heaving, my sword slick with ichor. The coast was littered with bodies—both human and not—but we were alive. For now.

I ran over to Orrin. He stumbled, wide-eyed and pale. Blood seeped through his fingers as he gripped his chest, his breath coming in shallow gasps. The deep gashes tore through flesh and muscle, and the sight of it churned my stomach. I dropped to my knees beside him, my blade still slick with ichor, and pressed a hand to his shoulder.

Orrin, barely older than a boy, looked up at me with wide, terrified eyes. His lips moved, but the only sound that came out was a wet gurgle. My throat tightened as I saw the truth written across his face—the wound was too deep.

Nyx crouched beside me, his expression grim. "Captain…"

I silenced him with a sharp glare, my mind racing for a solution. But as the moments passed, the reality of the situation sank in. The claws that had raked across him weren't just sharp—they carried the curse. We didn't know how it spread, but this wound… this was no ordinary injury.

Enric approached, but his steps faltered when he saw the gashes. His magic stirred the wind around us, a faint, uneasy rustle that mirrored my own turmoil. "We can't save him, not from this."

I clenched my jaw, fighting against the wave of fury and helplessness crashing over me. The boy's chest heaved as he tried to speak again, his eyes darting between me and the crew.

"Please…" he rasped, barely audible. "Don't… let me turn."

My breath caught, and the world seemed to narrow to just the two of us. The storm raged behind me, the wind howling through the cliffs, but all I could hear was the faint, desperate plea in his voice.

He knew.

My hand tightened on the hilt of my sword. The blade felt heavier than it ever had, the weight of what I had to do pressing down on my shoulders. Around us, the crew stood in somber silence, their expressions a mix of sorrow and grim understanding.

I met his gaze, my voice steady despite the ache in my chest. "You'll have honor, lad. You won't suffer."

His lips trembled, but he nodded, a single tear slipping down his cheek. "Thank you... Captain."

I rose to my feet, gripping the sword tightly. The crew parted, giving us space, their heads bowed in respect. Even Nyx and Enric stepped back, though their gazes lingered on the boy with unspoken sorrow.

The blade gleamed faintly in the moonlight as I raised it, my magic humming faintly beneath my skin. "You fought well, Orrin," I said, my voice carrying over the sound of the storm. "And you'll be remembered as one of The Tidecaller's own."

He closed his eyes, his lips moving in a silent prayer or perhaps a farewell.

I didn't hesitate. The blade came down cleanly, a single strike that ended his suffering before the curse could claim him.

The moment it was done, I stood there, the weight of the act pressing down on me like the tide. The storm seemed to ease for a moment, the winds softening, as if the sea itself mourned his loss.

Enric knelt beside the body, his magic stirring the air as he whispered a quiet blessing. The crew began to gather, their faces somber but resolute.

As I turned back to the cliffs, the storm surged again, mirroring the fury burning inside me. I couldn't let this happen again.

"Let's move," I said, my voice sharp with determination. "We're not stopping until we find her."

Nyx stepped closer, his expression grim. "The curse... it's spreading faster than we thought."

I nodded, wiping the blade clean in the coarse sand. "And we're running out of time."

The grit bit against the steel as I worked, each scrape a reminder of the lives taken—and the one I'd just ended. My hands moved on instinct, though my chest felt hollow. The boy deserved better, but the curse offered no mercy, and neither could I.

The air around me was thick with the stench of blood and sweat, mingling with the acrid tang of Shadowborne decay. The sand beneath my boots was wet, stained darker than the crimson coast's natural hue. Somewhere behind me, Nyx and Enric were securing the remaining perimeter.

The silence was heavy, punctuated only by the distant crash of waves and the faint rustle of wind through the mist. Enric joined us, his usually calm expression strained.

"We can't keep fighting like this," Enric said, his voice low but carrying the weight of truth. "The Shadowborne are relentless, and we still don't know how the curse spreads. A scratch? A bite? Proximity? We're guessing blind."

I turned to him, my jaw tightening. He wasn't wrong, but there was no room for retreat, no space for hesitation. Not with Briar out there, somewhere ahead of us. The thought of her alone, unarmed, possibly facing the same monsters we'd just fought, worried me.

310

"We don't stop," I said, my voice firm. "We push forward."

Nyx's tethers shifted uneasily, the faint hum of his magic brushing against my senses. "The crew's tired, Rhayne. They won't say it, but they're looking to you. We need a plan."

"They need rest," Enric added. "Even you can't carry them all."

I shook my head, the weight of leadership settling heavily on my shoulders. "They can rest when Briar is safe."

The words left me harsher than I intended, but I didn't care. Every moment we lingered here was a moment wasted, a moment Asher and his men dragged her further from me. The faint pulse of the bond between us still thrummed in my chest, a lifeline that refused to fade, but I knew better than to rely solely on that fragile connection. It wasn't enough—not yet.

Enric touched my arm, his magic sparking faintly against my skin. "We'll find her, My King. But we have to be smart about this. If we lose more men, we're no good to her— or to you."

I swallowed hard, my throat dry. They were right, damn them, and the logic stung like salt in an open wound. I exhaled sharply, running a hand over my face. "Fine."

Nyx tilted his head toward the jagged cliffs rising ahead. "There's cover up there. Enough for the crew to catch their breath."

I nodded once, curtly. "Do it. And keep your eyes sharp."

The two men moved to relay the orders, leaving me alone with the weight of my thoughts. The tide churned against the coast, the rhythmic crash of waves an echo of the storm still brewing in my veins. I turned my gaze toward the path ahead, the jagged rocks and crimson sands a relentless reminder of the fight still to come.

Briar's presence pulsed faintly at the edge of my awareness, a distant echo that refused to fade. She was alive. She had to be. But every step forward brought us closer to the unknown—closer to whatever Asher and his accomplices had planned.

I pressed my fingers against the hilt of my blade, the steel cool and reassuring beneath my grip. "Hold on, Briar," I muttered under my breath. "I'm coming."

The crew was quiet as we broke camp at the first light of dawn. The red sands of the Crimson Coast glimmered under the morning sun, stark and unforgiving. Despite the brief respite, tension clung to the air, a heavy weight on everyone's shoulders. The faint tang of Shadowborne decay still lingered, a grim reminder of what we'd faced the day before.

Nyx's tethers slid silently over the sand as he surveyed the horizon. "No signs of movement," he reported, his voice low but steady. "Whatever ambushed us last night isn't following."

I nodded, though my grip tightened on the hilt of my sword. The Shadowborne didn't care about time or reason. They'd come again if the opportunity arose, and we couldn't afford to be caught off guard.

I straightened, turning to look at the crew. Exhaustion lined their faces, but their resolve hadn't cracked. "She's close. I can feel it. And we don't leave this coast without her."

The murmurs of agreement that rippled through the crew bolstered my resolve. They didn't need speeches—they needed direction, and I'd give it to them.

Nyx stepped closer, his tethers curling around his wrist like restless snakes. "There's a path ahead, narrow but manageable. It'll take us higher into the cliffs."

"The higher we go, the more exposed we are," Enric cautioned, his magic flickering faintly in the breeze. "But it might also give us a vantage point to spot them."

The climb was grueling, the red sand giving way to jagged rocks that bit into our boots. The wind howled around us, carrying the salty tang of the sea and something else— something darker. I felt it in my chest, a faint echo of Briar's presence that pulsed like a heartbeat, guiding me forward. She was still alive. That much I knew. I'd know it until she wasn't.

The path narrowed as we ascended, forcing us to move single file. The cliffs loomed on either side, their shadows long and oppressive. The sense of being watched prickled at the back of my neck, but I pressed on, my focus unyielding.

At the crest of the ridge, Nyx froze, his tethers snapping taut around him. He raised a hand, signaling for us to stop. "There's something ahead," he whispered, his eyes narrowing as he peered through the haze.

I stepped up beside him, my magic stirring in response to the tension in the air. The landscape stretched before us—a narrow plateau littered with signs of recent activity. Boot prints marred the red sand, and scraps of fabric fluttered in the wind, caught on jagged rocks.

"They were here," Nyx confirmed, his voice tight. "Not long ago."

Enric crouched beside one of the prints, his fingers brushing the sand. "Two groups, by the looks of it. One leading, one following."

"They're moving fast," I said, my chest tightening.

"Captain," one of the crew called out, his voice urgent. He stood near the edge of the plateau, holding up a piece of torn fabric. It was dark, faded by the elements, but unmistakable.

It was from Briar's jacket. The same one I gave her from my chest. My family crest stitched into the fabric.

My heart thundered as I took it from him, the rough texture biting into my palm. She had been here.

"If I didn't know better, I'd say she left this," Nyx said quietly, his gaze sharp. "She's trying to leave a trail."

Knowing she knew I'd come for her made my heart swell. I turned my gaze toward the horizon, the cliffs stretching endlessly into the distance. The storm in my chest raged on, the pull of the bond guiding me forward. Briar was out there, and I wouldn't stop until I found her.

"He looked ready to set the world on fire, and for the first time, I believed he'd do it for me."

BRIAR

The night had been colder than any night I'd ever experienced. Morning was doing nothing to help warm me. I shivered and wrapped Rhayne's jacket around me tighter. My fingers were numb as I gripped the worn fabric.

The sound outside the cave was deafening, as if the squall itself was coming closer.

The stone walls of the cave trembled with a force that felt like the world itself was splitting apart. Dust rained down from the ceiling. The wind raged, screaming as if it carried the wrath of the gods. It was no ordinary storm—it felt alive, angry, purposeful. The kind of tempest that could tear ships apart and swallow men whole.

And then I heard it.

"Where is my wife?!"

The voice boomed across the cliffs, cutting through the storm like a blade. It wasn't just loud—it was thunderous, carrying with it an authority that seemed to shake the earth itself. My heart stopped, then raced as the word echoed in my mind: *wife.*

Rhayne.

I froze, my breath catching in my throat. The raw power in his voice was unmistakable, as was the undercurrent of fury that made my blood run cold. I clutched the rope binding me, my knuckles white as I fought to process what I'd just heard. The storm wasn't just nature's wrath—it was his. The Pirate King was here, and his fury felt as vast and unyielding as the sea he commanded.

Hope flared in my chest, fragile and wild, before being drowned out by an equally strong wave of fear. I had no doubt he would rip apart anything—or anyone—standing in his way. I'd seen him command storms before, watched the ocean itself bow to his will. But this... this was different. This wasn't the calculated, commanding man I'd come to know. This was something primal, untamed, and terrifying.

Another tremor rocked the walls, and I heard a guard outside mutter something, his voice tinged with fear. I couldn't make out the words, but I could feel the unease thick in the air. Whatever loyalty or courage they had was faltering in the face of Rhayne's wrath.

"Where is she?!"

His voice came again, more focused this time, and I flinched despite myself. It was as if he were speaking directly to me, his words reverberating in my chest. I felt a pull deep in my gut, something intangible but undeniable, like a thread tugging at the core of my being. My magic stirred, responding instinctively to his call. I didn't understand it, but I felt it as surely as I felt the cold stone beneath me.

He came for me.

The thought hit me like a hammer. He was here, tearing through whatever stood between us. For me. My chest tightened, my mind reeling. Why would he risk so much? Why unleash this kind of fury, this storm, for someone like me? I was just a thief, caught in a web of magic and misfortune. Yet here he was, calling for his wife with a ferocity that could split the heavens.

My throat tightened. *Wife.* That word was a noose, both binding and freeing in ways I couldn't fully comprehend. The bond between us—the marriage we'd been forced into—had always felt like a shackle. Yet now, hearing him claim me with such unyielding resolve, it didn't feel like a trap. It felt like... safety.

I shook my head, trying to banish the thought. I couldn't afford to think like that, to let hope take root. What if he didn't find me in time? What if Asher and his men took me further, or worse, used me as bait for whatever game they were playing?

But even as fear clawed at my mind, I couldn't shake the warmth blooming in my chest at the sound of his voice. For the first time since being dragged from Silverveil, I felt the stirrings of something I hadn't dared to hold onto—faith. Faith that he would find me, that he would move heaven and earth if that's what it took.

The storm intensified, the wind howling against the small opening of the cave. I craned my neck, trying to see through it, but all I caught were flashes of lightning, illuminating the jagged cliffs and the wild ocean beyond. The sheer magnitude of his power left me breathless.

"Where is my queen?!"

The shout echoed again, and this time, it wasn't fear that filled me—it was awe. I wasn't sure if I wanted to laugh or cry. Rhayne was terrifying and infuriating and more than a little reckless. But gods help me, he was here.

Tears pricked my eyes, unbidden and unwelcome. I swiped at them angrily, refusing to let the storm of emotions inside me match the one raging outside. There was no room for weakness here, not now. Not when Rhayne was risking everything to bring me back.

The guard outside the cave shouted something, but it was lost in the cacophony of wind and thunder. Another tremor shook the walls, dust falling from the ceiling like ash.

"Rhayne..." I whispered his name, the sound barely audible over the din. But somehow, I knew he would hear me. Or maybe he already had.

The walls trembled again, and distant shouts reached my ears, muffled but growing louder. My captors were scrambling. They'd underestimated him, thought they could keep me hidden, out of reach. They didn't understand who they were dealing with.

Another rumble shook the ground, this one closer. The sound of splintering wood and crashing stone made me flinch, but I couldn't tear my eyes away from the entrance.

And then I felt it—something deep and primal stirring within me. A pulse, faint but growing stronger, like a second heartbeat. It wasn't the crystal this time. No, this was something else. Something inside me. It thrummed in rhythm with the storm, with Rhayne's magic, as if answering his call.

I backed up against the far wall, my hands trembling. A guard stumbled into the cave with panic etched on his face. "Move!" he barked, grabbing me roughly by the arm. "We're leaving."

I twisted, trying to pull away, but he was stronger. "Let go of me!" I shouted, my voice rising over the chaos. The pulse inside me flared, and for a brief moment, the air around us seemed to hum.

The guard cursed, dragging me toward the outside. "We don't have time for this. That monster is going to bring the whole place down."

Monster. My lips pressed into a thin line. If only he knew the truth. Rhayne wasn't a monster—he was my husband.

We hadn't made it far when the another explosion of magic rippled across the ground and the stone walls around me. It wasn't a physical blast, but a surge of energy so fierce it left me gasping for breath. The walls cracked, bits of stone crumbling to the floor. The guard faltered, fear flashing in his eyes, and I took my chance. I slammed my elbow into his side with all the strength I could muster. He grunted, loosening his grip just enough for me to wrench free.

I didn't hesitate. I ran.

Outside was a mass of chaos. Shouts echoed from every direction, blending with the roar of the storm. The ground shook beneath me, the tremors growing more violent with every step. I had no plan, no idea where I was going. All I knew was that Rhayne was close, and I had to find him.

Another blast of magic rippled through the air, and I stumbled, catching myself against a tree. My vision blurred as the pulse inside me surged again, stronger this time. My magic. It wanted out.

The sounds of fighting grew louder, the clash of steel against steel ringing in the air. My heart leapt as I saw them—Rhayne and his crew, cutting through the enemy with a precision and ferocity that left me breathless. He was a force of nature, his blade moving faster than I could follow, his magic crackling like lightning in the air around him.

For a moment, I forgot to breathe. His presence was overwhelming, a storm made flesh, and every ounce of his fury was directed at those who had taken me. His voice boomed, commanding and unyielding, and the sight of him sent a jolt of something hot and fierce through me.

But I wasn't safe yet.

A figure loomed behind Rhayne, blade raised. I didn't think. The pulse inside me surged, and before I could stop it, the magic burst free. Despite still being bound together, a blinding light erupted from my hands, slamming into the attacker and sending him flying into the wall. He crumpled to the ground, unmoving.

A shimmer of the Veil cracked open where my magic had gone, revealing a splinter of something powerful. I gasped, watching as it stitched back together, closing tightly and vanishing from sight.

The light around my hands faded, leaving me shaking and breathless. My fingers tingled, the remnants of the magic sparking faintly before disappearing. I stared at them, horrified.

"Briar!"

Rhayne's voice pulled me back to reality. He was running toward me, his expression a mixture of relief and worry. I wanted to run to him, to throw myself into his arms, but my legs wouldn't move. My eyes stayed locked on my hands, the terror of what I'd just done stealing my breath.

"Briar," he called again, his voice softening as he closed the distance.

Before I could blink, his arms wrapped around me, pulling me into a crushing embrace. The force of it stole my breath, but it wasn't unwelcome. His hold wasn't just protective—it was grounding, solid, and real. The warmth of his body seeped into my cold, trembling frame, and for the first time in what felt like an eternity, I felt safe.

I buried my face in his chest, the scent of salt and storm clinging to him, and the tears I didn't know I'd been holding back spilled over. His hand came up to cradle the back of my head, his fingers threading gently through my hair.

"Briar," he murmured, his voice a rough whisper against my temple. "You're safe now. I've got you."

I pulled back slightly, just enough to look up at him. His storm-gray eyes locked onto mine, and for a moment, the rest of the world disappeared. There was no storm, no danger—just the weight of his gaze, heavy with emotion I couldn't quite unravel. Relief, worry, and... something deeper.

"Rhayne," I choked out, my voice trembling. "I—"

Before I could say another word, he cupped my face, his thumbs brushing away the tears that streaked my cheeks. His touch was firm but achingly gentle, and the intensity in his gaze stole whatever words I'd been about to say.

Then, without hesitation, he leaned down and kissed me.

It wasn't soft or tentative. It was fierce, consuming, as if he needed to prove to himself that I was really here, that I was alive and whole. His lips claimed mine with a passion that made my heart stutter, the desperation of the moment bleeding into every movement.

For a second, I forgot the fear, the pain, the chaos. All I felt was him—his strength, his warmth, his unwavering presence. My hands, trembling moments ago, found their way to his chest, clutching at his shirt as if letting go would send me spiraling back into the void.

When he finally pulled back, his forehead rested against mine, his breath coming in short, ragged bursts. His hands stayed on my face, holding me as if I might vanish if he let go.

"Are you hurt?"

I shook my head, swallowing hard. "No. But—Asher..."

"Where is he?" Rhayne's voice hardened, and the fury that had shaken the stronghold moments ago simmered dangerously beneath the surface.

I shook my head again, guilt curling in my stomach. "I don't know. He was with me, but when the fighting started, he..." My words faltered as shame burned my throat. "He must've slipped away."

Rhayne's jaw tightened, his gaze flicking past me to the cave I'd come from. His fingers flexed, and for a moment, I thought he might turn and charge after Asher on sheer will alone. But then his gaze softened, his focus shifting back to me.

"We'll deal with him," he said, though his tone carried the weight of a vow. "Right now, getting you out of here comes first."

The roar of battle ebbed slightly, though the tension in the air remained thick. Nyx appeared from the shadows, his magical tethers trailing faintly behind him like whispers of smoke. His expression was grim.

"There's no one left," he said. "But there is no sign of Asher."

A chill ran down my spine. There was one other unaccounted for. "Kael." I said it more under my breath, but Rhayne looked at me, cocking his head as if trying to understand. "I don't know who he is, but that's where Asher was taking me. He's the one we need to worry about. He's the one who shattered the Veil. He caused all of this and wants to destroy it completely."

Rhayne's eyes narrowed, his voice low. "He's behind this?"

I nodded. "Everything. The Veil. The curse. My father's death."

For a moment, Rhayne was silent, his expression a mask of control even as the storm in his eyes raged. I wanted to tell him everything right then and there, about my father's last words, about the truth of the Veil and what it meant for both of us. But there wasn't time—not yet.

I clenched my fists, pushing aside the gnawing ache in my chest. "I need my satchel," I said, my voice firmer now. "We can't let anyone get the crystal—or the map. If they get their hands on it, everything we're trying to stop will get worse."

Rhayne's gaze flicked to me, his intensity unwavering. "Can anyone else read the map?"

"I don't think so," I admitted. "But I'm not taking the chance."

A sudden burst of footsteps pulled our attention. Tavian emerged from the cave, my satchel clutched in his hands. His face was streaked with dirt and blood, but his grin was triumphant.

"Got it!" he called, jogging toward us.

Relief flooded through me as I reached out for the bag. The moment my fingers closed around it, I felt the faint pulse of the crystal inside, its magic humming in recognition. My heart skipped a beat, the connection between me and the Veil fragment sparking like a live wire.

But the relief was short-lived. Rhayne stepped closer, his hand brushing mine as he inspected the satchel. "If this Kael is as dangerous as you say, we need to move now. He won't stop until he gets what he wants."

29

"When I carried her back to the ship, the world around us didn't matter. She was safe."

RHAYNE

I was never letting her go. There was no magic strong enough, no force powerful enough, and absolutely no living creature man or otherwise that could rip me from her side.

I kept her close as we made our way back to the longboats, the storm finally easing around us. The air was thick with salt and the lingering charge of magic. Briar leaned into me, her steps faltering with exhaustion. I could see it in the way her shoulders sagged, the way her head tilted slightly against my arm. She wouldn't admit how much she was hurting, but I didn't need her to. I saw it. I felt it.

The moment she collapsed against me, I felt the fragile weight of her in my arms, her trembling breath brushing against my neck. Briar was too weak to stand, let alone walk back to the ship. Her defiance had carried her this far, but now it was up to me. I scooped her up, cradling her against my chest.

Her head rested against my shoulder, and the soft sound of her breathing, shallow and uneven, twisted something deep inside me. The storm of my magic still roiled just beneath the surface, begging for release, but I held it back. I needed clarity, not destruction. Briar needed me steady.

The trek back to the shore felt longer than it should have, each step a reminder of how vulnerable she was. Her wrists bore angry, raw marks from where the bindings had rubbed, and the smudges of dirt and blood on her skin told the story of her captivity. I gritted my teeth against the surge of rage that flared again. Those bastards would have paid twice over if I'd had more time.

"Rhayne," she whispered, her voice barely audible.

"I'm here," I said, my voice low but firm. I shifted her slightly, holding her closer. "I've got you."

Her eyes fluttered closed, exhaustion overtaking her again. The rise and fall of her chest against mine was a steady reassurance, but I couldn't stop glancing down at her, cataloging every bruise, every scrape. My mind whirred with a singular focus: get her back to The Tidecaller, where she could rest, where I could see for myself that she would recover.

By the time we reached the beach, the sky was darkening with sunset. The Tidecaller loomed in the distance, her masts a beacon against the horizon. Our crew worked quickly, preparing the longboats to take us aboard.

"My King," Enric murmured as he approached, his gaze flicking between me and Briar. "She'll be all right?"

"She will," I said, more for myself than him.

The longboat rocked slightly as I stepped in, but I kept her steady in my arms. Her head lolled against my chest, and I adjusted my hold, shielding her from the chill of the evening air. The rhythmic splash of the oars against the water was the only sound, and with every stroke, the tension in my chest began to ease.

When we finally boarded The Tidecaller, the crew parted instinctively, their gazes lingering on Briar. I didn't stop to address them. Instead, I carried her straight to our cabin.

Inside, the soft glow of a lantern illuminated the room. I laid her gently on the bed, her form almost lost among the blankets. For a moment, I just stood there, staring at her. The storm outside had calmed, but the one inside me still raged.

Her wrists drew my attention again—raw, inflamed, and smeared with dried blood. I fetched a basin of water and a clean cloth, my movements quick but careful. Returning to her side, I dipped the cloth into the water and wrung it out.

"Briar," I said softly, brushing a strand of hair from her face. Her eyes opened slowly, meeting mine with a flicker of awareness.

"You're fussing," she murmured, her lips curving in the faintest hint of a smile.

"And you're in no position to argue," I replied, my tone firm but edged with warmth.

She didn't resist as I gently took her hand, her wrist fitting far too easily in my grasp. I cleaned the wounds carefully, my touch as light as I could manage. Her sharp intake of breath made me pause.

"Sorry," I muttered.

"It's fine," she said, her voice steadier now. "I've had worse."

Her words were meant to reassure, but they only deepened my resolve. I finished with her wrists, then turned my attention to the other cuts and bruises that marred her skin.

"I need to see all of them," I said, my voice leaving no room for argument.

Her cheeks flushed, but she nodded. "Fine."

I helped her sit up, guiding her toward the small tub in the corner of the room. The crew had already filled it with warm water—an order I'd given before we'd even reached the ship.

"I can handle this part," she said, her voice a little stronger now, though there was still a flicker of hesitation in her eyes.

"No," I said firmly, meeting her gaze. "Not after what you've been through. Let me help."

She hesitated but didn't argue further. As she stepped into the water, I turned my back, giving her the space she needed to settle. When I turned around again, she was seated in the tub, the water lapping at her shoulders.

I knelt beside the tub, my hand brushing hers as I reached for the cloth. The moment was quiet, almost tender, and I found myself watching her—truly seeing her. The stubborn tilt of her chin, the fire that hadn't dimmed despite everything.

"Briar," I said softly, the name a vow on my lips.

She looked at me then, her blue eyes wide and searching. "Rhayne?"

"I almost lost you," I said, my voice rough. "I won't let it happen again."

Her breath hitched, and for a moment, the walls between us felt thinner than ever. I reached for her hand, lifting it to my lips. My kiss was light, a promise rather than a demand.

"You're mine, Briar," I said, my voice low but firm. "In every way that matters. This isn't just an alliance anymore."

Her gaze softened, her lips parting as if to respond. But instead of words, she leaned forward, her hand brushing against my cheek.

When her lips met mine, it was soft at first, hesitant. But as the kiss deepened, it carried all the unspoken words between us—the fear, the relief, the tentative beginnings of something more.

When we finally parted, her cheeks were flushed, her breathing uneven. "Rhayne..."

"Rest now," I said, brushing a thumb over her knuckles. "We'll talk more when you're stronger."

For the first time since I'd found her, she smiled—a real, genuine smile that lit up the room. And in that moment, I knew I'd do whatever it took to keep her safe, to keep her by my side.

The knock came before Corwin's familiar voice called through the door. "Captain, food's ready."

I turned to Briar, who was bundled in blankets on the bed, looking far too pale for my liking. "Come in," I called, keeping my voice steady despite the frustration simmering under my skin.

Corwin entered, carrying a tray laden with bread, cheese, and a steaming bowl of stew. His sharp eyes flicked to Briar, softening as he set the tray on the small table beside the bed. "For you, lass. You need to eat."

Briar murmured a quiet thanks, her voice hoarse from exhaustion. She shifted under the covers but made no move to sit up.

I grabbed the tray and settled it across her lap, crouching beside her to help. "Eat something," I said gently, brushing a stray lock of hair from her face.

She hesitated but picked up the spoon, dipping it into the stew. She barely managed a few bites before there was another knock at the door.

"Enter," I growled, already sensing it wouldn't be the last interruption.

Enric stepped in, his usual calm demeanor tinged with concern. His gaze darted to Briar, assessing her condition. "How's she holding up?"

"She's alive," I said curtly, my jaw tightening.

Briar lifted her spoon, attempting a weak smile. "I'm fine. Truly."

"You look like hell," Enric said bluntly, though his tone carried a trace of humor.

"She doesn't need reminders," I said, my voice cold enough to cut.

Enric raised his hands in mock surrender. "Just making sure our queen's still breathing. I'll leave you to it."

He ducked out just as Nyx entered, followed by Tavian. They barely waited for the door to close before crowding the small cabin.

Nyx's sharp gaze swept over Briar. "You gave us quite a scare," he said, his voice low but sincere.

Tavian nodded, his boyish face etched with worry. "I thought we'd lost you," he said, fiddling with the hem of his sleeve.

Briar looked overwhelmed but managed a soft laugh. "I'm tougher than I look."

I stood abruptly, towering over the intruders. "She needs rest, not all of you swarming in here like crows."

"But—" Tavian started, only to be silenced by a glare.

"She's fine," I said firmly, her health far too precious to me to allow them to linger any longer.

Before either could argue, Ciaus hobbled in, his bandages stark against his pale skin. "Wanted to see with my own eyes," he said, his voice rough but steady.

Briar's eyes softened at the sight of him. "You shouldn't be out of bed."

"It was nothing more than a mere scratch," he countered, leaning heavily on the doorframe.

That was enough. I stepped forward, herding them toward the exit with a pointed look. "Out. All of you."

Nyx chuckled, but didn't argue, ushering Tavian and Ciaus ahead of him. "Take care of her, Captain," he said, his voice laced with amusement.

Once the door closed behind them, silence finally settled. I turned back to Briar, who looked at me with a mixture of exhaustion and gratitude.

"They care," she said softly.

"I know," I replied, sitting beside her on the bed. "But they don't know when to leave well enough alone."

She smiled faintly and leaned back against the pillows, her eyes fluttering shut.

I stayed there, watching her until her breathing evened out, the lines of tension on her face easing. The storm in my chest hadn't settled—not entirely—but seeing her safe and finally resting calmed some part of me I hadn't realized was so deeply frayed.

Briar was my queen, my wife, my heartmate. And I'd guard her with everything I had.

The soft creak of wood pulled me from sleep. My eyes snapped open, instincts honed by years of vigilance kicking in. The moonlight filtered through the cabin's small window, casting pale streaks across the room. Briar was out of bed.

Her movements were careful, deliberate, as if she didn't want to wake me. She reached for her satchel, the faint glow of the map pulsing like a heartbeat in the dim cabin light. I watched her for a moment, my own pulse quickening—not from fear, but from the sight of her, the way determination and hesitation warred on her face. She didn't realize how much she carried, not just the map or the crystal, but the weight of everything between us.

"Briar," I said softly, my voice cutting through the quiet like a blade.

She froze, her hand hovering over the satchel. Slowly, she turned to face me, her expression equal parts guilt and defiance. "It's awake," she said, her voice barely above a whisper. "The map—it's trying to tell me something."

I pushed myself upright, the blanket pooling around my waist. "It can wait," I said firmly. "For one night, it can wait."

Her brow furrowed, her fingers curling into the strap of her bag. "But what if it can't? What if we miss something important—"

I was already out of bed, crossing the cabin to her. Gently but firmly, I took the satchel from her grip. "You're exhausted, Briar. You've barely eaten, barely rested. Whatever the map wants to show you, it will still be here tomorrow night."

Her lips pressed into a thin line, her shoulders tense. But when her gaze met mine, I saw the flicker of uncertainty beneath her stubbornness.

I set the satchel down, the map's glow dimming as I closed the flap. "Come back to bed," I said, my voice softer now. "You need this."

She hesitated, her arms wrapped protectively around herself. "I—"

I gently took her hand, careful of the bandages but let the warmth of her skin ground me. "Come," I murmured, leading her back toward the bed. She followed, though the tension in her body didn't completely ease until she was sitting on the edge of the mattress, her head bowed.

For a moment, we sat in silence, the distant crash of waves against the hull filling the space between us. When she finally spoke, her voice was quiet, weighted with something deeper. "I keep thinking about my father."

I stilled, watching her carefully. "What about him?"

She exhaled shakily, her fingers twisting in the blanket. "He left because of me. He knew they would come for me. He thought he could protect me by finding a way to fix the Veil—" Her voice broke, and she shook her head, her hair falling like a curtain around her face. "And now he's gone, and I'm still here, and nothing feels... fixed."

I reached for her, brushing a strand of hair behind her ear. "He was trying to protect you, Briar. That's not a weight you should carry."

She looked up at me then, her blue eyes glassy with unshed tears. "But I do. I carry all of it—the Veil, the crystal, this magic I don't understand. I don't even know who I am anymore."

"You're Briar Firethorn, daughter of Rowan and Selene Firethorn, thief extraordinaire, and wife of the Pirate King. You are my queen." I said, my voice steady. "You're stronger than you know. Stronger than the Veil. Stronger than this magic. And you're not carrying it alone."

I shifted, pulling back the blanket for her. "Come. Lie down." For a moment, I thought she might refuse, but then she exhaled a shuddering breath and moved to lie down.

When she stretched out, her back against the pillow, I sat for a moment longer, watching her in the dim light. Her eyes fluttered shut, but her breathing was shallow, restless. She wasn't going to fall asleep like this—not with whatever weight she was carrying. I eased down beside her, careful not to crowd her, and propped myself up on one elbow.

"You'll rest better if you let yourself breathe," I murmured, my hand brushing lightly against hers. She turned her face toward me, her eyes fluttering open again. There was something vulnerable in her gaze, and I couldn't look away, caught in the storm of it.

For a heartbeat, neither of us moved. Then, as if something inside her gave way, she shifted closer. Her head found its place against my chest, tentative at first, until she relaxed with a sigh. Her hand rested lightly over my ribs, her touch so delicate it sent a pang through me.

I lowered myself fully onto the bed, wrapping an arm around her as I pulled the blanket over both of us. She fit perfectly against me, as though this had always been meant to happen. I rested my chin lightly on the top of her head and felt her relax further, the weight of her body settling against mine.

For a long time, the silence stretched, broken only by the creak of the ship and the gentle lap of the waves against the hull. Her breathing evened, but I could feel the tension still coiled in her body, a storm yet to pass.

"I haven't told you how my father died," she murmured at last, her voice so quiet I almost missed it. Her fingers twisted in the fabric of my shirt, gripping it like an anchor.

I stayed still, giving her the space to speak. I'd learned long ago that sometimes silence carried more weight than words.

"He was a captive," she said, her voice trembling, each word laced with pain. "On that other ship." Her breath hitched, and I felt her tears against my chest before I heard the soft sob. "He was so beaten and sick. I tried to help him escape, I did… but…."

Her voice cracked on the last word, and my chest tightened. I couldn't imagine the weight of that memory, the helplessness she must have felt knowing she couldn't save him. My arms tightened around her instinctively, as though I could shield her from the ghosts of her past.

I ran a hand over her hair, smoothing the wild strands in a slow, steady rhythm. "You didn't deserve to carry that alone," I said, my voice rougher than I intended. "And he didn't deserve to die like that."

She shifted slightly, tilting her head to look up at me. Her eyes shimmered, unshed tears catching the moonlight. "I think he knew about you. Or maybe he knew you were coming?"

I cupped her cheek, brushing a stray tear away with my thumb. "Did you doubt it?"

For a moment, she didn't respond. Then she nestled back against me, her breath warm against my skin. "I don't think I ever truly gave up hope."

30

"She slipped through my fingers, and now I was left standing in the shadow of a monster I foolishly thought I could control."

ASHER

The silence after Rhayne's storm was deafening. My ears still rang with the echoes of his fury, and the sting of his power lingered in the air like the charge before lightning struck. I paced the dim cabin on the ship, my boots scuffing against the splintered floorboards.

I had nothing. No Briar. No Crystal. No leverage. Nothing.

Failure clawed at my chest, but the fear gnawing at the back of my mind wasn't of Rhayne. It was of him. Kael. The beastly shadow of a man I'd foolishly made a pact with. A predator in human skin. And now, with nothing to show for all my efforts, I was the prey.

The creak of the door snapped me from my thoughts, and I turned sharply. Kael stepped into the room, his hood pulled low, though it couldn't hide the glint of his eyes—cold and sharp as a predator's. His claws caught the faint light as he flexed his fingers, his movements slow, deliberate.

"I should kill you," Kael growled, his voice a guttural snarl that scraped along my nerves. "You promised me Briar."

I swallowed hard, fighting to keep my voice steady. "The Pirate King intervened. You saw what he did. He tore through my defenses like they were nothing."

Kael's lip curled, revealing sharp, inhuman teeth. "And yet you're still breathing. A pity."

I held my ground, though my pulse thundered in my ears. "You never told me Rhayne Whitehook was going to come for her."

He took a step closer, his claws clicking against the edge of the table as he loomed over me. "The Pirate King is the least of your worries."

I frowned, his words cutting through the haze of my panic. "I'm not fae. You can't infect me."

Kael stiffened, his claws retracting slightly as he straightened, a slight smirk twisting his features into a gruesome smile.

Magic unfurled around me, gripping my soul as if Kael could rip it from me without hesitation. I gasped as I was lifted from the ground by invisible hands choking the life out of me. I clutched at my chest, trying to break loose from the grasp.

He cocked his head. "I may not be able to infect you, but I can still kill you."

His magic released its hold on me, and I fell to the floor in a heap. I gasped for air. "Killing me won't get you what you want."

His gaze snapped to mine, a dangerous growl rumbling in his chest. "Maybe not. But it will be fun. For decades, I waited, banished to the Shadowborne realm like a criminal. All because I understood that mortals are beneath me. Beneath all fae." He crouched next to me, his voice like venom. "And I was right. You are nothing without me."

I staggered to my feet, standing over him. "I can see why you were tossed away and forgotten."

Kael's eyes glinted in the dim light. "I have never given a mortal a second chance, but you intrigue me. So I will make you a deal. You'll bring her back to me—or I'll tear you apart and find her myself."

The threat hung in the air like the blade of a guillotine. I nodded slowly, though my mind raced. Kael was a means to an end, a tool I could use to regain what I'd lost. But tools had a way of turning on their masters, and Kael was no ordinary beast.

"Fate wasn't supposed to look like this, wild, untamed, and wrapped in the arms of the man who turned my world upside down."

BRIAR

I lay in the silence of Rhayne's cabin, the rocking of the ship a steady rhythm that refused to lull me to sleep. My mind churned with too many unanswered questions. Why did he come for me? What was a heartmate? And why were my father's last words of Rhayne?

The faint creak of the door pulled my attention. Rhayne stepped inside, his presence as commanding as ever, even in the dim light of the lantern he carried.

"You're awake." He set the lantern down and met my gaze, his expression unreadable.

I pushed myself upright, my hands fidgeting with the edge of the blanket. "I couldn't sleep. Too much on my mind."

He crossed the room, sitting on the edge of the bed. "My little thief, your mind should never be so full you cannot sleep. Share with me. Give me the burden of carrying whatever weighs you down."

I hesitated, unsure how to begin, but the words tumbled out before I could stop them. "Why did you come for me? The bargain we made... it should be done. There was nothing forcing you to come for me."

Rhayne's jaw tightened, and for a moment, he said nothing. Then, his eyes met mine, steady and unflinching. "The bargain ended the same night it was made."

I blinked, his words sinking in. "What?"

"The night we made the bargain, I knew it wouldn't matter," he said, his voice low, steady. "I never intended to let you leave."

The air left my lungs in a rush, anger flaring hot in my chest. "You... you lied to me?"

"No," he said sharply, his tone softening almost immediately. "I would never force you to stay. Not then. Not now. But I couldn't let you go... not when I realized what you are to me."

His words hung in the air, heavy and unresolved. I searched his face, trying to understand what he wasn't saying. "What I am to you?" I asked cautiously.

He ran a hand over his face, his shoulders sagging slightly. "It was more than just vows to me, Briar. You are..." He stopped, his gaze flicking to mine, then away again, as if he couldn't bring himself to say it.

Frustration prickled under my skin. "What? What am I, Rhayne?"

Silence stretched between us until finally, he sighed. "You're my wife. That's real and binding, more than you understand. But you're also something more than that. Something I can't put into words."

His hesitation made my stomach twist. "Fine. But I have one more question? What is a heartmate?"

His head snapped toward me, his expression unreadable. For a moment, I thought he wouldn't answer, but then his voice dropped to a near whisper. "It's more than love. It's a bond beyond reason, beyond choice. A tether to the deepest part of your soul, something eternal and unyielding. Love can be fragile, fleeting—but a heartmate? It's an anchor, a force that doesn't waver, doesn't fade. It binds two souls so irrevocably, so completely that one cannot exist fully without the other. Briar," he whispered my name. "Without you I am incomplete."

My heart thudded heavily in my chest. "And you think..." I stopped myself, unwilling to finish the question, unsure if I wanted the answer.

He stepped closer, his presence overwhelming, his gaze unwavering. "I don't think, Briar. I know."

The room felt too small, the air too thick. I looked away, my fingers knotting in the fabric of my dress. "And what does that mean for me?"

"It means," he said, his voice soft but firm, "that no matter what choices you make, no matter where you go, I'll always come for you. Not because of duty. Because it's you."

My breath caught, emotions swirling too fast for me to catch hold of any of them. Anger. Confusion. And something softer, warmer, that I didn't dare name. "I... I don't know what to do with that."

"You don't have to," he said. "Not now. Not yet. But know this—I will never force you to stay. That choice is yours."

His words struck me like a blow I hadn't expected. I stared at him, his confession crashing against the walls I'd built to keep myself steady. My heart ached with the weight of it, and my mind rebelled against the impossibility of what he was asking me to accept.

"I need to think," I said, the words spilling out before I could stop them. My voice was steadier than I felt, but my hands betrayed me, trembling as I smoothed them over my shirt.

"Briar..." he started, then stopped himself.

The vulnerability in his tone made my chest tighten further, but I forced myself to move. Standing felt like wading through quicksand, every step away from him harder than it should've been. I needed space, air, anything to stop the chaos in my head.

The cabin door closed behind me with a soft click, and I stepped into the cool night. The wind caught my hair, whipping it against my face, but I barely noticed. I gripped the railing of the ship, the sea stretching endlessly before me. Waves crashed below, the sound a distant roar beneath the storm inside me.

What was I supposed to do with his words? That I was bound to him—not just by vows, but by something so much deeper it felt impossible to comprehend. A tether. A bond. A heartmate. My chest tightened, and I swallowed hard, my fingers gripping the railing until they ached.

Could I believe him? Could I trust what he felt for me? I had barely begun to understand this new life as his wife, let alone the weight of something as all-consuming as what he described. And yet... the way he looked at me, the way he said my name, made it hard to deny.

The wind picked up, cold and biting against my skin, but I stayed rooted in place, staring at the stars. They seemed so far away, like everything I wanted—answers, clarity, peace.

For now, all I could do was try to breathe through the storm, even as his words replayed in my mind, over and over again: *Without you I am incomplete.*

The ship swayed beneath me, but it wasn't just the water. *She* swayed. The Tidecaller's magic hummed softly, thrumming through the wood and into my fingertips as I leaned against the railing. It was faint, but undeniable, like the heartbeat of something ancient. Something alive. I could almost hear her, feel her watching me, waiting for something I couldn't name.

Then there was my own magic, bubbling just beneath the surface, restless and unformed. It didn't roar or demand— it simmered, waiting for me to reach out to it. But I couldn't. Not yet. It was too much, too unknown.

I pushed away from the railing, pacing the deck as the cool night air bit at my skin. I needed something tangible, something that made sense. My father had believed in me, trusted me to figure it out. But belief wasn't enough. Answers weren't going to fall into my lap—I had to find them. And the map was the only place to start.

I grabbed my satchel from where I'd left it and pulled out the map. Its surface glowed faintly in the moonlight, pulsing softly as though it was responding to me. With a deep breath, I unfolded it. The glow intensified, spreading across the parchment until the entire world shimmered before me.

Tiny markings darted across the map, winding along rivers, disappearing into mountains, and converging on larger markings that seemed to pulse with purpose. It was mesmerizing. Chaotic. But somehow, I knew it wasn't random. It all meant something.

The Veil.

I followed the marking with my fingers and watched as they lit up under my touch. The light rippled, rearranging itself with a fluid motion that made my breath hitch. The arrows twisted and danced, and then they stopped. A single arrow pulsed steadily, pointing directly behind me. Toward the cabin.

I stared at it, dumbfounded. "You've got to be kidding me," I muttered, holding the map closer. Its glow didn't waver, its intent clear.

I narrowed my eyes. "Really? After all this, you're telling me to go back *there*?" The map offered no response, of course, but its steady glow felt insistent, almost smug.

A laugh bubbled out of me, sharp and hollow. "You're awfully pushy for an enchanted piece of parchment, you know that?"

The map didn't change, but the glow seemed to intensify, as if it were doubling down on its answer. I sighed, rolling it up with more force than necessary. "Fine. But if this doesn't go well, I'm blaming you."

I tucked the map back into my satchel and leaned against the railing, the sea stretching out before me like an unspoken promise. It didn't help. The stars overhead glittered faintly, mocking my uncertainty with their unreachable stillness.

The Tidecaller hummed again beneath my feet, a steady pulse that matched the rhythm of my own restless thoughts. The answers I wanted weren't going to appear out of nowhere. I had to seek them. The map seemed certain it knew what I needed, even if I didn't agree. But for now, I could only follow its lead.

Straight back to the Rhayne.

I pushed off the railing and started toward the cabin.

I opened the door, stepping inside. Rhayne was exactly where I left him—leaning against the desk, his broad shoulders slumped slightly, his gaze fixed on the lantern's flickering light. He didn't look surprised to see me, but the tension in his posture eased the moment our eyes met. He'd been waiting.

"Decided to come back?" he asked, his tone carefully neutral, though his eyes betrayed something warmer. Relief? Worry?

I leaned against the doorframe, crossing my arms as if I hadn't just spent the past fifteen minutes battling my own indecision. "Not by choice. The map insisted." I yanked the rolled parchment from my satchel and waved it at him. "Apparently, it's got strong opinions about where I should be."

He stepped away from the desk, his gaze sharpening as it settled on me. "You were gone long enough to make me worry."

I rolled my eyes, even as his words sent an unexpected pang through my chest. "Worry? Really? I was on the deck, Rhayne, not dangling off the side of the ship."

"That doesn't mean I wasn't thinking about it," he muttered, his voice quieter, softer.

The vulnerability in his tone made me falter for just a moment. But I wasn't ready to face that—not yet. I tossed the map onto the desk with a flourish. "Well, you can relax now. The magical map brought me back in one piece. Feel free to thank it for its excellent work."

His lips twitched, but his eyes stayed serious. "You've got a talent for making me question every decision I've ever made."

A grin tugged at my lips, though my heart still pounded too fast. "Good. Keeps you on your toes."

"It does more than that." His voice was low, almost too quiet, and for a moment, his expression softened in a way that made my stomach twist. "Briar Firethorn, thief, pirate queen, bane of my sanity..."

"Wrong," I interrupted, stepping closer and raising an eyebrow. "That's not who I am anymore."

He arched a brow, curiosity sparking in his gaze. "No? Then enlighten me."

I tilted my head, letting a slow smile creep across my face as I closed the space between us. "I am Briar Whitehook, wife of Rhayne Whitehook, pirate queen, Veil guardian, and..." I paused for effect, tapping my chin with exaggerated thoughtfulness. "...the perpetual thorn in your side."

His laugh was low and rough, rolling through the cabin like distant thunder. "That last one's definitely true."

"I like to keep things interesting," I shot back, leaning casually against the desk.

"You do that, Briar." His voice softened, though the amusement still lingered in his eyes. "You've been doing that since the moment I met you."

The shift in his tone hit me like a wave, and for a moment, I couldn't hide from the weight of it. There was something in his gaze—something raw and unguarded—that made it hard to breathe.

I cleared my throat, desperate to shake the sudden tension. "Don't get too sentimental on me, Whitehook. The map says I'm supposed to be here, but it didn't say I have to like it."

His lips curved into a slow, infuriating smile. "You can pretend all you want, Briar. But you're here, and that means something."

"Does it?" I asked, tilting my head with mock curiosity. "Maybe it just means the map has a bad sense of humor."

"Or maybe it knows exactly what you need," he countered, his voice dropping into that low, steady tone that always managed to unnerve me.

I frowned, trying to ignore the way my pulse quickened. "What I need is to stop letting enchanted maps and self-righteous pirate kings tell me what to do."

Rhayne chuckled, shaking his head. "Keep telling yourself that, Briar. But I think you're starting to like being here."

"Even if I did, I would never admit it to you." I pushed off the wall, my steps slow and deliberate, closing the space between us.

Before I could take another step, Rhayne surged forward, his hands gripping my waist with a confidence that made my breath catch. He pulled me against him, his body solid and unyielding, his face just inches from mine. His gaze burned, a storm of emotions swirling in the depths of his eyes—desire, frustration, something deeper I couldn't name.

"Admit it or not," he murmured, his voice low and rough, "you were meant to be here."

I opened my mouth to argue, to deflect, but the words never came. His lips claimed mine, cutting off every thought, every protest. The kiss was slow at first, deliberate, like he was giving me the chance to pull away. But I didn't. I couldn't.

Heat coursed through me as I leaned into him, my hands finding their way to his chest, gripping the fabric of his shirt like it was the only thing keeping me grounded. His kiss deepened, his lips moving against mine with a need that stole the breath from my lungs.

His hands slid up my back, one tangling in my hair while the other held me closer. The world outside the cabin melted away, leaving only him—his touch, his warmth, the way he seemed to devour me like he'd been starving for this moment.

I should have pulled back. I should have said something snarky, something to regain control of the situation. But the way his mouth moved over mine, the way his fingers pressed into my skin, made it impossible to think of anything but him.

He broke the kiss just enough to catch his breath, his forehead resting against mine. "You're infuriating," he muttered, his voice thick with desire.

"Good," I whispered back, my lips brushing his as I spoke. "You're insufferable."

His laughter was low and rough, vibrating through me as he tilted his head and kissed me again, this time harder, deeper. The cabin felt too small, the air too thick, as my hands slid up to his shoulders, clutching at him like he was the only steady thing in my world.

He lifted me effortlessly, setting me on the desk behind him, his hands never leaving my body. His lips trailed along my jaw, down the curve of my neck, sending a shiver racing down my spine. I tilted my head, giving him access I couldn't believe I was offering, but the way he groaned against my skin erased any doubt.

"You drive me mad," he murmured against my collarbone, his voice barely more than a growl. "I can't get you out of my head."

"Good," I managed to say, though my voice was breathless, trembling under his touch. "I like it that way."

His lips returned to mine, stealing any chance I had to say more. The kiss was fire and hunger, leaving no space for hesitation. My hands tangled in his hair, pulling him closer as every nerve in my body screamed for him.

Time lost all meaning, the lines between us blurring until nothing else mattered. In that moment, there were no doubts, no questions—only him, only us, and the undeniable pull that tied us together, deeper than I could understand.

I was Briar Whitehook, heartmate of the Pirate King who was a better thief than me... he stole my heart with a bargain he never kept. And I would sail these seas, not as the woman I once was, but as the wife of the man who turned my world upside down and dared me to fight for it.

Together, we would face the unknown, bound by a love that defied reason and a destiny neither of us had chosen. The stars above and the tides below had set us on this path, and I knew there would be no turning back.

Whatever awaited us beyond the horizon, I would meet it head-on. Not just as Briar Whitehook, but as his equal, his partner, his match.

31.5

"I am Briar Whitehook, wife of the Pirate King, Queen of The Tidecaller, and a force of my own making."

BRIAR

The deck of The Tidecaller was quiet in the way that only followed chaos—a fragile kind of silence, where every creak of wood and hiss of the wind felt like a reminder of what they'd all just survived. The sea stretched calm and steady beneath a sky brushed with the fading glow of twilight, but it felt like the eye of the storm rather than the end of it. Something was coming. I could feel it in my bones.

Ciaus leaned against the railing near the ship's stern, his arm pressed protectively to his side where the bandages from his injury were hidden beneath his shirt. He was too pale for my liking, but he wore that expression most of the crew seemed to share—stoic, determined, and deeply unwilling to admit when he needed help.

I wasn't planning on approaching him. He didn't seem the type who appreciated small talk or company. But before I could talk myself out of it, my feet carried me toward him.

"You look like hell," I said, leaning casually against the railing beside him.

Ciaus snorted, the corner of his mouth twitching upward in something that might have been the ghost of a grin. "That's funny, coming from you."

I rolled my eyes, feigning indignation. "Touché."

For a moment, we stood in companionable silence, the wind tugging at my hair and the steady roll of the ship beneath us grounding me more than I cared to admit. My gaze flicked to his side, where his arm still rested. "How's the injury?"

"Better," he said shortly, though his tone didn't invite further questions. "The King, though—he'd prefer I stay out of the next fight."

"And are you going to listen?" I raised an eyebrow, already guessing the answer.

He gave me a sidelong glance, his lips curving into a faint, wry smile. "Not likely."

The honesty caught me off guard, and I let out a quiet laugh. "Well, don't keel over before we get wherever this map is dragging us."

His eyes flicked to the rolled parchment in my hands. "It's still glowing?"

"Like the blasted sun," I muttered, unrolling it against the railing. The lines on the map shimmered faintly in the fading light, their paths twisting and winding toward a pulsing mark farther west. It was mesmerizing and frustrating in equal measure, like a puzzle I was never meant to solve. "It's pointing us somewhere new, but I don't speak enchanted map, so your guess is as good as mine."

The sound of boots against the deck drew my attention. Tavian approached with a rope slung over his shoulder and an easy grin tugging at his lips.

"Well, well, if it isn't our fearless navigator," he said, tipping an imaginary hat to me.

"Fearless, huh?" I shot back. "That's generous."

Tavian shrugged, the grin widening. "You haven't run us into a kracken yet, so I'd say you're doing fine."

"High standards," I said dryly, though I couldn't help the faint smile that tugged at my lips.

Tavian's gaze shifted to Ciaus, his expression sobering. "How's the side?"

"Still attached," Ciaus replied with his usual bluntness.

Tavian narrowed his eyes, his tone more serious. "Try to keep it that way."

The two men exchanged a look that said more than words ever could—a mix of concern, camaraderie, and the kind of unspoken loyalty that only came from surviving battles together. Whatever history they shared, it ran deep.

"Don't suppose you've heard anything useful about where we're headed?" I asked Tavian, eager to shift the conversation.

"Useful? No," Tavian said, glancing toward the cabin where Rhayne was holed up. "But the Captain seems to think he can make hide or tail of it. He's been locked in there for hours, going over maps like a man possessed."

I sighed, tucking the glowing map under my arm. "Guess I'd better see what's so pressing."

"Good luck," Tavian said with a mock salute. "Try not to let him brood you to death."

I rolled my eyes, leaving them at the railing and headed toward the cabin.

The door creaked softly as I stepped inside, the warm glow of the lantern casting long shadows across the room.

Rhayne was at the desk, his broad shoulders hunched as he pored over a cluster of charts and the open journal that I'd seen him writing in earlier. He didn't look up right away, but the tension in his posture eased the moment he noticed me.

"You took your time," he said, his voice low and steady as always, but there was a hint of relief beneath it.

"I wasn't exactly rushing to get back here," I said, closing the door behind me with a soft click. "The map was very insistent, though. Practically dragged me."

He turned, leaning back against the desk and crossing his arms. The corner of his mouth twitched. "Did it now?"

"Don't look so smug," I said, walking toward him and tossing the map onto the desk beside him. "Your enchanted map has a real attitude problem. Always glowing, always pointing. You'd think it could at least use words to tell me what it wants."

"Words wouldn't make it less pushy," he replied, his eyes crinkling slightly with amusement.

I folded my arms, narrowing my eyes at him. "You're awfully calm for someone who sent me out there to deal with glowing maps and ominous seas."

His gaze softened, the teasing edge slipping away. "I was worried about you."

The sincerity in his tone made my breath hitch, but I quickly covered it with a scoff. "Worried? Please. I wasn't in any danger. You think I'd let some cursed map or restless tide get the better of me?"

His lips curved into a slow, infuriating smile. "Of course not. You're Briar Firethorn, the most stubborn thief I've ever met."

I rolled my eyes, stepping closer. "Wrong again, Captain. I'm Briar Whitehook, remember? Wife of Rhayne Whitehook, Pirate King, and..." I paused, tilting my head as if considering my next words. "...the pirate queen who's twice the trouble you bargained for."

His laughter was low and rich, rolling through the cabin like a warm tide. "I didn't bargain for you, Briar. I *lost* to you."

"Is that what you're calling it now?" I shot back, a smirk tugging at my lips. "Losing?"

He stepped forward, closing the space between us with an ease that made my pulse quicken. His eyes burned with something deeper than amusement now, something that sent a shiver down my spine. "If this is losing," he murmured, his voice dropping into that low, intimate tone that always managed to unnerve me, "then I don't ever want to win."

I swallowed hard, my witty retort dying on my tongue. The air between us was charged, heavy with the weight of everything unsaid. My heart thundered in my chest, but I didn't step back.

"Careful, Rhayne," I managed to say, my voice quieter now. "I might start believing you."

"Good," he said, his hands brushing against my waist as he leaned in closer. "Because I mean every word."

The warmth of his touch burned through the thin fabric of my shirt, and for a moment, I forgot how to breathe. His gaze held mine, steady and unrelenting, and the distance between us disappeared entirely as his lips brushed against mine.

For a moment, I froze, caught between the instinct to push him away and the undeniable pull that drew me closer.

But when his hand slid to the small of my back, anchoring me against him, the decision was made. I melted into him, my hands gripping his shirt like it was the only thing keeping me steady.

The kiss deepened, slow and deliberate, yet filled with a hunger that made my knees weak. His other hand came up, tangling in my hair, holding me in place as though he feared I might disappear. Every nerve in my body sparked to life, the warmth of him spreading through me like fire.

"Briar," he murmured against my lips, his voice rough and unsteady, like he was holding back a tide he couldn't control. My name on his lips made something in my chest tighten, and I pulled him closer, closing whatever space was left between us.

His kisses grew bolder, more demanding, and I matched him with a fierceness that surprised even me. My hands slid up to his shoulders, my fingers tangling in his hair, and he groaned softly in response, the sound vibrating through me in a way that made my heart race.

He lifted me effortlessly, his hands firm but careful as he placed me on the edge of the bed. His lips left mine, trailing down the curve of my jaw and along my neck, his breath hot against my skin. I tilted my head, giving him more access, and a soft gasp escaped me when his teeth grazed the sensitive spot just below my ear.

"You drive me mad," he murmured, his voice low and raw, as if the words were being torn from him. "Every moment since you walked onto this ship, I've fought to keep my distance. Losing you would destroy me."

His forehead rested lightly against mine, his breath warm against my skin. "But you're here, Briar. And every second I'm near you, I'm losing the battle. I tell myself I'm protecting you, but the truth is, I'm afraid of what happens if I let myself fall. And gods help me, I'm falling anyway."

The vulnerability in his tone cracked something inside me, leaving me breathless. His lips curved faintly, but it wasn't his usual confident grin. It was softer, almost hesitant. "But I can't keep pretending anymore. Not when every part of me is tethered to you."

His words hit me harder than I wanted to admit, but I didn't pull away. Instead, I tugged his face back to mine, claiming his mouth with a ferocity that made it clear I wasn't letting him go, either. For once, there were no questions, no doubts. Just us, tangled together in a moment that felt like it had been waiting for us all along.

The room felt smaller, the air heavier, as his hands roamed over me with a reverence that left me breathless. My own hands weren't still, sliding over the planes of his chest and down to his waist, committing every inch of him to memory. The fire between us burned brighter, hotter, until the rest of the world ceased to exist.

"Briar," he said again, pulling back just enough to rest his forehead against mine. His breath came in short, uneven bursts, his voice filled with something raw and vulnerable. "Tell me again..."

I met his gaze, my chest tight with the weight of his words. There was no escaping the truth—not for him, and not for me. "You're insufferable," I whispered, my voice steady despite the storm raging inside me.

"So you keep saying. Tell me anyway."

My lips grazed his as I matched his kiss. "I am Briar Whitehook, heartmate of the Pirate King."

His lips curved into a small, relieved smile before he kissed me again, this time slower, softer, but no less consuming. And as his hands drew me closer, grounding me in a way I hadn't thought possible, I let myself fall—not just into the kiss, but into him, into us.

The magic in the room pulsed, echoing as though the Veil itself approved of our union. A faint shimmer of light flickered beyond the window, revealing the rift we had been chasing. Just over the horizon—beyond the shoreline and mountains, deep within the heart of the Shadowmere Kingdom—something waited for us.

Something ancient. Something powerful. Something that felt both like a promise and a warning, its presence pressing against my senses even from this distance. Whatever it was, it held the answers we sought—or the end of everything we knew.

With the wind at my back and the sea beneath me, I sailed on, for a pirate's story is never truly done.

Acknowledgments

Writing a book is never a solo journey, and I am beyond grateful for the people who have supported me along the way.

To my family—your love, patience, and encouragement mean the world to me. To my husband, thank you for always believing in me, for putting up with my chaotic writing schedule, and for being my anchor when my imagination takes me out to sea. To my kids, who have grown into incredible humans, and to my bonus son, thank you for always cheering me on and embracing my stories.

To my readers—you are the reason these stories exist. Every message, review, and shared moment about my books keeps me going. Thank you for diving into my worlds, falling in love with my characters, and making this journey so special.

To my editor, beta readers, and critique partners—your insights, feedback, and keen eyes have shaped this book into something even better. I truly appreciate your time and dedication. A special thanks to Antoinette for putting up with my crazy deadlines!

To my fellow authors and the bookish community, your support, wisdom, and friendship make this career even more fulfilling. I'm so lucky to be part of such an amazing creative world.

Ashley, thank you for giving me the time to brainstorm and dive into this world. And yes, you were right... I was wrong. It is more than one book.

And finally, to the dreamers, the storytellers, and the ones who believe in magic—never stop chasing your stories. The world needs them.

PS. Jym, I stole the last of your "secret chocolate" during a late night writing session. Love you!

Author's Note

Dear Reader,

From the moment Briar and Rhayne's story took root in my imagination, I knew it would be filled with storms, fate, and the kind of love that refuses to be denied. I've always been drawn to tales of adventure, magic, and soul-deep bonds, and *On Fated Tides* became a whirlwind of all those things—wrapped in the mystery of the sea, the danger of the unknown, and the undeniable pull of heartmates.

This book is for the romantics, the dreamers, and those who believe in destiny. It's for those who long to stand at the edge of the world, to hear the whisper of the waves, and to fall hopelessly into a love story that feels bigger than time itself.

I can't begin to express my gratitude to you, my reader. Whether this is your first book of mine or you've been with me for a while, thank you for setting sail with me on this journey. Your love for these stories, your excitement, your messages, and your reviews mean more than I can ever say.

If you're anything like me, you're already wondering what's next. Fear not—Briar and Rhayne's journey is far from over. On Shadowed Shores is coming soon, bringing even greater stakes, deeper magic, and love that refuses to break, even in the face of darkness.

Until then, may the sea always call to you, and may you always chase the tides.

M.R. Polish

About the Author

M.R. Polish is an Amazon best-selling author with over 30 books published across multiple pen names. Known for her fantasy romance and captivating love stories, she weaves tales filled with fated mates, adventure, and powerful emotions, always delivering happily ever afters her readers crave. Her work includes fan-favorites like *Crown of Blood and Wings* and many more.

Out on the ocean is her favorite place to be, and if she could, she'd write from the deck of a cruise ship while exploring the world. But alas, adulting and responsibilities keep her (mostly) grounded.

M.R. is happily married to someone who would gladly follow her onto a ship and sail away. They have two fully grown adult children, one wonderful bonus son (son-in-law), and two more who are nearly out of the house. *GASP!* Family is at the heart of everything she does—whether it's crafting unforgettable love stories or planning the next great adventure.

Connect with M.R. Polish and explore her books at:

Thank you for reading!

I hope you enjoyed *On Fated Tides*, the first installment in *The Shattered Veil*. Briar and Rhayne's journey is just beginning, and the next chapter will bring even greater challenges, deeper bonds, and unexpected revelations.

If you're eager to continue their story, don't miss *On Shadowed Shores*, coming soon!

Want More?

Join my mailing list to receive updates on upcoming releases, exclusive sneak peeks, and special offers. You'll also gain access to bonus content, behind-the-scenes insights, and giveaways!

Sign up here: https://www.mrpolishauthor.com/newsletter

Let's Stay Connected

I'd love to hear what you thought of Briar and Rhayne's story! You can find me everywhere here:

Don't forget to leave a review! Reviews help authors like me reach more readers and mean the world to indie authors.

Also by M.R. Polish

Fantasy Romance – Fae, Pirates, Fated Mates
The Shattered Veil
On Fated Tides
On Shadowed Shores

Fantasy Romance – Vampire, Fated Mates
Ash Kingdom
Crown of Blood and Wings
The Fallen Ash Queen
Throne of Broken Wings

Fantasy Romance ~ Soulmates
Sandman saga
Shadow Moon
Day Break
Total Eclipse

Paranormal Romance ~ Stand Alone Novellas (shared world)
Pharos Hills Novellas
The Love Contract
A Delectable Bite
Changing Carma

Paranormal Romance ~ Stand Alone Novel (shared world)
Savage Vengeance

Paranormal Romance ~ Stand Alone Novel (shared world)
Ash and Scale

Paranormal Romance ~ Witches and Cowboys
Saddles and Spells Series
Saddles and Spells
Chaps and Cauldrons
Boots and Broomsticks
Pistols and Potions
Hats and Hexes
Ropes and Runes

Fantasy Romance ~ Greek Gods and Mermaids
Ageless Series
Ageless Sea
Endless Shores
Timeless Tides

Romantic Suspense ~ Stand Alone Novel
Change of Possession

Paranormal Romance ~Witches and Vampires
Wolf Series
Wolf Love
Wolf Spell
Wolf Dream
Wolf Fate

Dragon Fantasy - Epic (Co-Written with Bill Morgan)
Mysts of Santerrian
Mark of the Dragon
Orb of Incendia

Dark Romance / Mafia Romances (under Gracin Sawyer)

Men of Cardosa Ranch
Branding Lily
I'll Be What She Wants
Take Me Back
Whiskey burn

Want to be the first to know about new releases?

Sign up for my newsletter at **www.mrpolishauthor.com** and never miss an update!

Glossary & Pronunciation Guide

Welcome to the world of *The Shattered Veil*. Below is a guide to help with pronunciations and a glossary of key terms, locations, and magical elements in the story.

Pronunciation Guide

Briar (BRY-er) – The fierce, stubborn thief with a destiny greater than she knows.

Rhayne (RAIN) – The enigmatic fae pirate king, bound to the sea and its secrets.

Ciaus (KAI-us) – A cunning and loyal member of Rhayne's crew.

Nyx (NICKS) – A sharp-tongued rogue with a deadly skillset.

Tavian (TAY-vee-en) – A strategist with a past as murky as the deep.

Kael (KAY-el) – A powerful ancient fae, banished to the Shadowborne realm.

Asher (ASH-er) – A dangerous and calculating man working in the shadows.

Enric (EN-rick) – A man of unshaken loyalty, duty-bound to Rhayne and the kingdom he serves. Though his words are measured, his presence commands respect.

The Kraken (CRACK-en) – A well-known tavern in Everfell.

The Lore of the Sea & Shadows

Magic and the Veil

The Veil – A mystical barrier that once kept the Shadowborne Realm sealed away. Now ripped, its seams allow dark magic to seep into the world.

The Veil Guardians – Powerful fae created to protect the Veil and maintain the balance between realms. They were essential in keeping the Shadowborne realm sealed away.

The Shadowborne Realm – A place of exile, a prison or cursed plane of existence where banished fae and corrupted magic dwell.

Heartmates – A rare, soul-deep bond that ties two people together through fate and magic. It cannot be broken.

The Starlight Map – A powerful and elusive magical artifact that reveals what one desires or needs most but can only be read under starlight.

Those Who Shape Fate

Rhayne – King of the Nether Shores, bound to the sea and the magic that ties him to it. *The Tidecaller* answers to no one but him, its power woven into his own. He makes bargains that cannot be undone—those who strike a deal with him are bound, their fate tied to his whether they regret it or not.

Briar – A thief with quick hands, a sharp tongue, and a past that refuses to stay buried. She wants freedom, but fate has never cared much for what she wants.

Ciaus, Nyx, and Tavian – Crew brothers, and blades at Rhayne's back. They'd follow him into the depths if that's where the sea took them.

Kael – His name was lost to time for a reason. The Shadowborne follow him, and whatever he's planning, it won't end well for anyone.

Asher – A man who never reveals more than he has to. He watches, waits, and plays a game only he seems to understand.

Enric – Rhayne's second-in-command and a trusted friend. His loyalty is to his king first, his people second, and himself last.

Creatures of the Deep & Dark

The Shadowborne – They were once fae, but not anymore. The magic of the realm beyond twisted them, leaving them somewhere between fae and beast. Their former selves are trapped beneath dark magic, hidden away like a cruel joke.

Shadowborne Siren – No longer just a song upon the waves, but a hunger that calls men to their doom. Unlike their fae kin, these sirens do not sing to seduce—they sing to consume, their voices a lure that feeds upon life itself.

Places Where Destiny Unfolds

The Tidecaller – No ordinary ship, but a vessel of legend, woven with siren magic and heartwood. She sails only for Rhayne, and none who cross her decks leave unchanged.

Mistwood – A city swallowed by mist and magic. Lost, but not forgotten.

The Sliver – A thin place between realms, a borderland of magic and danger. It acts as a protective barrier between the Nether Shores and the mortal kingdoms.

The Nether Shores – The fae kingdom Rhayne swore to protect, though it falls ever closer to the sea's embrace.

Crimson Coast – A barren shore that stretches for miles with crimson colored sand. This land is as eerie as the stories that are told about it.

Arrowwood Forest – The trees are filled with silver leaves as sharp as the blades they resemble. Even the bravest tread carefully.

The Kraken – A tavern in Everfell with some of the best citrus rum (according to Briar).

The Waste – A land long abandoned to darkness, where the Shadowborne walk freely, waiting for something—or someone—to cross their path.

The tides have shifted... Here's a sneak peek at
On Shadowed Shores:

The sea calls.
The shadows answer.
But fate is not yet done with them.

Briar and Rhayne are no longer enemies, but the Veil remains in ruins, and the Shadowborne threat is only growing. With adversaries closing in and time slipping through their fingers, they must venture deep into treacherous lands—where old secrets rise and new dangers wait in the dark.

Bound by magic, love, and the weight of destiny, they'll face a test of their hearts and their power. But the sea is unforgiving, and not everyone who sets sail will make it back.

Made in United States
Troutdale, OR
03/22/2025

29895625R00225